Prescription for Entertainment

The Man without an Appetite—a view of surgery-from-the-inside-looking-out.

The Brothers—a gruesome voyage through the dark chambers of the supernatural, as a real ghoul stalks a modern hospital.

Compound B—a biting satire on the race problems of the future.

Bedside Manner—advanced medical science from a star culture eons older than ours is used to rebuild two victims of a space accident.

The Shopdropper—about a "narapoiac" who is convinced that *he is following someone* and that people are always plotting *to do him good*.

Bolden's Pets—in which a "positive parasite" enjoys dying for you rather than living off you!

—And the many other delightful tales in this anthology.

Great Science Fiction

About Doctors

Edited with an Introduction and

Story Prefaces by Groff Conklin

and Noah D. Fabricant, M. D.

COLLIER BOOKS • *NEW YORK*

COLLIER-MACMILLAN LTD. • *LONDON*

Library of Congress Catalog Card Number: 63-12790

FIRST EDITION 1963

FOURTH PRINTING 1966

The Macmillan Company, New York

Collier-Macmillan Canada Ltd., Toronto, Ontario

Printed in the United States of America

ACKNOWLEDGMENTS

Miles J. Breuer, M.D.—"The Man Without an Appetite." Copyright 1916 by *Bratrsky Věšnik*. Reprinted by permission of Julia E. Breuer.

Arthur C. Clarke—"Out of the Cradle, Endlessly Orbiting." Copyright 1959 by *Dude* Magazine. Reprinted by permission of the author and Scott Meredith Literary Agency, Inc., from *Dude*, March 1959, where it appeared as "Out of the Cradle."

Clifton L. Dance, M.D.—"The Brothers." Copyright 1952 by Clifton L. Dance, Jr. Reprinted by permission of the author from *Fantasy and Science Fiction*, June 1952.

Arthur Conan Doyle, M.D.—"The Great Keinplatz Experiment." Reprinted by permission of the Estate of Sir Arthur Conan Doyle.

David Harold Fink, M.D.—"Compound B." Copyright 1954 by Henry Holt, Inc. Copyright 1962 by David Harold Fink, M.D. Reprinted by permission of the author from *9 Tales of Space and Time*, edited by Raymond J. Healy, Holt, 1954.

David H. Keller, M.D.—"The Psychophonic Nurse." Copyright 1928 by Amazing Stories (E. P. Company), now published by Ziff-Davis Publishing Co. Reprinted from Keller, *Tales from Underwood*, Pellegrini and Cudahy, 1952, by permission of the author and August Derleth, Arkham House.

C. M. Kornbluth—"The Little Black Bag." Coypright 1950 by Street and Smith Publications, Inc. Reprinted by permission of Mary Kornbluth from *Astounding Science Fiction*, July 1950.

Murray Leinster—"Ribbon in the Sky." Copyright 1957 by Street and Smith Publications, Inc. Reprinted by permission of Will Jenkins from *Astounding Science Fiction*, June 1957.

Winston K. Marks—"Mate in Two Moves." Copyright 1954 by Galaxy Publishing Corp. Reprinted by permission of the author and Scott Meredith Literary Agency, Inc., from *Galaxy Science Fiction*, May 1954.

William Morrison—"Bedside Manner." Copyright 1954 by Galaxy Publishing Corp. Reprinted by permission of Joseph Samachson from *Galaxy Science Fiction*, May 1954.

Alan Nelson—"The Shopdropper." Copyright 1955 by Mercury Press. Reprinted by permission of the author from *Fantasy and Science Fiction*, January 1955.

Alan E. Nourse, M.D.—"Family Resemblance." Copyright 1953 by Street and Smith Publications, Inc. Reprinted by permission of Harry Altshuler from *Astounding Science Fiction*, April 1953.

Arthur Porges—"Emergency Operation." Copyright 1956 by Mercury Press, Inc. Reprinted by permission of Scott Meredith Literary Agency, Inc., from *Fantasy and Science Fiction*, May 1956.

J. R. Shango—"A Matter of Ethics." Copyright 1954 by J. R. Shango. Reprinted by permission of the author from *Fantasy and Science Fiction*, November 1954.

F. L. Wallace—"Bolden's Pets." Copyright 1955 by Galaxy Publishing Corp. Reprinted by permission of Harry Altshuler from *Galaxy Science Fiction*, October 1955.

J. A. Winter, M.D.—"Expedition Mercy." Copyright 1948 by Street and Smith Publications, Inc. Reprinted by permission of Marjorie R. Winter from *Astounding Science Fiction*, November 1948.

Contents

Contents

Introduction

FOR OVER A generation, now, science fiction has provided entertainment—and, not infrequently, enlightenment—for a large and growing audience of perceptive readers, many of them physicians. And a number of the writers, not a few of them medical men, have tried their hands at a special branch of this field of imaginative writing, the medical science fiction tale, and have delighted in exploring the medical possibilities, both good and bad, in the worlds of super-science and of the future.

As you will discover for yourself as you read this book, physicians still have a long way to go to equal the "achievements" of medical science fiction, despite recent advances in space medicine, electronic medicine, and the like. This is as it should be: for it is the function of science fiction to rove in the realms of the not-yet-achieved, the possible-but-not-probable, and even, once in a while, the completely unlikely.

In medical science fiction, for example, the sky is not the limit at all. In fact, the galaxy can barely contain it. Take, for example, William Morrison's "Bedside Manner," in which a completely alien, and possibly extragalactic, medical science is used to rescue and miraculously rebuild two victims of a space accident. On the other hand, it can deal with space history near at home, almost in our back yard, so to speak, as Arthur C. Clarke does in his charming story of one of the great medical events in the exploration of the moon.

Also still within the solar system, the pseudonymous physician who uses the name J. R. Shango offers a sharp critique of surgical practice in interplanetary space in his "A Matter of Ethics." And much farther out in the swirling pinwheel of our own galaxy, where planets of other stars offer strange and sometimes inimical life forms, the late Dr. J. A. Winter, in his "Expedition Mercy," relates some of the lethal effects that alien life can have on human beings, while in "Bolden's Pets," F. L. Wallace gives us a warm and compassionate picture of a self-sacrificing symbiote.

Medical science fiction, like science fiction of other varieties, is not limited to space travel, as this book well shows. Dr. David Harold Fink writes a biting satire on the race problems of the future in "Compound B"; Dr. Clifton Dance enters the realm of the supernatural with his tale of a "real" ghoul loose in a modern hospital; Dr. David H. Keller satirizes robots and unmaternal mothers in "The Psychophonic Nurse"; and Dr. Alan E. Nourse spoofs the pompous medical bureaucrat in his hilarious "Family Resemblance."

To show that imaginative medicine is not an invention of the twentieth century, we have included classic narratives by Edgar Allan Poe, Nathaniel Hawthorne, and Sir Arthur Conan Doyle, M.D., all from the nineteenth century, and all spellbinding tales.

For physicians and laymen everywhere, medical science fiction contains clues to some of our present far-out thinking about medicine. It is conceivable that the medicine in many of these tales may eventually come true. Who can say that it is impossible to eliminate neuroses (whether it would be a wise thing to do it or not is another matter), conquer cancer and the cardiovascular diseases, and postpone death for longer and longer periods? And who can deny that science fictioneers, laymen as well as those medically trained, might be able to provide answers to unsolved medical problems, ranging from allergy to surgery, from infection to genetics, from psychotherapy to epidemiology? Their ideas would have to be considered as clues to be followed up in endless laboratory research, but nevertheless they might trigger such vital discoveries, for it has happened before.

However, don't read this book hoping for a revelation of tomorrow's medical achievements; read it, rather, because it is fun to read, because it will relax tensions and expand the imagination. And if you come across a worthwhile idea once in a while, be it medical or social, don't be startled. Science fiction, medical and otherwise, is full of such intriguing surprises.

We have made no effort to arrange these stories in any medical or literary pattern; to do so would have been both forced and futile. We have left classification according to etiology, pathology, symptomatology, diagnosis, and treatment to the textbooks. We are after surprises and sensations here, not a parsing of the *materia medica*. What we have done instead is simply to arrange the stories in the alphabetical order of their authors' names. You will never know what is coming next in this medico-fantastic science fiction grab-bag. We hope you enjoy the stories as much as we have; and we assure you that if you indicate your pleasure in them by seeing to it that the book does well, we have plenty more first-rate tales of medical super-science in our inventory—more than enough for another collection!

GROFF CONKLIN
NOAH D. FABRICANT, M.D.

June 1962

THE MAN WITHOUT AN APPETITE

Miles J. Breuer, M.D.

We had originally planned to use Dr. Breuer's famous piece of medical science fiction describing an operation through the Fourth Dimension, entitled The Appendix and the Spectacles, *in this anthology. But while it was in the process of being prepared for publication, a collection entitled* The Mathematical Magpie (a pun on π), *edited by Clifton Fadiman, appeared, and "Appendix" was in it. Whereupon we wrote Dr. Breuer's widow and asked if she had a different medical story for us. She found the following remarkable tale in her husband's papers, and wrote: "It was first published in the Czech language in the* Bratrsky Věstník *in about 1916. . . . I think it was probably published in some science fiction magazine about 1924 or 1925, but I do not know." And the same goes for us, too. Nothing with this title appears in any bibliography of Dr. Breuer's short stories, and consequently we are unable to provide it with an American magazine credit. If anyone knows of its previous appearance in the English language, the editors would appreciate being informed about it.*

The Man Without an Appetite

UPON MY discharge from the Army after the close of the war, I remained for a year studying at universities in Vienna and Paris. Then I returned to Chicago and opened up an office on West 26th Street. Shortly afterwards I received my first professional caller, in the person of the fair wife and recent bride of my old chum, Doctor Volny. I greeted her warmly, as I had seen neither her nor her husband for many months. She seemed uneasy, but lost no time in coming to the point.

"Doctor," she said, "I'd like to have you advise me as a physician and as a friend. I am afraid that my husband is ill in some way."

"And of what does he complain?" I asked.

"He states that he never felt better than he does now, and he looks it. And yet, I am sure that he does not eat. He always turns the things over on his plate and dabs at them a few times, but when I carry the plate away, I can see that there is just as much on it as there was before. When I ask him what is the matter, he says that nothing is the matter, and pretends to eat, but I know that he eats nothing."

"Doesn't he perhaps eat elsewhere?"

She shook her pretty head.

"No. He would tell me about it if he did. He is not that kind. He confides everything to me, except his scientific work, which I do not understand. At first, naturally, I thought that it was my cooking that he did not like. But that is a foolish idea; I am not a silly sixteen-year-old girl. I am wise enough to be able to recognize the situation if that were the case; when I think it over, my common sense tells me that is not the reason. There must be some reason why he does not eat. He keeps making excuses—that he is not hungry; that he has eaten and I did not notice it; that he is dieting to avoid obesity; but it all sounds too thin."

I was compelled to explain to the anxious wife that before I could help her, I would have to look into her husband's condition more in detail, for which purpose I would have to see him personally.

"No—I am afraid to have you approach him that way. He would not like it. He insists there is nothing wrong with him, and indeed looks and acts perfectly healthy. I am only afraid lest it be the beginning of some terrible disease creeping upon him unnoticed. That would be quite possible; he is always working at strange things that would overtax the brains of a dozen ordinary people."

"Well," I said, "I'll have to visit him. That is the only way to get at the truth. It is a long time since I've seen him anyway, and I would like to see what he is about. I shall say nothing whatever of what you have told me, but shall watch him carefully."

She left me with an open invitation to dinner at their home whenever I could come. I sat for a while, immersed in a sea of recollections of my extraordinary friend. We had been roommates at college, where I had come to know his remarkable personality thoroughly. Since then, we had seen each other only briefly and rarely, but I had followed the newspaper reports about him during my European studies.

That such a hermit as I knew him to be could have blossomed out with as pretty a love affair as he had was a surprise to me. He had come into public notice in a romance such as I had thought was confined to the motion-picture screen; it was the last thing I would have expected from a mole like Volny. And yet, after I had thought the affair over and analyzed it, I was compelled to admit that it logically was just what could be expected. For, if there was any consistent characteristic that could be ascribed to him, it was that he invariably reached the goal he aimed at. He had a strictly scientific method of procedure in everything. He would define clearly just what it was that he wanted, learn all there was to be known about it, investigate all possible ways of accomplishing it, select the best, and then set about it with all his knowledge and strength. I have no doubt that his procedure in this affair of the heart could be classed with the rest of his scientific accomplishments in respect to the efficiency with which he carried it out.

I can omit a repetition of its details; my readers, if they live in the Middle West, have followed it all in the newspapers, which are my sole source of information. It first appeared in print when Winslow became involved, at which time various items leading up to the situation were published, including a description of the astonishing mental ability of Doctor Volny and his love for the pretty teacher at the Harrison High School —and she was indeed beautiful, as I knew from a long previous acquaintance with her. Her published photographs did not do her justice, for her charm lay not only in a pretty face, but in manner and carriage and speech, things that the camera cannot depict. The little love affair was like any other until Miss Holly, one Sunday afternoon, at a picnic at Riverside, met Winslow, son of the president of the Winslow Steamship Corporation. The newspapers had him accurately sized up, a typical worthless son of a busy wealthy father; he drank and gambled, associated with fast women, and had undermined his health with unmentionable diseases. Most of this came out later; at the start, this cultured, well-dressed, handsome, courtly young man made a pleasant and favorable impression on the young lady. Those who did not know him thoroughly thought him to be what his external appearance seemed to indicate: the perfect product of modern civilization. When it first seemed that he was about to win away the affections of Miss Holly, only a few cynics mentioned the fact that father's dollars counted for more, where a girl's heart was concerned, than the greatest brain the century had produced. Volny, however, needed no pity. He saw that it was time to act, and he acted at once. That he would be successful, I, who knew him the best, could readily have foretold. Winslow scattered money right and left in his efforts to maintain himself in the lady's graces, but apparently Volny succeeded in meeting the fundamental requirements, for his sweetheart remained faithful to him in spite of the extravagant courtship of his rival. When Winslow finally realized that he had failed, he acted like a man who had lost his reason. My personal opinion was that this misfortune merely displayed a weak spot in his heredity; a well-balanced man would not act as he did. He swore that some day he would kill Volny. And in fact he did once attack Volny at night in a lonely spot in the park, but he got his eyes blacked and his nose broken for his trouble. These are things well known to the newspaper reading public. Only I knew things about Volny that others did not know.

Yes, I must visit him. Now, that we were both well off in the world, we must talk over those old times when we were students together, bound together mainly by ties of poverty. Besides the fact that he had such a wonderful brain, I remember him also because he was so poor, poorer than I; and I often went hungry. He was hungry most of the time; and often I had shared my slender resources with him. He frequently deplored the fact that a man must eat; he would say that not only was it uncomfortable on the occasions when one had nothing to eat, but from the standpoint of natural laws, eating was very inefficient; plants are much better off because they can live without eating.

He was the most brilliant scientific student that had ever gone through the university. My own achievements in the scientific field were not inconsiderable, but I always regarded his brain as some supernatural miracle. How could I wonder at his wife because she sometimes feared for his reason? His wide knowledge in numerous scientific fields, the originality of his ideas, the clearness of his reasoning, and the astonishing skill with which he worked were no less surprising and interesting than the determination with which he concealed his abilities and his work and kept himself from becoming conspicuous. Everyone but myself considered him an obscure "grind."

I recollect a few incidents at the university which show what sort of a fellow he was. One afternoon, when the air was full of the excitement of the biggest football game of the year, and every one was wrought up to a keen pitch over the outcome of the game in progress, from janitors to professors, Volny was not to be found. I had not seen him since morning, but finally located him in a recess in one of the biological laboratories, surrounded by glass apparatus, with his head bent over a microscope.

"Football?" he mumbled absently. "Listen. Do you know

what abiogenesis is? Look here" I was so excited over the football game that I thought little of the moving specks that I saw until much later; and then I wondered what connection they had with abiogenesis—with that talk that we were hearing so much of at the time in the scientific world, about the creation of life in the laboratory without the help of preceding life.

It was not unusual for Volny to get some strange idea and then spend all of his time in working it out, to the detriment of his studies and his health. Once he spent two weeks of laborious experiment in establishing an error in a textbook of which a professor of his was the author; and when he had proved it to his own satisfaction, he put away his notes, and said nothing about it. That was the way he usually acted; he made no particular secret of his work, but he was disinclined to talk about it. Once he borrowed a cat from the zoology laboratory; later I saw it moving over a table covered with electrical apparatus; he manipulated switches and the cat jerked about with stiff, hideous motions.

"What's the matter with that cat?" I demanded. He looked at me with a smile.

"The assistant killed it last week for dissection," he replied.

When he got out of school, he did not have to beg for a position. During the next few years his reputation grew apace, and lucrative positions beckoned to him. For many years he was biochemist on the faculty at the University of Chicago. Then, shortly after the war began, he accepted the medical directorship of the Waldo S. Hunt Pharmaceutical Company. The war had increased the price of many drugs to such an extent that the company thought it worth while to pay him twenty-five thousand dollars a year to make use of his unusual abilities in the effort to work out better and cheaper methods of preparing expensive drugs for the American public. And what he must be accomplishing in this present position, with unlimited resources behind him, not even the most vivid imagination could picture.

And now, his wife thought that he did not eat, that he might be ill, or that his reason was in danger. What sort of experiments has he on his mind? was the first thing that occurred to me. I knew him. During the week following her visit to my office, I saw him at a meeting of the Chicago Medical Society. Yes, there was that same, thoughtful, absent-minded air about him, as though he were really somewhere else instead of here. We talked a moment after the meeting.

"I'm glad you're here, old man," he said. "I don't suppose I'll tell anyone else about it, but I always liked to show my playthings to you. You must come over some day, and I'll show you something that will surprise you. The most surprising thing I have ever done, I think. It is not merely of scientific interest; I think it would take anyone's breath away."

After the meeting, the usual dinner was served, but Volny excused himself, pleading urgent work. A few days later I met him in the street. I caught him by the arm.

"You're not often in this part of town," I said. "Come, let's go in here to Schnabel's and get our knees under a table—why, it's a hundred years since we've had a chat."

"Oh!" answered Volny, "I can't even dream of eating right now. I could more easily fly straight up in the air. Come and visit me at the laboratory; that will be best. When you see my experiments, you will understand. Then we can have a chat."

As I have said, I was rather curious as to what new marvel he might be working on. However, various little matters kept getting in the way and preventing my visit. I saw him several times, and observed him closely because of my promise to his wife. The Sunday afternoon when a group of us went to White City for a little recreation, he seemed his usual absent-minded self; he would rally occasionally for our benefit, and then lose himself again. When we sat down in a little bower to an elegant little table, he poked his food several times, and devoted himself to conversation so as to detract attention from his eating.

A week later he burst into my office.

"I've been wanting to come and see you—" I began.

"That can wait now," he said quickly. "I've got something else. We need you. I recollected your skill in animal experimentation, and recommended you. You can do the standardization." He spoke rapidly and gave no opportunity for reply. "Beede is coming too. There will be work for the three of us.

Yes, a new variety of ipecac. Great! We are to investigate it
—an expedition to the Gulf of Mexico."

"Yes," I said, "I can go. I cannot see that I am so busy
that I could not be spared. What's that? Friday? What's the
rush? Why, I haven't even seen your experiments!"

"I know. But there isn't time now. This is an important
thing. And interesting. Afterwards—"

The Waldo S. Hunt Company had equipped a little steamer,
and I was soon on it, with Volny, and a botanist by the name
of Beede, who in the course of a research trip among the
keys, had picked up reports of a wonderful plant that cured
dysentery and caused vomiting. He convinced himself that
some of the islands contained large quantities of the plant,
and brought back a supply of it with him. From this, Volny
succeeded in isolating substances so similar to emetin and
cephaelin that they were probably identical. That was important, because genuine ipecac and its active principle, emetin,
had risen 300 per cent in price since the war began, and could
hardly be gotten at all. Here was a possibility of opening a
new source of supply which would lower the price and furnish enough of the drug for all purposes. Incidentally I
learned that a certain firm had offered Volny a fabulous sum
for perfecting a cheapening of the manufacture of glycerin.
He refused. "More glycerin for explosives!" he exclaimed. "I'm
sick of this murdering. Here we have something that means
relief from suffering." We had complete laboratory equipment
on board for assaying, standardizing, and physiologically testing the plant, so that in case it proved to be useful we could
at once bring back a load with us.

It would be interesting to recount how we searched for
Beede's plant among the thousands of islands of the Gulf of
Mexico, and finally found a few islands quite covered with
it, but that does not belong here. We finally decided upon
one of them for a stopping place; a tiny little island which
had a supply of fresh water in the form of a few springs at
the base of its tiny mountain range. There was no harbor, and
laboratory work on board a swaying ship was impossible; we
therefore had to set up work on the shore in tents, a rather
laborious procedure. We set them up on a little knoll, a quar-

ter of a mile from the water's edge; behind them were three small palms and a spring, from which the surface sloped upwards to the middle ridge; from the latter we could see the further shore, some ten miles away. There were a few groups of trees, but altogether, it was a cheerless and desolate place. Everything was covered with Beede's plant, which he had named *Ipecacuanhua martialis*; there were reddish-green heads and bunches of it.

"Things are going fine," said Beede. "Look, here it is the evening of the second day, and there is Volny boiling ipecac already. But what does that fool captain mean by getting all of the ship's stores out on the beach?"

"He mumbled something about rearranging the cargo and ballast," I explained. "He had me there, for I know nothing about such things. Seems to me a queer looking guy, though."

The next morning the mate rushed into our tent.

"All the stores have been carried away by the tide!" he roared. "There isn't food enough for a sparrow."

"What's that?" shouted Beede and I in chorus. Volny looked up for a moment, and turned back to his glassware, apparently willing to trust the matter to us. We ran out on the shore and found only a few metal objects left. The ship was empty, save for its stone ballast. The men looked nervous and worried.

"And what does the captain say?" I asked of the mate.

"That he miscalculated," he answered, and there were some more mumbles that I could not understand.

I could not understand it. However, because there was not food enough for the ten men for even one day, there was no time for deliberation: we were compelled to get aboard the ship and turn full steam toward Tampa. All except Volny. Experiments in the tents were under way and could not be abandoned. There was no talking to him; he insisted on it, and stayed behind. We left him a loaf of bread and a can of beef, and hurried away, leaving him bent over a distillation flask of bubbling brown liquid.

That evening, Beede and I leaned against the ship's rail in the tropical moonlight, glad that one interminable day was over.

"It seems to me that man is crazy," said Beede. We were talking of the captain of the ship. "I am watching him, and he acts queer."

We had heard a loud laugh from the cabin where the captain sat alone. When Beede spoke, it was repeated.

"Aha, I heard you!" shouted the captain, appearing in the cabin door with an ugly leer on his bearded face. "Yes, I am crazy. He made me crazy, and now I've had my revenge!" He laughed again, sending chills down our backs. "No one on this ship, no one in the world, can find the island he is on, before he has starved his hated life out. Ho! ho! no one knows the position of the island but I, and I am crazy! Ha! ha! I've thrown the logbook into the sea! Now I'm going into the sea after it."

That last was a warning to us, and as he plunged toward the rail, we were ready for him; both of us bore him down to the deck. He roared and fought like a demon, but the commotion brought the crew to the scene, and soon he was tied hand and foot.

"Can you find the island?" I demanded of the mate.

He stared at me for a moment, and then gave orders to turn the ship about.

How can I describe our feverish efforts to find the island, and the four interminable weeks that followed? The mate did not find the island; we searched a dozen of them just exactly alike before hunger drove us back to Tampa. How many times during those hungry days did my hands ache to throttle the captain, who lay bound and raving in the cabin.

"I have it!" shouted Beede, gripping my arm. "You didn't know Winslow? Those eyes seemed familiar." We went into the cabin and studied the prisoner. "No doubt of it. He swore revenge on Volny, and it seems that he has succeeded." I could hardly resist the impulse to kick the man savagely in the ribs. Now I understood the whole affair of the lost supplies, and the low sum for which the Winslow Corporation had chartered the steamer.

When our hunger became so terrible that we had to give up and get to Tampa, we warmed up the telegraph wires at once. In a short time the whole country buzzed with the news, and all the vessels in the Gulf were keeping a lookout for Volny's island. A book could be made of this story: of the long, hopeless search among the thousands of islands in the West Indies; of the sums of money spent by the Waldo S. Hunt Company in the search; of the frantic distress of Volny's beautiful wife; of our hopeless hoping that Volny would find some way to keep alive on that desolate island; of the indignation of fifty* states against the son of the president of the Winslow Corporation; and of the wonderful experiments on the insane youth by Dussek, a psychologist at the University of Kansas, who eventually succeeded in winning the Waldo S. Hunt Company's reward for discovering the location of Volny's island. Full reports of his work are found elsewhere, of how he worked by suggestion on Winslow's raving brain, and carried it vividly, in imagination, through all the incidents of our original expedition with Volny, step by step to the island itself, and to the moment when the insane man imagined himself abandoned without supplies, on a sandy floor and surrounded by painted skies and seas; how he came within an ace of starving to death, but finally, by means of suggestion from Dussek, hit upon the idea of writing the position of his island on a page from his notebook and enclosing it in a bottle and throwing it into the sea, in the hope that it would bring him help—all in Dussek's laboratory. We were aboard a ship with steam up, awaiting the telegram from Dussek which would give us the latitude and longitude of the island.

Approaching the island with beating hearts, we expected to find the wrecks of the tents, and the bones of Volny whitening on the sand. Our astonishment knew no bounds when we saw the tents standing, with their guy-ropes taut, white against the yellow sand, and from one of them rolled a stream of black smoke. We hastened ashore.

We found Volny, sitting on a wooden packing-box, his hands in his pockets, his eyes on a bubbling distillation flask. We stood astonished in the door, unable to speak. His tall

* So in the original draft of this story, written in 1916!— *The Editors.*

figure was in perfect health; his cheeks full, his eyes bright; he whistled merrily and tapped his heel against the box.

"Volny!" I finally managed to gasp.

"We've got it!" he cried, as though nothing unusual had happened. "I have isolated plenty of emetin, and the process is not costly."

When we had recovered from our astonishment, we crowded around him, grasped his shoulders, and shook him.

"Starve to death—?" he repeated in confusion. "Eh? What did I eat? Well—I—that is. I didn't even—the fact is—I mean—well, I forgot—." He stopped, thoroughly confused. Then we saw, untouched, the meager supplies that we had left him, and gasped in amazement.

"Well, you needn't turn so pale," said Volny with a smile. "Although I couldn't understand what kept you from coming for so long. You all look so tired and worried." He turned to me. "You might have understood if you had come when I invited you—my experiments—"

"I don't get the connection at all," I said.

He laughed.

"Do you remember when we starved together in our student days, how I cursed hunger, and swore to get rid of it?"

"You mean—that you have accomplished—that you do not require food?"

"Well, yes, something like that, yes. Of course, I do require materials to furnish energy and repairs to the body. You know how plants accomplish that—by means of sunlight and water—they don't need to eat, that is, to put pieces of food into open mouths."

"By means of sunlight?" I repeated dazedly. "But you must have needed something. Where did you get it?"

"Very simple. Our foods contain only a few elements— carbon, hydrogen, oxygen, nitrogen and trace elements. These are found around us, in the air and in the water, in quantities so vast not all the people in the world could ever use them up. Twelve years ago I worked on the preparation of a substance which combines with the hemoglobin of the blood, and makes the latter able to do what the chlorophyll of plants does—take the required elements from air and water and combine them into the proper molecules to serve as food. The sunlight furnishes the power for this synthesis, just as it does in plants."

"In other words, you are a plant—"

"Yes, a holophyte. I must have daylight, or I would perish, but the high cost of living does not concern me. I haven't eaten for so long that my digestive apparatus is weak, and I depend entirely on my new method—and you can see how well this climate suits me."

Postscript

In her letter giving us permission to use this story. Dr. Breuer's widow Mrs. Julia E. Breuer wrote: "I always appreciate receiving copies of the books in which Dr. Breuer's stories appear, since I then can give them to the families of my two daughters, Rosalie Breuer Neligh, M.D., and Mildred Breuer Dale, M.D. Their older children are beginning to show interest in what Grandfather used to write. The oldest one, eleven years old, shows definite signs of having a knack for writing, although he is planning to go in for electronics and the sciences connected with space travel. The nine-year-old girl is planning on being a doctor, despite all her mother's efforts to discourage her; and the five-year-old boy says he is going to be a veterinarian—'because animals need it more!' " To which the editors of this anthology can only say, "More power to the Breuers, and especially to that very percipient five-year-old!"

OUT OF THE CRADLE, ENDLESSLY ORBITING

Arthur C. Clarke

"Medical science fiction?" you may say on a questioning note after you read this superbly turned-out little gem from the future history of space conquest. Give it a long second thought, though, and you will see that it is, indeed, the story of a medical miracle—even though there isn't an identified doctor in the cast. Put it this way: The anonymous physicians did all the constructive worrying—and that was plenty! The tale also tells of a crucial victory of the human race over the alien and inimical environment of the Cosmos. And the actual victor is so puny!

Out of the Cradle, Endlessly Orbiting

BEFORE WE START, I'd like to point out something that a good many people seem to have overlooked. The Twenty-first Century does *not* begin tomorrow; it begins a year later, on 1 January 2001. Even though the calendar reads 2000 from midnight, the old century still has twelve months to run. Every hundred years we astronomers have to explain this all over again, but it makes no difference. The celebrations start just as soon as the two zeros go up.

So you want to know my most memorable moment in fifty years of space exploration . . . I suppose you've already interviewed von Braun? How is he? Good; I've not seen him since that symposium we arranged in Astrograd on his eightieth birthday, the last time he came down from the Moon.

Yes—I've been present at some of the biggest moments in the history of space-flight, right back to the launching of the first Satellite. I was only twenty-five then, and a very junior mathematician at Kapustin Yar—not important enough to be in the control center during the countdown. But I heard the takeoff: it was the second most awe-inspiring sound I'd heard in my entire life. (The first? I'll come to that later.)

When we knew we'd hit orbit, one of the senior scientists called for his Zis and we drove into Stalingrad for a real party. Only the very top people had cars in the Worker's Paradise, you know; we made the hundred kilometer drive in just about the same time the Sputnik took for one circuit of Earth, and *that* was pretty good going. Someone calculated that the amount of vodka consumed the next day could have launched the satellite the Americans were building, but I don't think that was quite true.

Most of the history books say that the Space Age began then, on 4 October 1957; I'm not going to argue with them but I think the really exciting times came later. For sheer drama you can't beat the U.S. Navy's race to fish Dimitri Kalinin out of the South Atlantic, while the whole world waited to find if a human being could come back alive from space. Then there was Jerry Wingate's radio commentary, with all the adjectives which no network dared to censor, as he rounded the Moon and became the first man to see its hidden face. And, of course, only five years later, that TV broadcast from the cabin of the *Hermann Oberth* as she touched down on the plateau in the Bay of Rainbows where she still stands, an eternal monument to the men buried beside her.

Those were the great landmarks on the road to space, but you're wrong if you think I'm going to talk about them; for what made the greatest impact on me was something very, very different. I'm not even sure if I can share the experience, and if I succeed you won't be able to make a story out of it. Not a new one, anyway, for the papers were full of it at the time. But most of them missed the point completely: to them it was just good human interest material, nothing more.

The time was thirty years after the launching of Sputnik I, and by then, with a good many other people, I was on the Moon—and too important, alas, to be a real scientist any more. It had been a dozen years since I'd programmed an electronic computer; now I had the slightly more difficult task of programming human beings, since I was Chief Coordinator of Project Ares, the first manned expedition to Mars.

We were starting from the Moon, of course, because of the low gravity; it's about fifty times easier, in terms of fuel, to take off from there than from the Earth. We'd thought of constructing the ships in a satellite orbit, which would have cut fuel requirements even further, but when we looked into it the idea wasn't as good as it seemed. It's not easy to set up factories and machine shops in space; the absence of gravity is a nuisance rather than an advantage when you want things to stay put. By that time, at the end of the '80's, the First Lunar Base was getting well organized, with chemical processing plants and all kinds of small-scale industrial operations to turn out the things the colony needed. So we decided to use the existing facilities rather than set up new ones, at great difficulty and expense, out in space.

Alpha, Beta and Gamma, the three ships of the expedition,

were being built inside the ramparts of Plato, perhaps the most perfect of all the walled plains on this side of the Moon. It's so large that if you stood in the center you could never guess that you were inside a crater; the ring of mountains around you is hidden far below the horizon. The pressure-domes of the Base were about ten kilometers from the launching site, connected to it by one of those overhead cable systems that the tourists love to ride on, but which have ruined so much of the lunar scenery.

It was a rugged sort of life, in those pioneering days, for we had none of the luxuries everyone now takes for granted. Central Dome with its parks and lakes was still a dream on the architects' drawing boards; even if it had existed, we would have been too busy to enjoy it, for Project Ares devoured all our waking moments. It would be Man's first great leap into space; by that time we already looked on the Moon as no more than a suburb of Earth, a stepping-stone on the way to places that really mattered. Our beliefs were neatly expressed by that famous remark of Tsiolkovskii's, which I'd hung up for everyone to see as they entered my office:

EARTH IS THE CRADLE OF MANKIND
BUT ONE CANNOT LIVE IN THE
CRADLE FOREVER

(What was that? No—of *course* I never knew Tsiolkovskii! I was only four years old when he died in 1936!)

After half a lifetime of secrecy, it was good to be able to work freely with men of all nations, on a project that was backed by the entire world. Of my four chief assistants, one was American, one Indian, one Chinese and one Russian. We often congratulated ourselves on escaping from Security and the worst excesses of nationalism, and though there was plenty of good-natured rivalry among scientists from different countries, it gave a stimulus to our work. I sometimes boasted to visitors who remembered the bad old days, "There are no secrets on the Moon."

Well, I was wrong; there *was* a secret, and it was under my very nose—in my own office. Perhaps I might have suspected something if I hadn't been so immersed in the multitudinous details of Project Ares that I'd no opportunity of taking the wider view. Looking back on it afterwards, of course, there were all sorts of hints and warnings, but I never noticed any of them at the time.

True, I was vaguely aware that Jim Hutchins, my young American assistant, was becomingly increasingly abstracted, as if he had something on his mind. Once or twice I had to pull him up for some minor inefficiency: each time he looked hurt and promised it wouldn't happen again. He was one of those typical, clean-cut college boys the United States produces in such quantities—usually very reliable, but not exceptionally brilliant. He'd been on the Moon for three years and was one of the first to bring his wife up from Earth when the ban on nonessential personnel was lifted. I'd never quite understood how he'd managed that; he must have been able to pull some strings, but certainly he was the last person you'd expect to find at the center of a world-wide conspiracy. World-wide, did I say? No—it was bigger than that, for it extended all the way back to Earth. Dozens of people were involved, right up to the top brass of the Astronautics Authority. It still seems a miracle that they were able to keep the plot from leaking out.

The slow sunrise had been under way for two days, Earth time, and though the needle-sharp shadows were shortening, it was still five days to noon. We were ready to make the first static tests of Alpha's motors, for the power-plant had been installed and the framework of the ship was complete. It stood out there on the plain looking more like a half-built oil refinery than a spaceship, but to us it was beautiful with its promise of the future. It was a tense moment; never before had a thermonuclear engine of such size been operated, and despite all the safety precautions that had been taken, one could never be sure. . . . If anything went wrong now, it could delay Project Ares by years.

The count-down had already begun when Hutchins, looking rather pale, came hurrying up to me. "I have to report to Base at once," he said. "It's very important."

"More important than *this*?" I retorted sarcastically, for I was mighty annoyed.

He hesitated for a moment as if wanting to tell me something; then he replied, "I think so."

"O.K." I said, and he was gone in a flash. I could have questioned him, but one has to trust one's subordinates. As I went back to the central control panel, in rather a bad temper, I decided that I'd had enough of my temperamental young American and would ask for him to be transferred. It was odd, though—he'd been as keen as anybody on this test, and now he was racing back to Base on the cable-car. The blunt cylinder of the shuttle was already half way to the nearest suspension tower, sliding along its almost invisible wires like some strange bird skimming across the lunar surface.

Five minutes later, my temper was even worse. A group of vital recording instruments had suddenly backed up, and the whole test would have to be postponed for at least three hours. I stormed around the blockhouse telling everyone who would listen (and of course everyone had to) that we used to manage things much better at Kapustin Yar. I'd quieted down a bit and we were on our second round of coffee when the "General Attention" signal sounded from the speakers. There's only one call with a higher priority than that—the wail of the emergency alarms, which I'd heard just twice in all my years in the Lunar Colony, and hope never to hear again.

The voice that echoed through every enclosed space on the Moon, and over the radios of every worker out on the soundless plains, was that of General Moshe Stein, Chairman of the Astronautics Authority. (There were still lots of courtesy titles around in those days, though they didn't mean anything any more.)

"I'm speaking from Geneva," he said, "and I have an important announcement to make. For the last nine months, a great experiment has been in progress. We have kept it secret for the sake of those directly involved, and because we did not wish to raise false hopes or fears. Not long ago, you will remember, many experts refused to believe that men could survive in space; this time, also, there were pessimists who doubted if we could take the next step in the conquest of the universe. We have proved that they were wrong; for now I would like to introduce you to George Jonathan Hutchins—first Citizen of Space."

There was a click as the circuit was rerouted, followed by a pause full of indeterminate shufflings and whisperings. And then, over all the Moon and half the Earth came the noise I promised to tell you about—the most awe-inspiring sound I've ever heard in my life.

It was the thin cry of a new-born baby—the first child in all the history of mankind to be brought forth on another world than Earth. We looked at each other in the suddenly silenced blockhouse, and then at the ships we were building out there on the blazing lunar plain. They had seemed so important, a few minutes ago. They still were—but not as important as what had happened over in Medical Center, and would happen again billions of times on countless worlds down all the ages to come.

For that was the moment, gentlemen, when I knew that Man had *really* conquered Space.

THE BROTHERS

Clifton Dance, Jr., M.D.

In this collection of stories, anything goes. Possibilities and impossibilities; nirvanas and nightmares; science and sorcery. Dr. Dance, a practicing anesthesiologist, takes us on a gruesome voyage through the dark chambers of the supernatural in this goosepimply tale of a thoroughly unco (and uncooperative) patient. It is hardly what one would call conventional science fiction—but then, who cares? It is a dreadfully convincing "entertainment," nonetheless!

The Brothers

"HERE HE IS, Doc." Reardon's heavy cop's voice sounded clearly relieved to be turning the prisoner over.

The sleep-narrowed eyes of the intern looked at what had been brought him at 3 A.M. Not usually much at that hour on the psycho service. Occasional would-be suiciders, paraphrenic drunks, senile wanderers. Usually got a fair night's sleep. Not up suturing all night like the surgery boys, or catching preemies on OB.

"What did he do?" he asked the cop.

"Well, he claims he lives in the Ridgewood Cemetery over on Andrews Avenue. He was just inside the fence, sitting on a grave, when we found him."

The intern gazed at him solemnly. "Did you check with the caretaker?"

"Yeah, and he doesn't know anything about him."

The intern addressed the prisoner. "What's your name?"

"Joseph Walder."

"How old are you?"

"I was fifty-six."

Was! The intern turned the word over in his mind, then decided it was too early in the morning to quibble about grammar.

"Where do you live?"

"I dwell in the Ridgewood Cemetery."

The intern, Brandt, absorbed this statement silently. He shifted slightly on his stool and leaned forward, grasping the man's arm, feeling the thin sticklike bones under the coat sleeve. His voice was young, sincere, and as authoritative as he could make it.

"Look here, Joseph. You say you live in the Ridgewood Cemetery. The officers here have checked with the caretaker and he doesn't know you. How do you explain that?"

"They don't understand." There was a rusty, throaty quality to his voice.

"What do you do in the Ridgewood Cemetery?"

The dry looking lips separated and the yellow teeth came slowly into view. It wasn't quite a grin. The man said nothing.

The intern shifted slightly again, uneasily, and looked at the cops and then back to the prisoner.

"Do you have any relatives we could call to come and take you home?"

The man looked straight at him with those curiously wide blank eyes, the pupils so dilated there was hardly any iris to be seen.

"You could not call them," he said.

Brandt tried once more.

"Where else do you live, besides the cemetery?"

The man barely moved his shoulders, causing a filmy fall of dust particles.

Brandt closed his eyes for a moment as though trying to think of some way out of the thing, some way to solve the problem quickly and get back to bed.

"Mrs. Jamison," he called to the nurse. "Do we have a bed in a closed ward?"

Mrs. Jamison looked at a big card on the desk before her.

"H 12," she said.

"Fine," Brandt said. "We'll put you up for the night, Joseph, and in the morning perhaps we can straighten this out."

Walder walked into the ward and undressed when they told him to. He said nothing to their comments about his clothes and the filth. They were good clothes. Digging is hard work and even the best material will wear. And the dirt— good clean earth. They didn't understand. He'd never expected them to. He'd been a fool back there with the police and the doctor. He should never have told them those things.

But it had been such an awful surprise. He hadn't noticed the police until they were right next to him. Then they spoke so fast he couldn't keep up; years of habit had slowed his thought processes to the somber pace of Ridgewood. He was so frantic to get away that he told them the first thing he thought of and that happened to be the truth.

He should have stayed deeper. But like all the brothers in Ridgewood, except perhaps old Phidias, he was hoping to find a way to fare in the living world. He must be stupid, stupid as some of the higher brothers had told him he was, for look what had happened to him. A wave of sheer hopelessness and futility swept over him. He must get out of here and back to Ridgewood. He must! He must! The idea pushed everything else out of his mind and he numbly let the orderlies guide him into the white tiled room. They stood him in the shower and he felt the strange warm water running all over him, over his long-cold flesh. It stirred him oddly, as though his body was remembering things of long ago. Things of warmth. Then they put him between smooth white sheets, smelling of the iron, and put sideboards on the bed. For hours he lay there, sensing the aliens living all around him, feeling their constant pumping vibrations, louder and louder, almost overwhelming him; making him want to jump up and try the heavy mesh over the window, shake it and see if he could get out; making him want to pull at the wire door and call the orderly to let him out, out of the hospital, back to where he belonged.

Dr. Brandt, the intern, came in early so he could complete his notes on the new admission and do a physical before rounds. The patient was apparently still delusional this morning. Ridgewood Cemetery was it? May be some kind of addiction, cerebral arteriosclerosis, or paresis. It could be lots of things. But which one? Be glad when this service was over, sleep or no sleep. These guys gave him the creeps. Lives in a cemetery! Now a gall bladder that doesn't empty can be cut out. But what can you cut out of a guy who thinks he lives in a cemetery?

Like an immense icicle it flew into Walder's mind, pure cold slender thought. It happened while the doctor was tapping on his back, and startled Walder so that he stopped breathing and the doctor had to tell him rather impatiently to start up again. It seemed to come from one of the floors above, high up and to the left. *"Only one all night and he's full of radioactive iodine. Thyrogenic carcinoma is bitter enough, Satan knows, without loading it with halogenated gamma rays. To hell with . . ."* It mumbled off till he could no longer perceive it. Hope surged up in him like a palpable substance. A brother! A brother! Somewhere up there in the hospital itself. He had but to contact him and he would get him out of here and find him a place in this world. This seemed to be a brother of tremendous brilliance and force; his thoughts, strong and clear, filled Walder's system to its fullest resonance, sounding like a bell when you're right in the bell tower, all pervasive, overwhelmingly powerful. If Walder only had a fraction of that power he could summon the brother himself. But no, he knew he could never make himself heard, particularly now, weak and confused as he was. Unlike some of the more powerful brothers who could use the telepathic voice by intention, it was in him, like in most, usually subliminal, becoming apparent only in periods of high sensual excitement. He was really very poor telepathically, though sometimes, he reflected, that had proved an advantage; he recalled the time he had found the fat one in the new Sherrington plot . . . he'd had more than he wanted by the time his radiations were strong enough to bring the rest of them scuttering down upon his find.

But a brother! A brother right here in the hospital . . .

Brandt went methodically over the patient. Chest clear to percussion and auscultation. Definite bradycardia and the cardiac sounds had a hesitant, tired quality. They somehow made him think of the word "dusty," though he'd never heard that term used in physical diagnosis. Words, words—he was getting as balmy as the psych staff. Wished he was back on the path service, much as he hated the fragrances of the post room. At least there you had something concrete to work with. What was it old Mayer, the pathology chief, used to say? Something about necromancy and alchemy being required courses for all psychiatrists. Well, that Fuchs, the psych chief, was a necromancer if there ever was one.

Seemed to know what you were thinking before you opened your mouth. And from one sentence he could deduce the state of your past relations with your sisters. Like to see what he would make of this old bird! Brandt did a brief neurological and went back to the nurses' station to write up Walder. Except for the bradycardia, the halitosis, and the mydriasis the physical exam was essentially normal. Emaciated of course. That odor though, worse than a lung abscess. Teeth seemed OK. Have to rule out that lung abscess as well as an esophageal diverticulum. Better have a chest ray. He wrote the order on the chart and glanced through the nurses' notes. Nothing unusual. Wouldn't eat his breakfast. Well, lots of them won't eat at first. This guy didn't seem to be the nervous type though. He'd be all right.

Who could it be? A patient? An orderly? A doctor? Some visitor? At the last thought Walder almost panicked. He must get to him before he got away! He was in a fever of anxiety until he perceived some low, almost unintelligible mumblings from about the same place. Seemed to be about hobnails and livers and he could make no sense of it at all. He watched everyone the orderly let through the locked wire door, and tried to make out those passing in the hall beyond. He must let the brother know he was here. For the brother might be anyone—that orderly, that student, that doctor across the ward! These worldly brothers were ingenious beyond belief; they had to be. Their disguises could probably fool him easily. His only chance was to reveal himself enough to have the brother recognize him. But he must remember not to reveal too much. His head ached with all this thinking. Why, oh why did he ever leave Ridgewood?

If he'd only been content to stay deep, like old Phidias! But no, he'd thought that by observing the living ones he could discover a way to fare in their world. It was with this in mind that he'd left the older burial grounds in the center of Ridgewood and made his way to the edge. He'd seen others leave and knew of their successes. Like that Matthew Shayne. Was it seventeen years ago he'd left? Now look at him! Driving in as bold as brass with the caskets and lowering them into the ground and looking mournful in his morning coat. And how the brothers laughed at the rubbish Shayne stuffed the coffins with, and how they cursed him for leaving nothing but chitterlings for them. Still, he always remembered to leave those, and there was never a trace of formalin about them, so the brothers were grateful. Oh, it was a sorry lot to be at the bottom of the order, forced to eke out an existence on the wrecks morticians left. If only Walder had been a little cleverer perhaps he, too, could have found a way like Brother Matthew. Perhaps he would yet with the help of this brother he'd . . . *"Fool, Fool! Three months you've been here and you can't recognize a fibroblast! See those giant cells, and the collagenous fibers? Epulis, epulis, epulides! Idiot residents, idiot . . ."* The brother was angry. His thoughts clanged through Walder's system, driving out everything else. Then gradually they sank and disappeared.

Martin, the resident on the closed wards, worked his way around the hall, hearing the interns' work-ups of the cases, dictating progress notes and orders. He stopped by Brandt's new admission and looked at him. It's strange how often the first impression one gets is right. This patient just lay there, not even looking at him. Waxen flexibility, psychomotor retardation, masklike facies . . . the terms rolled across Martin's mind, calling up other phrases, other symptoms, other ideas—all leading to a diagnosis. A schiz, he thought, this one will turn out to be a catatonic schiz.

"All right, Brandt," he said, and listened attentively to the admission note, the history and physical.

"What do you think it is, Brandt?"

"Well, sir, fifty-six is a little early for senile dementia, but he sure looks a lot older."

He certainly does, thought Martin, and picked up one of the patient's hands. The nails were dirty, coarse and rough like a laborer's.

"Is that all you've got to say?"

"Well, yes sir, I guess I'd make that number one and rule out paresis."

"You would, eh?" It was hard to tell from Martin's voice what he thought of the diagnosis. He spoke to the patient.

What's your name? Where are you? What year is this? What state is this? He was satisfied with the answers, which were given in an even, throaty voice with no hesitation.

"I'd say he was fairly well oriented, Brandt. One of the most frequent characteristics of senility is disorientation. Now we'll try him a little further and see what we get."

"Where were you born?"

"Detroit."

"When?"

"1807."

1807! Martin stopped and thought about it. This was 1952. He moved around to where he could see the patient's face better.

"And how old are you?"

"I was fifty-six."

"Probably, but how old are you now?"

"One doesn't get any older after that happens."

"What happens?"

What happens? Walder repeated the question inanely to himself. How could he tell this one what it was like? He musn't tell him. He'd told enough already for a brother to recognize him. Perhaps he was toying with him; a joke like they sometimes played on him in Ridgewood, as when Shayne had lain down in a coffin and they had led him to believe Shayne was a new one for him.

"I do not think you would understand."

Martin didn't like that too well. He looked at Brandt and then back at the patient.

"Where do you live?"

"Ridgewood Cemetery."

"Now, listen—" he glanced at the chart, "Mr. Walder. This is a hospital. We don't have time to joke. We know you don't live in the cemetery so why don't you tell us where you do live? We're your friends, we want to help you, get you home again."

The sepulchral voice was so faint Martin had to strain to hear it. "You do not understand. You could not understand."

It was the wrong thing to say. Martin just looked at the patient and moved on to the next bed.

"Better get a dental refer on him, Brandt."

"His teeth seem OK, sir. I thought a chest plate might show something."

"Lungs, teeth . . . something's sure rotten. Get it cleaned up so the rest of these patients can breathe."

"Yes, sir," Brandt said.

Why didn't the brother come? Walder caught his thoughts at odd times during the day, sometimes nearer, sometimes further. Odd, jumbled words and phrases that meant nothing to Walder. Strange ideas of little colored circles and irregular boxes with dots and lines in them and sometimes wiggling little things. There were mutterings of leukemoid and meta-myelocyte, safranin, myxomas, Anitschow nuclei and chroma-tolysis. All sorts of strange stuff that sounded at times like a foreign language. Then late in the afternoon the radiations suddenly came in even louder than in the morning. *"Beautiful, beautiful. We just cut out this little infarct and we have at least 300 grams of delicious myocardium left."* He must be quite excited to have such volume! After that Walder heard no more till morning. Apparently the brother left the hospital at night, so he wasn't a patient. It narrowed down to an orderly, doctor, or student. Judging from the day's reception he wandered all over the building, but spent most of the time upstairs someplace.

A brother of such power would be a valuable ally. He must be high in the empire. He could certainly think of a place for Walder in this world. The hardest part always was leaving the cemetery. Now that Walder had done that they would surely recognize his worth and find him a place. Never had any brother returned to the cemetery. Walder thought of the various positions he might aspire to. There was the mortuary of course, and hadn't Brother Malachy found an excellent place as a morgue attendant? Wonderful stories had come back from a brother who was with a Graves Registration Unit, actually working for the government. "Working" he called it! Walder meditated happily for a moment on such a future. Then the driving hunger within him called him back.

The brother must find him soon or it would be too late. He might perish for lack of sustenance! Or he might even be exposed for what he was! There were dreadful tales of what was done to brothers who were found out by the living ones.

Without the consoling intrusions of the brother's thoughts the nights became horrible wastelands of hopelessness and despair. Slowly, ever slowly, the hours passed by, measured loudly, constantly by that living pumping around him. Nowhere any silence, any peace, any food, only the violent, harsh rhythms of the living. Perhaps the old man in the corner . . . he seemed only partially alive and he pumped and beat more slowly, more weakly than the rest. Part of the man seemed still and quiet and almost ready. Soon perhaps . . . The hunger was burning within Walder. He could feel himself withering, dying out. If only he had heeded the others and stayed deeper. Now, locked in this place of the living, he would starve and be lost forever—for who had ever risen twice!

Two days later Walder's clinical story was the same. He hadn't eaten anything since admission and he looked it. Brandt took him off the house diet list and ordered a select diet. The dietitian called him up at noon. You could order a select diet easily enough, but how could you make the patient select it? Brandt called Martin and Martin called the chief resident.

"Why won't you eat, old man?" Rawlings was a clubby type, but one of the smartest residents ever to hit the institution.

"I don't care for that stuff."

"What would you like?" asked Rawlings.

Walder looked at him, estimated him, weighed his possibilities, then knew he was not the one.

He shook his head.

"Tube feed him," said Rawlings. He took the chart and glanced through it. "Tarry stools, eh. You take any pills, old man? No." Rawlings inclined his head at the medical student who was clerking on the ward. "What'll cause tarry stools?"

The student thought a moment. "Tarry stools could be caused by iron medication or blood . . . those are the commonest ones."

Rawlings nodded in approval and spoke to Brandt. "Better check on him and see if he's bleeding from somewhere in the GI tract." Something in the work-up caught his interest and he read more slowly. Reflectively, he closed the chart and came over to the foot of the bed, looking down at Walder. His hand rested on Walder's foot, and finally he patted it quite gently and said softly, "I'll be seeing you again, old man." He winked at Brandt and left, walking rather slowly, which was unusual for him.

Brandt jotted down the request for a gastrointestinal investigation, and got the tube. Passing a tube is no fun for anybody connected with it. It goes through a nostril, through the nasopharynx, oropharynx, and down the esophagus—if one is lucky. Brandt chilled the tube in a pan of ice and lubricated it with mineral oil, but on the first pass it curled up in the pharynx. That was enough for Walder. He whispered hoarsely to Brandt that he would eat for him if he would only get him what he could eat.

"And what do you eat?"

"Meat," said Walder. "Old meat."

"How old?"

"The older, the better."

"Well, that's easy. I'll have the chef get you an old gamy steak."

"And," said Walder, "he must not cook it."

"If you want it raw, you can have it raw." Brandt was obliging.

"And," said Walder, "it must not be an animal steak."

"What must it be?" asked Brandt, beginning to doubt.

Walder hesitated a moment, looked at the intern, then looked at the tube. The answer came softly in his cavernous whisper, "Human meat."

Brandt cleared his throat as authoritatively as he could. "All right now, Mr. Walder, let's try this tube once more. Just relax."

They tube fed him. But everything went right through undigested. And Walder got weaker and weaker. They had medical consultants in and they talked about sprue, anemias, anastomotic short circuits in the intestinal tract, and they shook their heads. The chest ray was negative. His GI series were within normal limits. He just seemed to be starving to death.

Then the case in the corner across the ward, the one with glycemic gangrene of the leg, died.

Walder felt it happen. It was a little after 1 A.M. The pumping became fainter in the corner, and finally it skipped a few times and then stopped altogether. Walder could sense the dead one across the ward. For some time now he'd known the leg was dead. But now he knew that all of the man was dead. Slowly, creakingly he got up and slid over the edge of the bed. Straight across the ward he went, like a thirsty animal nearing a spring. And it was as he thought. Almost a full hour passed before he heard the orderly coming down the hall. By the time the door was unlocked he was back in bed.

Presiding at the special meeting was Dr. Heinrich Fuchs, chief of the psychiatric service, a wise and learned man. He'd seen and heard a great many things and what he hadn't seen or heard himself, he'd read about. But, he had said, never before had he known of a thing like this happening in a hospital. In cemeteries, yes, but never in a hospital.

Dr. Mayer, the pathologist, who always personally checked every cadaver in the hospital, was finishing his report. "I would say the marks were those of human teeth. An area 12 centimeters by 9 centimeters on the anterior aspect of the thigh was denuded of skin and the underlying portions of the rectus femoris, vastus intermedius and sartorius muscles were apparently devoured, exposing about five centimeters of femur. Tentative bites appear to have been made on the neck, chest and upper extremities. Through the jugular vein, apparently, most of the blood was drained off."

The abundant use of "apparently" was characteristic of Mayer's professionally conservative attitude, but his opinion as to the physical factors involved settled the matter, for he examined more bodies than all the other men put together. Numerically, his autopsy record was unrivaled in the world. He put down the notes he had been referring to and looked quizzically at the assemblage. "Is it not strange that so many seemingly inexplicable happenings occur on the psychiatric wards?" He paused for a moment: "Perhaps where science ends, the mysterious begins."

Fuchs was on his feet instantly, his choleric color almost concealing the frenzied pumping of the distended artery on his forehead. But before he could manage coherent speech the Chief of Staff smoothly intervened, calming Fuchs and reminding Mayer that his last remarks were out of order.

This was not the first time dissension had bloomed between the psychiatrist and the pathologist. Their enmity was a byword in the hospital. It was true, of course, that things difficult to understand sometimes occurred in the psychiatric wards, and Fuchs was a figure about whom a host of legends had sprung up, legends ranging from his obsession with the color purple to his ability to dominate student nurses. Much of his success with patients was believed to be due to his phenomenal power as a hypnotist, but many thought there was an element that went beyond the science of hypnosis. In fact, there were several things about him that seemed beyond the scientific pale, especially of that science which can be seen in the test tube. He practised in a world of fears, delusions, dreams, and moods.

Mayer, on the other hand, was a strict materialist, scientifically precise and often boastful of the fact that his reports never described anything that could not be demonstrated in the laboratory. The personalities of the two men seemed as much of an antithesis as did their chosen fields. On several previous occasions they had almost come to blows, and many otherwise dull clinics had been enlivened by the sparks of their conflict.

The Chief of Staff deftly guided the discussion back to the events of the previous night and briefly reviewed the pathological findings.

After a silence, Rawlings spoke. "Necrophagy."

But it didn't seem to relieve the conclave very much.

"Fortunately," said Fuchs, who had almost subsided to his normal color, "it is a closed ward. That narrows our list down considerably. Just the patients in that ward and the attendants having keys to it. I suggest we make rounds on the ward."

Fuchs led the procession and Rawlings followed, briefing the chief on each patient as they reached the bed. When they came to Walder, Fuchs seemed to increase in alertness. "That odor," he said, his Germanic accent harshening the words in his excitement.

"He's had that right along," said Rawlings, "in spite of massive doses of chlorophyll. We thought it had improved slightly, but it does seem worse today. I'm afraid you'll have to rule him out, however. He hasn't eaten since admission, his pulse has been imperceptible at the wrist for two days, his blood pressure has dropped below eighty systolic and his respirations were so bad yesterday we've had an oxygen tent standing by *pro re nata.*" He lowered his voice and turned away from the patient. "We've expected him to go anytime, and I doubt he has the strength to speak, much less to eat."

Fuchs reached over and grasped the patient's wrist, feeling for the pulsations of the radial artery. Walder opened his eyes. For a long moment Fuchs looked at him. Walder's pulse was strong and full.

"Lie still, brother!" spoke the silent voice. Clear and impelling the radiations came to him from one among the group of white-coated men by the beside. "Breathe slowly and quietly, do not speak, do not move! We can save you if only you will be still."

Walder sought him with his eyes and probed for him with his senses. Then, Walder found his brother. It was the odor that had concealed him at first, the acrid, biting tang of formaldehyde. Walder lay quietly.

Fuchs moved on to the next bed, and the next, until they completed the ward. Then he took the patients' charts and went to his office.

At noon he went to the Ridgewood Cemetery and spent a

short time looking at the records. After that, he spent a little longer period at the Bureau of Vital Statistics.

That afternoon he visited the ward. He went straight to Walder's bed.

"When were you born, Joseph Walder?"

Walder opened his eyes and looked at him for a long time, seeing the bright glitter of understanding in his eyes, feeling the tremendous pressure of Fuchs' perceptiveness. The doctor spoke again.

"It was in 1807. And you died in 1863." The doctor leaned over Walder, staring, deep, deep into his eyes.

"You are a ghoul, Joseph Walder." His voice was little more than a whisper. "A ghoul, Joseph Walder." A trace of a smile seemed to twist the doctor's lips, and his eyelids widened suddenly showing a clear ring of white entirely around the iris.

Then, as abruptly as he had come, Fuchs turned and left.

Brandt was pondering the latest report from the lab. Walder's stools were black as tar again. But clinically the patient seemed much improved. It was all screwed up. Brandt would really have liked to see the results of a sternal puncture, the peripheral blood picture being as confused as it was. But when the hematologist had tried to get a specimen this afternoon, Walder had taken one look at the shiny sternal punch poised over his breast bone and, yelling something about an iron spike, he'd gone over the sideboards and climbed halfway up the mesh screen on the window. It took four orderlies to get him down and frightened that poor epileptic in the next bed into one hell of a seizure. After that Fuchs had bounced in and muttered over him a while and then had him transferred to room 101, a locked private. And Fuchs had kept the chart. How the devil could you write progress notes without a chart to write them on? Thank God, Brandt thought, he only had four more days on this service. He didn't care if he never saw another psycho in his life.

At the evening meeting of the staff Fuchs told them he had good reason to believe he'd found the patient responsible, but that he must check further before he could definitely say. He wanted time to study the case a little more. He assured the staff there would be no more such incidents, staking his professional reputation on it. But he begged for a little time.

"Perhaps then . . ." he hesitated, choosing his words carefully . . . "we can publish a case history that will startle the entire medical world." His voice became almost confidential. "I believe I have discovered proof of a concept long thought by the medical profession to be purely mythological. I have now only a hypothesis," he hastened to add. "But give me a little time and I'll have facts that anybody can demonstrate in any laboratory."

He accompanied this last remark with a scathing look at Mayer.

His words caused a quick buzz of excitement, with someone calling for an immediate explanation. The surgical chief asked for a résumé of the post mortem findings. Dr. Mayer repeated those details in his slow, carefully emotionless voice. At the end of the factual report, he was asked for his opinion. Removing his thin pince nez, he began to clean them as he continued speaking in his calculated, measured phrases.

"I have personally supervised every necropsy performed in this hospital in the past fourteen years. Before that I was at other institutions. I have seen a small number of similar instances. In every case they were traced to patients either temporarily deranged or purely psychotic. I believe in this instance we will find the same agents at work. We must not let the relative bizarreness of this incident cloud our critical judgment, our common sense. Mythology has no place in a hospital. Not even in the psychiatric ward."

As a rule such a remark would have brought Fuchs sputtering red-faced to his feet. He defended jealously the status of psychiatry as a science, and he and Mayer had long been at verbal scalpels' points over the issue. But tonight, oddly enough, there was no such response, somewhat to the disappointment of the younger members of the staff. Fuchs bowed slightly in the direction of the pathologist and presented his final plea. "All I ask, gentlemen, is a little time."

There was little more discussion. Everything seemed to

have been said. Even Rawlings, who was usually very out-spoken for a resident, had surprisingly little to say. He had seemed quite preoccupied all evening. In the end the staff voted Fuchs full power to act as he saw fit, reserving his explanation for not more than two weeks. Few placed much credence in his vague hypothesis, but could see no harm re-sulting from investigation.

When the meeting broke up, the doctors went their various ways out of the hospital. All but one. Quietly he unlocked the door of 101 and let himself in. Without turning on the lights he went directly to Walder's bedside.

The silent voice spoke again. *"You have acted unwisely, brother. You and your stupidity have threatened the security of the entire under empire. Scientific proof and exposure of your existence would lead to extensive investigation in many realms. No one would be safe. Our years of painstaking work would go for nought. I aid you in leaving here, more out of regard for all of us, than for you."*

Quietly he waited while Walder put on the rough clothing he had brought him. Then he unlocked the window and the heavy mesh guard. *"Ridgewood is three blocks east. No one will disturb you if you do not idle."*

Joseph came over and looked at the moon, clear and pale through the window, without glass or mesh to obstruct its cold, dead radiance. How differently he had pictured this moment. Instead of a place in this world he was being sent back to the cemetery, back to the reek of formalin, and dry cotton waste, and digging in the hard ground. But he bowed his head, for this brother was high in the empire and wise in the ways of this world.

"Remember, brother," came the whisper, *"stay away from the edge of the cemetery."*

Joseph Walder stepped out the window and Dr. Mayer watched him cross the hospital yard and turn up Andrews Avenue toward the cemetery. The doctor muttered several things to himself with a vehemence that would have startled his associates, accustomed as they were to his calm, dispas-sionate manner. He locked the door of the room and went to his lab to pick up the heart and pair of kidneys that he'd asked the diener to freeze for him so that he could take them home to dissect and study. They were in the freezing compartment wrapped in tinfoil. He weighed the package tentatively in his hands and the troubled look occasioned by Walder seeped out of his eyes. He put on his hat and coat rather quickly and as he went out the door on his way home he was almost humming.

THE GREAT KEINPLATZ EXPERIMENT

Sir Arthur Conan Doyle, M.D.

Few people know that the great creator of Sherlock Holmes was at one time a practicing physician, although not for very long: only until he found writing was more rewarding psychologically and, possibly, financially. Even fewer of those who love him as a master of the detective story know that he was also a topnotch, tongue-in-cheek, pseudo-science writer: but such is the case. In the story you are about to read, you will find Sir Arthur making excellent fun out of the standard mystico-philosophico-autocratic German medical professor (of physiology, etcetera) and the equally standard, boorish, harum-scarum, beer-drinking German student, and telling a thoroughly bizarre scientific fairy tale in the process. Incidentally, for a more modern approach to the idea dwelt on herewith, take a look at H. F. Heard's "The Swap,"* which is a remarkably different handling of the same concept Doyle deals with in "The Great Keinplatz Experiment."

* In *The Supernatural Reader*, edited by Groff Conklin. Collier Books AS392X, New York, 1962.

The Great Keinplatz Experiment

OF ALL THE sciences which have puzzled the sons of men, none had such an attraction for the learned Professor von Baumgarten as those which relate to psychology and the ill-defined relations between mind and matter. A celebrated anatomist, a profound chemist, and one of the first physiologists in Europe, it was a relief for him to turn from these subjects and to bring his varied knowledge to bear upon the study of the soul and the mysterious relationship of spirits. At first, when as a young man he began to dip into the secrets of mesmerism, his mind seemed to be wandering in a strange land where all was chaos and darkness, save that here and there some great unexplainable and disconnected fact loomed out in front of him. As the years passed, however, and as the worthy Professor's stock of knowledge increased, for knowledge begets knowledge as money bears interest, much which had seemed strange and unaccountable began to take another shape in his eyes. New trains of reasoning became familiar to him, and he perceived connecting links where all had been incomprehensible and startling. By experiments which extended over twenty years, he obtained a basis of facts upon which it was his ambition to build up a new exact science which should embrace mesmerism, spiritualism, and all cognate subjects. In this he was much helped by his intimate knowledge of the more intricate parts of animal physiology which treat of nerve currents and the working of the brain; for Alexis von Baumgarten was Regius Professor of Physiology at the University of Keinplatz, and had all the resources of the laboratory to aid him in his profound researches.

Professor von Baumgarten was tall and thin, with a hatchet face and steel-grey eyes, which were singularly bright and penetrating. Much thought had furrowed his forehead and contracted his heavy eyebrows, so that he appeared to wear a perpetual frown, which often misled people as to his character, for though austere he was tender-hearted. He was popular among the students, who would gather round him after his lectures and listen eagerly to his strange theories. Often he would call for volunteers from amongst them in order to conduct some experiment, so that eventually there was hardy a lad in the class who had not, at one time or another, been thrown into a mesmeric trance by his Professor.

Of all these young devotees of science there was none who equalled in enthusiasm Fritz von Hartmann. It had often seemed strange to his fellow-students that wild, reckless Fritz, as dashing a young fellow as ever hailed from the Rhinelands, should devote the time and trouble which he did in reading up abstruse works and in assisting the Professor in his strange experiments. The fact was, however, that Fritz was a knowing and long-headed fellow. Months before he had lost his heart to young Elise, the blue-eyed, yellow-haired daughter of the lecturer. Although he had succeeded in learning from her lips that she was not indifferent to his suit, he had never dared announce himself to her family as a formal suitor. Hence he would have found it a difficult matter to see his young lady had he not adopted the expedient of making himself useful to the Professor. By this means he frequently was asked to the old man's house, where he willingly submitted to be experimented upon in any way as long as there was a chance of his receiving one bright glance from the eyes of Elise or one touch of her little hand.

Young Fritz von Hartmann was a handsome lad enough. There were broad acres, too, which would descend to him when his father died. To many he would have seemed an eligible suitor; but Madame frowned upon his presence in the house, and lectured the Professor at times on his allowing such a wolf to prowl around their lamb. To tell the truth, Fritz had an evil name in Keinplatz. Never was there a riot or a duel, or any other mischief afoot, but the young Rhinelander figured as a ringleader in it. No one used more free and violent language, no one drank more, no one played cards more habitually, no one was more idle, save in the one solitary subject. No wonder, then, that the good Frau Professorin gathered her Fräulein under her wing, and resented the attentions of such a *mauvais sujet*. As to the worthy lecturer, he was too much engrossed by his strange studies to form an opinion upon the subject one way or the other.

For many years there was one question which had continually obtruded itself upon his thoughts. All his experiments and his theories turned upon a single point. A hundred times a day the Professor asked himself whether it was possible for the human spirit to exist apart from the body for a time and then to return to it once again. When the possibility first suggested itself to him his scientific mind had revolted from it. It clashed too violently with preconceived ideas and the prejudices of his early training. Gradually, however, as he proceeded farther and farther along the pathway of original research, his mind shook off its old fetters and became ready to face any conclusion which could reconcile the facts. There were many things which made him believe that it was possible for mind to exist apart from matter. At last it occurred to him that by a daring and original experiment the question might be definitely decided.

"It is evident," he remarked in his celebrated article upon invisible entities, which appeared in the *Keinplatz wochenliche Medicalschrift* about this time, and which surprised the whole scientific world—"it is evident that under certain conditions the soul or mind does separate itself from the body. In the case of a mesmerised person, the body lies in a cataleptic condition, but the spirit has left it. Perhaps you reply that the soul is there, but in a dormant condition. I answer that this is not so, otherwise how can one account for the condition of clairvoyance, which has fallen into disrepute through the knavery of certain scoundrels, but which can easily be shown to be an undoubted fact. I have been able myself, with a sensitive subject, to obtain an accurate description of what was going on in another room or another house. How can such knowledge be accounted for on any hypothesis save that the soul of the subject has left the body and is wandering through space? For a moment it is recalled by the voice of the operator and says what it has seen, and then wings its way once more through the air. Since the spirit is by its very nature invisible, we cannot see these comings and goings, but we see their effect in the body of the subject, now rigid and inert, now struggling to narrate impressions which could never have come to it by natural means. There is only one way which I can see by which the fact can be demonstrated. Although we in the flesh are unable to see these spirits, yet our own spirits, could we separate them from the body, would be conscious of the presence of others. It is my intention, therefore, shortly to mesmerise one of my pupils. I shall then mesmerise myself in a manner which has become easy to me. After that, if my theory holds good, my spirit will have no difficulty in meeting and communing with the spirit of my pupil, both being separated from the body. I hope to be able to communicate the result of this interesting experiment in an early number of the *Keinplatz wochenliche Medicalschrift.*"

When the good Professor finally fulfilled his promise, and published an account of what occurred, the narrative was so extraordinary that it was received with general incredulity. The tone of some of the papers was so offensive in their comments upon the matter that the angry savant declared that he would never open his mouth again, or refer to the subject in any way—a promise which he has faithfully kept. This narrative has been compiled, however, from the most authentic sources, and the events cited in it may be relied upon as substantially correct.

It happened, then, that shortly after the time when Professor von Baumgarten conceived the idea of the above-mentioned experiment, he was walking thoughtfully homewards after a long day in the laboratory, when he met a crowd of roystering students who had just streamed out from a beerhouse. At the head of them, half-intoxicated and very noisy, was young Fritz von Hartmann. The Professor would have passed them, but his pupil ran across and intercepted him.

"Heh! my worthy master," he said, taking the old man by the sleeve, and leading him down the road with him. "There is something that I have to say to you, and it is easier for me to say it now, when the good beer is humming in my head, than at another time."

"What is it, then, Fritz?" the physiologist asked, looking at him in mild surprise.

"I hear, mein Herr, that you are about to do some wondrous experiment in which you hope to take a man's soul out of his body, and then to put it back again. Is it not so?"

"It is true, Fritz."

"And have you considered, my dear sir, that you may have some difficulty in finding some one on whom to try this? *Potztausend!* Suppose that the soul went out and would not come back? That would be a bad business. Who is to take the risk?"

"But, Fritz," the Professor cried, very much startled by this view of the matter, "I had relied upon your assistance in the attempt. Surely you will not desert me. Consider the honour and glory."

"Consider the fiddlesticks!" the student cried angrily. "Am I to be paid always thus? Did I not stand two hours upon a glass insulator while you poured electricity into my body? Have you not stimulated my phrenic nerves, besides ruining my digestion with a galvanic current round my stomach? Four-and-thirty times you have mesmerised me, and what have I got from all this? Nothing. And now you wish to take my soul out, as you would take the works from a watch. It is more than flesh and blood can stand."

"Dear, dear!" the Professor cried in great distress. "That is very true, Fritz. I never thought of it before. If you can but suggest how I can compensate you, you will find me ready and willing."

"Then listen," said Fritz solemnly. "If you will pledge your word that after this experiment I may have the hand of your daughter, then I am willing to assist you; but if not, I shall have nothing to do with it. These are my only terms."

"And what would my daughter say to this?" the Professor exclaimed, after a pause of astonishment.

"Elise would welcome it," the young man replied. "We have loved each other long."

"Then she shall be yours," the physiologist said with decision, "for you are a good-hearted young man, and one of the best neurotic subjects that I have ever known—that is when you are not under the influence of alcohol. My experiment is to be performed upon the fourth of next month. You will attend at the physiological laboratory at twelve o'clock. It will be a great occasion, Fritz. Von Gruben is coming from Jena, and Hinterstein from Basle. The chief men of science of all South Germany will be there."

"I shall be punctual," the student said briefly; and so the two parted. The Professor plodded homeward, thinking of the great coming event, while the young man staggered along after his noisy companions, with his mind full of the blue-eyed Elise, and of the bargain which he had concluded with her father.

The Professor did not exaggerate when he spoke of the widespread interest excited by his novel psychological experiment. Long before the hour had arrived the room was filled by a galaxy of talent. Besides the celebrities whom he had mentioned, there had come from London the great Professor Lurcher, who had just established his reputation by a remarkable treatise upon cerebral centers. Several great lights of the Spiritualistic body had also come a long distance to be present, as had a Swedenborgian minister, who considered that the proceedings might throw some light upon the doctrines of the Rosy Cross.

There was considerable applause from this eminent assembly upon the appearance of Professor von Baumgarten and his subject upon the platform. The lecturer, in a few well-chosen words, explained what his views were, and how he proposed to test them. "I hold," he said, "that when a person is under the influence of mesmerism, his spirit is for the time released from his body, and I challenge any one to put forward any other hypothesis which will account for the fact of clairvoyance. I therefore hope that upon mesmerising my young friend here, and then putting myself into a trance, our spirits may be able to commune together, though our bodies lie still and inert. After a time nature will resume her sway, our spirits will return into our respective bodies, and all will be as before. With your kind permission, we shall now proceed to attempt the experiment."

The applause was renewed at this speech, and the audience settled down in expectant silence. With a few rapid passes the Professor mesmerised the young man, who sank back in his chair, pale and rigid. He then took a bright globe of glass from his pocket, and by concentrating his gaze upon it and making a strong mental effort, he succeeded in throwing himself into the same condition. It was a strange and impressive sight to see the old man and the young sitting together in the same cataleptic condition. Whither, then, had their souls fled? That was the question which presented itself to each and every one of the spectators.

Five minutes passed, and then ten, and then fifteen, and then fifteen more, while the Professor and his pupil sat stiff and stark upon the platform. During that time not a sound was heard from the assembled savants, but every eye was bent upon the two pale faces, in search of the first signs of returning consciousness. Nearly an hour had elapsed before the patient watchers were rewarded. A faint flush came back to the cheeks of Professor von Baumgarten. The soul was coming back once more to its earthly tenement. Suddenly he stretched out his long thin arms, as one awaking from sleep, and rubbing his eyes, stood up from his chair and gazed about him as though he hardly realized where he was. *"Tausend Teufel!"* he exclaimed, rapping out a tremendous South German oath, to the great astonishment of his audience and to the disgust of the Swedenborgian. "Where the Henker am I then, and what in thunder has occurred? Oh yes, I remember now. One of these nonsensical mesmeric experiments. There is no result this time, for I remember nothing at all since I became unconscious; so you have had all your long journeys for nothing, my learned friends, and a very good joke too;" at which the Regius Professor of Physiology burst into a roar of laughter and slapped his thigh in a highly indecorous fashion. The audience were so enraged at this unseemly behaviour on the part of their host, that there might have been a considerable disturbance, had it not been for the judicious interference of young Fritz von Hartmann, who had now recovered from his lethargy. Stepping to the front of the platform, the young man apologised for the conduct of his companion. "I am sorry to say," he said, "that he is a harum-scarum sort of fellow, although he appeared so grave at the commencement of this experiment. He is still suffering from mesmeric reaction, and is hardly accountable for his words. As to the experiment itself, I do not consider it to be a failure. It is very possible that our spirits may have been communing in space during this hour; but, unfortunately, our gross bodily memory is distinct from our spirit, and we cannot recall what has occurred. My energies shall now be devoted to devising some means by which spirits may be able to recollect what occurs to them in their free state, and I trust that when I have worked this out, I may have the pleasure of meeting you all once again in this hall, and demonstrating to you the result." This address, coming from so young a student, caused considerable astonishment among the audience, and some were inclined to be offended, thinking that he assumed rather too much importance. The majority, however, looked upon him as a young man of great promise, and many comparisons were made as they left the hall between his dignified conduct and the levity of his professor, who during the above remarks was laughing heartily in a corner, by no means abashed at the failure of the experiment.

Now although all these learned men were filing out of the lecture-room under the impression that they had seen nothing of note, as a matter of fact one of the most wonderful things in the whole history of the world had just occurred before their very eyes. Professor von Baumgarten had been so far correct in his theory that both his spirit and that of his pupil had been for a time absent from the body. But here a strange and unforeseen complication had occurred. In their return the spirit of Fritz von Hartmann had entered into the body of Alexis von Baumgarten, and that of Alexis von Baumgarten had taken up its abode in the frame of Fritz von Hartmann. Hence the slang and scurrility which issued from the lips of the serious Professor, and hence also the weighty words and grave statements which fell from the careless student. It was an unprecedented event, yet no one knew of it, least of all those whom it concerned.

The body of the Professor, feeling conscious suddenly of a great dryness about the back of the throat, sallied out into the street, still chuckling to himself over the result of the experiment, for the soul of Fritz within was reckless at the thought of the bride whom he had won so easily. His first impulse was to go up to the house and see her, but on second thought he came to the conclusion that it would be best to stay away until Madame Baumgarten should be informed by her husband of the agreement which had been made. He therefore made his way down to the Grüner Mann, which was one of the favourite trysting-places of the wilder students, and ran, boisterously waving his cane in the air, into the little parlour, where sat Spiegel and Müller and half a dozen other boon companions.

"Ha, ha! my boys," he shouted. "I knew I should find you here. Drink up, every one of you, and call for what you like, for I'm going to stand treat to-day."

Had the green man who is depicted upon the signpost of that well-known inn suddenly marched into the room and called for a bottle of wine, the students could not have been more amazed than they were by this unexpected entry of their revered professor. They were so astonished that for a minute or two they glared at him in utter bewilderment without being able to make any reply to his hearty invitation.

"Donner und Blitzen!" shouted the Professor angrily. "What the deuce is the matter with you, then? You sit there like a set of stuck pigs staring at me. What is it then?"

"It is the unexpected honour," stammered Spiegel, who was in the chair.

"Honour—rubbish!" said the Professor testily. "Do you think that just because I happen to have been exhibiting mesmerism to a parcel of old fossils, I am therefore too proud to associate with dear old friends like you? Come out of that chair, Spiegel, my boy, for I shall preside now. Beer, or wine, or schnapps, my lads—call for what you like, and put it all down to me."

Never was there such an afternoon in the Grüner Mann. The foaming flagons of lager and the green-necked bottles of Rhenish circulated merrily. By degrees the students lost their shyness in the presence of their Professor. As for him, he shouted, he sang, he roared, he balanced a long tobacco-pipe upon his nose, and offered to run a hundred yards against any member of the company. The Kellner and the barmaid whispered to each other outside the door their astonishment at such proceedings on the part of a Regius Professor of the ancient University of Keinplatz. They had still more to whisper about afterwards, for the learned man cracked the Kellner's crown, and kissed the barmaid behind the kitchen door.

"Gentlemen," said the Professor, standing up, albeit somewhat totteringly, at the end of the table, and balancing his high old-fashioned wine glass in his bony hand, "I must now explain to you what is the cause of this festivity."

"Hear! hear!" roared the students, hammering their beer glasses against the table; "a speech, a speech!—silence for a speech!"

"The fact is, my friends," said the Professor, beaming through his spectacles, "I hope very soon to be married."

"Married!" cried a student, bolder than the others. "Is Madame dead, then?"

"Madame who?"

"Why, Madame von Baumgarten, of course."

"Ha, ha!" laughed the Professor; "I can see, then, that you know all about my former difficulties. No, she is not dead, but I have reason to believe that she will not oppose my marriage."

"That is very accommodating of her," remarked one of the company.

"In fact," said the Professor, " I hope that she will now be induced to aid me in getting a wife. She and I never took to each other very much; but now I hope all that may be ended, and when I marry she will come and stay with me."

"What a happy family!" exclaimed some wag.

"Yes, indeed; and I hope you will come to my wedding, all of you. I won't mention names, but here is to my little bride!" and the Professor waved his glass in the air.

"Here's to his little bride!" roared the roysterers, with shouts of laughter. "Here's her health. *Sie soll leben—Hoch!*" And so the fun waxed still more fast and furious, while each young fellow followed the Professor's example, and drank a toast to the girl of his heart.

While all this festivity had been going on at the Grüner Mann, a very different scene had been enacted elsewhere. Young Fritz von Hartmann, with a solemn face and a reserved manner, had, after the experiment, consulted and adjusted some mathematical instruments; after which, with a few peremptory words to the janitor, he had walked out into the street and wended his way slowly in the direction of the house of the Professor. As he walked he saw Von Althaus, the professor of anatomy, in front of him, and quickening his pace he overtook him.

"I say, Von Althaus," he exclaimed, tapping him on the sleeve, "you were asking me for some information the other day concerning the middle coat of the cerebral arteries. Now I find—"

"Donnerwetter!" shouted Von Althaus, who was a peppery old fellow. "What the deuce do you mean by your impertinence! I'll have you up before the Academical Senate for this, sir;" with which threat he turned on his heel and hurried away. Von Hartmann was much surprised at this reception. "It's on account of this failure of my experiment," he said to himself, and continued moodily on his way.

Fresh surprises were in store for him, however. He was hurrying along when he was overtaken by two students. These youths, instead of raising their caps or showing any other sign of respect, gave a wild whoop of delight the instant that they saw him, and rushing at him, seized him by each arm and commenced dragging him along with them.

"Gott in Himmel!" roared Von Hartmann. "What is the meaning of this unparalleled insult? Where are you taking me?"

"To crack a bottle of wine with us," said the two students. "Come along! That is an invitation which you have never refused."

"I never heard of such insolence in my life!" cried Von Hartmann. "Let go my arms! I shall certainly have you rusticated for this. Let me go, I say!" and he kicked furiously at his captors.

"Oh, if you choose to turn ill-tempered, you may go where you like," the students said, releasing him. "We can do very well without you."

"I know you. I'll pay you out," said Von Hartmann furiously, and continued in the direction which he imagined to be his own home, much incensed at the two episodes which had occurred to him on the way.

Now, Madame von Baumgarten, who was looking out of the window and wondering why her husband was late for dinner, was considerably astonished to see the young student come stalking down the road. As already remarked, she had a great antipathy to him, and if ever he ventured into the house it was on sufferance, and under the protection of the Professor. Still more astonished was she, therefore, when she beheld him undo the wicket-gate and stride up the garden path with the air of one who is master of the situation. She could hardly believe her eyes, and hastened to the door with all her maternal instincts up in arms. From the upper windows the fair Elise had also observed this daring move upon the part of her lover, and her heart beat quick with mingled pride and consternation.

"Good day, sir," Madame von Baumgarten remarked to the intruder, as she stood in gloomy majesty in the open doorway.

"A very fine day indeed, Martha," returned the other. "Now, don't stand there like a statue of Juno, but bustle about and get the dinner ready, for I am well-nigh starved."

"Martha! Dinner!" ejaculated the lady, falling back in astonishment.

"Yes, dinner, Martha, dinner!" howled Von Hartmann, who was becoming irritable. "Is there anything wonderful in that request when a man has been out all day? I'll wait in the dining-room. Anything will do. *Schinken,* and sausage, and prunes—any little thing that happens to be about. There you are, standing staring again. Woman, will you or will you not stir your legs?"

This last address, delivered with a perfect shriek of rage, had the effect of sending good Madame von Baumgarten flying along the passage and through the kitchen, where she locked herself up in the scullery and went into violent hysterics. In the meantime Von Hartmann strode into the room and threw himself down upon the sofa in the worst of tempers.

"Elise!" he shouted. "Confound the girl! Elise!"

Thus roughly summoned, the young lady came timidly downstairs and into the presence of her lover. "Dearest!" she cried, throwing her arms round him, "I know this is all done for my sake. It is a *ruse* in order to see me."

Von Hartmann's indignation at this fresh attack upon him was so great that he became speechless for a minute from rage, and could only glare and shake his fists, while he struggled in her embrace. When he at last regained his utterance, he indulged in such a bellow of passion that the young lady dropped back, petrified with fear, into an arm-chair.

"Never have I passed such a day in my life," Van Hartmann cried, stamping upon the floor. "My experiment has failed. Von Althaus has insulted me. Two students have dragged me along the public road. My wife nearly faints when I ask her for dinner, and my daughter flies at me and hugs me like a grizzly bear."

"You are ill, dear," the young lady cried. "Your mind is wandering. You have not even kissed me once."

"No, and I don't intend to either," Von Hartmann said with decision. "You ought to be ashamed of yourself. Why don't you go and fetch my slippers, and help your mother to dish the dinner?"

"And is it for this," Elise cried, burying her face in her handkerchief—"is it for this that I have loved you passionately for upwards of ten months? Is it for this that I have braved my mother's wrath? Oh, you have broken my heart; I am sure you have!" and she sobbed hysterically.

"I can't stand much more of this," roared Von Hartmann furiously. "What the deuce does the girl mean? What did I do ten months ago which inspired you with such a particular affection for me? If you are really so very fond, you would do better to run away down and find the *Schinken* and some bread, instead of talking all this nonsense."

"Oh, my darling!" cried the unhappy maiden, throwing herself into the arms of what she imagined to be her lover. "You do but joke in order to frighten your little Elise."

Now it chanced that at the moment of this unexpected embrace Von Hartmann was still leaning back against the end of the sofa, which, like much German furniture, was in a somewhat rickety condition. It also chanced that beneath this end of the sofa there stood a tank full of water in which the physiologist was conducting certain experiments upon the ova of fish, and which he kept in his drawing room in order to ensure an equable temperature. The additional weight of the maiden, combined with the impetus with which she hurled herself upon him, caused the precarious piece of furniture to give way, and the body of the unfortunate student was hurled backwards into the tank, in which his head and shoulders were firmly wedged, while his lower extremities flapped helplessly about in the air. This was the last straw. Extricating himself with some difficulty from his unpleasant position, Von Hartmann gave an inarticulate yell of fury, and dashing out of the room, in spite of the entreaties of Elise, he seized his hat and rushed off into the town, all dripping and dishevelled, with the intention of seeking in some inn the food and comfort which he could not find at home.

As the spirit of Von Baumgarten encased in the body of Von Hartmann strode down the winding pathway which led down to the little town, brooding angrily over his many wrongs, he became aware that an elderly man was approaching him who appeared to be in an advanced state of intoxication. Von Hartmann waited by the side of the road and watched this individual, who came stumbling along, reeling from one side of the road to the other, and singing a student song in a very husky and drunken voice. At first his interest was merely excited by the fact of seeing a man of so venerable an appearance in such a disgraceful condition, but as he approached nearer, he became convinced that he knew the other well, though he could not recall when or where he had met him. This impression became so strong with him, that when the stranger came abreast of him he stepped in front of him and took a good look at his features.

"Well, sonny," said the drunken man, surveying Von Hartmann and swaying about in front of him, "where the *Henker* have I seen you before? I know you as well as I know myself. Who the deuce are you?"

"I am Professor von Baumgarten," said the student. "May I ask who you are? I am strangely familiar with your features."

"You should never tell lies, young man," said the other. "You're certainly not the Professor, for he is an ugly snuffy old chap, and you are a big broad-shouldered young fellow. As to myself, I am Fritz von Hartmann at your service."

"That you certainly are not," exclaimed the body of Von Hartmann. "You might very well be his father. But hullo, sir, are you aware that you are wearing my studs and my watch-chain?"

"*Donnerwetter!*" hiccoughed the other. "If those are not the trousers for which my tailor is about to sue me, may I never taste beer again."

Now as Von Hartmann, overwhelmed by the many strange things which had occurred to him that day, passed his hand over his forehead and cast his eyes downwards, he chanced to catch the reflection of his own face in a pool which the rain had left upon the road. To his utter astonishment he perceived that his face was that of a youth, that his dress was that of a fashionable young student, and that in every way he was the antithesis of the grave and scholarly figure in which his mind was wont to dwell. In an instant his active brain ran over the series of events which had occurred and sprang to the conclusion. He fairly reeled under the blow.

"*Himmel!*" he cried, "I see it all. Our souls are in the wrong bodies. I am you and you are I. My theory is proved—but at what an expense! Is the most scholarly mind in Europe to go about with this frivolous exterior? Oh the labours of a lifetime are ruined!" and he smote his breast in his despair.

"I say," remarked the real Von Hartmann from the body of the professor, "I quite see the force of your remarks, but don't go knocking my body about like that. You received it in an excellent condition, but I perceive that you have wet it and bruised it, and spilled snuff over my ruffled shirt-front."

"It matters little," the other said moodily. "Such as we are so must we stay. My theory is triumphantly proved, but the cost is terrible."

"If I thought so," said the spirit of the student, "it would be hard indeed. What could I do with these stiff old limbs, and how could I woo Elise and persuade her that I was not her father? No, thank Heaven, in spite of the beer which has upset me more than ever it could upset my real self, I can see a way out of it."

"How?" gasped the Professor.

"Why, by repeating the experiment. Liberate our souls once more, and the chances are that they will find their way back into their respective bodies."

No drowning man could clutch more eagerly at a straw than did Von Baumgarten's spirit at this suggestion. In feverish haste he dragged his own frame to the side of the road and threw it into a mesmeric trance; he then extracted the crystal ball from the pocket, and managed to bring himself into the same condition.

Some students and peasants who chanced to pass during the next hour were much astonished to see the worthy Professor of Physiology and his favourite student both sitting upon a very muddy bank and both completely insensible. Before the hour was up quite a crowd had assembled, and they were discussing the advisability of sending for an ambulance to convey the pair to hospital, when the learned savant opened his eyes and gazed vacantly around him. For an instant he seemed to forget how he had come there, but next moment he astonished his audience by waving his skinny arms above his head and crying out in a voice of rapture, *"Gott sei gedankt!* I am myself again. I feel I am!" Nor was the amazement lessened when the student, springing to his feet, burst into the same cry, and the two performed a sort of *pas de joie* in the middle of the road.

For some time after that people had some suspicion of the sanity of both the actors in this strange episode. When the Professor published his experiences in the *Medicalschrift* as he had promised, he was met by an intimation, even from his colleagues, that he would do well to have his mind cared for, and that another such publication would certainly consign him to a madhouse. The student also found by experience that it was wisest to be silent about the matter.

When the worthy lecturer returned home that night he did not receive the cordial welcome which he might have looked for after his strange adventures. On the contrary, he was roundly upbraided by both his female relatives for smelling of drink and tobacco, and also for being absent while a young scapegrace invaded the house and insulated its occupants. It was long before the domestic atmosphere of the lecturer's house resumed its normal quiet, and longer still before the genial face of Von Hartmann was seen beneath its roof. Perseverance, however, conquers every obstacle, and the student eventually succeeded in pacifying the enraged ladies and in establishing himself upon the old footing. He has now no longer any cause to fear the enmity of Madame, for he is Hauptmann von Hartmann of the Emperor's own Uhlans, and his loving wife Elise has already presented him with two little Uhlans as a visible sign and token of her affection.

COMPOUND B

David Harold Fink, M.D.

Here a serious-minded physician sets to work on some of the refractory materials of reality out of which science fiction sometimes is made. (Everything in this story is possible.) We must add that he makes a pretty unsavory pot of message from it, too. His protagonists are distinctly unpleasant, his plot sinister, and his dénouement devastating. That someone lived to tell the story at all is a miracle of the fictioneer's art. And then there is the sting in the tail, the story's last paragraph. Read it over, all about the "fifth freedom," and perhaps copy it out and give it to your friends. It might *do some good.*

Compound B

IF THE discoveries of Dr. Max Murdock had not been hidden behind the coconut palm curtain in the late 1960's, World War III might have been averted. As it happened, the hoarding of his scientific discovery set back the progress of world unity and civilization by hundreds of years and, what is worse, permanently impoverished the limited resources of this poor planet by loosing atomic warfare in its almost unlimited destructiveness.

I came upon the discoveries of Dr. Murdock while participating as literary editor for an archeological project in the Mantu Islands, which rise above the blue waters of the South Pacific a few hundred miles south and west of New Guinea. No human life remained upon these once-populous lands. With her inexorable vegetable logic, Nature had taken over to destroy and absorb almost every trace of man's invasion of her domain. Only some concrete caves remained, mutely to tell the tragic defeat of man's high hopes; and it was within these bleak caves that we found a crude but usable chemistry laboratory and the records from which I pieced together the story of the life and death of Dr. Max Murdock.

I am a novelist. I can tell a story only in my own way. I hope that I may be permitted to set down in narrative form the drama which was played out to its tragic conclusion five hundred years ago, roughly between 1965 and 1975.

The Murdocks were on their way to the Mantu Islands. They had sailed on a ship, the *Lurline*, to Hawaii where they spent ten days waiting for the freighter which was to take them to Sydney, Australia. In Hawaii they had whiled away the time sight-seeing and shopping. They had not enjoyed this; Dr. Murdock was indifferent and bored, while Mrs. Murdock worried so much over the price of every purchase that its ownership gave her no feeling of pleasure. It was with relief that they boarded the British freighter which was to take them to Sydney. They settled down to endure the heat and the empty passage of time with stoical equanimity.

The trip seemed endless and endlessly boring. However, when they reached Sydney, their luck seemed to turn. When they inquired at the booking office, they found that a Dutch tramp steamer would leave Sydney in two days; it would stop at the Mantu Islands to pick up copra. They engaged passage at once and for the first time in three weeks they smiled spontaneously.

"Anyhow," exclaimed Mrs. Murdock as she paid for the tickets, "it won't cost us much to live there."

"Missionaries?" inquired the booking agent as he filled out the necessary forms.

"Yes," replied Dr. Murdock decisively as his wife hesitated with her answer.

"My husband's a doctor," Mrs. Murdock volunteered.

The booking agent looked at them curiously. What, he wondered, could induce apparently sane people to leave their comfortable living to take residence among such unsavory people as the Mantus? Once he had employed a Mantu boy as a house servant when he lived in New Guinea and he had not been able to tolerate the Melanesian lad for a week. "Well," he said, "they need something in those Mantu Islands. Not very nice people, you know."

"They have souls to be saved," Dr. Murdock replied tartly.

The booking agent did not reply. "Those Americans," he was thinking. "All they think about is saving the almighty dollar and souls. No sense of humor."

Dr. and Mrs. Murdock had been missionaries for two months. It was the cleaning woman's feeble-minded son who had been the unlikely instrument that turned them into this field, so foreign to their natures. Neither of them took religion seriously; neither of them liked people as individuals. Yet here they were in Sydney, eager to embark on a ship which was to carry them into the most intimate relationships with their fellow man.

Dr. Murdock was afraid of people because he did not understand them. People are really very simple except to those who, like Dr. Murdock, think that people are very complex and unpredictable.

But Dr. Murdock thought he liked people. He took a deep and intelligent interest in social problems. He read the weekly news magazines avidly to keep himself informed of what people were doing. He formed decided opinions on politics. He loved mankind but loved no individual man, woman, or child. In short, he suffered from that deformity of spirit we call intellectualism. Like the midget and bearded lady in the circus, he prided himself on his deformity. "I," he said, "am an intellectual."

He had begun his career as a biological chemist, but because he wanted to do something great for humanity, he studied medicine. He felt that by combining these skills and sciences he could invent a drug which would lift humanity out of its doldrums and into a place where life could be lived pleasantly, without needless friction and suffering. And with his singleness of purpose, his dedication to his idea, his implacable perseverance, he did invent just such a medicine.

It was this invention which led to his becoming a missionary to the Mantu Melanesians in the South Pacific.

For fifteen years he had been working in the little laboratory which he had improvised in his Los Angeles home when on a certain fateful Thursday morning his wife interrupted him.

"Sally is here," she said. "I need seventeen dollars. We didn't pay her last week."

Sally was the colored cleaning woman who came in once a week to help Mrs. Murdock.

"I have it! I have it!"

Mrs. Murdock waited impatiently while the doctor examined a purple liquid in an Ehrlenmeyer flask which he held up to the light.

"I have it!" he repeated.

"Well, give it to me then," Mrs. Murdock said.

For the first time Dr. Murdock heard his wife. "Give you what?" he asked.

"The seventeen dollars."

"What seventeen dollars?"

"The seventeen dollars we owe Sally. This is her day for cleaning the house. You told me you had it."

Dr. Murdock's face lost its glow of exhilaration.

"Oh," he said, "I meant that my experiment worked. The new catalyst worked. I've got it." He held up the flask and swirled the purple solution around.

"Do you know what this is?" he asked. "This is the drug that will save the world from its own stupidity. It will transform even a moron into a genius."

"Don't you have the seventeen dollars?" asked Mrs. Murdock.

Dr. Murdock shook his head. "No. As a matter of fact, I have only two dollars, but I expect to collect something in the office this afternoon. We'll get by."

Mrs. Murdock sighed. "But what in the world will I tell Sally? We didn't pay her last week, either."

They both thought deeply, and then Dr. Murdock sighed.

"It's always money, money, money. The love of money is the root of all evil."

This reflection did not bring happiness to Mrs. Murdock who was thinking that the lack of money was the root of all her evils. However, she was thinking fast and practically.

"Sally has a feeble-minded son. I wonder . . ."

Dr. Murdock snatched at the conversation. "We'll give her some of this. Her son will be the first to be cured."

Mrs. Murdock was still thinking about the seventeen dollars and beyond that to eight dollars and fifty cents a week for the weeks stretching ahead.

"Are you sure it will work?" she asked.

"I'm positive," Dr. Murdock replied. "This solution . . ." and he swirled it in front of his wife's eyes, "this beautiful purple solution contains di-alpha-hydrobenzol-glutamic acid hydrochloride. Synthesizing it had to wait upon my invention of the catalyst."

Mrs. Murdock was still thinking and she wanted time to organize her thoughts, so she asked, "What's a catalyst?" She hardly listened while the doctor explained that a catalyst is an agent that facilitates a chemical reaction without participation in the reaction itself. "It sort of introduces and joins two substances without becoming friendly or joining with either of them." He added jocosely, "Like a minister at a wedding."

Mrs. Murdock asked, "I wonder what it would be worth to Sally?"

"Oh give her some and we'll pay her next time."

Mrs. Murdock had other ideas but she did not express them. "Put some of it in a bottle and I'll see what I can do."

Sally's son, Abraham Burns, was indeed a moron. Although the lad was sixteen years old, he had the intelligence of a six-year-old. According to law he had to attend school until he reached the age of eighteen, so he had been put in an un-graded room to vegetate until he could be discharged into the world to make his dim way as best he could.

The day after his mother had given him a teaspoonful of the purple medicine, he disappeared from school.

For two weeks he was nowhere to be found. During this time his mother was frantic. She rightly blamed Dr. and Mrs. Murdock for his disappearance. Mrs. Murdock blamed her husband, who forsook his laboratory for his office, not so much for the money, but more to escape his wife's sharp tongue.

When Abraham returned to his home, he was hungry and tired but there was a new look in his eyes.

"Where you been?" his mother demanded.

"Library," the boy replied as he gulped down his corn-bread and boiled pork. "Can I have some more pork, ma?"

His mother gave him another serving. "What you been doin' in the library? Do you know the law's been around here looking for you?"

"Law don't bother me none," he replied with a laugh. "I'm goin' to school this afternoon and when I get there, I'm goin' to give that old principal a piece of my mind. The idea of him puttin' me in an ungraded room! Why I'm smarter than he'll ever dream of bein'."

Sally had never heard her son talk like this. Somehow it frightened her and she felt chills run up her legs and down her back.

"No good your talking like white folks," she said. "Mind what you say to that principal or you'll get in trouble."

When Sally came to work for the Murdocks the following Thursday, she was beside herself with excitement. "God bless you, Dr. Murdock," she said over and over. "I'll work for you free the rest of my life. You don't know what you've done for my boy."

What Dr. Murdock had done for her boy seemed no less than a miracle. Abraham had indeed seen the principal but he did not get into trouble. Instead, he was given a battery of psychological tests which, the psychologist said, indicated that the boy was a near-genius. He was also given tests in English, history, spelling, arithmetic, and other subjects and as a result of his performance, he was promoted from the ungraded room to the tenth grade.

"Well, that's fine," said Mrs. Murdock who was thinking that she would be spared the necessity of asking the doctor for eight dollars and fifty cents every Thursday. "That's just fine, Sally, and you won't have to work for us the rest of your life without pay. If you just come here every Thursday for a year, we'll feel that you've paid us in full." She turned to her husband. "You better take a dose of that medicine yourself," she said.

Dr. Murdock did, but whether he had already reached his peak of intelligence or whether some other cause was operative, he did not know. At any rate he saw no change in himself.

He gave the medicine to his patients but the results were disappointing. Why, he wondered, had it worked so well on Abraham Burns and upon no one else? He set out to investigate, much to the disgust of Mrs. Murdock who resented the time this took away from his practice.

Dr. Murdock decided to give his medicine to a second and a third colored moron. Again the results were astounding. One teaspoonful of the purple liquid changed the moron into a near-genius.

"It works on Negroes but not on white people," he said. "There must be something present in Negro blood which is absent from white blood, and it is this something, this x-factor, which unites with my compound to make them intelligent. But what can this x-factor be?"

The question did not interest Mrs. Murdock, but nevertheless she thought she saw possibilities in Dr. Murdock's compound.

"There should be a good market for this," she said. "There are lots of stupid colored people and you should get at least a thousand dollars for everyone you help. People are more stupid than you think. Especially, colored people."

Dr. Murdock shook his head. "That's not the way medicine is practiced," he told her. "In the first place, we doctors do not patent our discoveries, nor do we keep them secret. We give them freely to the world."

"A fine idea," Mrs. Murdock sneered, "and in the meantime who supports the doctor's wife and children?"

Dr. Murdock could not answer this one, so he evaded the question by observing that they had no children and for a time the argument turned upon the question as to who was to blame. Finally, Dr. Murdock returned to the subject nearest his heart. "I can't publicize this discovery," he said. "It would defeat my purpose. Not just the colored peoples of this earth but all people must be made intelligent. The world has become so complicated," he continued as he warmed up to his favorite topic, "that mankind lacks the intelligence to create and repair its social machinery. In other words, people are too dumb to govern themselves and smart men are too evil to be entrusted with the government of their fellows. Democracy is the answer, but democracy cannot succeed until all men are intelligent."

Mrs. Murdock interrupted his soliloquy. "You just don't want me to have anything," she said. "Here I live in this damned old shack without even a washing machine and all you worry about is social machinery. A lot of good that does me."

"I do worry about you," Dr. Murdock insisted. "All right. Suppose I gave this compound to the black races. How long, do you suppose, could you hire Sally? With this drug," and here he held up his purple compound, "the blacks would dominate the earth. No white boy would have a chance to get into medical school, into law school, or to study engineering. The blacks would run everything. And Sally, why, you'd be working for Sally instead of Sally working for you. Don't tell me I don't think about you."

The thought of working for Sally made Mrs. Murdock shudder. She hated Negroes.

Furthermore, she knew from her twenty years of experience as Dr. Murdock's wife that it would be useless to argue with him. He would never commercialize his compound by selling it to Negroes.

"Well, to hell with it, then," she exclaimed. Defeated, she slammed the door as she left the room.

Dr. Murdock followed her to the kitchen. "Do you know what I'm going to do?" he asked her.

"Go to work?" Mrs. Murdock asked, half sneeringly and half hopefully.

"I'll tell you what I'm going to do. I'm going to invent a compound which will make the white race intelligent. Compound B."

"And in the meantime," Mrs. Murdock asked with exasperation which she controlled only by clenching her fists, "And in the meantime will you please tell me how we're going to live?"

The question of how Dr. Murdock was going to finance his research involved a few months of acrimonious discussion between himself and his wife.

Dr. Murdock was convinced that Negro blood contained an x-factor which, uniting with his compound, transformed them into geniuses. He was determined to discover this x-factor, and to do so, he would have to study the composition of Negro blood. But where and how? He confided his problem to his wife. Eventually, it was she who hit upon a practical solution.

Both of them had been graduated from an Evangelical college which supported a medical school. Both the college and medical school had been created for the purpose of training missionaries. This fact occurred to Mrs. Murdock during one of her long, sleepless nights and in the morning she said to her husband, "We're going to be missionaries. You can live with your colored people and practice medicine for free. But we're going to be paid out of the missionary funds. Then you can fool around with your damn Compound B all you like. And the fewer patients you have, the better I'll like it."

Mrs. Murdock was a determined woman and not without resources in persuasion. It was through her efforts that Dr. and Mrs. Murdock found themselves in Sydney, Australia, waiting for the ship which was to take them to the Mantu Islands to bring religion and medicine to the heathens and an opportunity for research to Dr. Max Murdock.

On the deck of the Dutch tramp steamer, Mrs. Clara Murdock contemplated her future with ever-increasing anxiety. Had she done the right thing in uprooting her husband by taking him to the South Pacific to continue his search for Compound B? Were they on another wild goose chase?

She remembered the time when her husband had brought up his idea for making Compound A, the one which had cured Abraham Burns of feeble-mindedness. He had exclaimed, "This will save the world. Everyone will be super-intelligent. No more stupidity anywhere. You'll be rich. You'll be able to do anything you want to do." That was fifteen years ago, and she had fallen into the trap. Money, fame, power—these were the baits at which she always snapped. And now, fifteen years later, she was as far from wealth, fame, and power as she always had been. She was the wife of an obscure missionary doctor, on her way to the Mantu settlements and to God knows what hardships.

They had come so close to success in Compound A, the one which turned a lot of ordinary chemicals into the compound that could make geniuses out of Negro morons. Why couldn't he have hit upon a drug that would work on white folk?

Sweating in the deck chair under the tropical sun, she fell into her favorite fantasy, the one in which she had a million dollars and an assured income of fifty thousand dollars a year. She saw herself presiding over a beautiful home, complete with servants, a large electric freezer and a heated swimming pool. What entertaining she would do! What celebrities in bathing suits would bask in the California sunshine, reclining on gaily colored deck chairs arranged with calculated casualness in her friendly patio. Would she serve cocktails? Of course. Not that she would drink, but why be narrow-minded? Narrow-mindedness is the only luxury that a millionaire cannot afford.

But how to get the million dollars? Mrs. Murdock turned from her fantasy to purposive planning. First: let Dr. Max Murdock invent his Compound B. Second: form a nonprofit corporation, a foundation, and turn the brain-producing medicine over to the non-profit corporation. By doing this, all profits from its sale would be tax-free. Mrs. Murdock had studied accounting and business administration while at college; she understood the trickeries and shady by-passes of finance. Finally, she, Mrs. Max Murdock, would be the president of the non-profit corporation; and as president she would get a salary of fifty thousand dollars a year for life. Dr. Max Murdock would also receive a large salary and have a beautiful laboratory in which to continue his research work. Away from home, of course.

She sighed. It was a beautiful dream, a beautiful iridescent soap bubble, but it all hung upon that old Compound B, as a beautiful iridescent soap bubble hangs upon an ugly clay pipe. Could Dr. Murdock create the clay pipe?

And what about the Mantus? What were they like? Would they allow the Murdocks to live in peace and quiet so that Dr. Murdock could put together the pipe upon which her soap bubble must depend? The remark made by the booking agent in Sydney had disquieted her. She decided to find out more about these black heathens from the captain of this Dutch tramp steamer on which she was traveling. He had done business with them for years. He ought to know.

"They are very honest," the captain told her. "They are trained from infancy never to touch anything that belongs to another person. On all this earth, and I've been around, you can depend on that, I've never found more honest, reliable people. Why, do you know," he went on, "they can't stand being in debt. Do something for one of them and he can't stand it until he does something of equal value for you."

Mrs. Murdock nodded her head understandingly. "I don't like to be under obligation to anyone, myself," she confided.

"Of course, I don't like to be taken for a sucker, either," she added.

The captain did not like Mrs. Murdock's autobiographical interpolation; it interrupted his chain of thought. If she had been a pretty, young woman it would be different. The autobiography of an attractive woman furnishes the would-be seducer with cues, indications as to what to do or say next. The captain looked at Mrs. Murdock while she was talking and he reflected that twenty years earlier things might have been different. At this late day he wanted none of her comments about herself.

"They are very moral, too," he went on. "No hanky-panky. The girls are all virtuous and the people, men and women, are very prudish. Taboo, you know. Marriage with them is all business. The parents arrange the marriages for their children and exchange property. Marriage with them gets to be a kind of business alliance between families. They don't go for any romantic nonsense."

"What do they do for a living?"

"Traders, mostly. Be careful of them; they'll trade you out of your eyeteeth. They have about two hundred settlements where they set up stores. They buy and sell to the other Melanesian tribes. Sometimes they buy land and work plantations. The Mantus are landlords and overseers; the more primitive Melanesians do the work. They are practically European in their outlook. All they care about is money and property and getting ahead."

Mrs. Murdock felt relieved. "I think I'll like them even if they are black," she said. "I was afraid that they'd be quite uncivilized. After all, they can't help being black."

The Murdocks had been established in their tropical island home for seven months and during that time much had happened to confuse and worry Mrs. Murdock. Now, seated before her portable typewriter and making her first report to the Board of Missions, she hardly knew what to tell and what not to tell the Missionary Board. From the veranda she could see the sparkling Pacific through the grove of coconut palms which surrounded the house. Peace and calm lay all about her but there was no peace and calm in Clara Murdock's mind.

"The Mantus are very hospitable people," she wrote, *"and they are most grateful for the medical services of Dr. Murdock. Within a week after we arrived, they selected a beautiful building site for our mission and built us a most suitable place in which to live and work for their salvation."* The Missionary Board would be glad to know this, she reflected and then she exclaimed out loud, "What a lie!"

What really happened was this. When their belongings in many trunks and crates were put ashore, Paytone, the richest man on the island, approached them to ask their purpose in coming to the islands. When they told him that their intention was to bring the blessings of modern medicine and science to the Mantus, Paytone observed that their services would not be in demand and that they, the Murdocks, would not be able to earn a living. Fortunately, Mrs. Murdock had been prepared by the Dutch steamer captain for just such a reception. She replied that they possessed independent means and were prepared to pay their own way. At once, the black man became conciliatory and even obsequious. "Like a real estate salesman in Los Angeles," Mrs. Murdock told her husband.

Paytone and Mrs. Murdock were quick to reach an understanding, and as they did so, they discovered that despite their difference in color, they were kindred spirits. Paytone was a short, thick-set Melanesian. His shoulders were broad; his chest was barrel-shaped; and although he was forty-five years old, his arms and legs were as heavily muscled as an American wrestler. His features, while not fine, were not coarse. Mrs. Murdock reflected that if he were not black, she could like him, he looked so like an American business executive. He had worked in Australia during his adolescence and young manhood and spoke English with only a slight Australian accent. Mrs. Murdock soon found herself enjoying her business relationship with him.

Together they found a home site in a palm grove on a hilltop overlooking the Pacific. Paytone would not sell, but agreed to rent the property and build a house after Mrs. Murdock's specifications. Mrs. Murdock was delighted. That very afternoon a group of Melanesians brought bamboo and lumber to the site; within three days the house was completed and their goods were moved in.

Paytone had carried out his part of the bargain with scrupulous exactness. Dr. Murdock had his laboratory, complete with shelves and tables. Mrs. Murdock had her kitchen equipped with kerosene stove and kerosene-activated refrigerator. These two pieces of equipment fascinated Paytone, who inspected their every detail. He took more than a builder's casual interest in the house and its furnishings.

Mrs. Murdock returned her attention to the letter she was trying to write. The Dutch tramp steamer would arrive any day now; she must make herself finish it.

"Dr. Murdock has discovered a medicine which makes these blacks much more intelligent," she wrote. *"He treated the son of the richest man in the Islands, one Paytone. The results were astounding. Paytone demanded some of this medicine for himself, and ever since he received it, he has been a different man."*

At least this much, she reflected, was true. Paytone had vainly tried to put his own business sense into the thick head of his youngest son, but the boy's skull was simply impenetrable. But after taking one teaspoonful of Compound A, the boy took to business as a fly to honey.

Paytone had been delighted. Consistent with his attitude of not being able to tolerate an obligation, he insisted on the Murdocks' living rent-free in the home he had built for them. He also inquired into the cost of a dose of this purple liquid for himself. Payment in sago and yams was agreed upon and Paytone was given two teaspoonsful of the purple liquid. The following day he asked Mrs. Murdock to teach him to read and write.

"I have been teaching the most influential man on these islands to read and write," she went on. *"Both Dr. Murdock and I feel that the conversion of the Mantus can best be accomplished through adult education. If,"* she paused and x-ed out the 'if.' *"After we convert the adults, they can cooperate with us in teaching the children."*

She then typewrote a list of titles of books to be sent to her.

They included such subjects as philosophy, art, and fictional literature.

"*Their conversion,*" she went on, "*depends upon their acceptance of Western ideas. Their religion makes it impossible for them to accept the blessings of modern medicine. This religion is a kind of ethical spiritism. They believe that all disease is a punishment visited upon them by their recently deceased relatives because of some transgression of their moral code. Cure of disease is in the hands of these spirits, whose favor depends upon their confessing their sins and turning away from evil. All good that comes to them they attribute to these spirits who reward the living for having followed in the path of virtue.*

"*Until they realize that modern medicine and not virtue can cure disease and that modern science rather than their virtues can bring them wealth, we cannot teach them to be Christians.*"

She typed on, "*You can have no idea of the hold their religion has upon them. They do not steal, they pay their debts, they work hard and save and live pure lives. Girls and boys do not speak to each other after the age of puberty and married women never speak to men other than their husbands—all because of fear of offending their recently dead relatives. However, we'll change all that after we educate them.*"

She rested for a minute and added, "*Dr. Murdock keeps busy with his scientific research and medicine. He seems much happier here doing God's work than he was when he practiced medicine in Los Angeles.*"

She ended her letter with a sigh of relief. It was almost time for Paytone to come for his lessons. He had already mastered reading and writing and a course in bookkeeping. They were now studying a college text book titled, *Modern Banking and Finance,* and both were finding the work exhilarating and exciting.

When Paytone came to discuss modern banking and finance with Mrs. Murdock, her husband was working in his laboratory with his assistant, Hargo, a Melanesian lad whom he had trained to help him. He had given the boy the purple solution and so had nothing to complain of in regard to Hargo's capacity to learn. Already he had taught the black boy the equivalent of two years of college work in mathematics and chemistry. Hargo was now ready to study calculus, the theory of least squares, and physical chemistry. Dr. Murdock felt himself being crowded by the boy's eagerness.

When the doctor heard Paytone's voice, he went out to the veranda to greet him. He always felt that Paytone treated him with ill-concealed, amused contempt, but he was used to such treatment at the hands of his wife's friends, so while inwardly cursing himself for his awkward stiffness, he made his usual attempt to appear friendly. He envied Paytone's urbanity and social ease.

"I see you're hard at work," Paytone observed. "You are really one of us at heart. We have a saying, 'The departed spirit will always reward a hard worker.' "

When Dr. Murdock only nodded his head in reply, Paytone went on, "What are you working at?"

For reasons of his own, Dr. Murdock had kept the object of his research a secret. He was secretive by nature, because he was the type who loses interest in a project once he has talked about it; besides, his training in research chemistry had taught him never to share an idea until it was ready for the scientific journals. Sad experience had shown him that other research scientists are always ready to pounce upon any discovery to claim it for their own. Secrecy, or perhaps the need for secrecy, was the principal social disease of the twentieth century. Now, of course, such secrecy is unthinkable. So, at Paytone's question, Dr. Murdock felt himself tighten up and draw within himself like a snail curling up in its shell.

"It's just a research project," he replied while he shot a meaningful look at his wife, warning her not to talk. Then he said, "Well, I'll leave you two alone now; I've got to get back to work."

As he left he heard Paytone's low voice, saying, "The doctor keeps pretty busy. My people keep asking me why he takes their blood. They wonder just what he's up to." Dr. Murdock did not catch his wife's reply.

That afternoon Hargo noticed that the doctor was absent-minded; and, with cause. Dr. Murdock had only half his mind on his work for he could not ignore the recurrent thought that something important in his life was being discussed on the veranda. He was relieved, therefore, when after two hours he heard Paytone shout, "Good-by, Doctor." He dismissed Hargo hurriedly and, still wearing his laboratory coat, he went to the kitchen where Mrs. Murdock was getting ready to prepare their dinner.

"What's the score?" he asked. "When is Mr. Mantu going to let us set up our clinic and school?"

"Never," she snapped. "You and your damned Compound B. You and your mysterious element in the Melanesian blood, your x-factor. Do you know that we're practically prisoners?"

"How are we prisoners? We can leave on the Dutch steamer any time we want. That is," he added, "any time it lands here."

"It won't land here. Paytone has moved his warehouse to another island. He took my letter to give to the captain. And he made me order a lot of books and magazines on physics, chemistry, and mathematics. He's using us, that's what he's doing. And when he has no more use for us, it's curtains for us both. Now you know the score."

"But why?"

She sat down at her kitchen table. "I'll tell you why. It's because of the books I taught him to read. They've upset his mind. He told me all about it. Bitter? You'd have thought I poisoned him. And I taught him arithmetic and accounting, the damned black heathen. God, how I hate Negroes."

Dr. Murdock sat down at the table. "It just doesn't add up," he said. "Can you tell me what it's all about without getting so emotional about it all? And please make it short."

"He told me the story of his life, practically," she said. "Paytone's a money-lender, a banker, but he charges only about three hundred per cent. He finances young couples who want to marry. They spend five years working to pay him back. And he doesn't need collateral, either. On these islands, when a man and woman go into debt to marry, their families, including uncles and aunts and cousins, even, are obliged to pay off that debt. It's part of their silly religion. They believe that even their dead ancestors, spirits, are interested or involved in payment of their debts. With a religion like that, they don't need courts and judges and sheriffs and lawyers and police. So you see why he doesn't want us to influence their religion. If his people lost their religion, there would be anarchy unless he organized a government to control the people by force. And that he doesn't want. It's wasteful, he says. So there goes our mission. He is going to keep these heathens ignorant and superstitious. He won't let us preach the truth."

"We've got to get out of here," Dr. Murdock said.

"How? Swim to Australia? And he took all my books. He doesn't want the people to read books. Only technical books. And those are only for the few whom he selects."

"Well, those few will be educated," observed the doctor. "He won't have power over them."

"That's what I told him. But he's a slick one. You never should have given him that purple medicine. You sure cooked our goose."

"And what else did this usurer have to say?"

"He told me that he would allow mathematicians to read books on mathematics; the physicists books on physics, the chemists books on chemistry. In that way they will all be such specialists that their science won't conflict with their religion. Why, do you know what he's done? He has a chain of sixty-two stores. Each storekeeper thinks he owns his own store, but all of them are so much in debt to him that it will take generations to pay him off. Well, he's taught all these storekeepers to add and substract and to write about twenty words, like yams, coconuts, pigs, and so forth. He had the nerve to say that all they needed to know was the three R's and bookkeeping; that frills in education would unsettle their minds. So there goes our school. He took away all my books. He called them foreign 'isms'—'not for my people,' he said."

Dr. Murdock shook his head. "I still don't get it," he said. "If he feels that way about us, why doesn't he kill us and be done with it?"

"Because he needs your Compound A medicine. It wears off in two weeks, you know that. So he has to depend on you to refill his empty think-tank. And he wants you to develop a few

more geniuses he can control. He wants me to teach them to
read their scientific books and he wants you to set up their
laboratories. If they ever catch on to how you make Compound A, we're through. Now do you understand?"

Dr. Murdock thought his wife had never looked so hateful
as at this moment.

"I suppose you've blabbed your big mouth to Hargo about
Compound A," she said.

The doctor shook his head slowly. "No," he replied. "He
isn't ready yet." He nodded his head slowly again. "Look, all
isn't lost. As long as I have Compound A, they need me, as
you say, to refill their think-tanks. And Hargo will never learn
how I put it together. I'll see to that. Meanwhile, we'll figure
out a way to get away from here." He paused. "We must get
out of here. The very existence of mankind depends on us.
Society is running a race between destruction and the acquisition of intelligence. We'll figure out a way to escape. We
must."

"Yes, we'll figure out a way. Well, you do your figuring
and I'll do mine. And you'd better hurry up with your Compound B and get some brains for yourself or we'll never
escape from this damn island."

Paytone had made one remark that Mrs. Murdock did not
relay to her husband. He had said, "You destroyed my faith,
my belief in my religion when you gave me your purple medicine and your books. You changed me. Now I hardly know
what to believe. I no longer believe that the spirits of my ancestors are watching me to punish or reward. Spirits do not
exist. But what is left for me to believe in? Only myself. Yes, I
believe in myself, in my own power to get things done. Personal power, that's all that remains that is worth anything to
me. I can't enjoy anything else—only power. And power is
what I'm going to get, more and more and more power." He
had turned on her with ferocity and added, "But don't touch
the faith of my people. Religion is good for them, it's good
for me to have them steeped in tradition. The more firmly
they believe, the better it will be for them—and for me."

Somehow Mrs. Murdock sensed that he had given her a
hold over him, but how she could use that hold, she did not

know. She must think about it. Meanwhile, she felt it best not to mention this to her husband. She knew that somehow she could turn this knowledge to her advantage; just how would have to wait upon future events. But that she would find a way to escape from her prison, she had no doubt. As for Dr. Murdock, well, she thought, let him look out for himself.

She had to wait five months for her opportunity to talk to Paytone at any length. She continued to teach scientific English to the group of eight young men whom Paytone had selected to receive Compound A, but only occasionally did she see him, and then only briefly, when he came for his bimonthly medication or stopped to talk with her about the progress of her students. Aside from her teaching and the little housework required to maintain their home, she had little to do to occupy her time, and she found it hard to control her impatience and frustration.

At last, however, she had her chance. After avoiding her for five months, Paytone called upon her after receiving his teaspoonful of the purple Compound A. As he dropped into a chair on the veranda, she noted with satisfaction that he seemed to be prepared to talk with her at length. It was at this time that she learned why he wanted power and what he intended to do with it.

Paytone began with his customary bluntness. "I need American dollars."

"Dollars?"

"Dollars. You Americans know what dollars are. It's all you live for."

"You Mantus seem to have a fairly acute sense of property."

"With us it's different. With us, property has only spiritual significance. We save and invest to please the spirits who want our children to have it better than they did. We do not dissipate wealth in pleasure and display. I've read about you Americans, with your thousand-dollar dinners and the like."

"But you told me you no longer believe in spirits. They're a myth."

"I want dollars because I want power. Once I was powerless, defenseless. Now things are different. I have a few scores to settle with those whites who ground me down. But I need more power and that means more dollars. With enough dollars, I'll get even with a few white people. I owe it to them."

He went on to tell her how at the age of fourteen he had shipped on an English pearler.

"Pearler?" she interrupted.

"Diving for pearls," he explained. He described the wormy food, the vermin-infested sleeping quarters, the brutal treatment he had received. "When I jumped ship in Port Moresby in New Guinea, it was no better," he went on. "The English are all alike. And in Australia, no better. They think a black man is someone they are entitled to enslave. Look at South Africa. When I read *Cry, the Beloved Country*, my blood boiled. And I understand you have a black minority in your country. How are they treated?"

Her mind traveled back to the day when her husband refused to make Compound A available to all Negroes and she kept silent.

"So I'll show them. I'll even things up. But first, I need dollars. And you are the only one who can help me. You know the ropes, as we sailors say."

Mrs. Murdock felt that at last her moment had come. She was not disturbed in the least by Paytone's revengeful purposes; in fact, with an indifferent kind of understanding she felt somewhat in sympathy with his purpose. But his feelings did not particularly interest her. What was exciting her was the prospect of getting money and the opportunity to use it. Suddenly she found herself having difficulty with her breathing. She wiped her forehead with her handkerchief and then she dried her sweating palms. This was it, the moment she had long waited for. She asked herself how much dare she ask. She pulled herself together with effort and tried to control the tremor in her voice.

"How much is there in it for me?" she asked.

"How much do you want?" Paytone countered.

How much dare she ask? She hesitated a moment and then took confidence from the fact that she was in the driver's seat. He needed her. Drawing a deep breath, she said, "How about thirty per cent?"

"I was planning on offering you ten per cent," Paytone replied. "This thing I have in mind will run into millions. Ten millions or thirty millions—what difference can it make to you? You white Americans think of nothing but your comfort, pleasure, and ostentation. Ten million dollars will get you more than you can use. You can't spend it all. You love money for what you can spend on yourself. For my purposes, every penny counts."

"And another thing," Mrs. Murdock added. "Safe-conduct to any part of the world where I may choose to go."

Paytone nodded his head. "Of course," he agreed. "A one-way ticket to any port you choose. It's ten per cent, then, up to but not more than ten million dollars?"

Mrs. Murdock put out her hand. "It's a deal," she said. "And not a word about this to Dr. Murdock. He doesn't understand these things."

Paytone grinned. He understood Mrs. Murdock.

"Now," she said briskly, "let's see the books. What have you been up to?"

Paytone told her what he had done to date. "I've settled two thousand Mantus in New Guinea," he said. "There were Melanesians there, primitive peoples, but we displaced them. No violence. We just resettled them on our own islands."

He chuckled, "Right under the noses of the English and the Dutch. To them, one Melanesian is the same as another. We're all black trash. But someday they'll find out otherwise. I'll show them who's trash."

He went on to tell her how he had imported some modern farm equipment which had greatly increased the productivity of his people. They now had more copra for export. "Another thing," he added. "It isn't good for people to live in luxury. So we have lowered the age of marriage to twelve for girls and fourteen for young men. When people marry young, they don't learn so much and they are happier. It's better so." He went on, "So our agriculture now supports a larger population. But farming does not bring in enough dollars. Our population grows with modern agricultural methods, but dollars come in too slowly. What can we do?"

Mrs. Murdock thought for a moment. "We must manufacture," she said. "Look. The Western world uses pearl buttons.

You people are all sailors; you swim like fish. Can't you get mother-of-pearl?"

"Too slow," Paytone replied. "We are mining mother-of-pearl and I've wanted to build two factories, one in British and one in Dutch New Guinea. But it will be years before these operations pay off in the kind of money I'm thinking about."

"But all business enterprises have to start on a small scale."

"Not mine. I don't think in terms of nickels and dimes." He looked at her searchingly. "Are you sure you can't think of anything that will be faster and bigger?"

She shook her head.

"There are fifteen million Negroes in the United States," he said musingly. "Couldn't we find something they would buy?"

Light dawned on Mrs. Murdock. It was Compound A that he wanted.

"There's that purple medicine you take," she said.

"Yes," Paytone replied. "That might do. We could mix it with alcohol and export it as wine. At a profit, say, of one dollar a pint, to begin with. Later, we'll double the price. Fifteen million customers, fifty dollars apiece—yes, four hundred and fifty million dollars a year would be a good start. Do you have the formula?"

Mrs. Murdock never did know where Paytone built the factories in which he made Compound A. All she knew was that the dollars came rolling in, and rolling in fast.

The first pearl-button factory was incorporated in British New Guinea and the second one was incorporated in Dutch New Guinea. Then came a lumber mill which exported fine hardwoods. Then came a shipping company, and the Mantus had a merchant marine.

Concrete, steel, machinery of all kinds were imported for the big dam in the Owen Stanley Mountains. "It won't be long now," Paytone informed her, "and we'll be generating electricity. With electricity, we'll really be in business. You've done your share. Don't you want to go back to the United States?"

This question had often occurred to Mrs. Murdock. She

could go back, but from where she viewed the situation, the prospect did not look good. Compound A had revolutionized the social situation there.

It had turned out just as Dr. Murdock had predicted. One-third of the Congress of the United States was composed of colored men. They were crowding whites out of the professions, arts, sciences, and high places in business. Racial tensions were creating an explosive situation.

She knew that if people found out that she was responsible for the distribution of Compound A to the colored people, her life would not be worth a nickel. Even Dr. Murdock did not know that she had sold his formula. If they returned to the United States, he would be quick to discover the truth and for her, the results would be disastrous. She had burned her bridges and she knew that Paytone knew it.

"I suppose I could go back to America," she said, "but I'm happy here, working with you."

The dam was constructed and the electric generators were installed. Cattle ranches, meat-packing plants, tanneries were added to the rapidly expanding economy. All were owned by Paytone and Mrs. Murdock.

They worked well together. Paytone gave his time to supervising and improving management; Mrs. Murdock attended to financing their many enterprises. Her husband she saw hardly at all.

Eight years had passed since they had come to the South Pacific. Three of them had been spent on their obscure island; during the last five they lived in New Guinea.

Dr. Murdock now had a large, well-equipped laboratory, but he still made up his Compound A in his home. Paytone had kept his promise to Mrs. Murdock not to tell the doctor of their agreement, so the doctor never suspected that Paytone was exporting his formula.

Nevertheless, events in the United States worried him. "Something is happening back home," he told his wife. "Someone has made a formula something like mine and is distributing it to the colored people. Otherwise, how do you account for their sudden rise to power?"

"Nonsense," Mrs. Murdock exclaimed. "You inventors are all paranoid. The Negro is just being given a fair chance and of course some of them are coming to the top."

"I hope you're right," Dr. Murdock replied. "If Compound A or anything like it ever got into South Africa, it would blow the lid right off the world. By comparison, earlier revolutions would look like church socials."

When Mrs. Murdock reported this conversation to Paytone, he grunted. "Compound A will be distributed in South Africa," he said. "The British will find out that the black man is not to be trifled with."

Mrs. Murdock said nothing. She was beginning to find that out for herself. Nevertheless, she enjoyed the power and prestige given her through her partnership with Paytone.

Dr. Murdock worked longer and harder to create the formula for Compound B. "I must even things up between the races," he told Hargo. "Otherwise it's disaster for all of us." His face had become thin and lined with anxiety; his nerves were so on edge that he was controlling himself only by strenuous effort.

One day after work he came home and called to his wife. He found her in her sitting room which she had converted into an office.

"I'm moving right along," he told her. "Hargo has discovered the secret of skin pigmentation."

Mrs. Murdock was waiting in her study at home for a report from her representative at the United Nations. Now almost entirely Melanesian, the natives of New Guinea had petitioned for an end to British and Dutch colonialism, and it seemed probable that the Melanesians would be given complete control of this large area of the earth's land surface. It would be the beginning of a larger expansion. There were Tasmania, New Zealand, Australia, to be settled, overrun, and taken over. Dreaming of these possibilities, waiting for news from New York, she hardly heard her husband.

"You mean he's learned how to make Compound A?" she asked.

"No, don't you ever listen? He's discovered the secret of skin pigmentation. It's a great step forward."

He went on to explain that skin pigmentation depends upon the deposition of a dark pigment, melanin, in the skin. Why does melanin settle in the skin of Melanesians and other black races but not in the skin of the white race? "It's due to an hereditary difference in function of the pituitary gland. The pituitary gland of the dark races secretes a chromatophototropic hormone, melaninine. Hargo isolated it. Then he discovered its chemical formula. Together we synthesized it. We make it artificially, in quantity. After twenty-three years of work, we are now on the edge of success."

"What the hell does all this mean?" Mrs. Murdock asked irritably. "Melaninine! What good is it?" She picked up her telephone and dialed her operator.

The doctor took a corked test tube from his coat pocket. He produced a syringe, filled it from the test tube and, before Mrs. Murdock knew what he was up to, he had injected the solution into her arm. "I'll show you what it's good for," he said.

As the telephone fell from her hand, he shouted, "Now you'll find out what melaninine is good for. It will turn you black."

"How dare you stick me with a needle!"

"That's melaninine," the doctor shouted. "The pituitary chromatophototropic hormone. You always hated the black race. Now you're going to find out what it's like to be black. You'll turn black."

"I don't believe it," she said. "You've gone crazy. Why in hell did you stick me with a needle, you lunatic? Are you trying to poison me?"

"You'll see. Tomorrow you'll start turning black. Of course, the pigmentation will fade. Like suntan. But you'll find out what it's good for, this great scientific discovery. Perhaps you'll learn not to ask silly questions."

Mrs. Murdock replaced the telephone in its cradle and thought quickly. He had said that the pigmentation would fade, like suntan. Then no irreparable harm had been done. And what would Paytone say? She could imagine the expression on his face when he would see her a black woman. Would he despise her as he despised the women of his own race? "Stupid," he called them. Suddenly an idea occurred to Mrs. Murdock. "Would Compound A work on me?" she asked. "Or is that another silly question?"

Immediately Dr. Murdock's manner changed. Without answering, he rushed to the kitchen and brought back a glass containing his purple Compound A. His hand shook as he handed it to her. "This may be it," he said. "Drink it. If it works, we may have the missing ingredient in Compound B. I still may be in time to save the world from its own stupidity."

She drained the glass. "If it works it will be the first good thing you've ever done for me. Even so, I don't know whether I want to become a black genius. Why can't you invent something to help white people? Physician, heal thyself."

Dr. Murdock ignored this last thrust.

"If this works on you, I have the problem solved," he said. "Don't you see? It will prove that melaninine contains two fractions—one which causes melanin to be deposited in the skin and another which acts with Compound A to increase intelligence. We can separate these two fractions, add the intelligence factor to Compound A, and the world will be saved. Man will at last have the brains he needs to manage his own society."

"If it works," said Mrs. Murdock. "If." She reached for the telephone and dialed her operator. "Give me New York, United States of America," she ordered.

It worked. When she woke up the following morning, her head was surprisingly clear. Ideas occurred to her that, she realized, had never before entered her mind. For a moment she could not understand what had happened. She was still the same woman, only, somehow, more so. The difference, she thought, between wine and brandy. She had become a distillate of her previous self. "That Compound A," she thought, "that blessed Compound A. No wonder Paytone loved it."

Two weeks later while she was in her office telephoning the British foreign minister in London, Paytone walked in on her. He heard her say, "No, we don't want independence. All we ask is what the Dutch have given our people—dominion status. Yes. Certainly. Of course we want to belong to the British Commonwealth of Nations. No. No property rights will be disturbed. English investments will not only be safe, they will be made more attractive to English capital. Yes. Talk it over with the Prime Minister and the Cabinet. Yes. We'll withdraw our complaints at the UN Assembly. Yes. I'll call New York at once."

Paytone frowned as he listened. "Why not complete independence?" he asked. "Why should we Melanesians always be the tail on the white man's kite?" He paused and added, "I hate white people."

Mrs. Murdock dialed her operator and asked to be connected with New York. While she waited for the call to be put through, she said, "Because as members of the Dutch colonial system, we'll have easy access to Indonesia. As members of the British Commonwealth of Nations, we'll have easy access and equal rights in New Zealand and Australia. As a racial group rather than as a national group, we can infiltrate everywhere. No tariff boundaries. No exclusion on account of color. In time, we'll take over the world."

"Take over the world?"

"That's right. Now we have New Guinea. But what's that? It will be worth about a billion dollars. Do you know that in the United States any one of six corporations is worth more than a billion dollars? If my plans work out as I know they will, we'll control them all and more besides."

"Your plans and my plans are different," Paytone objected. "I want to show certain white people that they can't push me around." He noted the change of expression on her face. "Not that there is anything personal, you understand. You are different from your race. The fact is, some of my best friends are whites." He looked at her more closely. "You know," he said, you are becoming more beautiful every day. Your skin is much darker than it used to be."

Something awoke in Mrs. Murdock that had lain dormant for many years. It was a powerful surge of impulse that frightened her but made her feel ecstatically happy. She knew that she must say something, something to please Paytone, something that would arouse his masculinity.

"Your plans come first," she said. "I know exactly how you feel."

As she said those words, she knew that she had made her far-reaching decision, had made her last irrevocable choice, had crossed her Rubicon. It flashed through her mind that she must cultivate Hargo to make sure of a continuous supply of that chromatophototropic hormone, melaninine. She had been using it, off and on, for two weeks and her skin had become a few shades darker. She decided that henceforth she would inject herself with the hormone regularly. Her husband had told her that the pigmentation of her skin would be temporary, like suntan. Well, suntan can be as permanent as one's exposure to the sun's rays. She smiled as these thoughts ran through her head.

"What's so funny?" Paytone asked.

She flashed him a bright, mischievous smile.

"I was just thinking of a remark Dr. Murdock made. It was about something being only temporary and it just occurred to me that temporary is a relative state. How long is temporary?"

Dr. Max Murdock contemplated with mixed emotions the change he had induced in his wife. The success of his hormone, melaninine, elated him, and yet he could not reconcile himself to his wife's change in color. "You could let your skin fade," he told her. "You take melaninine just to annoy me."

"But if I let my color fade, Compound A wouldn't help me," she pointed out, "and I like being a genuis. Until you make Compound B, I'll stay black." She did not mention Paytone's new interest in her as a woman. After all, she thought, what the doctor doesn't know won't hurt him.

"I hope we'll soon have Compound B," Dr. Murdock assured her. "Then you can let your skin return to its natural color."

"Is that all you have to worry about? I'm satisfied with being dark-skinned as long as it helps Compound A to work on me. Brains are more important than skin color. You wouldn't know, of course, from personal experience."

As usual Dr. Murdock ignored the jibe. In twenty-three

years of married life, he reflected, a man learns to overlook many unpleasant things.

"I have lots to worry about," he replied. "Too much. I don't like the way the world is going. This atomic weapon race is going to end in disaster. Time is running out on me. Unless I can give Compound B to the world in time to establish a rule of reason, there won't be a human race to give it to."

But Mrs. Murdock was studying the statistics of the woolen industry in Australia and she didn't hear him.

Mrs. Murdock had told Paytone that her husband was trying to create a Compound B, one which would transform any white man or woman into a genius. "It has something to do with a pituitary hormone, one that he calls the x-factor," she said.

Paytone knew all about it. "What a man," she exclaimed. "You keep track of everything."

"You think I ought to kill him," Paytone said. "That's what a white man would do. But we Melanesians don't do things that way."

She noted the inclusive word, "we," and felt warm all over. "No," she lied, "we don't," and she waited for him to continue.

"When the time comes," Paytone assured her, "I'll know what to do and how to do it."

It was that very evening when an excited and worried Dr. Murdock returned home. He sought his wife immediately. He showed her a note written to him by Hargo. "That damn Melanesian," he shouted, "He's run off with my discovery, my life-work, my Compound B."

"What happened? Stop pulling at your ear and talk sense. Just what happened? Get hold of yourself, you fool, and quit cursing these Melanesians. I won't have it."

"That's because you're one now, yourself. You're on his side. The whole world can blow itself up and go to hell for all you care." He sat down and drummed the floor with his foot. "That damned black bastard. He stole my Compound B, the one thing that I've worked for all my life, the only thing in this world I give a damn about."

Mrs. Murdock expressed surprise. Now she understood what Paytone had meant when he said he'd know what to do should Dr. Murdock succeed in making Compound B. She decided to play dumb.

"Then you did make Compound B?"

"Yes, I did make Compound B. What do you think I'm talking about?"

"And where did Hargo go?"

Dr. Murdock gave her the paper he held in his hand and she read it. Hargo had written that he had to return to the Mantu Islands where Dr. Murdock's researches in the South Pacific had begun.

Mrs. Murdock now had the entire picture straight in her own mind, and she knew exactly what to do. She must adopt the role of the dumb but loyal wife. She decided to play it straight.

"He'll be back, won't he? Besides, does it matter much? What you did once, you can do again. I mean, it's in your head, isn't it?"

"No, it's not in my head. We did the work together. Furthermore, I don't write down what I can keep in my head."

He walked to the door, opened it, looked out, and then closed it. "That Hargo," he repeated. "And we made Compound B. It will work on anyone, regardless of skin color. The drug that could have saved the world."

"Well, moaning and groaning won't help. Dinner is served. Let's eat."

"I don't want to eat. I can't eat."

"I know just how you feel. Well, we must get your notes back. One thing is sure: Hargo won't destroy them. He's too much the scientist to do that." She gave her voice the optimistic note. "We'll get them back. If Hargo's on the Mantu Islands, that's the place for you to go. Let's see Paytone right now and make arrangements."

Paytone listened patiently to their story. From his face and manner, no one would have suspected that he had engineered

Hargo's leaving with the records. In the end he agreed to loan Dr. Murdock his private airplane and pilot to fly to the Mantu Islands.

"You are going with me, of course," Dr. Murdock said to his wife.

"But I have work to do. I can't leave here."

"Then I won't go, either," the doctor declared. "It's your duty to be with me when I confront Hargo. I'll need you as a witness."

Mrs. Murdock looked at Paytone for guidance, but he kept his face blank and he said nothing. What did he want her to do? She studied his face, his posture, for a cue but he continued to maintain his noncommittal pose. She had to choose; but she had to make the right choice and do it in exactly the right way.

She wanted to be rid of Dr. Murdock and to win Paytone. But suppose that Paytone did not want her? Then it would be to her advantage to have the formula for Compound B, the drug which would be invaluable to the white races.

Finally she turned to her husband. "All right," she snarled, "I'll go with you if you must have someone to hold your hand and fight your battles."

Their old home in the Mantu Islands had not changed. The kerosene stove and refrigerator in the kitchen were spotlessly clean. Someone had put the house in order before their arrival. The cupboards were stocked with canned food; fresh yams were in the bin. Mrs. Murdock opened the door of the refrigerator and saw that someone had provided her with a freshly caught fish.

Dr. Murdock went to his laboratory. Everything was in perfect order. And on the laboratory table lay the records and notes which Hargo had taken with him.

Suddenly the truth dawned upon them. "We're back where we started from," Mrs. Murdock wailed. "We're prisoners again."

So that is how the Murdocks returned to their home on the Mantu Islands. That Mrs. Murdock became white again is a matter of record. It is also a matter of record that both the doctor and his wife continued to live on their little island until all life there was wiped out during World War III.

Nor did Paytone live long to enjoy his economic power in New Guinea and Australia. It is true that he became the wealthiest man in Australia and took pleasure in making life miserable for those white men whom he could impoverish. He had quite a reputation for being a man of unusual mental powers and of ability to surround himself with brilliant assistants, black, of course, and devoutly religious. But it is one thing to have great power; it is quite another thing to dominate a continent permanently. And by a strange quirk of fate, the same atomic war that wiped out the Murdocks brought sudden death to Paytone.

It seems strange to us today in 2466 that anyone could want to keep secret a discovery as important as Dr. Murdock's, a discovery that has done for mankind just what Dr. Murdock said it would do, namely, make the human race intelligent enough to govern itself. But we must remember that the twentieth century was the age of secrecy, in science, in politics, in business, and even in art. It was the age of the iron curtain, the bamboo curtain, and security regulations in every so-called civilized society. It is interesting to note that when they talked about the various freedoms, no one mentioned freedom from stupidity. Indeed, a careful study of available records indicates that, in that age, no one believed it possible that he might be stupid. In those days, five hundred years ago, people even thought that the possession of a television set and atomic weapons was evidence of their sanity and wisdom.

RAPPACCINI'S DAUGHTER

Nathaniel Hawthorne

As far as we know, this first-rate toxicological fantasy by one of America's greatest writers has never before appeared in a science fiction anthology. (We may be wrong, of course.) The omission is all the more surprising because this story of a truly fanatic physician-"scientist" is so compellingly told, with such a stately and yet vivid style. The pace is grave and measured, as befits the high tragedy of the narrative, and as is to be expected from the period in which it was written (the 1840's)—but: read it slowly, savoring as you read, and you will find it very much worth your while.

Rappaccini's Daughter

A YOUNG MAN, named Giovanni Guasconti, came, very long ago, from the more southern region of Italy, to pursue his studies at the University of Padua. Giovanni, who had but a scanty supply of gold ducats in his pocket, took lodgings in a high and gloomy chamber of an old edifice which looked not unworthy to have been the palace of a Paduan noble, and which, in fact, exhibited over its entrance the armorial bearings of a family long since extinct. The young stranger, who was not unstudied in the great poem of his country, recollected that one of the ancestors of this family, and perhaps an occupant of this very mansion, had been pictured by Dante as a partaker of the immortal agonies of his Inferno. These reminiscences and associations, together with the tendency to heartbreak natural to a young man for the first time out of his native sphere, caused Giovanni to sigh heavily as he looked around the desolate and ill-furnished apartment.

"Holy Virgin, signor!" cried old Dame Lisabetta, who, won by the youth's remarkable beauty of person, was kindly endeavoring to give the chamber a habitable air, "what a sigh was that to come out of a young man's heart! Do you find this old mansion gloomy? For the love of Heaven, then, put your head out of the window, and you will see as bright sunshine as you have left in Naples."

Guasconti mechanically did as the old woman advised, but could not quite agree with her that the Paduan sunshine was as cheerful as that of southern Italy. Such as it was, however, it fell upon a garden beneath the window and expended its fostering influences on a variety of plants, which seemed to have been cultivated with exceeding care.

"Does this garden belong to the house?" asked Giovanni.

"Heaven forbid, signor, unless it were fruitful of better pot herbs than any that grow there now," answered old Lisabetta. "No; that garden is cultivated by the own hands

111

of Signor Giacomo Rappaccini, the famous doctor, who, I warrant him, has been heard of as far as Naples. It is said that he distils these plants into medicines that are as potent as a charm. Oftentimes you may see the signor doctor at work, and perchance the signora, his daughter, too, gathering the strange flowers that grow in the garden."

The old woman had now done what she could for the aspect of the chamber; and, commending the young man to the protection of the saints, took her departure.

Giovanni still found no better occupation than to look down into the garden beneath his window. From its appearance, he judged it to be one of those botanic gardens which were of earlier date in Padua than elsewhere in Italy or in the world. Or, not improbably, it might once have been the pleasure-place of an opulent family; for there was the ruin of a marble fountain in the centre, sculptured with rare art, but so wofully shattered that it was impossible to trace the original design from the chaos of remaining fragments. The water, however, continued to gush and sparkle into the sunbeams as cheerfully as ever. A little gurgling sound ascended to the young man's window, and made him feel as if the fountain were an immortal spirit that sung its song unceasingly and without heeding the vicissitudes around it, while one century imbodied it in marble and another scattered the perishable garniture on the soil. All about the pool into which the water subsided grew various plants, that seemed to require a plentiful supply of moisture for the nourishment of gigantic leaves, and, in some instances, flowers gorgeously magnificent. There was one shrub in particular, set in a marble vase in the midst of the pool, that bore a profusion of purple blossoms, each of which had the lustre and richness of a gem; and the whole together made a show so resplendent that it seemed enough to illuminate the garden, even had there been no sunshine. Every portion of the soil was peopled with plants and herbs, which, if less beautiful, still bore tokens of assiduous care, as if all had their individual virtues, known to the scientific mind that fostered them. Some were placed in urns, rich with old carving, and others in common garden pots; some crept serpent-like along the ground or climbed on high, using whatever means of ascent was offered them. One plant had wreathed itself round a statue of Vertumnus, which was thus quite veiled and shrouded in a drapery of hanging foliage, so happily arranged that it might have served a sculptor for a study.

While Giovanni stood at the window he heard a rustling behind a screen of leaves, and became aware that a person was at work in the garden. His figure soon emerged into view, and showed itself to be that of no common laborer, but a tall, emaciated, sallow, and sickly-looking man, dressed in a scholar's garb of black. He was beyond the middle term of life, with gray hair, a thin, gray beard, and a face singularly marked with intellect and cultivation, but which could never, even in his more youthful days, have expressed much warmth of heart.

Nothing could exceed the intentness with which this scientific gardener examined every shrub which grew in his path: it seemed as if he was looking into their inmost nature, making observations in regard to their creative essence, and discovering why one leaf grew in this shape and another in that, and wherefore such and such flowers differed among themselves in hue and perfume. Nevertheless, in spite of this deep intelligence on his part, there was no approach to intimacy between himself and these vegetable existences. On the contrary, he avoided their actual touch or the direct inhaling of their odors with a caution that impressed Giovanni most disagreeably; for the man's demeanor was that of one walking among malignant influences, such as savage beasts, or deadly snakes, or evil spirits, which, should he allow them one moment of license, would wreak upon him some terrible fatality. It was strangely frightful to the young man's imagination to see this air of insecurity in a person cultivating a garden, that most simple and innocent of human toils, and which had been alike the joy and labor of the unfallen parents of the race. Was this garden, then, the Eden of the present world? And this man, with such a perception of harm in what his own hands caused to grow,—was he the Adam?

The distrustful gardener, while plucking away the dead leaves or pruning the too luxuriant growth of the shrubs, defended his hands with a pair of thick gloves. Nor were these his only armor. When, in his walk through the garden, he came to the magnificent plant that hung its purple gems beside the marble fountain, he placed a kind of mask over his mouth and nostrils, as if all this beauty did but conceal a deadlier malice; but, finding his task still too dangerous, he drew back, removed the mask, and called loudly, but in the infirm voice of a person affected with inward disease,—

"Beatrice! Beatrice!"

"Here am I, my father. What would you?" cried a rich and youthful voice from the window of the opposite house—a voice as rich as a tropical sunset, and which made Giovanni, though he knew not why, think of deep hues of purple or crimson and of perfumes heavily delectable. "Are you in the garden?"

"Yes, Beatrice," answered the gardener, "and I need your help."

Soon there emerged from under a sculptured portal the figure of a young girl, arrayed with as much richness of taste as the most splendid of the flowers, beautiful as the day, and with a bloom so deep and vivid that one shade more would have been too much. She looked redundant with life, health, and energy; all of which attributes were bound down and compressed, as it were, and girdled tensely, in their luxuriance, by her virgin zone. Yet Giovanni's fancy must have grown morbid while he looked down into the garden; for the impression which the fair stranger made upon him was as if here were another flower, the human sister of those vegetable ones, as beautiful as they, more beautiful than the richest of them, but still to be touched only with a glove, nor to be approached without a mask. As Beatrice came down the garden path, it was observable that she handled and inhaled the odor of several of the plants which her father had most sedulously avoided.

"Here, Beatrice," said the latter, "see how many needful offices require to be done to our chief treasure. Yet, shattered as I am, my life might pay the penalty of approaching it so closely as circumstances demand. Henceforth, I fear, this plant must be consigned to your sole charge."

"And gladly will I undertake it," cried again the rich tones of the young lady, as she bent towards the magnificent plant and opened her arms as if to embrace it. "Yes, my sister, my splendor, it shall be Beatrice's task to nurse and serve thee; and thou shalt reward her with thy kisses and perfumed breath, which to her is as the breath of life."

Then, with all the tenderness in her manner that was so strikingly expressed in her words, she busied herself with such attentions as the plant seemed to require; and Giovanni, at his lofty window, rubbed his eyes and almost doubted whether it were a girl tending her favorite flower, or one sister performing the duties of affection to another. The scene soon terminated. Whether Dr. Rappaccini had finished his labors in the garden, or that his watchful eye had caught the stranger's face, he now took his daughter's arm and retired. Night was already closing in; oppressive exhalations seemed to proceed from the plants and steal upward past the open window; and Giovanni, closing the lattice, went to his couch and dreamed of a rich flower and beautiful girl. Flower and maiden were different, and yet the same, and fraught with some strange peril in either shape.

But there is an influence in the light of morning that tends to rectify whatever errors of fancy, or even of judgment, we may have incurred during the sun's decline, or among the shadows of the night, or in the less wholesome glow of moonshine. Giovanni's first movement, on starting from sleep, was to throw open the window and gaze down into the garden which his dreams had made so fertile of mysteries. He was surprised and a little ashamed to find how real and matter-of-fact an affair it proved to be, in the first rays of the sun which gilded the dew-drops that hung upon leaf and blossom, and, while giving a brighter beauty to each rare flower, brought everything within the limits of ordinary experience. The young man rejoiced that, in the heart of the barren city, he had the privilege of overlooking this spot of lovely and luxuriant vegetation. It would serve, he said to himself, as a symbolic language to keep him in communion with Nature. Neither the sickly and thought-worn Dr. Giacomo Rappaccini, it is true, nor his brilliant daughter, were now visible; so that

Giovanni could not determine how much of the singularity which he attributed to both was due to their own qualities and how much to his wonder-working fancy; but he was inclined to take a most rational view of the whole matter. In the course of the day he paid his respects to Signor Pietro Baglioni, professor of medicine in the university, a physician of eminent repute, to whom Giovanni had brought a letter of introduction. The professor was an elderly personage, apparently of genial nature, and habits that might almost be called jovial. He kept the young man to dinner, and made himself very agreeable by the freedom and liveliness of his conversation, especially when warmed by a flask or two of Tuscan wine. Giovanni, conceiving that men of science, inhabitants of the same city, must needs be on familiar terms with one another, took an opportunity to mention the name of Dr. Rappaccini. But the professor did not respond with so much cordiality as he had anticipated.

"Ill would it become a teacher of the divine art of medicine," said Professor Pietro Baglioni, in answer to a question of Giovanni, "to withhold due and well-considered praise of a physician so eminently skilled as Rappaccini; but, on the other hand, I should answer it but scantily to my conscience were I to permit a worthy youth like yourself, Signor Giovanni, the son of an ancient friend, to imbibe erroneous ideas respecting a man who might hereafter chance to hold your life and death in his hands. The truth is, our worshipful Dr. Rappaccini has as much science as any member of the faculty—with perhaps one single exception—in Padua, or all Italy; but there are certain grave objections to his professional character."

"And what are they?" asked the young man.

"Has my friend Giovanni any disease of body or heart, that he is so inquisitive about physicians?" said the professor, with a smile. "But as for Rappaccini, it is said of him—and I, who know the man well, can answer for its truth—that he cares infinitely more for science than for mankind. His patients are interesting to him only as subjects for some new experiment. He would sacrifice human life, his own among the rest, or whatever else was dearest to him, for the sake of adding so much as a grain of mustard seed to the great heap of his accumulated knowledge."

"Methinks he is an awful man indeed," remarked Guasconti, mentally recalling the cold and purely intellectual aspect of Rappaccini. "And yet, worshipful professor, is it not a noble spirit? Are there many men capable of so spiritual a love of science?"

"God forbid," answered the professor, somewhat testily; "at least, unless they take sounder views of the healing art than those adopted by Rappaccini. It is his theory that all medicinal virtues are comprised within those substances which we term vegetable poisons. These he cultivates with his own hands, and is said even to have produced new varieties of poison, more horribly deleterious than Nature, without the assistance of this learned person, would ever have plagued the world withal. That the signor doctor does less mischief than might be expected with such dangerous substances is undeniable. Now and then, it must be owned, he has effected, or seemed to effect, a marvellous cure; but, to tell you my private mind, Signor Giovanni, he should receive little credit for such instances of success,—they being probably the work of chance,—but should be held strictly accountable for his failures, which may justly be considered his own work."

The youth might have taken Baglioni's opinions with many grains of allowance had he known that there was a professional warfare of long continuance between him and Dr. Rappaccini, in which the latter was generally thought to have gained the advantage. If the reader be inclined to judge for himself, we refer him to certain black-letter tracts on both sides, preserved in the medical department of the University of Padua.

"I know not, most learned professor," returned Giovanni, after musing on what had been said of Rappaccini's exclusive zeal for science,—"I know not how dearly this physician may love his art; but surely there is one object more dear to him. He has a daughter."

"Aha!" cried the professor, with a laugh. "So now our friend Giovanni's secret is out. You have heard of this daughter, whom all the young men in Padua are wild about, though not half a dozen have ever had the good hap to see her face. I know little of the Signora Beatrice save that Rappaccini is said to have instructed her deeply in his science, and that, young and beautiful as fame reports her, she is already qualified to fill a professor's chair. Perchance her father destines her for mine! Other absurd rumors there be, not worth talking about or listening to. So now, Signor Giovanni, drink off your glass of lachryma."

Guasconti returned to his lodgings somewhat heated with the wine he had quaffed, and which caused his brain to swim with strange fantasies in reference to Dr. Rappaccini and the beautiful Beatrice. On his way, happening to pass by a florist's, he bought a fresh bouquet of flowers.

Ascending to his chamber, he seated himself near the window, but within the shadow thrown by the depth of the wall, so that he could look down into the garden with little risk of being discovered. All beneath his eye was a solitude. The strange plants were basking in the sunshine, and now and then nodding gently to one another, as if in acknowledgement of sympathy and kindred. In the midst, by the shattered fountain, grew the magnificent shrub, with its purple gems clustering all over it; they glowed in the air, and gleamed back again out of the depths of the pool, which thus seemed to overflow with colored radiance from the rich reflection that was steeped in it. At first, as we have said, the garden was a solitude. Soon, however,—as Giovanni had half hoped, half feared, would be the case,—a figure appeared beneath the antique sculptured portal, and came down between the rows of plants, inhaling their various perfumes as if she were one of those beings of old classic fable that lived upon sweet odors. On again beholding Beatrice, the young man was even startled to perceive how much her beauty exceeded his recollection of it; so brilliant, so vivid, was its character, that she glowed amid the sunlight, and, as Giovanni whispered to himself, positively illuminated the more shadowy intervals of the garden path. Her face being now more revealed than on the former occasion, he was struck by its expression of simplicity and sweetness,—qualities that had not entered into his idea of her character, and which made him ask anew what manner of mortal she might be. Nor did he fail again to observe, or imagine, an analogy between the beautiful girl and the gorgeous shrub that hung its gemlike flowers over the fountain, —a resemblance which Beatrice seemed to have indulged a fantastic humor in heightening, both by the arrangement of her dress and the selection of its hues.

Approaching the shrub, she threw open her arms, as with a passionate ardor, and drew its branches into an intimate embrace—so intimate that her features were hidden in its leafy bosom and her glistening ringlets all intermingled with the flowers.

"Give me thy breath, my sister," exclaimed Beatrice; "for I am faint with common air. And give me this flower of thine, which I separate with gentlest fingers from the stem and place it close beside my heart."

With these words the beautiful daughter of Rappaccini plucked one of the richest blossoms of the shrub, and was about to fasten it in her bosom. But now, unless Giovanni's draughts of wine had bewildered his senses, a singular incident occurred. A small orange-colored reptile, of the lizard or chameleon species, chanced to be creeping along the path, just at the feet of Beatrice. It appeared to Giovanni,—but, at the distance from which he gazed, he could scarcely have seen anything so minute,—it appeared to him, however, that a drop or two of moisture from the broken stem of the flower descended upon the lizard's head. For an instant the reptile contorted itself violently, and then lay motionless in the sunshine. Beatrice observed this remarkable phenomenon, and crossed herself, sadly, but without surprise; nor did she therefore hesitate to arrange the fatal flower in her bosom. There it blushed, and almost glimmered with the dazzling effect of a precious stone, adding to her dress and aspect the one appropriate charm which nothing else in the world could have supplied. But Giovanni, out of the shadow of his window, bent forward and shrank back, and murmured and trembled.

"Am I awake? Have I my senses?" said he to himself. "What is this being? Beautiful shall I call her, or inexpressibly terrible?"

Beatrice now strayed carelessly through the garden, approaching closer beneath Giovanni's window, so that he was compelled to thrust his head quite out of its concealment in order to gratify the intense and painful curiosity which she excited. At this moment there came a beautiful insect over the garden wall; it had, perhaps, wandered through the city, and found no flowers or verdure among those antique haunts of men until the heavy perfumes of Dr. Rappaccini's shrubs had lured it from afar. Without alighting on the flowers, this winged brightness seemed to be attracted by Beatrice, and lingered in the air and fluttered about her head. Now, here it could not be but that Giovanni Guasconti's eyes deceived him. Be that as it might, he fancied that, while Beatrice was gazing at the insect with childish delight, it grew faint and fell at her feet; its bright wings shivered; it was dead—from no cause that he could discern, unless it were the atmosphere of her breath. Again Beatrice crossed herself and sighed heavily as she bent over the dead insect.

An impulsive movement of Giovanni drew her eyes to the window. There she beheld the beautiful head of the young man—rather a Grecian than an Italian head, with fair, regular features, and a glistening of gold among his ringlets—gazing down upon her like a being that hovered in mid air. Scarcely knowing what he did, Giovanni threw down the bouquet which he had hitherto held in his hand.

"Signora," said he, "there are pure and healthful flowers. Wear them for the sake of Giovanni Guasconti."

"Thanks, signor," replied Beatrice, with her rich voice, that came forth as it were like a gush of music, and with a mirthful expression half childish and half woman-like. "I accept your gift, and would fain recompense it with this precious purple flower; but if I toss it into the air it will not reach you. So Signor Guasconti must even content himself with my thanks."

She lifted the bouquet from the ground, and then, as if inwardly ashamed at having stepped aside from her maidenly reserve to respond to a stranger's greeting, passed swiftly homeward through the garden. But few as the moments were, it seemed to Giovanni, when she was on the point of vanishing beneath the sculptured portal, that his beautiful bouquet was already beginning to wither in her grasp. It was an idle thought; there could be no possibility of distinguishing a faded flower from a fresh one at so great a distance.

For many days after this incident the young man avoided the window that looked into Dr. Rappaccini's garden, as if something ugly and monstrous would have blasted his eyesight had he been betrayed into a glance. He felt conscious of having put himself, to a certain extent, within the influence of an unintelligible power by the communication which he had opened with Beatrice. The wisest course would have been, if his heart were in any real danger, to quit his lodgings and Padua itself at once; the next wiser, to have accustomed himself, as far as possible, to the familiar and daylight view of Beatrice—thus bringing her rigidly and systematically within the limits of ordinary experience. Least of all, while avoiding her sight, ought Giovanni to have remained so near this extraordinary being that the proximity and possibility even of intercourse should give a kind of substance and reality to the wild vagaries which his imagination ran riot continually in producing. Guasconti had not a deep heart—or, at all events, its depths were not sounded now; but he had a quick fancy, and an ardent southern temperament, which rose every instant to a higher fever pitch. Whether or no Beatrice possessed those terrible attributes, that fatal breath, the affinity with those so beautiful and deadly flowers which were indicated by what Giovanni had witnessed, she had at least instilled a fierce and subtle poison into his system. It was not love, although her rich beauty was a madness to him; nor horror, even while he fancied her spirit to be imbued with the same baneful essence that seemed to pervade her physical frame; but a wild offspring of both love and horror that had each parent in it, and burned like one and shivered like the other. Giovanni knew not what to dread; still less did he know what to hope; yet hope and dread kept a continual warfare in his breast, alternately vanquishing one another and starting up afresh to renew the contest. Blessed are all simple emotions, be they dark or bright! It is the lurid intermixture of the two that produces the illuminating blaze of the infernal regions.

Sometimes he endeavored to assuage the fever of his spirit by a rapid walk through the streets of Padua or beyond its gates: his footsteps kept time with the throbbings of his brain, so that the walk was apt to accelerate itself to a race. One day he found himself arrested; his arm was seized by a portly personage, who had turned back on recognizing the young man and expended much breath in overtaking him.

"Signor Giovanni! Stay, my young friend!" cried he. "Have you forgotten me? That might well be the case if I were as much altered as yourself."

It was Baglioni, whom Giovanni had avoided ever since their first meeting, from a doubt that the professor's sagacity would look too deeply into his secrets. Endeavoring to recover himself, he stared forth wildly from his inner world into the outer one and spoke like a man in a dream.

"Yes; I am Giovanni Guasconti. You are Professor Pietro Baglioni. Now let me pass!"

"Not yet, not yet, Signor Giovanni Guasconti," said the professor, smiling, but at the same time scrutinizing the youth with an earnest glance. "What! did I grow up side by side with your father? and shall his son pass me like a stranger in these old streets of Padua? Stand still, Signor Giovanni; for we must have a word or two before we part."

"Speedily, then, most worshipful professor, speedily," said Giovanni, with feverish impatience. "Does not your worship see that I am in haste?"

Now, while he was speaking there came a man in black along the street, stooping and moving feebly like a person in inferior health. His face was all overspread with a most sickly and sallow hue, but yet so pervaded with an expression of piercing and active intellect that an observer might easily have overlooked the merely physical attributes and have seen only this wonderful energy. As he passed, this person exchanged a cold and distant salutation with Baglioni, but fixed his eyes upon Giovanni with an intentness that seemed to bring out whatever was within him worthy of notice. Nevertheless, there was a peculiar quietness in the look, as if taking merely a speculative, not a human, interest in the young man.

"It is Dr. Rappaccini!" whispered the professor when the stranger had passed. "Has he ever seen your face before?"

"Not that I know," answered Giovanni, starting at the name.

"He *has* seen you! he must have seen you!" said Baglioni, hastily. "For some purpose or other, this man of science is making a study of you. I know that look of his! It is the same that coldly illuminates his face as he bends over a bird, a mouse, or a butterfly, which, in pursuance of some experiment, he has killed by the perfume of a flower; a look as deep as Nature itself, but without Nature's warmth of love. Signor Giovanni, I will stake my life upon it, you are the subject of one of Rappaccini's experiments!"

"Will you make a fool of me?" cried Giovanni, passionately. "*That,* signor professor, were an untoward experiment."

"Patience! patience!" replied the imperturbable professor. "I tell thee, my poor Giovanni, that Rappaccini has a scientific interest in thee. Thou hast fallen into fearful hands! And the Signora Beatrice,—what part does she act in this mystery?"

But Guasconti, finding Baglioni's pertinacity intolerable, here broke away, and was gone before the professor could again seize his arm. He looked after the young man intently and shook his head.

"This must not be," said Baglioni to himself. "The youth is the son of my old friend, and shall not come to any harm from which the arcana of medical science can preserve him. Besides, it is too insufferable an impertinence in Rappaccini, thus to snatch the lad out of my own hands, as I may say, and make use of him for his infernal experiments. This daughter of his! It shall be looked to. Perchance, most learned Rappaccini, I may foil you where you little dream of it!"

Meanwhile Giovanni had pursued a circuitous route, and at length found himself at the door of his lodgings. As he crossed the threshold he was met by old Lisabetta, who smirked and smiled, and was evidently desirous to attract his attention; vainly, however, as the ebullition of his feelings had momentarily subsided into a cold and dull vacuity. He turned his eyes full upon the withered face that was puckering itself into a smile, but seemed to behold it not. The old dame, therefore, laid her grasp upon his cloak.

"Signor! signor!" whispered she, still with a smile over the whole breadth of her visage, so that it looked not unlike a grotesque carving in wood, darkened by centuries. "Listen, signor! There is a private entrance into the garden!"

"What do you say?" exclaimed Giovanni, turning quickly about, as if an inanimate thing should start into feverish life. "A private entrance into Dr. Rappaccini's garden?"

"Hush! hush! not so loud!" whispered Lisabetta, putting her hand over his mouth. "Yes; into the worshipful doctor's garden, where you may see all his fine shrubbery. Many a young man in Padua would give gold to be admitted among those flowers."

Giovanni put a piece of gold into her hand.

"Show me the way," said he.

A surmise, probably excited by his conversation with Baglioni, crossed his mind, that this interposition of old Lisabetta might perchance be connected with the intrigue, whatever were its nature, in which the professor seemed to suppose that Dr. Rappaccini was involving him. But such a suspicion, though it disturbed Giovanni, was inadequate to restrain him. The instant that he was aware of the possibility of approaching Beatrice, it seemed an absolute necessity of his existence to do so. It mattered not whether she were angel or demon; he was irrevocably within her sphere, and must obey the law that whirled him onward, in ever-lessening circles, towards a result which he did not attempt to foreshadow; and yet, strange to say, there came across him a sudden doubt whether this intense interest on his part were not delusory; whether it were really of so deep and positive a nature as to justify him in now thrusting himself into an incalculable position; whether it were not merely the fantasy of a young man's brain, only slightly or not at all connected with his heart.

He paused, hesitated, turned half about, but again went on.

His withered guide led him along several obscure passages, and finally undid a door, through which, as it was opened, there came the sight and sound of rustling leaves, with the broken sunshine glimmering among them. Giovanni stepped forth, and, forcing himself through the entanglement of a shrub that wreathed its tendrils over the hidden entrance, stood beneath his own window in the open area of Dr. Rappaccini's garden.

How often is it the case that, when impossibilities have come to pass and dreams have condensed their misty substance into tangible realities, we find ourselves calm, and even coldly self-possessed, amid circumstances which it would have been a delirium of joy or agony to anticipate! Fate delights to thwart us thus. Passion will choose his own time to rush upon the scene, and lingers sluggishly behind when an appropriate adjustment of events would seem to summon his appearance. So was it now with Giovanni. Day after day his pulses had throbbed with feverish blood at the improbable idea of an interview with Beatrice, and of standing with her, face to face, in this very garden, basking in the Oriental sunshine of her beauty, and snatching from her full gaze the mystery which he deemed the riddle of his own existence. But now there was a singular and untimely equanimity within his breast. He threw a glance around the garden to discover if Beatrice or her father were present, and, perceiving that he was alone, began a critical observation of the plants.

The aspect of one and all of them dissatisfied him; their gorgeousness seemed fierce, passionate, and even unnatural. There was hardly an individual shrub which a wanderer, straying by himself through a forest, would not have been startled to find growing wild, as if an unearthly face had glared at him out of the thicket. Several also would have shocked a delicate instinct by an appearance of artificialness indicating that there had been such commixture, and, as it were, adultery, of various vegetable species, that the production was no longer of God's making, but the monstrous offspring of man's depraved fancy, glowing with only an evil mockery of beauty. They were probably the result of experiment, which in one or two cases had succeeded in mingling plants individually lovely into a compound possessing the questionable and ominous character that distinguished the whole growth of the garden. In fine, Giovanni recognized but two or three plants in the collection, and those of a kind that he well knew to be poisonous. While busy with these contemplations he heard the rustling of a silken garment, and, turning, beheld Beatrice emerging from beneath the sculptured portal.

Giovanni had not considered with himself what should be his deportment; whether he should apologize for his intrusion into the garden, or assume that he was there with the privity at least, if not by the desire, of Dr. Rappaccini or his daughter; but Beatrice's manner placed him at his ease, though leaving him still in doubt by what agency he had gained admittance. She came lightly along the path and met him near the broken fountain. There was surprise in her face, but brightened by a simple and kind expression of pleasure.

"You are a connoisseur in flowers, signor," said Beatrice, with a smile, alluding to the bouquet which he had flung her from the window. "It is no marvel, therefore, if the sight of my father's rare collection has tempted you to take a nearer view. If he were here, he could tell you many strange and interesting facts as to the nature and habits of these shrubs; for he has spent a lifetime in such studies, and this garden is his world."

"And yourself, lady," observed Giovanni, "if fame says true,—you likewise are deeply skilled in the virtues indicated by these rich blossoms and these spicy perfumes. Would you deign to be my instructress, I should prove an apter scholar than if taught by Signor Rappaccini himself."

"Are there such idle rumors?" asked Beatrice, with the music of a pleasant laugh. "Do people say that I am skilled in my father's science of plants? What a jest is there! No; though I have grown up among these flowers, I know no more of them than their hues and perfume; and sometimes methinks I would fain rid myself of even that small knowledge. There are many flowers here, and those not the least brilliant, that shock and offend me when they meet my eye. But pray, signor, do not believe these stories about my science. Believe nothing of me save what you see with your own eyes."

"And must I believe all that I have seen with my own eyes?" asked Giovanni, pointedly, while the recollection of former scenes made him shrink. "No, signora; you demand too little of me. Bid me believe nothing save what comes from your own lips."

It would appear that Beatrice understood him. There came a deep flush to her cheek; but she looked full into Giovanni's eyes, and responded to his gaze of uneasy suspicion with a queenlike haughtiness.

"I do so bid you, signor," she replied. "Forget whatever you may have fancied in regard to me. If true to the outward senses, still it may be false in its essence; but the words of Beatrice Rappaccini's lips are true from the depths of the heart outward. Those you may believe."

A fervor glowed in her whole aspect and beamed upon Giovanni's consciousness like the light of truth itself; but while she spoke there was a fragrance in the atmosphere around her, rich and delightful, though evanescent, yet which the young man, from an indefinable reluctance, scarcely dared to draw into his lungs. It might be the odor of the flowers. Could it be Beatrice's breath which thus embalmed her words with a strange richness, as if by steeping them in her heart? A faintness passed like a shadow over Giovanni and flitted away; he seemed to gaze through the beautiful girl's eyes into her transparent soul, and felt no more doubt or fear.

The tinge of passion that had colored Beatrice's manner vanished; she became gay, and appeared to derive a pure delight from her communion with the youth not unlike what the maiden of a lonely island might have felt conversing with a voyager from the civilized world. Evidently her experience of life had been confined within the limits of that garden. She talked now about matters as simple as the daylight or summer clouds, and now asked questions in reference to the city, or Giovanni's distant home, his friends, his mother, and his sisters—questions indicating such seclusion, and such lack of familiarity with modes and forms, that Giovanni responded as if to an infant. Her spirit gushed out before him like a fresh rill that was just catching its first glimpse of the sunlight and wondering at the reflections of earth and sky which were flung into its bosom. There came thoughts, too, from a deep source, and fantasies of a gemlike brilliancy, as if diamonds and rubies sparkled upward among the bubbles of the fountain. Ever and anon there gleamed across the young man's mind a sense of wonder that he should be walking side by side with the being who had so wrought upon his imagination, whom he had idealized in such hues of terror, in whom he had positively witnessed such manifestations of dreadful attributes,—that he should be conversing with Beatrice like a brother, and should find her so human and so maidenlike. But such reflections were only momentary; the effect of her character was too real not to make itself familiar at once.

In this free intercourse they had strayed through the garden, and now, after many turns among its avenues, were come to the shattered fountain, beside which grew the magnificent shrub, with its treasury of glowing blossoms. A fragrance was diffused from it which Giovanni recognized as identical with that which he had attributed to Beatrice's breath, but incomparably more powerful. As her eyes fell upon it, Giovanni beheld her press her hand to her bosom as if her heart were throbbing suddenly and painfully.

"For the first time in my life," murmured she, addressing the shrub, "I had forgotten thee."

"I remember, signora," said Giovanni, "that you once promised to reward me with one of these living gems for the bouquet which I had the happy boldness to fling at your feet. Permit me now to pluck it as a memorial of this interview."

He made a step towards the shrub with extended hand; but Beatrice darted forward, uttering a shriek that went through his heart like a dagger. She caught his hand and drew it back with the whole force of her slender figure. Giovanni felt her touch thrilling through his fibres.

"Touch it not!" exclaimed she, in a voice of agony. "Not for thy life! It is fatal!"

Then, hiding her face, she fled from him and vanished beneath the sculptured portal. As Giovanni followed her with his eyes, he beheld the emaciated figure and pale intelligence of Dr. Rappaccini, who had been watching the scene, he knew not how long, within the shadow of the entrance.

No sooner was Guasconti alone in his chamber than the image of Beatrice came back to his passionate musings, invested with all the witchery that had been gathering around it ever since his first glimpse of her, and now likewise imbued with a tender warmth of girlish womanhood. She was human; her nature was endowed with all gentle and feminine qualities; she was worthiest to be worshipped; she was capable, surely, on her part, of the height and heroism of love. Those tokens which he had hitherto considered as proofs of a frightful peculiarity in her physical and moral system were now either forgotten, or, by the subtle sophistry of passion transmitted into a golden crown of enchantment, rendering Beatrice the more admirable by so much as she was the more unique. Whatever had looked ugly was now beautiful; or, if incapable of such a change, it stole away and hid itself among those shapeless half ideas which throng the dim region beyond the daylight of our perfect consciousness. Thus did he spend the night, nor fell asleep until the dawn had begun to awake the slumbering flowers in Dr. Rappaccini's garden, whither Giovanni's dreams doubtless led him. Up rose the sun in his due season, and, flinging his beams upon the young man's eyelids, awoke him to a sense of pain. When thoroughly aroused, he became sensible of a burning and tingling agony in his hand—in his right hand—the very hand which Beatrice had grasped in her own when he was on the point of plucking one of the gemlike flowers. On the back of that hand there was now a purple print like that of four small fingers, and the likeness of a slender thumb upon his wrist.

Oh, how stubbornly does love,—or even that cunning semblance of love which flourishes in the imagination, but strikes no depth of root into the heart,—how stubbornly does it hold its faith until the moment comes when it is doomed to vanish into thin mist! Giovanni wrapped a handkerchief about his hand and wondered what evil thing had stung him, and soon forgot his pain in a reverie of Beatrice.

After the first interview, a second was in the inevitable

course of what we call fate. A third; a fourth; and a meeting with Beatrice in the garden was no longer an incident in Giovanni's daily life, but the whole space in which he might be said to live; for the anticipation and memory of that ecstatic hour made up the remainder. Nor was it otherwise with the daughter of Rappaccini. She watched for the youth's appearance, and flew to his side with confidence as unreserved as if they had been playmates from early infancy—as if they were such playmates still. If, by any unwonted chance, he failed to come at the appointed moment, she stood beneath the window and sent up the rich sweetness of her tones to float around him in his chamber and echo and reverberate throughout his heart: "Giovanni! Giovanni! Why tarriest thou? Come down!" And down he hastened into that Eden of poisonous flowers.

But, with all this intimate familiarity, there was still a reserve in Beatrice's demeanor, so rigidly and invariably sustained that the idea of infringing it scarcely occurred to his imagination. By all appreciable signs, they loved; they had looked love with eyes that conveyed the holy secret from the depths of one soul into the depths of the other, as if it were too sacred to be whispered by the way; they had even spoken love in those gushes of passion when their spirits darted forth in articulated breath like tongues of long-hidden flame; and yet there had been no seal of lips, no clasp of hands, nor any slightest caress such as love claims and hallows. He had never touched one of the gleaming ringlets of her hair; her garment —so marked was the physical barrier between them—had never been waved against him by a breeze. On the few occasions when Giovanni had seemed tempted to overstep the limit, Beatrice grew so sad, so stern, and withal wore such a look of desolate separation, shuddering at itself, that not a spoken word was requisite to repel him. At such times he was startled at the horrible suspicions that rose, monster-like, out of the caverns of his heart and stared him in the face; his love grew thin and faint as the morning mist, his doubts alone had substance. But, when Beatrice's face brightened again after the momentary shadow, she was transformed at once from the mysterious, questionable being whom he had watched with so much awe and horror; she was now the beautiful and unsophisticated girl whom he felt that his spirit knew with a certainty beyond all other knowledge.

A considerable time had now passed since Giovanni's last meeting with Baglioni. One morning, however, he was disagreeably surprised by a visit from the professor, whom he had scarcely thought of for whole weeks, and would willingly have forgotten still longer. Given up as he had long been to a pervading excitement, he could tolerate no companions except upon condition of their perfect sympathy with his present state of feeling. Such sympathy was not to be expected from Professor Baglioni.

The visitor chatted carelessly for a few moments about the gossip of the city and the university, and then took up another topic.

"I have been reading an old classic author lately," said he, "and met with a story that strangely interested me. Possibly you may remember it. It is of an Indian prince, who sent a beautiful woman as a present to Alexander the Great. She was as lovely as the dawn and gorgeous as the sunset; but what especially distinguished her was a certain rich perfume in her breath—richer than a garden of Persian roses. Alexander, as was natural to a youthful conqueror, fell in love at first sight with this magnificent stranger; but a certain sage physician, happening to be present, discovered a terrible secret in regard to her."

"And what was that?" asked Giovanni, turning his eyes downward to avoid those of the professor.

"That this lovely woman," continued Baglioni, with emphasis, "had been nourished with poisons from her birth upward, until her whole nature was so imbued with them that she herself had become the deadliest poison in existence. Poison was her element of life. With that rich perfume of her breath she blasted the very air. Her love would have been poison—her embrace death. Is not this a marvellous tale?"

"A childish fable," answered Giovanni, nervously starting from his chair. "I marvel how your worship finds time to read such nonsense among your graver studies."

"By the by," said the professor, looking uneasily about

him, "what singular fragrance is this in your apartment? Is it the perfume of your gloves? It is faint, but delicious; and yet, after all, by no means agreeable. Were I to breathe it long, methinks it would make me ill. It is like the breath of a flower; but I see no flowers in the chamber."

"Nor are there any," replied Giovanni, who had turned pale as the professor spoke; "nor, I think, is there any fragrance except in your worship's imagination. Odors, being a sort of element combined of the sensual and the spiritual, are apt to deceive us in this manner. The recollection of a perfume, the bare idea of it, may easily be mistaken for a present reality."

"Ay; but my sober imagination does not often play such tricks," said Baglioni; "and, were I to fancy any kind of odor, it would be that of some vile apothecary drug, wherewith my fingers are likely enough to be imbued. Our worshipful friend Rappaccini, as I have heard, tinctures his medicaments with odors richer than those of Araby. Doubtless, likewise, the fair and learned Signora Beatrice would minister to her patients with draughts as sweet as a maiden's breath; but woe to him that sips them!"

Giovanni's face evinced many contending emotions. The tone in which the professor alluded to the pure and lovely daughter of Rappaccini was a torture to his soul; and yet the intimation of a view of her character, opposite to his own, gave instantaneous distinctness to a thousand dim suspicions, which now grinned at him like so many demons. But he strove hard to quell them and to respond to Baglioni with a true lover's perfect faith.

"Signor professor," said he, "you were my father's friend; perchance, too, it is your purpose to act a friendly part towards his son. I would fain feel nothing towards you save respect and deference; but I pray you to observe, signor, that there is one subject on which we must not speak. You know not the Signora Beatrice. You cannot, therefore, estimate the wrong—the blasphemy, I may even say—that is offered to her character by a light or injurious word."

"Giovanni! my poor Giovanni!" answered the professor,

with a calm expression of pity, "I know this wretched girl far better than yourself. You shall hear the truth in respect to the poisoner Rappaccini and his poisonous daughter; yes, poisonous as she is beautiful. Listen; for, even should you do violence to my gray hairs, it shall not silence me. That old fable of the Indian woman has become a truth by the deep and deadly science of Rappaccini and in the person of the lovely Beatrice."

Giovanni groaned and hid his face.

"Her father," continued Baglioni, "was not restrained by natural affection from offering up his child in this horrible manner as the victim of his insane zeal for science; for, let us do him justice, he is as true a man of science as ever distilled his own heart in an alembic. What, then, will be your fate? Beyond a doubt you are selected as the material of some new experiment. Perhaps the result is to be death; perhaps a fate more awful still. Rappaccini, with what he calls the interest of science before his eyes, will hesitate at nothing."

"It is a dream," muttered Giovanni to himself; surely it is a dream."

"But," resumed the professor, "be of good cheer, son of my friend. It is not yet too late for the rescue. Possibly we may even succeed in bringing back this miserable child within the limits of ordinary nature, from which her father's madness has estranged her. Behold this little silver vase! It was wrought by the hands of the renowned Benvenuto Cellini, and is well worthy to be a love gift to the fairest dame in Italy. But its contents are invaluable. One little sip of this antidote would have rendered the most virulent poisons of the Borgias innocuous. Doubt not that it will be as efficacious against those of Rappaccini. Bestow the vase, and the precious liquid within it, on your Beatrice, and hopefully await the result."

Baglioni laid a small, exquisitely wrought silver vial on the table and withdrew, leaving what he had said to produce its effect upon the young man's mind.

"We will thwart Rappaccini yet," thought he, chuckling to himself, as he descended the stairs; "but, let us confess the truth of him, he is a wonderful man—a wonderful man indeed; a vile empiric, however, in his practice, and therefore not to be tolerated by those who respect the good old rules of the medical profession."

Throughout Giovanni's whole acquaintance with Beatrice, he had occasionally, as we have said, been haunted by dark surmises as to her character; yet so thoroughly had she made herself felt by him as a simple, natural, most affectionate, and guileless creature, that the image now held up by Professor Baglioni looked as strange and incredible as if it were not in accordance with his own original conception. True, there were ugly recollections connected with his first glimpses of the beautiful girl; he could not quite forget the bouquet that withered in her grasp, and the insect that perished amid the sunny air, by no ostensible agency save the fragrance of her breath. These incidents, however, dissolving in the pure light of her character, had no longer the efficacy of facts, but were acknowledged as mistaken fantasies, by whatever testimony of the senses they might appear to be substantiated. There is something truer and more real than what we can see with the eyes and touch with the finger. On such better evidence had Giovanni founded his confidence in Beatrice, though rather by the necessary force of her high attributes than by any deep and generous faith on his part. But now his spirit was incapable of sustaining itself at the height to which the early enthusiasm of passion had exalted it; he fell down, grovelling among earthly doubts, and defiled therewith the pure whiteness of Beatrice's image. Not that he gave her up; he did but distrust. He resolved to institute some decisive test that should satisfy him, once for all, whether there were those dreadful peculiarities in her physical nature which could not be supposed to exist without some corresponding monstrosity of soul. His eyes, gazing down afar, might have deceived him as to the lizard, the insect, and the flowers; but if he could witness, at the distance of a few paces, the sudden blight of one fresh and healthful flower in Beatrice's hand, there would be room for no further question. With this idea he hastened to the florist's and purchased a bouquet that was still gemmed with the morning dew-drops.

It was now the customary hour of his daily interview with

Beatrice. Before descending into the garden, Giovanni failed not to look at his figure in the mirror,—a vanity to be expected in a beautiful young man, yet, as displaying itself at that troubled and feverish moment, the token of a certain shallowness of feeling and insincerity of character. He did gaze, however, and said to himself that his features had never before possessed so rich a grace, nor his eyes such vivacity, nor his cheeks so warm a hue of superabundant life.

"At least," thought he, "her poison has not yet insinuated itself into my system. I am no flower to perish in her grasp."

With that thought he turned his eyes on the bouquet, which he had never once laid aside from his hand. A thrill of indefinable horror shot through his frame on perceiving that those dewy flowers were already beginning to droop; they wore the aspect of things that had been fresh and lovely yesterday. Giovanni grew white as marble, and stood motionless before the mirror, staring at his own reflection there as at the likeness of something frightful. He remembered Baglioni's remark about the fragrance that seemed to pervade the chamber. It must have been the poison in his breath! Then he shuddered—shuddered at himself. Recovering from his stupor, he began to watch with curious eye a spider that was busily at work hanging its web from the antique cornice of the apartment, crossing and recrossing the artful system of interwoven lines—as vigorous and active a spider as ever dangled from an old ceiling. Giovanni bent towards the insect, and emitted a deep, long breath. The spider suddenly ceased its toil; the web vibrated with a tremor originating in the body of the small artisan. Again Giovanni sent forth a breath, deeper, longer, and imbued with a venomous feeling out of his heart: he knew not whether he were wicked, or only desperate. The spider made a convulsive gripe with his limbs and hung dead across the window.

"Accursed! accursed!" muttered Giovanni, addressing himself. "Hast thou grown so poisonous that this deadly insect perishes by thy breath?"

At that moment a rich, sweet voice came floating up from the garden.

"Giovanni! Giovanni! It is past the hour! Why tarriest thou? Come down!"

"Yes," muttered Giovanni again. "She is the only being whom my breath may not slay! Would that it might!"

He rushed down, and in an instant was standing before the bright and loving eyes of Beatrice. A moment ago his wrath and despair had been so fierce that he could have desired nothing so much as to wither her by a glance; but with her actual presence there came influences which had too real an existence to be at once shaken off: recollections of the delicate and benign power of her feminine nature, which had so often enveloped him in a religious calm; recollections of many a holy and passionate outgush of her heart, when the pure fountain had been unsealed from its depths and made visible in its transparency to his mental eye; recollections which, had Giovanni known how to estimate them, would have assured him that all this ugly mystery was but an earthly illusion, and that, whatever mist of evil might seem to have gathered over her, the real Beatrice was a heavenly angel. Incapable as he was of such high faith, still her presence had not utterly lost its magic. Giovanni's rage was quelled into an aspect of sullen insensibility. Beatrice, with a quick spiritual sense, immediately felt that there was a gulf of blackness between them which neither he nor she could pass. They walked on together, sad and silent, and came thus to the marble fountain and to its pool of water on the ground, in the midst of which grew the shrub that bore gem-like blossoms. Giovanni was affrighted at the eager enjoyment—the appetite, as it were—with which he found himself inhaling the fragrance of the flowers.

"Beatrice," asked he, abruptly, "whence came this shrub?"

"My father created it," answered she, with simplicity.

"Created it! created it!" repeated Giovanni. "What mean you, Beatrice?"

"He is a man fearfully acquainted with the secrets of Nature," replied Beatrice; "and, at the hour when I first drew breath, this plant sprang from the soil, the offspring of his science, of his intellect, while I was but his earthly child. Approach it not!" continued she, observing with terror that

Giovanni was drawing nearer to the shrub. "It has qualities that you little dream of. But I, dearest Giovanni,—I grew up and blossomed with the plant and was nourished with its breath. It was my sister, and I loved it with a human affection; for, alas!—hast thou not suspected it?—there was an awful doom."

Here Giovanni frowned so darkly upon her that Beatrice paused and trembled. But her faith in his tenderness reassured her, and made her blush that she had doubted for an instant.

"There was an awful doom," she continued, "the effect of my father's fatal love of science, which estranged me from all society of my kind. Until Heaven sent thee, dearest Giovanni, oh, how lonely was thy poor Beatrice!"

"Was it a hard doom?" asked Giovanni, fixing his eyes upon her.

"Only of late have I known how hard it was," answered she, tenderly. "Oh, yes; but my heart was torpid, and therefore quiet."

Giovanni's rage broke forth from his sullen gloom like a lightning flash out of a dark cloud.

"Accursed one!" cried he, with venomous scorn and anger. "And, finding thy solitude wearisome, thou hast severed me likewise from all the warmth of life and enticed me into thy region of unspeakable horror!"

"Giovanni!" exclaimed Beatrice, turning her large bright eyes upon his face. The force of his words had not found its way into her mind; she was merely thunderstruck.

"Yes, poisonous thing!" repeated Giovanni, beside himself with passion. "Thou hast done it! Thou hast blasted me! Thou hast filled my veins with poison! Thou hast made me as hateful, as ugly, as loathsome and deadly a creature as thyself— a world's wonder of hideous monstrosity! Now, if our breath be happily as fatal to ourselves as to all others, let us join our lips in one kiss of unutterable hatred, and so die!"

"What has befallen me?" murmured Beatrice, with a low moan out of her heart. "Holy Virgin, pity me, a poor heart-broken child!"

"Thou,—dost thou pray?" cried Giovanni, still with the same fiendish scorn. "Thy very prayers, as they come from thy lips, taint the atmosphere with death. Yes, yes; let us pray! Let us to church and dip our fingers in the holy water at the portal! They that come after us will perish as by a pestilence! Let us sign crosses in the air! It will be scattering curses abroad in the likeness of holy symbols!"

"Giovanni," said Beatrice, calmly, for her grief was beyond passion, "why dost thou join thyself with me thus in those terrible words? I, it is true, am the horrible thing thou namest me. But thou,—what hast thou to do, save with one other shudder at my hideous misery to go forth out of the garden and mingle with thy race, and forget that there ever crawled on earth such a monster as poor Beatrice?"

"Dost thou pretend ignorance?" asked Giovanni, scowling upon her. "Behold! this power have I gained from the pure daughter of Rappaccini."

There was a swarm of summer insects flitting through the air in search of the food promised by the flower odors of the fatal garden. They circled round Giovanni's head, and were evidently attracted towards him by the same influence which had drawn them for an instant within the sphere of several of the shrubs. He sent forth a breath among them, and smiled bitterly at Beatrice as at least a score of the insects fell dead upon the ground.

"I see it! I see it!" shrieked Beatrice. "It is my father's fatal science! No, no, Giovanni; it was not I! Never! never! I dreamed only to love thee and be with thee a little time, and so to let thee pass away, leaving but thine image in mine heart; for, Giovanni, believe it, though my body be nourished with poison, my spirit is God's creature, and craves love as its daily food. But my father,—he has united us in this fearful sympathy. Yes; spurn me, tread upon me, kill me! Oh, what is death after such words as thine? But it was not I. Not for a world of bliss would I have done it."

Giovanni's passion had exhausted itself in its outburst from his lips. There now came across him a sense, mournful, and not without tenderness, of the intimate and peculiar relationship between Beatrice and himself. They stood, as it were, in an utter solitude, which would be made none the less solitary by the densest throng of human life. Ought not, then, the desert of humanity around them to press this insulated pair closer together? If they should be cruel to one another, who was there to be kind to them? Besides, thought Giovanni, might there not still be a hope of his returning within the limits of ordinary nature, and leading Beatrice, the redeemed Beatrice, by the hand? O, weak, and selfish, and unworthy spirit, that could dream of an earthly union and earthly happiness as possible, after such deep love had been so bitterly wronged as was Beatrice's love by Giovanni's blighting words! No, no; there could be no such hope. She must pass heavily, with that broken heart, across the borders of Time—she must bathe her hurts in some fount of paradise, and forget her grief in the light of immortality, and *there* be well.

But Giovanni did not know it.

"Dear Beatrice," said he, approaching her, while she shrank away as always at his approach, but now with a different impulse, "dearest Beatrice, our fate is not yet so desperate. Behold! there is a medicine, potent, as a wise physician has assured me, and almost divine in its efficacy. It is composed of ingredients the most opposite to those by which thy awful father has brought this calamity upon thee and me. It is distilled of blessed herbs. Shall we not quaff it together, and thus be purified from evil?"

"Give it me!" said Beatrice, extending her hand to receive the little silver vial which Giovanni took from his bosom. She added, with a peculiar emphasis, "I will drink; but do thou await the result."

She put Baglioni's antidote to her lips; and, at the same moment, the figure of Rappaccini emerged from the portal and came slowly towards the marble fountain. As he drew near, the pale man of science seemed to gaze with a triumphant expression at the beautiful youth and maiden, as might an artist who should spend his life in achieving a picture or a group of statuary and finally be satisfied with his success. He paused; his bent form grew erect with conscious power; he spread out his hands over them in the attitude of a father imploring a blessing upon his children; but those were the same hands that had thrown poison into the stream of their lives. Giovanni trembled. Beatrice shuddered nervously, and pressed her hand upon her heart.

"My daughter," said Rappaccini, "thou art no longer lonely

in the world. Pluck one of those precious gems from thy sister shrub and bid thy bridegroom wear it in his bosom. It will not harm him now. My science and the sympathy between thee and him have so wrought within his system that he now stands apart from common men, as thou dost, daughter of my pride and triumph, from ordinary women. Pass on, then, through the world, most dear to one another and dreadful to all besides!"

"My father," said Beatrice, feebly,—and still as she spoke she kept her hand upon her heart,—"wherefore didst thou inflict this miserable doom upon thy child?"

"Miserable!" exclaimed Rappaccini. "What mean you, foolish girl? Dost thou deem it misery to be endowed with marvellous gifts against which no power nor strength could avail an enemy—misery, to be able to quell the mightiest with a breath—misery, to be as terrible as thou art beautiful? Wouldst thou, then, have preferred the condition of a weak woman, exposed to all evil and capable of none?"

"I would fain have been loved, not feared," murmured Beatrice, sinking down upon the ground. "But now it matters not. I am going, father, where the evil which thou hast striven to mingle with my being will pass away like a dream—like the fragrance of these poisonous flowers, which will no longer taint my breath among the flowers of Eden. Farewell, Giovanni! Thy words of hatred are like lead within my heart; but they, too, will fall away as I ascend. Oh, was there not, from the first, more poison in thy nature than in mine?"

To Beatrice,—so radically had her earthly part been wrought upon by Rappaccini's skill,—as poison had been life, so the powerful antidote was death; and thus the poor victim of man's ingenuity and of thwarted nature, and of the fatality that attends all such efforts of perverted wisdom, perished there, at the feet of her father and Giovanni. Just at that moment Professor Pietro Baglioni looked forth from the window, and called loudly, in a tone of triumph mixed with horror, to the thunderstricken man of science,—

"Rappaccini! Rappaccini! and is *this* the upshot of your experiment!"

THE PSYCHOPHONIC NURSE

David H. Keller, M.D.

After reading this story, one can only conclude that Dr. Keller (born in 1880 and as of spring, 1962, still enjoying life and writing neat hand-penned letters from Stroudsburg, Pennsylvania) had little use for either automation or successful businesswomen—at least when he wrote about them. Certainly he comes out powerfully against even successful robots (although when he wrote about his synthetic nurse and his surrogate papa the term "robot" was as yet generally unknown to American readers, since it had been invented only five years previously), and much in favor of undiluted mother (and father) love. For that matter, we go along with him on both counts, up to a point at least, and we think you will, too!

The Psychophonic Nurse

"I'M MAD! JUST PLAIN MAD!" cried Susanna Teeple.

"Well, it can't be helped now," replied her husband. "I'm just as sorry as you are about it, but the baby is here now and some one has to take care of it."

"I admit all that," said Susanna. "I want her to be well cared for, but I have my work to do and now I have a real chance to make good money writing regularly for the *Business Woman's Advisor*. I can easily make a thousand dollars a month if I can only find time to do the work. I simply *can't* do my work and care for the baby. It was all a great mistake, having the baby now."

"But I make enough to hire a nurse," insisted Teeple.

"Certainly, but where can I find one? The women who need the money are all working seven hours a day and all the good nurses are in hospitals. I have searched all over town and they just laugh when I start talking to them."

"Take care of her yourself. Systematize the work. Budget your time, and make out a definite daily programme. Would you like me to employ an efficiency engineer? I have just had a man working along those lines in my factory. Bet he could help you a lot. Investigate the modern electrical machinery for taking care of the baby. Jot down your troubles and my inventor will start working on them."

"You talk just like a man!" replied the woman in cold anger. "Your suggestions prove you have no idea whatever of the problem of caring for a three-weeks-old baby. I've used all the brains I have, and it takes me exactly seven hours a day. If the seven hours would all come in sequence, I could spare them, but during the last three days, since I've kept count, I've been interrupted from my writing exactly one hundred and ten times every twenty-four hours and only about five per cent of those interruptions could have been avoided. The baby has to be fed, changed, and washed and the bottles must be sterilized, the crib fixed, and the nursery cleaned, and

just when I have her all right she regurgitates and then everything has to be done all over again. I just wish you had to
take care of her for twenty-four hours, then you'd know more
than you do now. I've tried some of those electrical machines
you speak of: had them sent on approval, but they weren't
satisfactory. The vacuum evaporator clogged up with talcum
powder and the curd extractor worked all right so long as it
was over the mouth, but once the baby turned her head and
the machine nearly pulled her ear off, before I found out why
she was crying so. It would be wonderful if a baby could
be cared for by machinery, but I'm afraid it will never be
possible."

"I believe it will," said Teeple. "Of course, even if the machine worked perfectly, it couldn't supply a mother's love."

"That idea of mother-love belongs to the dark ages," sneered
the disappointed woman. "We know now that a child doesn't
know what love is till it develops the ability to think. Women
have been deceiving themselves. They believed their babies
loved them because they wanted to think so. When my child is
old enough to know what love is, I'll be properly demon-
strative—and not before. I've read very carefully what Hug-
Hellmuth has written about the psychology of the baby and
no child of mine is going to develop unhealthy complexes
because I indulged in untimely love and unnecessary caresses.
I noticed that you've kissed it when you thought I wasn't
watching. How would you feel if, because of those kisses,
your daughter developed an Oedipus complex when she
reached maturity? I differ with you in regard to the machine;
it will never be possible to care for a baby by machinery!"

"I believe it will!" insisted Teeple doggedly.

That evening he boarded the air-express for New York City.
When he returned, after some days of absence, he was very
uncommunicative in regard to the trip and what he had accomplished. Mrs. Teeple continued to take very good care of
her baby, and also lost no opportunity of letting her husband
realize what a sacrifice she was making for her family. Teeple
continued to preserve a dignified silence. Then, about two
weeks after his New York trip, he told his wife to go out for

the afternoon. He would stay home and be nurse, just to see how it would go. After giving a thousand detailed instructions, Mrs. Teeple left.

On her return, she found her husband calmly reading in the library. Going to the nursery, she found the baby asleep and by the side of the crib she saw a fat, black woman, clad in the spotless uniform of a graduate nurse. She seemed as fast asleep as the child. Surprised, Mrs. Teeple went to her husband.

"Well, what does this mean?" she demanded.

"That, my dear, is our new nurse."

"Where did you get her?"

"I bought her in New York. In fact, I had her made to order."

"You what?" asked the astonished woman.

"I had her made to order by the Eastinghouse Electric Company. You see, she's just a machine nurse, but as she doesn't eat anything, is on duty twenty-four hours a day, and draws no salary, she's cheap at the price I paid."

"Are you insane, or am I?"

"Neither. Certainly not your husband. Let me show you how she works. She's made of a combination of springs, levers, acoustic instruments, and by means of tubes such as are used in the radio, she's very sensitive to sounds. She's connected to the house current by a long, flexible cord, which supplies her with the necessary energy. To simplify matters, I had the orders put into numbers instead of sentences. *One* mean that the baby is to be fed; *seven* that she's to be changed. *Twelve* that it's time for a bath. I had a map made showing the exact position of the baby, the pile of clean diapers, the full bottles of milk, the clean sheets, in fact, everything needed to care for the baby during the twenty-four hours. In the morning, all you have to do is see that everything needed is in its place. At six o'clock you go into the nursery and say *one* in a loud, clear voice. The nurse reaches over to the row of bottles, picks up one and puts the nipple in the baby's mouth. At the end of ten minutes it takes the empty bottle and puts it back in the row. At six-thirty, you say clearly and distinctly, *seven.* The nurse removes the wet diaper, takes a can of talcum, uses it, puts it back, takes a diaper, and pins it on the baby. Then she sits down."

"I think you're drunk!" said the woman, coolly.

"Not at all. You feel of her and see. She's just a lot of rods and wires and machinery. I had her padded and made with a face because I thought she'd look more natural that way."

"Suppose all that you say is true. How can it help me? I have to see what the baby needs, then look through the book and see what number to say and then, I suppose, I have to stay and watch the old thing work. I wanted a chance to work at my books and this—why, it's ridiculous!"

Teeple laughed.

"You're a nice little woman, Susanna, but you certainly lack imagination. When I ordered this machine, I thought about all that and so I bought a phonograph with clock attachment. It will run for twenty-four hours without attention. Then I had a baby doctor work out a twenty-four hour programme of infant activity for different ages. Our baby is about two months old. You put this phonograph with the two-month record on it in the nursery. At six in the morning you see that all the supplies for that day are in the proper place; you see that the Psychophonic Nurse is in her proper place; the baby must also be in her proper place. Then you attach the current to the phonograph and the nurse and start the record. At definite periods of the twenty-four hours the phonograph will call out a number and the nurse will do what is necessary for that hour. It will feed the baby just so often and change it just so often and bathe it just so often. You start it at six and leave it alone till six the next morning."

"That sounds fine," said the wife, sarcastically, "but suppose the baby gets wet between times? Suppose it starts to cry?"

"I thought of that, too. In every diaper there is a fine copper wire. When that becomes wet a delicate current is sent—you understand I mean an electrical current, not a watery one—to an amplifier and a certain sound is made, and the nurse will properly react to that sound. We have also provided for crying. When the baby does that, the nurse will pick the little one up and rock her to sleep."

"But the books say that spoils the baby!"

"I know. I thought of that. But then, the poor little thing has to have some love and affection in her life and so I thought it wouldn't harm it any to be rocked now and then. That was one reason why I had the padding made the way I did. I bet it will be mighty comfortable for the child. Then again, you know I had a black mammy and I wanted my child to have one, too."

"Well," said the woman, petulantly, "show me how the thing works. I've a lot of writing to do and unless I do it, they'll hire some one else."

After two hours of close observation, she had to admit that the nurse was just as capable of mechanically looking after the needs of a baby as she was. In fact, the cleverness of the performance made her gasp with astonishment. After each series of complicated acts, the machine went back to the chair and sat down.

The husband was triumphant.

"She does the work nicely," he said. "Naturally, there's no intelligence, but none is needed in the early months of child-care."

The Psychophonic Nurse performed her duties in a way that would have been a credit to any woman. Of course there were times when things didn't go as well as they should, but the fault was always with the human side of the arrangement and not the mechanical. Usually the mother was to blame because she didn't put the supply of food or clothes in exactly the right place and once a new servant played havoc by cleaning the room and putting the nurse and the chair on the wrong side of the crib. Still, with a little supervision and care, things went very well indeed, and in a very short time the baby became accustomed to her black mammy and the mother was satisfied to spend a few minutes every morning arranging supplies and then leave the two alone for the rest of the day. Every two weeks a new record was placed in the phonograph, for it was determined that it was necessary to make a change in the program at least that often.

Mrs. Teeple, thoroughly happy with her new freedom, now

devoted her entire time to literature. Her articles, which appeared in the Saturday issue of *The Business Woman's Advisor,* were brilliant and aroused the most favorable comment from all parts of the world. An English firm asked her to write a book on *Woman, the Conqueror,* and so relieved was she of household worries, that at once she started to pound out the introduction on her noiseless, electrical typewriter. Once in a while she felt the need of exercise and would stroll around the house, and occasionally look into the nursery. Now and then she would pick the little one up. As the child grew older, this made her cry, so the mother decided that it was best not to interfere with the daily routine.

In spite of their efforts to conceal the activity of their new assistant, the news spread through the little town. The neighbors called, and while they had all kinds of excuses, there was no doubt about what it was they really wanted to see. Of course, opinions differed, and rather sharply. There were some of the older women who fearlessly denounced such conduct as unconditionally bad, but most of the women were secretly jealous and demanded that their husbands also buy a mechanical nursemaid.

The news spread beyond the confines of the town. Descriptions of a most interesting and erroneous nature began to appear in the newspapers. Finally, to avoid unscientific criticism, Mrs. Teeple wrote a full account of the way she was raising her child and sold it to the *New York Comet,* fully illustrated, for five thousand dollars. At once the Eastinghouse Electric Company was swamped with orders which they simply filed for future delivery. The entire machine was covered with patents and these were all the property of Teeple, who, for the time being, merely said that he wanted to make further studies before he would consider the sale of his rights.

For several months it seemed the discussion would never end. College debating teams selected as their subject, *Shall the Child of the Future Be Raised by the Mother or by a Psychophonic Nurse?* The leaders of the industrial world spent anxious evenings wondering whether such an invention would not simplify the labor problem. Very early in the social furor that was aroused, Henry Cecil, who had taken the place of Wells as an author of scientifiction, wrote a number of brilliant articles in which he showed a world where all the work was done by similar machines. Not only the work of nurses, but of mechanics, day laborers, and farmers could be done by machinery. He told of an age when mankind, relieved of the need to labor, could enter into a golden age of ease. The working day would be one hour long. Each mechanician would go to the factory, oil and adjust a dozen automamatons, see that they had the material for twenty-four hours production, and then turn on the electric current and leave them working till the next day.

Life, Henry Cecil said, would not only become easier, but also better in every way. Society, relieved of the necessity of paying labor, would be able to supply the luxuries of life to everyone. No more would women toil in the kitchen and men on the farm. The highest civilization could be attained because mankind would now have time and leisure to play.

And in his argument he showed that, while workmen in the huge assembling plants had largely become machines in their automatic activities, still they had accidents, sickness, and discontent, ending in troublesome strikes. These would all be avoided by mechanical workmen; of course, for a while there would have to be human supervision, but if it were possible to make a machine that would work, why not make one that would supervise the work of other machines? If one machine could use raw material, why couldn't other machines be trained to distribute the supplies and carry away the finished product? Cecil foresaw the factory of the future running twenty-four hours a day and seven days a week, furnishing everything necessary for the comfort of the human race. At once the ministers of the Gospel demanded a six-day week for the machines, and a proper observance of the Sabbath.

Strange though it may seem, all this discussion seemed natural to the general public. For years they had been educated to use electrical apparatus in their homes. The scrubbing and polishing of floors, washing of dishes, washing and ironing of clothes, the sewing of clothes, grass cutting, cleaning of the furniture, had all been done by electricity for many years. In every department of the world's activity, the white servant, electricity, was in common use. In a little western town a baby was actually being cared for by a Psychophonic Nurse. If one baby, why not all babies? If a machine could do that work, why couldn't machines be made to do all other kinds of work?

The lighter fiction began to use the idea. A really clever article appeared in *The London Spode,* the magazine of society in England. It commented on the high cost of human companionship, and how much the average young woman demanded of her escort, not only in regard to the actual cash expenditure, but also of his time. When he should be resting and gaining strength for his labors in the office, she demanded long evenings at the theater or dance or petting parties in lonely automobiles. The idea was advanced that every man should have a psychophonic affinity. He could take her to the restaurant, but she wouldn't eat, at the theater she could be checked with his opera cloak and top hat. If he wanted to dance, she would dance with him and she would stop just when he wanted her to and then, in his apartment, he could pet her and she would pet him and there would be no scandal. He could buy her in a store, blonde or brunette and when he was tired of her, trade her in for the latest model, with the newest additions and latest line of phonographic chatter records. Every woman could have a mechanical lover. He could do the housework in the daytime while she was at the office, and at night he could act as escort in public or pet her in private. The phonograph would declare a million times, "I love you," and a million times his arms would demonstrate the truth of the declaration. For some decades the two sexes had become more and more discontented with each other. Psychophonic lovers would solve all difficulties of modern social life.

Naturally, this issue of the *Spode* was refused admission to the United States on the grounds that it contained immoral literature. At once it was extensively bootlegged and read by millions of people, who otherwise would never have heard of it. A new phrase was added to the slang. Men who formerly were called "dumbbells," "creeps," or "drips," were now referred to as "psychophonic affinities." If a man was duller than usual, his girl friend would say, "Get a better electric attachment. Your radio tubes are wearing out and your wires are rusting. It's about time I exchanged you for a newer model."

In the meantime, life in the Teeple home was progressing as usual. Mrs. Teeple had all the time she wanted for her literary work and was making a name for herself in the field of letters. She was showing her husband and friends just what a woman could do, if she had leisure to do it. She felt that in no way was she neglecting her child. One hour every morning was spent in preparing the supplies and the modified milk for the following twenty-four hours. After that she felt perfectly safe in leaving the child with the mechanical nurse; in fact, she said that she felt more comfortable than if the baby were being cared for by an ignorant, uninterested girl.

The baby soon learned that the black woman was the one who did everything for her and all the love of the child was centered on her nurse. For some months it did not seem to realize much more than that it was being cared for in a very competent manner and was always very comfortable. Later it found out that this care would not come unless it was in a very definite position on the bed. This was after it had started to roll around. Dimly it must have found out that the nurse had certain limitations, for it began to learn to always return to its correct position in the middle of the crib. Naturally, difficulties arose while she was learning to do this. Once she was upside down and the nurse was absolutely unable to pin on the diaper, but the baby, frightened, started to cry and the machine picked it up and, by a clever working of the mechanism, put her down in the right position. By the time the baby was a year old a very good working partnership had been formed between the two and at times the nurse was even teaching the little child to eat with a spoon and drink out of a cup. Of course various adjustments had to be made from time to time, but this was not a matter of any great difficulty.

Tired with the day's work, Mrs. Teeple always slept soundly. Her husband, on the other hand, often wandered around the house during the night, and on such occasions developed the habit of visiting the nursery. He would sit there silently for hours, watching the sleeping baby and the sleepless nurse.

This did not satisfy him, so his next step was to disconnect the electric current which activated the nurse. Now, with the phonograph quiet and the nurse unable to respond to the stimuli from the baby and the phonograph, the father took care of the child. Of course, there was not much to do, but it thrilled him to do even that little, and now, for nearly a half year, the three of them led a double life. The machine sat motionless all night till life was restored in the early morning, when Teeple connected her to an electric socket. The baby soon learned the difference between the living creature who so often cared for it at night and the black mammy, and while she loved the machine woman, still she had a different kind of affection for the great warm man who so tenderly and awkwardly did what was needful for her comfort during the dark hours of the night. She had special sounds that she made just for him and, to her delight, he answered her and somehow, the sounds he made pulled memories of similar sounds from the deep well of her inherited memory and by the time she was a year old she knew many words which she only used in the darkness—talking with the man—and she called him *Father*.

He thrilled when he held her little soft body close to his own and felt her little hand close around his thumb. He would wait till she was asleep and then silently kiss her on the top of her head, well-covered with soft new hair, colored like the sunshine. He told her over and over that he loved her, and gradually she learned what the words meant and cooed her appreciation. They developed little games to be played in the darkness, and very silently, because no matter how happy they were, they must never, never wake mother, for if she knew what was going on at night, they could never play again.

The man was happy in his new companionship with his baby. He told himself that those hours made life worth while.

After some months of such nocturnal activity, Mrs. Teeple observed that her husband came to the breakfast table rather sleepy. As she had no actual knowledge of how he spent his nights, it was easy for her to imagine. Being an author, imagination was one of her strongest mental faculties. Being a woman, it was necessary for her to voice these suspicions.

"You seem a bit sleepy mornings. Are you going out with another woman?"

Teeple looked at her with narrowing eyelids.

"What if I am?" he demanded. "That was part of our companionate wedding contract—that we could do that sort of thing if we wanted to."

As this was the truth, Susanna Teeple knew she had no argument, but she wasn't ready to stop talking.

"I should think that the mere fact that you are the father of an innocent child should keep your morals high. Think of her and your influence on her."

"I do think of that. In fact, only yesterday I arranged to have some phonograph records made that, in addition to everything else, would teach the baby to talk. I've asked an old friend of mine who teaches English at Harvard to make that part of the record, so that from the first, the baby's pronunciation will be perfect. I am also considering having another Psychophonic Nurse made with man's clothes. The black mammy needs some repairs, and it's about time our child had the benefit of a father's love. It needs the masculine influence. I'll have it made my size and we can dress it in some of my clothes and have an artist paint a face that looks like me. That way the child will gradually grow to know me and by the time she's three years old I'll be able to play with her and she'll be friendly instead of frightened. In the twilight, the neighbors will think that I'm taking the child out in the baby carriage for an airing and will give me credit for being a real father."

The wife looked at him. At times she just did not understand him.

It was a few days after this conversation that Mrs. Teeple called her husband at the factory.

"I wish you'd come home as soon as you can."

"What's the matter?"

"I think the baby has nephritis."

"What's that?"

"It's a disease I've just been reading about. I happened to

go into the nursery and the mammy has had to change the baby twenty-seven times since this morning."

Teeple assured his wife that he would be right home and that she should leave everything just as it was. He lost no time making it home; since he had been taking care of the baby at night, she had become very precious to him.

His wife met him at the door.

"How do you know mammy had to change her so often?"

"I counted the napkins, and the awful part was that many of them were not moist, just mussed up a little."

Teeple went to the nursery. He watched the baby for some minutes in silence. Then he took her hand, and finally he announced his decision.

"I don't think there's anything wrong with her."

"Of course you ought to know. You are such an expert on baby diseases." His wife was sarcastic.

"Oh! I'm not a doctor, but I do have a lot of common sense. Tomorrow is Sunday. Instead of golfing, I'll stay home and observe her. You leave the typewriter alone for a day and stay with me, won't you?"

"I wish I could, but I'm just finishing my book, *Perfect Harmony between Parent and Child*, and I must finish it before Monday morning, so you'll have to do your observing by yourself. I think, however, that it would be best for you to send for a doctor."

It did not take long for Teeple to find out what was wrong. The baby was learning to talk and had developed a habit of saying, very often, sounds that were very similar to *Seven*. This was the sound to which the Psychophonic Nurse had been attuned to react by movements resulting in a change of napkins. The baby had learned the sound from the phonograph and was imitating it so perfectly that the machine reacted to it, being unable to tell that it was not the voice from the phonograph, or the electrical stimulus from the wet pad. When Teeple found out what was the trouble, he had to laugh in spite of his serious thoughts. A very simple change in the mechanism blotted out the sound *Seven*, and cured the baby's nephritis.

Two weeks later, the inventor introduced his wife to the

new male nurse who was to be a father substitute. Machinery had been put into a form about the size of Teeple, the face was rather like his and he wore a blue serge suit that had become second best the previous year.

"This is a very simple machine," Teeple told his wife. "For the present it will be used only to take the baby out in the new baby-carriage which holds storage batteries and a small phonograph. We'll put the baby in the carriage and attach Jim Henry to the handles, pointing him down the country lane, which fortunately is smooth, straight as an arrow, and but little used. We attach the storage batteries to him and to the phonograph, which at once gives the command, 'Start.' Then, after a half hour, it will give the command, 'About Face—Start,' and in exactly another half hour, when it is exactly in front of the house, it will give the command 'Halt.' Then you or the servant will have to come out and put everything away and put the baby back in the crib under the care of the mechanical nurse. This will give baby an hour's exercise and fresh air. Of course she can be given an extra hour if you think it best. If you have an early supper and start the baby and Jim Henry out just as the sun is setting, the neighbors will think that it is really a live father who is pushing the carriage. Rather clever, don't you think?"

"I think it's a good idea for the baby to be outdoors every day. The rest of it, having it look like you, seems idiotic. Are you sure the road is safe?"

"Certainly. You know it's hardly used except by pedestrians and everyone will be careful when they meet a little baby in a carriage. There are no deep gutters, the road is level, there are no houses and no dogs. Jim Henry will take it for an hour's airing and bring it back safely. You don't suppose that I'd deliberately advise anything that would harm the child, do you?"

"Oh! I suppose not, but you're so queer sometimes."

"I may seem queer, but I assure you I've a good reason for everything I do."

Anyone watching him closely that summer would have seen that this last statement was true. He insisted on an early supper, five at the latest, and then he always left the house, giving one excuse or another, usually an important engagement at the facory. He made his wife promise that after supper she would at once start Jim Henry out with the baby in the carriage. Mrs. Teeple was glad enough to do this, as it gave her an hour's uninterrupted period to work in her study. The mechanical man would start briskly down the road and in a few minutes disappear into a clump of willows. Here Teeple sat waiting. He also was dressed in a blue serge suit. He would make the mechanical man lifeless by disconnecting the storage batteries, lay him carefully amid the willows and, taking his place, would happily push the carriage down the road. He would leave the phonograph attached to the battery. When it called "About Face," he would turn the carriage around and start for home. When he reached the willows, he would attach the mechanical nurse to the carriage and let it take the baby home. Sometimes when it was hot, the baby, the father, and Jim Henry would rest on a blanket, in the shade of the willows. Teeple would read poetry to his child and teach her new words, while Jim Henry would lie quietly near them, a look of happy innocence on his unchanging face.

The few neighbors who were in the habit of using that road after supper became accustomed to seeing the little man in the blue serge suit taking care of the baby. They complimented him in conversations with their wives and the ladies lost no time in relaying the compliment to Mrs. Teeple, who smiled in a very knowing way and said in reply, "It certainly is wonderful to have a mechanical husband. Have you read my new book, *Happiness in the Home?* It's arousing a great deal of interest in the larger cities."

She told her husband what they said and he also smiled. Almost all the men he had met during the evening hour were Masons and he knew they could be trusted.

When the baby was a year and a half old, Mrs. Teeple decided it was time to make a serious effort to teach the child to talk. She told her husband that she wanted to do this herself and was willing to take fifteen minutes a day from her literary work for this duty. She asked him if he had any suggestions. If not, she was willing, and able, to assume the entire responsibility. He replied that he had been reading up on this subject and would write out a list of twenty words which were very easy for a baby to learn. He did this, and that night she met him with a very grandiose air and stated that she had taught the baby to say all twenty of the words perfectly in one lesson. She believed she would write an article on the subject. It was very interesting to see how eager the child was to learn. Teeple simply grinned. The list he had given her was composed of words that he and the baby had been working with for some months, not only at night, but also during the evening hour under the willows.

By that fall, Mrs. Teeple was convinced that Watson, in his book, *Psychological Care of Infant and Child,* was absolutely right when he wrote that every child would be better if it were raised without the harmful influence of mother-love. She wrote him a long personal letter about her experience with the Psychophonic Nurse. He replied that he was delighted, and asked her to write a chapter for the second edition of his book. "I have always known," he wrote at the end of the letter, "that a mechanical nurse was better than an untrained mother. Your experience proves this to be the truth. I wish you could persuade your husband to put the machine on the market and make it available to millions of mothers who want to do the right thing, but have not the necessary intelligence. Every child is better without a love-life. Your child will grow into an adult free from complexes."

Mr. Teeple smiled even more broadly when he read that letter.

It was a pleasant day in early November. If anything, the day was too warm. There was no wind and the sky over western Kansas was dull and coppery. Teeple asked for a supper earlier than usual and at once left the house, telling his wife that the Masons were having a very special meeting and that he had promised to attend. Thoroughly accustomed to his being away from home in the evening, Mrs. Teeple prepared Jim Henry and started him down the road, pushing the little carriage with the happy baby safely strapped in. Then she went back to her work.

Jim Henry had left the house at five-fifteen. At five-forty-five he would turn around, and at six-fifteen be back with the baby. It was a definite programme and she had learned, by experience, that it worked safely one hundred per cent of the time. At five-thirty a cold wind began to whine around the house and she closed all the windows. It grew dark and then, without warning, started to snow. By five-forty-five the house was engulfed in the blizzard that was sweeping down from Alaska. The wind tore the electric light poles down and the house was left in darkness.

Susanna Teeple thought of her child in a baby carriage out in the storm in the care of an electrical nurse. Her first impulse was to telephone her husband at the lodge, but she at once found out that the telephone wires had been broken at the same time that the light wires had snapped. She found the servant-girl crying and frightened in the kitchen and realized that she could expect no help from her.

Wrapping a shawl around her shoulders, she opened the front door and started down the road to find her baby. Five minutes later she was back in the house, breathless and hysterical with fright. It took her another five minutes to close and fasten the door. The whole house swayed under the impact of the wind. Outside she heard trees snapping and cracking. A crash on top of the house told of the fall of a chimney. She tried to light a lamp, but even in the house the flame could not live. Going to her bedroom, she found an electric torch and, turning it on, she put it in the window and started to pray. She had not prayed for years; since early adolescence she had prided herself on the fact that she had learned to live without a creator whose very existence she doubted. Now she was on her knees. Sobbing, she sank to the floor and, stuporous with grief, fell asleep.

As was his nightly custom, Teeple waited in the willows for Jim Henry and the baby carriage. He disconnected the mechanical man and put him under a blanket by the roadside; then he started down the road, singing foolish songs to the baby as they went together into the sunset. He had not gone far when the rising wind warned him of the approaching storm and at once he turned the carriage and started towards home. In five minutes he had all he could do to push the carriage in the teeth of the wind. Then came the snow, and he knew that only by the exercise of all his adult intelligence could he save the life of his child. There was no shelter except the clump of willows. Every effort had to be made to reach those bushy trees, Jim Henry, and the blanket that covered him. One thousand feet lay between the willows and the Teeple home and the man knew that if the storm continued they could easily die, trying to cover that last thousand feet. It was growing dark so fast that it was a serious question if he could even find the clump of willows. He realized that if he once left the road, they were doomed.

He stopped for a few seconds, braced himself against the wind, took off his coat and wrapped it around the crying child. Then he went on, fast as he could, breathing when possible, and praying continuously. There were occasional short lulls in the gale. He finally reached the willows, and instinct helped him find Jim Henry, still covered by the blanket, which was now held to the ground by a foot of snow.

The man wrapped the baby up as well as he could, put the pillow next to Jim Henry, now partly uncovered, laid the baby on the pillow and crawled next to her, pulled the blanket over all three as best he could, and started to sing. The carriage, no longer held, was blown far over the prairie. In a half hour, Teeple felt the weight and the warmth of the blanket of snow. He believed that the baby was asleep. Unable to do anything more, he also fell asleep. In spite of everything, he was happy and told himself it was a wonderful thing to be a father.

During the night the storm passed and the morning came clear, with sunshine on the snow drifts. Mrs. Teeple awoke, built a fire, helped the servant prepare breakfast, and then went for help. The walking was hard, but she finally reached the next house. The woman was alone, her husband having gone to the Masonic lodge the night before. The two of them went on to the next house, and to the next and finally in the distance they found the entire lodge brotherhood breaking their way through the snow-drifts They had been forced to spend the entire night at the hall, but had had a pleasant time in spite of their anxiety. To Mrs. Teeple's surprise, her husband was not with them. She told her story and appealed for help. The master of the lodge listened in sympathetic silence.

"Mr. Teeple was not at the lodge last night," he finally said. "I believe he was with the baby."

"That's impossible!" exclaimed the hysterical woman. "The baby was out with the new model Psychophonic Nurse. Mr. Teeple never goes out with the baby. In fact, he knows nothing about the baby. He never notices her in any way."

The master looked at his senior warden, and they exchanged unspoken words. Then he looked at the members of his lodge. They were all anxious to return to their families, but there were several who were not married. He called these by name, asked them to go to his home with him for coffee, and then join him in the hunt for the baby. Meantime he urged Mrs. Teeple to go home and get the house warm and breakfast ready. She could do no good by staying out in the cold.

The master of the lodge knew Teeple. He had often seen him under the willows talking to the baby. Instinctively he went there first, followed by the young men. Breaking their way through the drifts, they finally arrived at the clump of trees and there found what they were looking for—a peculiar hillock of snow, which, when it was broken into, revealed a blanket, and under the blanket a crying baby, a sick man, and a mechanical nurse. The baby, on the pillow, wrapped up in her father's coat, and protected on one side by his body and on the other by the padded and clothed Jim Henry, and kept fairly warm. Teeple, on the outside, without a coat and barely covered by the edge of the blanket, had become thoroughly chilled.

It was days before he recovered from his pneumonia and weeks before he had much idea of what had happened or of his muttering conversations while sick. For once in his life, thoroughly uninhibited, he revealed everything he had been thinking of during the past fifteen months—spoke without reservation or regard for the feelings of his wife—and, above all else, he told of his great love for his child and how he had cared for it during the dark hours of the night and the twilight hour after supper.

Stunned, Susanna Teeple heard him talk. Silent by his bedside, she heard him bare his soul and she realized, even though the knowledge tortured her, that her ambition had been the means of estranging her husband and her child, and that to both of them she was practically a stranger. During the first days of her husband's illness she had placed the entire care of the child in the hands of the black mammy. Later it was necessary to hire nurses to care for her husband, and as he grew stronger, there was less and less work for the wife. Restless, she went to the kitchen, but there a competent servant was doing the work: in the sick-room, graduate nurses cared for her husband; in the nursery, her baby was being tended by a machine, and her little one would cry when she came near, protesting the presence of a stranger. The only place where she had work to do and was needed was in her study, and there the orders for magazine articles were accumulating.

She tried her soul. As judge, witness, and prosecutor, she tried her soul and knew that she had failed.

Finally Teeple crawled out of bed and sat in the sunshine. The house was still. One day the nurses were discharged, and his wife brought him his meals on a tray. Soon he was able to walk, and just as soon as he could do so, unobserved by his wife, he visited the nursery. Black mammy was gone. The baby, on a blanket, was playing contentedly on the floor. Teeple did not disturb her, but went to his wife's study. Her desk was free of papers, the typewriter was in its case and on the table lay a copy of Griffith's book *The Care of the Baby*. He was much puzzled, so he carried his investigations to the kitchen. His wife was there with a clean white apron on, beating eggs for a cake.

She was singing a bye-low-babykin-bye-low song, and to Teeple came a memory of how she used to sing that song before they were married. He hadn't heard her sing it since. Thinking quickly, he tried to reason out the absence of the nurses and the black mammy and the servant-girl, the empty desk and the closed typewriter, and then it came to him —just what it all meant; shyly, he called across the kitchen, "Hullo, Mother!"

She looked at him brightly, even though the tears did glisten in her eyes, as she replied, "Hullo, Daddy, dear."

And that was the end of the Psychophonic Nurse.

THE LITTLE BLACK BAG

C. M. Kornbluth

It may not be very politic of us to say so, but we wonder if the late Cyril Kornbluth, who was one of science fiction's great satirists, did not have something in his theory that "the more people there are, the lower the average I.Q." In any event, in the present story he wrote bitterly and with passion of the crimes against humanity that stupidity can perpetrate. (Page Dr. Fink and his Compound B!) *Kornbluth, who died at the age of 34, in 1958, was persecuted by a persistent premonition that mankind was debasing itself by the absence of any attempt at selective breeding, plus a horrifying kind of auto-intoxication called "popular education." The results, as far as the medical profession is concerned, are shown in a sufficiently dreadful way in the famous tale reprinted below . . . Also shown, as a byproduct, are some of the untoward results of travel through time—even though the traveling is done by an inanimate object.*

The Little Black Bag

OLD DR. FULL felt the winter in his bones as he limped down the alley. It was the alley and the back door he had chosen rather than the sidewalk and the front door because of the brown paper bag under his arm. He knew perfectly well that the flat-faced, stringy-haired women of his street and their gap-toothed, sour-smelling husbands did not notice if he brought a bottle of cheap wine to his room. They all but lived on the stuff themselves, varied by whiskey when pay checks were boosted by overtime. But Dr. Full, unlike them, was ashamed. A complicated disaster occurred as he limped down the littered alley. One of the neighborhood dogs—a mean little black one he knew and hated, with its teeth always bared and always snarling with menace—hurled at his legs through a hole in the board fence that lined his path. Dr. Full flinched, then swung his leg in what was to have been a satisfying kick to the animal's gaunt ribs. But the winter in his bones weighed down the leg. His foot failed to clear a half-buried brick, and he sat down abruptly, cursing. When he smelled unbottled wine and realized his brown paper package had slipped from under his arm and smashed, his curses died on his lips. The snarling black dog was circling him at a yard's distance, tensely stalking, but he ignored it in the greater disaster.

With stiff fingers as he sat on the filth of the alley, Dr. Full unfolded the brown paper bag's top, which had been crimped over, grocer-wise. The early autumnal dusk had come; he could not see plainly what was left. He lifted out the jug-handled top of his half gallon, and some fragments, and then the bottom of the bottle. Dr. Full was far too occupied to exult as he noted that there was a good pint left. He had a problem, and emotions could be deferred until the fitting time.

The dog closed in, its snarl rising in pitch. He set down the bottom of the bottle and pelted the dog with the curved triangular glass fragments of its top. One of them connected, and the dog ducked back through the fence, howling. Dr. Full then placed a razor-like edge of the half-gallon bottle's foundation to his lips and drank from it as though it were a giant's cup. Twice he had to put it down to rest his arms, but in one minute he had swallowed the pint of wine.

He thought of rising to his feet and walking through the alley to his room, but a flood of well-being drowned the notion. It was, after all, inexpressibly pleasant to sit there and feel the frost-hardened mud of the alley turn soft, or seem to, and to feel the winter evaporating from his bones under a warmth which spread from his stomach through his limbs.

A three-year-old girl in a cut-down winter coat squeezed through the same hole in the board fence from which the black dog had sprung its ambush. Gravely she toddled up to Dr. Full and inspected him, with her dirty forefinger in her mouth. Dr. Full's happiness had been providentially made complete; he had been supplied with an audience.

"Ah, my dear," he said hoarsely. And then: "Preposterous accusation. 'If that's what you call evidence,' I should have told them, 'you better stick to your doctoring.' I should have told them: 'I was here before your County Medical Society. And the License Commissioner never proved a thing on me. So, gennulmen, doesn't it stand to reason? I appeal to you as fellow memmers of a great profession—' "

The little girl, bored, moved away, picking up one of the triangular pieces of glass to play with as she left. Dr. Full forgot her immediately, and continued to himself earnestly: "But so help me, they *couldn't* prove a thing. Hasn't a man got any *rights?*" He brooded over the question, of whose answer he was so sure, but on which the Committee on Ethics of the County Medical Society had been equally certain. The winter was creeping into his bones again, and he had no money and no more wine.

Dr. Full pretended to himself that there was a bottle of whiskey somewhere in the fearful litter of his room. It was an old and cruel trick he played on himself when he simply had to be galvanized into getting up and going home. He might freeze there in the alley. In his room he would be bitten by bugs and would cough at the moldy reek from his sink, but he would not freeze and be cheated of the hundreds of bottles of wine that he still might drink, the thousands of hours of glowing content he still might feel. He thought about that bottle of whiskey—was it back of a mounded heap of medical journals? No; he had looked there last time. Was it under the sink, shoved well to the rear, behind the rusty drain? The cruel trick began to play itself out again. Yes, he told himself with mounting excitement, yes, it might be! Your memory isn't so good nowadays, he told himself with rueful good-fellowship. You know perfectly well you might have bought a bottle of whiskey and shoved it behind the sink drain for a moment just like this.

The amber bottle, the crisp snap of the sealing as he cut it, the pleasurable exertion of starting the screw cap on its threads, and then the refreshing tangs in his throat, the warmth in his stomach, the dark, dull happy oblivion of drunkenness—they became real to him. You *could* have, you know! You *could* have! he told himself. With the blessed conviction growing in his mind—It *could* have happened, you know! It *could* have!—he struggled to his right knee. As he did, he heard a yelp behind him, and curiously craned his neck around while resting. It was the little girl, who had cut her hand quite badly on her toy, the piece of glass. Dr. Full could see the spilling bright blood down her coat, pooling at her feet.

He almost felt inclined to defer the image of the amber bottle for her, but not seriously. He knew that it was there, shoved well to the rear under the sink, behind the rusty drain where he had hidden it. He would have a drink and then magnanimously return to help the child. Dr. Full got to his other knee and then his feet, and proceeded at a rapid totter down the littered alley toward his room, where he would hunt with calm optimism at first for the bottle that was not there, then with anxiety, and then with frantic violence. He would hurl books and dishes about before he was done looking for the amber bottle of whiskey, and finally would beat his swollen knuckles against the brick wall until old scars on them opened and his thick old blood oozed over his hands. Last of all, he would sit down somewhere on the floor, whimpering, and would plunge into the abyss of turbulent nightmare that was his sleep.

After twenty generations of shilly-shallying and "we'll cross that bridge when we come to it," genus homo had bred himself into an impasse. Dogged biometricians had pointed out with irrefutable logic that mental subnormals were outbreeding mental normals and supernormals, and that the process was occurring on an exponential curve. Every fact that could be mustered in the argument proved the biometricians' case, and led inevitably to the conclusion that genus homo was going to wind up in a preposterous jam quite soon. If you think that had any effect on breeding practices, you do not know genus homo.

There was, of course, a sort of masking effect produced by that other exponential funtion, the accumulation of technological devices. A moron trained to punch an adding machine seems to be a more skillful computer than a medieval mathematician trained to count on his fingers. A moron trained to operate the twenty-first century equivalent of a linotype seems to be a better typographer than a Renaissance printer limited to a few fonts of movable type. This is also true of medical practice.

It was a complicated affair of many factors. The supernormals "improved the product" at greater speed than the subnormals degraded it, but in smaller quantity because elaborate training of their children was practiced on a custom-made basis. The fetish of higher education had some weird avatars by the twentieth generation: "colleges" where not a member of the student body could read words of three syllables; "universities" where such degrees as "Bachelor of Typewriting," "Master of Shorthand" and "Doctor of Philosophy (Card Filing)" were conferred, with the traditional pomp. The handful of supernormals used such devices in order that the vast majority might keep some semblance of a social order going.

Some day the supernormals would mercilessly cross the bridge; at the twentieth generation they were standing irresolutely at its approaches wondering what had hit them. And the ghosts of twenty generations of biometricians chuckled malignantly.

It is a certain Doctor of Medicine of this twentieth generation that we are concerned with. His name was Hemingway —John Hemingway, B.Sc., M.D. He was a general practitioner, and did not hold with running to specialists with every trifling ailment. He often said as much, in approximately these words: "Now, uh, what I mean is you got a good old G.P. See what I mean? Well, uh, now a good old G.P. don't claim he knows all about lungs and glands and them things, get me? But you got a G.P., you got, uh, you got a, well, you got a . . . *all-around man!* That's what what you got when you got a G.P.—you got a all-around man."

But from this, do not imagine that Dr. Hemingway was a poor doctor. He could remove tonsils or appendixes, assist at practically any confinement and deliver a living, uninjured infant, correctly diagnose hundreds of ailments and prescribe and administer the correct medication or treatment for each. There was, in fact, only one thing he could not do in the medical line, and that was, violate the ancient canons of medical ethics. And Dr. Hemingway knew better than to try.

Dr. Hemingway and a few friends were chatting one evening when the event occurred that precipitates him into our story. He had been through a hard day at the clinic, and he wished his physicist friend Walter Gillis, B.Sc., M.Sc., Ph.D., would shut up so he could tell everybody about it. But Gillis kept rambling on, in his stilted fashion: "You got to hand it to old Mike; he don't have what we call the scientific method, but you got to hand it to him. There this poor little dope is, puttering around with some glassware and I come up and I ask him, kidding of course, 'How's about a time-travel machine, Mike?' "

Dr. Gillis was not aware of it, but "Mike" had an I.Q. six times his own, and was—to be blunt—his keeper. "Mike" rode herd on the pseudo-physicists in the pseudo-laboratory, in the guise of a bottle-washer. It was a social waste—but as has been mentioned before, the supernormals were still standing at the approaches to a bridge. Their irresolution led to many such preposterous situations. And it happens that "Mike," having grown frantically bored with his task, was malevolent enough to—but let Dr. Gillis tell it:

"So he gives me these here tube numbers and says, 'Series circuit. Now stop bothering me. Build your time machine, sit down at it and turn on the switch. That's all I ask.' "

"Say," marveled a brittle and lovely blonde guest, "you remember real good, don't you, doc?" She gave him a melting smile.

"Heck," said Gillis modestly, "I always remember good. It's what you call an inherent facility. And besides I told it quick to my secretary, so she wrote it down. I don't read so good, but I sure remember good, all right. Now, where was I?"

Everybody thought hard, and there were various suggestions:

"Something about bottles, doc?"

"You was starting a fight. You said 'time somebody was traveling.' "

"Yeah—you called somebody a swish. Who did you call a swish?"

"Not swish—*switch.*"

Dr. Gillis' noble brow grooved with thought, and he declared: "Switch is right. It was about time travel. What we call travel through time. So I took the tube numbers he gave me and I put them into the circuit-builder, I set it for 'series' and there it is—my time-travelling machine. It travels things through time real good." He displayed a box.

"What's in the box?" asked the lovely blonde.

Dr. Hemingway told her: "Time travel. It travels things through time."

"Look," said Gillis, the physicist. He took Dr. Hemingway's little black bag and put it on the box. He turned on the switch and the little black bag vanished.

"Say," said Dr. Hemingway, "that was, uh, swell. Now bring it back."

"Huh?"

"Bring back my little black bag."

"Well," said Dr. Gillis, "they don't come back. I tried it backwards and they don't come back. I guess maybe that dummy Mike give me a bum steer."

There was wholesale condemnation of "Mike" but Dr. Hemingway took no part in it. He was nagged by a vague feeling that there was something he would have to do. He reasoned: "I am a doctor, and a doctor has got to have a little black bag. I ain't got a little black bag—so ain't I a doctor no more?" He decided that this was absurd. He *knew* he was a doctor. So it must be the bag's fault for not being there. It was no good, and he would get another one tomorrow from that dummy Al, at the clinic. Al could find things good, but he was a dummy—never liked to talk sociable to you.

So the next day Dr. Hemingway remembered to get another little black bag from his keeper—another little black bag with which he could perform tonsillectomies, appendectomies and the most difficult confinements, and with which he could diagnose and cure his kind until the day when the supernormals could bring themselves to cross that bridge. Al was kinda nasty about the missing little black bag, but Dr. Hemingway didn't exactly remember what had happened, so no tracer was sent out, so—

Old Dr. Full awoke from the horrors of the night to the horrors of the day. His gummy eyelashes pulled apart convulsively. He was propped against a corner of his room, and something was making a little drumming noise. He felt very cold and cramped. As his eyes focused on his lower body, he croaked out a laugh. The drumming noise was being made by his left heel, agitated by fine tremors against the bare floor. It was going to be the D.T.'s again, he decided dispassionately. He wiped his mouth with his bloody knuckles, and the fine tremor coarsened; the snare-drum beat became louder and slower. He was getting a break this fine morning, he decided sardonically. You didn't get the horrors until you had been tightened like a violin string, just to the breaking point. He had a reprieve, if a reprieve into his old body with the blazing, endless headache just back of the eyes and the screaming stiffness in the joints were anything to be thankful for.

There was something or other about a kid, he thought vaguely. He was going to doctor some kid. His eyes rested on a little black bag in the center of the room, and he forgot about the kid. "I could have sworn," said Dr. Full, "I hocked that two years ago!" He hitched over and reached the bag, and then realized it was some stranger's kit, arriving here he did not know how. He tentatively touched the lock and it snapped open and lay flat, rows and rows of instruments and medications tucked into loops in its four walls. It seemed vastly larger open than closed. He didn't see how it could possibly fold up into that compact size again, but decided it was some stunt of the instrument makers. Since his time—that made it worth more at the hock shop, he thought with satisfaction.

Just for old times' sake, he let his eyes and fingers rove over the instruments before he snapped the bag shut and headed for Uncle's. More than a few were a little hard to recognize—exactly that. You could see the things with blades for cutting, the forceps for holding and pulling, the retractors for holding fast, the needles and gut for suturing, the hypos —a fleeting thought crossed his mind that he could peddle the hypos separately to drug addicts.

Let's go, he decided, and tried to fold up the case. It didn't fold until he happened to touch the lock, and then it folded all at once into a little black bag. Sure have forged ahead, he thought, almost able to forget that what he was primarily interested in was its pawn value.

With a definite objective, it was not too hard for him to get to his feet. He decided to go down the front steps, out the front door and down the sidewalk. But first—

He snapped the bag open again on his kitchen table, and pored through the medication tubes. "Anything to sock the autonomic nervous system good and hard," he mumbled. The tubes were numbered, and there was a plastic card which seemed to list them. The left margin of the card was a rundown of the systems—vascular, muscular, nervous. He followed the last entry across to the right. There were columns for "stimulant," "depressant," and so on. Under "nervous system" and "depressant" he found the number 17, and shakily located the little glass tube which bore it. It was full of pretty blue pills and he took one.

It was like being struck by a thunderbolt.

Dr. Full had so long lacked any sense of well-being except the brief glow of alcohol that he had forgotten its very nature. He was panic-stricken for a long moment at the sensation that spread through him slowly, finally tingling in his fingertips. He straightened up, his pains gone and his leg tremor stilled.

That was great, he thought. He'd be able to *run* to the hock shop, pawn the little black bag and get some booze. He started down the stairs. Not even the street, bright with mid-morning sun, into which he emerged made him quail. The little black bag in his left hand had a satisfying, authoritative weight. He was walking erect, he noted, and not in the somewhat furtive crouch that had grown on him in recent years. A little self-respect, he told himself, that's what I need. Just because a man's down doesn't mean—

"Docta, please-a come wit'!" somebody yelled at him, tugging his arm. "Da litt-la girl, she's-a burn' up!" It was one of the slum's innumerable flat-faced, stringy-haired women, in a slovenly wrapper.

"Ah, I happen to be retired from practice—" he began hoarsely, but she would not be put off.

"In by here, Docta!" she urged, tugging him to a doorway. "You come look-a da litt-la girl. I got two dolla, you come look!" That put a different complexion on the matter. He allowed himself to be towed through the doorway into a mussy, cabbage-smelling flat. He knew the woman now, or rather knew who she must be—a new arrival who had moved in the other night. These people moved at night, in motorcades of battered cars supplied by friends and relations, with furniture lashed to the tops, swearing and drinking until the small hours. It explained why she had stopped him: she did not yet know he was old Dr. Full, a drunken reprobate whom nobody would trust. The little black bag had been his guarantee, outweighing his whiskey face and stained black suit.

He was looking down on a three-year-old girl who had, he rather suspected, just been placed in the mathematical center of a freshly changed double bed. God knew what sour and dirty mattress she usually slept on. He seemed to recognize her as he noted a crusted bandage on her right hand. Two dollars, he thought— An ugly flush had spread up her pipe-stem arm. He poked a finger into the socket of her elbow, and felt little spheres like marbles under the skin and ligaments roll apart. The child began to squall thinly; beside him, the woman gasped and began to weep herself.

"Out," he gestured briskly at her, and she thudded away, still sobbing.

Two dollars, he thought— Give her some mumbo jumbo, take the money and tell her to go to a clinic. Strep, I guess, from that stinking alley. It's a wonder any of them grow up. He put down the little black bag and forgetfully fumbled for his key, then remembered and touched the lock. It flew open, and he selected a bandage shears, with a blunt wafer for the lower jaw. He fitted the lower jaw under the bandage, trying not to hurt the kid by its pressure on the infection, and began to cut. It was amazing how easily and swiftly the shining shears snipped through the crusty rag around the wound. He hardly seemed to be driving the shears with fingers at all. It almost seemed as though the shears were driving his fingers instead as they scissored a clean, light line through the bandage.

Certainly have forged ahead since my time, he thought— sharper than a microtome knife. He replaced the shears in their loop on the extraordinarily big board that the little black bag turned into when it unfolded, and leaned over the wound. He whistled at the ugly gash, and the violent infection which had taken immediate root in the sickly child's thin body. Now what can you do with a thing like that? He pawed over the contents of the little black bag, nervously.

If he lanced it and let some of the pus out, the old woman would think he'd done something for her and he'd get the two dollars. But at the clinic they'd want to know who did it and if they got sore enough they might send a cop around. Maybe there was something in the kit—

He ran down the left edge of the card to "lymphatic" and read across to the column under "infection." It didn't sound right at all to him; he checked again, but it still said that. In the square to which the line and column led were the symbols: "IV-g-3cc." He couldn't find any bottles marked with Roman numerals, and then noticed that that was how the hypodermic needles were designated. He lifted number IV from its loop, noting that it was fitted with a needle already and even seemed to be charged. What a way to carry those things around! So—three c.c.'s of whatever was in hypo number IV ought to do something or other about infections settled in the lymphatic system—which, God knows, this one was. What did the lower-case "g" mean, though? He studied the glass hypo and saw letters engraved on what looked like a rotating disk at the top of the barrel. They ran from "a" to "i," and there was an index line engraved on the barrel on the opposite side from the calibrations.

Shrugging, old Dr. Full turned the disk until "g" coincided with the index line, and lifted the hypo to eye level. As he pressed in the plunger he did not see the tiny thread of fluid squirt from the tip of the needle. There was a sort of dark mist for a moment about the tip. A closer inspection showed that the needle was not even pierced at the tip. It had the usual slanting cut across the bias of the shaft, but the cut did not expose an oval hole. Baffled, he tried pressing the plunger again. Again *something* appeared around the tip and vanished. "We'll settle this," said the doctor. He slipped the needle into the skin of his forearm. He thought at first that he had missed—that the point had glided over the top of his skin instead of catching and slipping under it. But he saw a tiny blood-spot and realized that somehow he just hadn't felt the puncture. Whatever was in the barrel, he decided, couldn't do him any harm if it lived up to its billing

—and if it could come out through a needle that had no hole. He gave himself three c.c. and twitched the needle out. There was the swelling—painless, but otherwise typical.

Dr. Full decided it was his eyes or something, and gave three c.c. of "g" from hypodermic IV to the feverish child. There was no interruption to her wailing as the needle went in and the swelling rose. But a long instant later, she gave a final gasp and was silent.

Well, he told himself, cold with horror, you did it that time. You killed her with that stuff.

Then the child sat up and said: "Where's my mommy?"

Incredulously, the doctor seized her arm and palpated the elbow. The gland infection was zero, and the temperature seemed normal. The blood-congested tissues surrounding the wound were subsiding as he watched. The child's pulse was stronger and no faster than a child's should be. In the sudden silence of the room he could hear the little girl's mother sobbing in her kitchen, outside. And he also heard a girl's insinuating voice:

"She gonna be O.K., doc?"

He turned and saw a gaunt-faced, dirty-blonde sloven of perhaps eighteen leaning in the doorway and eying him with amused contempt. She continued: "I heard about you, *Doctor* Full. So don't go try and put the bite on the old lady. You couldn't doctor up a sick cat."

"Indeed?" he rumbled. This young person was going to get a lesson she richly deserved. "Perhaps you would care to look at my patient?"

"Where's my mommy?" insisted the little girl, and the blonde's jaw fell. She went to the bed and cautiously asked: "You O.K. now, Teresa? You all fixed up?"

"Where's my mommy?" demanded Teresa. Then, accusingly, she gestured with her wounded hand at the doctor. "You *poke* me!" she complained, and giggled pointlessly.

"Well—" said the blond girl, "I guess I got to hand it to you, doc. These loud-mouth women around here said you didn't know your . . . I mean, didn't know how to cure people. They said you ain't a real doctor."

"I *have* retired from practice," he said. "But I happened

to be taking this case to a colleague as a favor, your good mother noticed me, and—" a deprecating smile. He touched the lock of the case and it folded up into the little black bag again.

"You stole it," the girl said flatly.

He sputtered.

"Nobody'd trust you with a thing like that. It must be worth plenty. You stole that case. I was going to stop you when I come in and saw you working over Teresa, but it looked like you wasn't doing her any harm. But when you give me that line about taking that case to a colleague I know you stole it. You gimme a cut or I go to the cops. A thing like that must be worth twenty–thirty dollars."

The mother came timidly in, her eyes red. But she let out a whoop of joy when she saw the little girl sitting up and babbling to herself, embraced her madly, fell on her knees for a quick prayer, hopped up to kiss the doctor's hand, and then dragged him into the kitchen, all the while rattling in her native language while the blond girl let her eyes go cold with disgust. Dr. Full allowed himself to be towed into the kitchen, but flatly declined a cup of coffee and a plate of anise cakes and St. John's Bread.

"Try him on some wine, ma," said the girl sardonically.

"Hyass! Hyass!" breathed the woman delightedly. "You like-a wine, docta?" She had a carafe of purplish liquid before him in an instant, and the blond girl snickered as the doctor's hand twitched out at it. He drew his hand back, while there grew in his head the old image of how it would smell and then taste and then warm his stomach and limbs. He made the kind of calculation at which he was practiced; the delighted woman would not notice as he downed two tumblers, and he could overawe her through two tumblers more with his tale of Teresa's narrow brush with the Destroying Angel, and then—why, then it would not matter. He would be drunk.

But for the first time in years, there was a sort of counter-image: a blend of the rage he felt at the blond girl to whom he was so transparent, and of pride at the cure he had just effected. Much to his own surprise, he drew back his hand from the carafe and said, luxuriating in the words: "No, thank you. I don't believe I'd care for any so early in the day." He covertly watched the blond girl's face, and was gratified at her surprise. Then the mother was shyly handing him two bills and saying: "Is no much-a money, docta—but you come again, see Teresa?"

"I shall be glad to follow the case through," he said. "But now excuse me—I really must be running along." He grasped the little black bag firmly and got up; he wanted very much to get away from the wine and the older girl.

"Wait up, doc," said she, "I'm going your way." She followed him out and down the street. He ignored her until he felt her hand on the black bag. Then old Dr. Full stopped and tried to reason with her:

"Look, my dear. Perhaps you're right. I might have stolen it. To be perfectly frank, I don't remember how I got it. But you're young and you can earn you're own money—"

"Fifty-fifty," she said, "or I go to the cops. And if I get another word outta you, it's sixty-forty. And you know who gets the short end, don't you, doc?"

Defeated, he marched to the pawnshop, her impudent hand still on the handle with his, and her heels beating out a tattoo against his stately tread.

In the pawnshop, they both got a shock.

"It ain't stendard," said Uncle, unimpressed by the ingenious lock. "I ain't never seen one like it. Some cheap Jap stuff, maybe? Try down the street. This I never could sell."

Down the street they got an offer of one dollar. The same complaint was made: "I ain't a collecta, mista—I buy stuff that got resale value. Who could I sell this to, a Chinaman who don't know medical instruments? Every one of them looks funny. You sure you didn't make these yourself?" They didn't take the one-dollar offer.

The girl was baffled and angry; the doctor was baffled too, but triumphant. He had two dollars, and the girl had a half-interest in something nobody wanted. But, he suddenly marveled, the thing had been all right to cure the kid, hadn't it?

"Well," he asked her, "do you give up? As you see, the kit is practically valueless."

She was thinking hard. "Don't fly off the handle, doc. I don't get this but something's going on all right . . . would those guys know good stuff if they saw it?"

"They would. They make a living from it. Wherever this kit came from—"

She seized on that, with a devilish faculty she seemed to have of eliciting answers without asking questions. "I thought so. You don't know either, huh? Well, maybe I can find out for you. C'mon in here. I ain't letting go of that thing. There's money in it—some way, I don't know how, there's money in it." He followed her into a cafeteria and to an almost-empty corner. She was oblivious to stares and snickers from other customers as she opened the little black bag— it almost covered a cafeteria table—and ferreted through it. She picked out a retractor from a loop, scrutinized it, contemptuously threw it down, picked out a speculum, threw it down, picked out the lower half of an O.B. forceps, turned it over, close to her sharp young eyes—and saw what the doctor's dim old ones could not have seen.

All old Dr. Full knew was that she was peering at the neck of the forceps and then turned white. Very carefully, she placed the half of the forceps back in its loop of cloth and then replaced the retractor and the speculum. "Well?" he asked. "What did you see?"

" 'Made in U.S.A.,' " she quoted hoarsely. " 'Patent Applied for July 2450.' "

He wanted to tell her she must have misread the inscription, that it must be a practical joke, that—

But he knew she had read correctly. Those bandage shears: they *had* driven his fingers, rather than his fingers driving them. The hypo needle that had no hole. The pretty blue pill that had struck him like a thunderbolt.

"You know what I'm going to do?" asked the girl, with sudden animation. "I'm going to go to charm school. You'll like that, won't ya, doc? Because we're sure going to be seeing a lot of each other."

Old Dr. Full didn't answer. His hands had been playing idly with that plastic card from the kit on which had been printed the rows and columns that had guided him twice before. The card had a slight convexity; you could snap the convexity back and forth from one side to the other. He noted, in a daze, that with each snap a different text appeared on the cards. *Snap.* "The knife with the blue dot in the handle is for tumors only. Diagnose tumors with your Instrument Seven, the Swelling Tester. Place the Swelling Tester—" *Snap.* "An overdose of the pink pills in Bottle 3 can be fixed with one white pill from Bottle—" *Snap.* "Hold the suture needle by the end without the hole in it. Touch it to one end of the wound you want to close and let go. After it has made the knot, touch it—" *Snap.* "Place the top half of the O.B. Forceps near the opening. Let go. After it has entered and conformed to the shape of—" *Snap.*

The slot man saw "FLANNERY 1—MEDICAL" in the upper left corner of the hunk of copy. He automatically scribbled "trim to .75" on it and skimmed it across the horseshoe-shaped copy desk to Piper, who had been handling Edna Flannery's quack-exposé series. She was a nice youngster, he thought, but like all youngsters she over-wrote. Hence, the *"trim."*

Piper dealt back a city hall story to the slot, pinned down Flannery's feature with one hand and began to tap his pencil across it, one tap to a word, at the same steady beat as a teletype carriage traveling across the roller. He wasn't exactly reading it this first time. He was just looking at the letters and words, they conformed to *Herald* style. The steady tap of his pencil ceased at intervals as it drew a black line ending with a stylized letter "d" through the word "breast" and scribbled in "chest" instead, or knocked down the capital "E" in "East" to lower case with a diagonal, or closed up a split word—in whose middle Flannery had bumped the space bar of her typewriter—with two curved lines like parentheses rotated through ninety degrees. The thick black pencil zipped a ring around the "30" which, like all youngsters, she put at the end of her stories. He turned back to the first page for the second reading. This time the pencil drew lines with the stylized "d's" at the end of them through adjectives and whole phrases, printed big "L's" to mark paragraphs, hooked some of Flannery's own paragraphs together with swooping recurved lines.

At the bottom of "FLANNERY ADD 2—MEDICAL" the pencil slowed down and stopped. The slot man, sensitive to the rhythm of his beloved copy desk, looked up almost at once. He saw Piper squinting at the story, at a loss. Without wasting words, the copy reader skimmed it back across the Masonite horseshoe to the chief, caught a police story in return and buckled down, his pencil tapping. The slot man read as far as the fourth add, barked at Howard, on the rim: "Sit in for me," and stumped through the clattering city room toward the alcove where the managing editor presided over his own bedlam.

The copy chief waited his turn while the make-up editor, the pressroom foreman and the chief photographer had words with the M.E. When his turn came, he dropped Flannery's copy on his desk and said: "She says this one isn't a quack."

The M.E. read:

"FLANNERY 1—MEDICAL, by Edna Flannery, *Herald* Staff Writer.

"The sordid tale of medical quackery which the *Herald* has exposed in this series of articles undergoes a change of pace today which the reporter found a welcome surprise. Her quest for the facts in the case of today's subject started just the same way that her exposure of one dozen shyster M.D.'s and faith-healing phonies did. But she can report for a change that Dr. Bayard Kendrick Full is, despite unorthodox practices which have drawn the suspicion of the rightly hypersensitive medical associations, a true healer living up to the highest ideals of his profession.

"Dr. Full's name was given to the *Herald's* reporter by the ethical committee of a county medical association, which reported that he had been expelled from the association on July 18, 1941 for allegedly 'milking' several patients suffering from trivial complaints. According to sworn statements in the committee's files, Dr. Full had told them they suffered from cancer, and that he had a treatment which would prolong their lives. After his expulsion from the association, Dr. Full dropped out of their sight—until he opened a midtown 'sanitarium' in a brownstone front which had for years served as a rooming house.

"The *Herald's* reporter went to that sanitarium, on East 89th Street, with the full expectation of having numerous imaginary ailments diagnosed and of being promised a sure cure for a flat sum of money. She expected to find unkempt quarters, dirty instruments and the mumbo-jumbo paraphernalia of the shyster M.D. which she had seen a dozen times before.

"She was wrong.

"Dr. Full's sanitarium is spotlessly clean, from its tastefully furnished entrance hall to its shining, white treatment rooms. The attractive, blond receptionist who greeted the reporter was soft-spoken and correct, asking only the reporter's name, address and the general nature of her complaint. This was given, as usual, as 'nagging backache.' The receptionist asked the *Herald's* reporter to be seated, and a short while later conducted her to a second-floor treatment room and introduced her to Dr. Full.

"Dr. Full's alleged past, as described by the medical society spokesman, is hard to reconcile with his present appearance. He is a clear-eyed, white-haired man in his sixties, to judge by his appearance—a little above middle height and apparently in good physical condition. His voice was firm and friendly, untainted by the ingratiating whine of the shyster M.D. which the reporter has come to know too well.

"The receptionist did not leave the room as he began his examination after a few questions as to the nature and location of the pain. As the reporter lay face down on a treatment table the doctor pressed some instrument to the small of her back. In about one minute he made this astounding statement: 'Young woman, there is no reason for you to have any pain where you say you do. I understand they're saying nowadays that emotional upsets cause pains like that. You'd better go to a psychologist or psychiatrist if the pain keeps up. There is no physical cause for it, so I can do nothing for you.'

"His frankness took the reporter's breath away. Had he guessed she was, so to speak, a spy in his camp? She tried again: 'Well, doctor, perhaps you'd better give me a physical checkup, I feel run-down all the time, besides the pains. Maybe I need a tonic.' This is never-failing bait to shyster M.D.'s—an invitation for them to find all sorts of mysterious conditions wrong with a patient, each of which 'requires' an expensive treatment. As explained in the first article of this series, of course, the reporter underwent a thorough physical checkup before she embarked on her quack-hunt, and was found to be in one hundred percent perfect condition, with the exception of a 'scarred' area at the bottom tip of her left lung resulting from a childhood attack of tuberculosis and a tendency toward 'hyperthyroidism'—overactivity of the thyroid gland which makes it difficult to put on weight and sometimes causes a slight shortness of breath.

"Dr. Full consented to perform the examination, and took a number of shining, spotlessly clean instruments from loops in a large board literally covered with instruments—most of them unfamiliar to the reporter. The instrument with which he approached first was a tube with a curved dial in its surface and two wires that ended on flat disks growing from its ends. He placed one of the disks on the back of the reporter's right hand and the other on the back of her left. 'Reading the meter,' he called out some number which the attentive receptionist took down on a ruled form. The same procedure was repeated several times, thoroughly covering the reporter's anatomy and thoroughly convincing her that the doctor was a complete quack. The reporter had never seen any such diagnostic procedure practiced during the weeks she put in preparing for this series.

"The doctor then took the ruled sheet from the receptionist, conferred with her in low tones and said: 'You have a slightly overactive thyroid, young woman. And there's something wrong with your left lung—not seriously, but I'd like to take a closer look.'

"He selected an instrument from the board which, the reporter knew, is called a 'speculum'—a scissorlike device which spreads apart body openings such as the orifice of the ear, the nostril and so on, so that a doctor can look in during an examination. The instrument was, however, too large to be an aural or nasal speculum but too small to be anything else. As the *Herald's* reporter was about to ask further questions, the attending receptionist told her: 'It's customary for us to blindfold our patients during lung examinations—do you mind?' The reporter, bewildered, allowed her to tie a spotlessly clean bandage over her eyes, and waited nervously for what would come next.

"She still cannot say exactly what happened while she was blindfolded—but X rays confirm her suspicions. She felt a cold sensation at her ribs on the left side—a cold that seemed to enter inside her body. Then there was a snapping feeling, and the cold sensation was gone. She heard Dr. Full say in a matter-of-fact voice: 'You have an old tubercular scar down there. It isn't doing any particular harm, but an active person like you needs all the oxygen she can get. Lie still and I'll fix it for you.'

"Then there was a repetition of the cold sensation, lasting for a longer time. 'Another batch of alveoli and some more vascular glue,' the *Herald's* reporter heard Dr. Full say, and the receptionist's crisp response to the order. Then the strange sensation departed and the eye-bandage was removed. The reporter saw no scar on her ribs, and yet the doctor assured her: 'That did it. We took out the fibrosis—and a good fibrosis it was, too; it walled off the infection so you're still alive to tell the tale. Then we planted a few clumps of alveoli —they're the little gadgets that get the oxygen from the air you breathe into your blood. I won't monkey with your thyroxin supply. You've got used to being the kind of person you are, and if you suddenly found yourself easy-going and all the rest of it, chances are you'd only be upset. About the backache: just check with the county medical society for the name of a good psychologist or psychiatrist. And look out for quacks; the woods are full of them.'

"The doctor's self-assurance took the reporter's breath away. She asked what the charge would be, and was told to pay the receptionist fifty dollars. As usual, the reporter delayed paying until she got a receipt signed by the doctor himself, detailing the services for which it paid. Unlike most, the doctor cheerfully wrote: 'For removal of fibrosis from left lung and restoration of alveoli,' and signed it.

"The reporter's first move when she left the sanitarium was to head for the chest specialist who had examined her in preparation for this series. A comparison of X rays taken on the day of the 'operation' and those taken previously would, the *Herald's* reporter then thought, expose Dr. Full as a prince of shyster M.D.'s and quacks.

"The chest specialist made time on his crowded schedule for the reporter, in whose series he has shown a lively interest from the planning stage on. He laughed uproariously in his staid Park Avenue examining room as she described the weird procedure to which she had been subjected. But he did not laugh when he took a chest X ray of the reporter, developed it, dried it and compared it with the ones he had taken earlier. The chest specialist took six more X rays that afternoon, but finally admitted that they all told the same story. The *Herald's* reporter has it on his authority that the scar she had eighteen days ago from her tuberculosis is now gone and has been replaced by healthy lung-tissue. He declares that this is a happening unparalleled in medical history. He does not go along with the reporter in her firm conviction that Dr. Full is responsible for the change.

"The *Herald's* reporter, however, sees no two ways about it. She concludes that Dr. Bayard Kendrick Full—whatever his alleged past may have been—is now an unorthodox but highly successful practitioner of medicine, to whose hands the reporter would trust herself in any emergency.

"Not so is the case of 'Rev.' Annie Dimsworth—a female harpy who, under the guise of 'faith' preys on the ignorant and suffering who come to her sordid 'healing parlor' for help and remain to feed 'Rev.' Annie's bank account, which now totals up to $53,238.64. Tomorrow's article will show, with photostats of bank statements and sworn testimony that—"

The managing editor turned down "FLANNERY LAST ADD—MEDICAL" and tapped his front teeth with a pencil, trying to think straight. He finally told the copy chief: "Kill the story. Run the teaser as a box." He tore off the last paragraph—the "teaser" about "Rev." Annie—and handed it to the desk man, who stumped back to his Masonite horseshoe.

The make-up editor was back, dancing with impatience as he tried to catch the M.E.'s eye. The interphone buzzed with the red light which indicated that the editor and publisher wanted to talk to him. The M.E. thought briefly of a special series on this Dr. Full, decided nobody would believe it and that he probably was a phony anyway. He spiked the story on the "dead" hook and answered his interphone.

Dr. Full had become almost fond of Angie. As his practice had grown to engross the neighborhood illnesses, and then to a corner suite in an uptown taxpayer building, and finally to the sanitarium, she seemed to have grown with it. Oh, he thought, we have our little disputes—

The girl, for instance, was too much interested in money. She had wanted to specialize in cosmetic surgery—removing wrinkles from wealthy old women and what not. She didn't realize, at first, that a thing like this was in their trust, that they were the stewards and not the owners of the little black bag and its fabulous contents.

He had tried, ever so cautiously, to analyze them, but without success. All the instruments were slightly radioactive, for instance, but not quite so. They would make a Geiger-Mueller counter indicate, but they would not collapse the leaves of an electroscope. He didn't pretend to be up on the latest developments, but as he understood it, that was just plain *wrong*. Under the highest magnification there were lines on the instruments' super-finished surfaces: incredibly fine lines, engraved in random hatchments which made no particular sense. Their magnetic properties were preposterous. Sometimes the instruments were strongly attracted to magnets, sometimes less so, and sometimes not at all.

Dr. Full had taken X rays in fear and trembling lest he disrupt whatever delicate machinery worked in them. He was *sure* they were not solid, that the handles and perhaps the blades must be mere shells filled with busy little watch-works —but the X rays showed nothing of the sort. Oh, yes—and they were always sterile, and they wouldn't rust. Dust *fell* off them if you shook them: now, that was something he understood. They ionized the dust, or were ionized themselves, or something of the sort. At any rate, he had read of something similar that had to do with phonograph records.

She wouldn't know about that, he proudly thought. She kept the books well enough, and perhaps she gave him a useful prod now and then when he was inclined to settle down. The move from the neighborhood slum to the uptown quarters had been her idea, and so had the sanitarium. Good; good; it enlarged his sphere of usefulness. Let the child have her mink coats and her convertible, as they seemed to be calling roadsters nowadays. He himself was too busy and too old. He had so much to make up for.

Dr. Full thought happily of his Master Plan. She would not like it much but she would have to see the logic of it. This marvelous thing that had happened to them must be handed on. She was herself no doctor; even though the instruments practically ran themselves, there was more to doctoring than skill. There were the ancient canons of the healing art. And so, having seen the logic of it, Angie would yield; she would assent to his turning over the little black bag to all humanity.

He would probably present it to the College of Surgeons, with as little fuss as possible—well, perhaps a *small* ceremony, and he would like a souvenir of the occasion, a cup or a framed testimonial. It would be a relief to have the thing out of his hands, in a way; let the giants of the healing art decide who was to have its benefits. No; Angie would understand. She was a goodhearted girl.

It was nice that she had been showing so much interest in the surgical side lately—asking about the instruments, reading the instruction card for hours, even practicing on guinea pigs. If something of his love for humanity had been communicated to her, old Dr. Full sentimentally thought, his life would not have been in vain. Surely she would realize that a greater good would be served by surrendering the instruments to wiser hands than theirs, and by throwing aside the cloak of secrecy necessary to work on their small scale.

Dr. Full was in the treatment room that had been the brownstone's front parlor; through the window he saw Angie's yellow convertible roll to a stop before the stoop. He liked the way she looked as she climbed the stairs; neat, not flashy, he thought. A sensible girl like her, she'd understand. There was somebody with her—a fat woman, puffing up the steps, overdressed and petulant. Now, what could she want?

Angie let herself in and went into the treatment room, followed by the fat woman. "Doctor," said the blonde girl gravely, "may I present Mrs. Coleman?" Charm school had not taught her everything, but Mrs. Coleman, evidently *nouveau riche*, thought the doctor, did not notice the blunder.

"Miss Aquella told me *so* much about you, doctor, and your remarkable system!" she gushed.

Before he could answer, Angie smoothly interposed: "Would you excuse us for just a moment, Mrs. Coleman?"

She took the doctor's arm and led him into the reception hall. "Listen," she said swiftly, "I know this goes against your grain, but I couldn't pass it up. I met this old thing in the exercise class at Elizabeth Barton's. Nobody else'll talk to her there. She's a widow. I guess her husband was a black marketeer or something, and she has a pile of dough. I gave her a line about how you had a system of massaging wrinkles out. My idea is, you blindfold her, cut her neck open with the Cutaneous Series knife, shoot some Firmol into the muscles, spoon out some of that blubber with an Adipose Series curette and spray it all with Skintite. When you take the blindfold off she's got rid of a wrinkle and doesn't know what happened. She'll pay five hundred dollars. Now, don't say 'no,' doc. Just this once, let's do it my way, can't you? I've been working on this deal all along too, haven't I?"

"Oh," said the doctor, "very well." He was going to have to tell her about the Master Plan before long anyway. He would let her have it her way this time.

Back in the treatment room, Mrs. Coleman had been thinking things over. She told the doctor sternly as he entered: "Of course, your system is permanent, isn't it?"

"It is, madam," he said shortly. "Would you please lie down there? Miss Aquella, get a sterile three-inch bandage

for Mrs. Coleman's eyes." He turned his back on the fat
woman to avoid conversation, and pretended to be adjusting
the lights. Angie blindfolded the woman, and the doctor selected the instruments he would need. He handed the blond
girl a pair of retractors, and told her: "Just slip the corners
of the blades in as I cut—" She gave him an alarmed look,
and gestured at the reclining woman. He lowered his voice:
"Very well. Slip in the corners and rock them along the
incision. I'll tell you when to pull them out."

Dr. Full held the Cutaneous Series knife to his eyes as he
adjusted the little slide for 3 cm. depth. He sighed a little
as he recalled that its last use had been in the extirpation of
an "inoperable" tumor of the throat.

"Very well," he said, bending over the woman. He tried
a tentative pass through her tissues. The blade dipped in and
flowed through them, like a finger through quicksilver, with
no wound left in the wake. Only the retractors could hold the
edges of the incision apart.

Mrs. Coleman stirred and jabbered: "Doctor, that felt so
peculiar! Are you sure you're rubbing the right way?"

"Quite sure, madam," said the doctor wearily. "Would you
please try not to talk during the massage?"

He nodded at Angie, who stood ready with the retractors.
The blade sank in to its three centimeters, miraculously cutting only the dead horny tissues of the epidermis and the
live tissue of the dermis, pushing aside mysteriously all major
and minor blood vessels and muscular tissue, declining to
affect any system or organ except the one it was—tuned to,
could you say? The doctor didn't know the answer, but he
felt tired and bitter at this prostitution. Angie slipped in the
retractor blades and rocked them as he withdrew the knife,
then pulled to separate the lips of the incision. It bloodlessly
exposed an unhealthy string of muscle, sagging in a dead-
looking loop from blue-gray ligaments. The doctor took a
hypo, Number IX, pre-set to "g" and raised it to his eye-
level. The mist came and went; there probably was no possibility of an embolus with one of these gadgets, but why take
chances? He shot one c.c. of "g"—identified as "Firmol" by

the card—into the muscle. He and Angie watched as it tightened up against the pharynx.

He took the Adipose Series curette, a small one, and spooned out yellowish tissue, dropping it into the incinerator box, and then nodded to Angie. She eased out the retractors and the gaping incision slipped together into unbroken skin, sagging now. The doctor had the atomizer—dialed to "Skintite"—ready. He sprayed, and the skin shrank up into the new firm throat line.

As he replaced the instruments, Angie removed Mrs. Coleman's bandage and gayly announced: "We're finished! And there's a mirror in the reception hall—"

Mrs. Coleman didn't need to be invited twice. With incredulous fingers she felt her chin, and then dashed for the hall. The doctor grimaced as he heard her yelp of delight, and Angie turned to him with a tight smile. "I'll get the money and get her out," she said. "You won't have to be bothered with her any more."

He was grateful for that much.

She followed Mrs. Coleman into the reception hall, and the doctor dreamed over the case of instruments. A ceremony, certainly—he was *entitled* to one. Not everybody, he thought, would turn such a sure source of money over to the good of humanity. But you reached an age when money mattered less, and when you thought of these things you had done that *might* be open to misunderstanding if, just if, there chanced to be any of that, well, that judgment business. The doctor wasn't a religious man, but you certainly found yourself thinking hard about some things when your time drew near—

Angie was back, with a bit of paper in her hands. "Five hundred dollars," she said matter-of-factly. "And you realize, don't you, that we could go over her an inch at a time—at five hundred dollars an inch?"

"I've been meaning to talk to you about that," he said.

There was bright fear in her eyes, he thought—but why?

"Angie, you've been a good girl and an understanding girl, but we can't keep this up forever, you know."

"Let's talk about it some other time," she said flatly. "I'm tired now."

"No—I really feel we've gone far enough on our own. The instruments—"

"Don't say it, doc!" she hissed. "Don't say it, or you'll be sorry!" In her face there was a look that reminded him of the hollow-eyed, gaunt-faced, dirty-blonde creature she had been. From under the charm-school finish there burned the guttersnipe whose infancy had been spent on a sour and filthy mattress, whose childhood had been play in the littered alley and whose adolescence had been the sweatshops and the aimless gatherings at night under the glaring street lamps.

He shook his head to dispel the puzzling notion. "It's this way," he patiently began. "I told you about the family that invented the O.B. forceps and kept them a secret for so many generations, how they could have given them to the world but didn't?"

"They knew what they were doing," said the guttersnipe flatly.

"Well, that's neither here nor there," said the doctor, irritated. "My mind is made up about it. I'm going to turn the instruments over to the College of Surgeons. We have enough money to be comfortable. You can even have the house. I've been thinking of going to a warmer climate, myself." He felt peeved with her for making the unpleasant scene. He was unprepared for what happened next.

Angie snatched the little black bag and dashed for the door, with panic in her eyes. He scrambled after her, catching her arm, twisting it in a sudden rage. She clawed at his face with her free hand, babbling curses. Somehow, somebody's finger touched the little black bag, and it opened grotesquely into the enormous board, covered with shining instruments, large and small. Half a dozen of them joggled loose and fell to the floor.

"*Now* see what you've done!" roared the doctor, unreasonably. Her hand was still viselike on the handle, but she was standing still, trembling with choked-up rage. The doctor bent stiffly to pick up the fallen instruments. Unreasonable girl! he thought bitterly. Making a scene—

Pain drove in between his shoulderblades and he fell face-down. The light ebbed. "Unreasonable girl!" he tried to croak. And then: "They'll know I tried, anyway—"

Angie looked down on his prone body, with the handle of the Number Six Cautery Series knife protruding from it. "—will cut through all tissues. Use for amputations before you spread on the Re-Gro. Extreme caution should be used in the vicinity of vital organs and major blood vessels or nerve trunks—"

"I didn't mean to do that," said Angie, dully, cold with horror. Now the detective would come, the implacable detective who would reconstruct the crime from the dust in the room. She would run and turn and twist, but the detective would find her out and she would be tried in a court-room before a judge and jury; the lawyer would make speeches, but the jury would convict her anyway, and the headlines would scream: "BLOND KILLER GUILTY!" and she'd maybe get the chair, walking down a plain corridor where a beam of sunlight struck through the dusty air, with an iron door at the end of it. Her mink, her convertible, her dresses, the handsome man she was going to meet and marry—

The mist of cinematic clichés cleared, and she knew what she would do next. Quite steadily, she picked the incinerator box from its loop in the board—a metal cube with a different-textured spot on one side. "—to dispose of fibroses or other unwanted matter, simply touch the disk—" You dropped something in and touched the disk. There was a sort of soundless whistle, very powerful and unpleasant if you were too close, and a sort of lightless flash. When you opened the box again, the contents were gone. Angie took another of the Cautery Series knives and went grimly to work. Good thing there wasn't any blood to speak of— She finished the awful task in three hours.

She slept heavily that night, totally exhausted by the wringing emotional demands of the slaying and the subsequent horror. But in the morning, it was as though the doctor had never been there. She ate breakfast, dressed with unusual care—and then undid the unusual care. Nothing out of the ordinary, she told herself. Don't do one thing different from the way you would have done it before. After a day or two, you can phone the cops. Say he walked out spoiling for a drunk, and you're worried. But don't rush it, baby—*don't rush it*.

Mrs. Coleman was due at 10:00 a.m. Angie had counted on being able to talk the doctor into at least one more five-hundred-dollar session. She'd have to do it herself now—but she'd have to start sooner or later.

The woman arrived early. Angie explained smoothly: "The doctor asked me to take care of the massage today. Now that he has the tissue-firming process beginning, it only requires somebody trained in his methods—" As she spoke, her eyes swiveled to the instrument case—open! She cursed herself for the single flaw as the woman followed her gaze and recoiled.

"What are those things!" she demanded. "Are you going to cut me with them? I *thought* there was something fishy—"

"Please, Mrs. Coleman," said Angie, "please, *dear* Mrs. Coleman—you don't understand about the . . . the massage instruments!"

"Massage instruments, my foot!" squabbled the woman shrilly. "That doctor *operated* on me. Why, he might have killed me!"

Angie wordlessly took one of the smaller Cutaneous Series knives and passed it through her forearm. The blade flowed like a finger through quicksilver, leaving no wound in its wake. *That* should convince the old cow!

It didn't convince her, but it did startle her. "What did you do with it? The blade folds up into the handle—that's it!"

"Now look closely, Mrs. Coleman," said Angie, thinking desperately of the five hundred dollars. "Look very closely and you'll see that the, uh, the sub-skin massager simply slips beneath the tissues without doing any harm, tightening and firming the muscles themselves instead of having to work through layers of skin and adipose tissue. It's the secret of the doctor's method. Now, how can outside massage have the effect that we got last night?"

Mrs. Coleman was beginning to calm down. "It *did* work, all right," she admitted, stroking the new line of her neck. But your arm's one thing and my neck's another! Let me see you do that with your neck!"

Angie smiled—

Al returned to the clinic after an excellent lunch that had almost reconciled him to three more months he would have to spend on duty. And then, he thought, and then a blessed year at the blessedly supernormal South Pole working on his specialty—which happened to be telekinesis exercises for ages three to six. Meanwhile, of course, the world had to go on and of course he had to shoulder his share in the running of it.

Before settling down to desk work he gave a routine glance at the bag board. What he saw made him stiffen with shocked surprise. A red light was on next to one of the numbers— the first since he couldn't think when. He read off the number and murmured "O.K., 674,101. That fixes *you*." He put the number on a card sorter and in a moment the record was in his hand. Oh, yes—Hemingway's bag. The big dummy didn't remember how or where he had lost it; none of them ever did. There were hundreds of them floating around.

Al's policy in such cases was to leave the bag turned on. The things practically ran themselves, it was practically impossible to do harm with them, so whoever found a lost one might as well be allowed to use it. You turn it off, you have a social loss—you leave it on, it may do some good. As he understood it, and not very well at that, the stuff wasn't "used up." A temporalist had tried to explain it to him with little success that the prototypes in the transmitter *had been transducted* through a series of point-events of transfinite cardinality. Al had innocently asked whether that meant prototypes had been stretched, so to speak, through all time, and the temporalist had thought he was joking and left in a huff.

"Like to see him do this," thought Al darkly, as he telekinized himself to the combox, after a cautious look to see that there were no medics around. To the box he said: "Police chief," and then to the police chief: "There's been a homicide committed with Medical Instrument Kit 674,101. It was lost some months ago by one of my people, Dr. John Hemingway. He didn't have a clear account of the circumstances."

The police chief groaned and said: "I'll call him in and question him." He was to be astonished by the answers, and was to learn that the homicide was well out of his jurisdiction.

Al stood for a moment at the bag board by the glowing red light that had been sparked into life by a departing vital force giving, as its last act, the warning that Kit 674,101 was in homicidal hands. With a sigh, Al pulled the plug and the light went out.

"Yah," jeered the woman. "You'd fool around with my neck, but you wouldn't risk your own with that thing!"

Angie smiled with serene confidence a smile that was to shock hardened morgue attendants. She set the Cutaneous Series knife to 3 centimeters before drawing it across her neck. Smiling, knowing the blade would cut only the dead horny tissue of the epidermis and the live tissue of the dermis, mysteriously push aside all major and minor blood vessels and muscular tissue—

Smiling, the knife plunging in and its microtome-sharp metal shearing through major and minor blood vessels and muscular tissue and pharynx, Angie cut her throat.

In the few minutes it took the police, summoned by the shrieking Mrs. Coleman, to arrive, the instruments had become crusted with rust, and the flasks which had held vascular glue and clumps of pink, rubbery alveoli and spare gray cells and coils of receptor nerves held only black slime, and from them when opened gushed the foul gases of decomposition.

RIBBON IN THE SKY

Murray Leinster

In this story the Old Master, who has been writing science fiction longer than almost anyone alive today (he published his first s.f. in 1915!), introduces us to the Interstellar Medical Service, here represented by a single physician-pilot-sociologist-teacher, and his small furry companion who is cryptically described as a tormal. *In his inimitable fashion Leinster gives us a vividly real and warmly human picture of space medicine as it may turn out to be when we really hit space—not just the few puny hundreds of miles above the earth's surface we have reached thus far—and treats of the future of the parsecs that will eventuate when—and if—we discover and utilize one of science fiction's most beloved and farthest-out gadgets, the faster-than-light interstellar overdrive, whatever that may be. Hasten the day!*

Ribbon in the Sky

I

"An error is a denial of reality, but mistakes are mere mental malfunctionings. In an emergency, a mistake may be made because of the need for precipitate action. There is no time to choose the best course: something must be done at once. Most mistakes, however, are made without any such exterior pressure. One accepts the first-imagined solution to a problem without examining it, either out of an urgent desire to avoid the labor of thinking, or out of impassioned reluctance to think about the matter at hand when prettier and more pleasurable other things can be contemplated . . ."

The Practice of Thinking
Fitzgerald

IT TURNED OUT afterward that somebody had punched the wrong button in a computer. It was in a matter in which mistakes are not permissible, but just as nothing can be manufactured without an ordinary hammer figuring somewhere in the making or the making-ready-to-make, so nothing can be done without a fallible human operating at some stage of the proceedings. And humans make mistakes casually, oddhandedly, with impartial lack of malice, and unpredictability. So . . .

Calhoun heard the tape-speaker say, *"When the gong sounds, breakout will follow in five seconds."* Then it made solemn ticking noises while Calhoun yawned and put aside the book, "The Practice of Thinking," that he'd been studying. Study was a necessity in his profession. Besides, it helped to pass the time in overdrive. He went to the control-desk chair and strapped in. Murgatroyd the *tormal* uncoiled his tail from about his nose and stood up from where he was catching twenty winks. He padded to the place under Calhoun's chair

199

where there were things to grab hold of, if necessary, with four black paws and a prehensile tail.

"Chee," said Murgatroyd conversationally in his shrill treble.

"I agree," Calhoun told him gravely. "Stone walls do not a prison make, nor Med Ship hulls a cage. But it will be good to get outside for a change."

The tape-speaker ticked and tocked and ticked and tocked. There was the sound of a gong. A voice said, *"Five—four—three—two—one—"*

The ship came out of overdrive. Calhoun winced and swallowed. Nobody ever gets used to going into overdrive or coming out of it. One is hideously dizzy for an instant, and his stomach has a brief but violent urge to upchuck, and no matter how often one has experienced it, it is necessary to fight a flash of irrational panic caused by the two sensations together.

But after an instant Calhoun stared about him as the vision-screens came to life. They showed the cosmos outside the Med Ship. It was a perfectly normal cosmos—not at all the cosmos of overdrive—but it looked extremely wrong to Calhoun. He and Murgatroyd and the Med Ship were in emptiness. There were stars on every hand, and they were of every conceivable color and degree of brightness. But each one of them was a point of light, and a point only.

This, obviously, was not what he'd expected. These days ships do not stop to view the universe from the monstrous loneliness which is Between-the-Stars. All ships go into overdrive as near their port of departure as they can. Usually it is something like five or six planetary diameters out from the local spaceport. All ships come out of overdrive as near their destinations as computation makes possible. They do not stop to look at scenery on the way. It isn't good for humans to look at stars when there are only stars to see. The sight has a tendency to make them feel small. Too small. Men have been known to come out of such an experience gibbering.

Calhoun scowled at the sight of Between-the-Stars. This was not good. But he wasn't frightened—not yet. There should have been a flaming sun somewhere nearby and bright crescents or half-disks or mottled cloudy planets swimming within view. The sun should have been the star Merida, and Calhoun should land in commonplace fashion on Merida II and make a routine planetary health check on a settled, complacent population, and presently he should head back to Med Headquarters with a report containing absolutely nothing of importance. But he couldn't do any of these things. He was in purely empty space. It was appalling.

Murgatroyd jumped up to the arm of the control-chair, to gaze wisely at the screens. Calhoun continued to scowl. Murgatroyd imitated him with a *tormal's* fine complacency in duplicating a man's actions. What he saw meant nothing to him, of course. But he was moved to comment.

"Chee," he said shrilly.

"To be sure," agreed Calhoun. "That is a very sage observation, Murgatroyd. But I deplore the situation that calls for it. Somebody's bilged on us."

Murgatroyd liked to think that he was carrying on a conversation. He said:

"Chee-chee! Chee-chee-chee!"

"No doubt," conceded Calhoun. "But this is a mess! Hop down and let me try to get out of it."

Murgatroyd disappointedly hopped to the floor. He watched with bright eyes as Calhoun went to the emergency-equipment locker and brought out the apparatus designed to take care of a state of things like this. If the situation wasn't too bad, correcting it should be simple enough. If it was too bad, it could be fatal.

The average separation of stars throughout the galaxy is something like four or five light-years. The distance between sol-type stars is on an average very much higher, and with certain specific exceptions habitable planets are satellites of sol-type suns. But only a fraction of the habitable planets are colonized, and when a ship has traveled blind, in overdrive, for two months or more its pilot cannot simply look astern and recognize his point of departure. There's too much scenery in between. Further, nobody can locate himself by the use of star-maps unless he knows where something on the star-map is, with reference to himself. Which makes a star-map not always useful.

But the present blunder might not be serious. If the Med Ship had come out into normal space no more than eight to ten light-years from Merida, Calhoun might identify that sun by producing parallax. He could detect relative distances for a much greater range. But it was to be hoped that his present blunder was small.

He got out the camera with its six lenses for the six vision-screens which showed space in all directions. He clamped it in place and snapped a plate. In seconds he had everything above third magnitude faithfully recorded in its own color, and with relative brightnesses expressed in the size of the dots of tint. He put the plate aside and said:

"Overdrive coming, Murgatroyd."

He pressed the short-hop button and there was dizziness and nausea and a flash of fear—all three sensations momentary. Murgatroyd said, "*Chee*" in a protesting tone, but Calhoun held down the button for an accurate five minutes. He and Murgatroyd gulped together when he let up the button again and all space whirled and nausea hit as before. He took another plate of all the heavens, made into one by the six-lensed camera. He swung the ship by ninety degrees and pressed the short-hop button a second time. More dizziness and panic and digestive revolt. In five minutes it was repeated as the ship came out to normal space yet again.

"*Chee-chee!*" protested Murgatroyd. His furry paws held his round little belly against further insult.

"I agree," said Calhoun. "I don't like it either. But I want to know where we are—if anywhere."

He set up the comparator and inserted the three plates. Each had images of each of the six vision-screens. When the instrument whirred, each of the plates in turn was visible for part of a second. Extremely remote stars would not jiggle perceptibly—would not show parallax—but anything within twenty light-years should. The jiggling distance could be in-creased by taking the plates still farther apart. This time, though, there was one star which visibly wavered in the comparator. Calhoun regarded it suspiciously.

"We're Heaven knows where," he said dourly. "Somebody really messed us up! The only star that shows parallax isn't Merida. In fact, I don't believe in it at all! Two plates show it as a sol-class sun and the third says it's a red dwarf!"

On the face of it, such a thing was impossible. A sun cannot be one color as seen from one spot, and another color seen from another. Especially when the shift of angle is small.

Calhoun made rough computations. He hand-set the overdrive for something over an hour's run in the direction of the one star-image which wabbled and thereby beckoned. He threw the switch. He gulped, and Murgatroyd acted for a moment as if he intended to yield unreservedly to the nausea of entering overdrive. But he refrained.

There was nothing to do but kill time for an hour. There was a microreel of starplates, showing the heavens as photographed with the same galactic co-ordinates from every visited sol-class star in this sector of the galaxy. Fewer than one in forty had a colonized planet, but if the nearest had been visited before, and if the heavens had been photographed there, by matching the stars to the appropriate plate he could find out where he was. Then a star-map might begin to be of some use to him. But he had still to determine whether the error was in his astrogation unit, or in the data fed to it. If the first, he'd be very bad off indeed. If the second, he could still be in a fix. But there was no point in worrying while in overdrive. He lay down on his bunk and tried to concentrate again on the book he'd laid aside.

"*Human error, moreover,*" he read, "*is never purely random. The mind tends to regard stored data as infallible and to disregard new data which contradicts it . . .*" He yawned, and skipped. "*. . . So each person has a personal factor of error which is not only quantitative but qualitative . . .*"

He read on and on, only half absorbing what he read. But a man who has reached the status of a Med Ship man in the Interstellar Medical Service hasn't finished learning. He's still away down the ladder of rank. He has plenty of studying ahead of him before he gets very far.

The tape speaker said, "*When the gong sounds, breakout will be five seconds off.*" It began to *tick-tock*, slowly and deliberately. Calhoun got into the control seat and strapped in. Murgatroyd went to position underneath the chair. The voice said, "*Five—four—three—two—one—*"

The little Med Ship came out of overdrive, and instantly its emergency rockets kicked and Murgatroyd held desperately fast. Then the rockets went off. There'd been something unguessable nearby—perhaps cometary debris at the extremest outer limit of a highly eccentric orbit. Now there was a starfield and a sun within two light-hours. But if Calhoun had stared, earlier, when there was no sun in sight at all, now he gazed blankly at the spectacle before him.

It was a yellow sun—a sol-type star with a barely perceptible disk. There were planets. Calhoun saw immediately one gas-giant near enough to be more than a point, and a sliver of light which was the crescent of another more nearly in line toward the sun. But he gazed at a belt, a band, a ribbon of shining stuff which was starkly out of all reason.

It was a thin curtain of luminosity circling this yellow star. It was not a ring from the breakup of a satellite within Roche's Limit. There were two quite solid planets inside it and nearer to the star. It was a thin, wide, luminous golden ribbon which looked like something that needed a flatiron to smooth it out. It looked like an incandescent smoke ring. An unimaginable rocket with a flat exhaust could have made it while chasing its tail around the sun. But that couldn't have happened, either.

Calhoun stared for seconds.

"Now," he said, "I've seen everything!" Then he grunted as realization came. "And we're all right, Murgatroyd! It's not our computers that went wrong. Somebody fed them wrong data. We arrived where we aimed for, and there'll be a colonized planet somewhere around."

He unlimbered the electron telescope and began a search. But he couldn't resist a closer look at the ribbon in space. It had the structure of a slightly wrinkled ribbon without beginning or end. It had to be a complex of solid particles, of course, and an organization of solid particles cannot exist in space without orbital motion. But orbits would smooth out in the course of thousands of revolutions around a primary. This was not smoothed out. It was relatively new.

"It's sodium dust," said Calhoun appreciatively. "Or maybe potassium. Hung out there on purpose. Particles small enough to have terrific surface and reflective power, and big enough not to be pushed out of orbit by light-pressure. Clever, Murgatroyd! At a guess it'll have been put out to take care of the climate on a planet just inside it. Which would be—there! Let's go look!"

He was so absorbed in his admiration that the almost momentary overdrive-hop needed for approach went nearly unnoticed. He even realized—his appreciation increasing—that this cloud of tiny particles accounted for the red-dwarf appearance on one of the plates he'd taken. Light passing through widely dispersed and very small particles turns red. From one position, he'd photographed through this dust cloud.

The ribbon was a magnificent idea—the more magnificent because of its simplicity. It would reflect back otherwise wasted sun-heat to a too-cold planet and make it warmer. There was probably only an infinitesimal actual mass of powder in the ring, at that. Tens or scores of tons in all. Hardly more.

The planet for which it had been established was the third world out. As is usual with sol-class systems, the third planet's distance from the sun was about a hundred twenty million miles. It had icecaps covering more than two-thirds of its surface. The sprawling white fingers of glaciation marked mountain chains and highlands nearly to the equator. But there was some blue sea, and green vegetation in a narrow belt of tropicality.

Calhoun jockeyed the Med Ship to position for a landing call. This was not Merida II, but there should be a colony here. That glowing ribbon had not been hung out for nothing.

"Med Ship Esclipus Twenty," he said confidently into the spacephone mike. "Calling ground. Requesting co-ordinates for landing. My mass is fifty tons. Repeat, five-oh tons. Purpose of landing, to find out where I am and how to get where I belong."

There was a clicking. Calhoun repeated the call. He heard murmurings which were not directed into the transmitter on the planet. He heard an agitated, *"How long since a ship landed?"* Another voice was saying fiercely, *"Even if he doesn't come from Two City or Three City, who knows what sickness—"* There was sudden silence, as if a hand had been clapped over the microphone below. Then a long pause. Calhoun made the standard call for the third time.

"Med Ship Esclipus Twenty," said the spacephone speaker grudgingly, *"You will be allowed to land. Take position—"* Calhoun blinked at the instructions he received. The co-ordinates were not the normal galactic ones. They gave the local time at the spaceport, and the planetary latitude. He was to place himself overhead. He could do it, of course, but the instructions were unthinkable. Galactic co-ordinates had been used ever since Calhoun had known anything about such matters. But he acknowledged the instructions. Then the voice from the speaker said truculently: *"Don't hurry! We might change our minds! And we have to figure settings for an only fifty-ton ship, anyhow."*

Calhoun's mouth dropped open. A Med Ship was welcome everywhere, these days. The Interstellar Medical Service was one of those overworked, understaffed, kicked-around organizations which is everywhere taken for granted. Like breathable air, nobody thought to be grateful for it—but nobody was suspicious of it, either.

The suspicion and the weird co-ordinates and the ribbon in space combined to give Calhoun a highly improbable suspicion. He looked forward with great interest to this landing. He had not been ordered to land here, but he suspected that a Med Ship landing was a long, long time overdue.

"I forgot to take star-pictures," he told Murgatroyd, "but a ribbon like this would have been talked about if it had been reported before. I doubt star-pictures would do us any good. The odds are our only chance to find out where we are is to ask." Then he shrugged his shoulders. "Anyhow this won't be routine!"

"*Chee!*" agreed Murgatroyd, profoundly.

II

"An unsolvable but urgent problem may produce in a society, as in an individual, an uncontrollable emotional tantrum, an emotional denial of the problem's existence, or purposive research for a solution. In olden days, the first reaction produced mass-tantrums then called 'wars.' The second produced frenziedly dogmatic ideologies. The third produced modern civilization. All three reactions still appear in individuals. If the first two should return to societies, as such . . ."

The Practice of Thinking
Fitzgerald

The descent, at least, was not routine. It was nerve-racking. The force-field from the planet's giant steel landing grid reached out into space and fumbled for the Med Ship. That was clumsily done. When it found the ship, it locked on. And that was awkwardly handled. The rest was worse. Whoever handled the controls, aground, was hopelessly inept. Once the Med Ship's hull-temperature began to climb, and Calhoun had to throw on the spacephone and yelp for caution. He did not see as much of the nearing planet as he'd have liked.

At fifty miles of height, the last trace of blue sea vanished around the bulge of the world. At twenty miles, the mountain chains were clearly visible, with their tortured, winding ice rivers which were glaciers. At this height three patches of green were visible from aloft. One, directly below, was little more than a mile in diameter and the landing grid was its center and almost its circumference. Another was streaky and long, and there seemed to be heavy mist boiling about it and above it. The third was roughly triangular. They were many miles apart. Two of them vanished behind mountains as the ship descended.

There were no cities in view. There were no highways.

This was an ice world with bare ground and open water at its equator only. The spaceport was placed in a snow-ringed polar valley.

Near landing, Calhoun strapped in because of the awkwardness with which the ship was lowered. He took Murgatroyd on his lap. The small craft bounced and wabbled as unskilled hands let it down. Presently, Calhoun saw the angular girders of the landing grid's latticed top rise past the opened ports. Seconds later, the Med Ship bumped and slid and bounced heart-stoppingly. Then it struck ground with a violent jolt.

Calhoun got his breath back as the little ship creaked and adjusted itself to rest on its landing fins after some months in space.

"*Now,*" said the voice in the spacephone speaker, "*now stay in your ship. Our weapons are bearing on you. You may not come out until we've decided what to do about you.*"

Calhoun raised his eyebrows. This was very unusual indeed. He glanced at the external field indicator. The landing grid field was off. So the operator bluffed. In case of need Calhoun could blast off on emergency rockets and probably escape close-range weapons anyhow—if there were any—and he could certainly get around the bulge of the world before the amateur at the grid's controls could hook on to him again.

"Take your time," he said with irony. "I'll twiddle my fingers. I've nothing better to do!"

He freed himself from his chair and went to a port to see. He regarded the landscape about him with something like unbelief.

The landing grid itself was a full mile across and half as high. It was a vast, circular frame of steel beams reaching heavenward, with the curiously curving copper cables strung as they had to be to create the special force-field which made space transportation practical. Normally such gigantic structures rose in the centers of spaceport cities. They drew upon the planet's ionosphere for power to lift and land cargo ships from the stars, and between-times they supplied energy for manufactures and the operation of cities. They were built, necessarily, upon stable bedrock formations, and for convenience were usually located where the cargoes to be shipped would require least surface transportation.

But here there was no city. There was perhaps a thousand acres of greenness—a mere vague rim around the outside of the grid. There was a control-room building to one side, of course. It was solidly built of stone, but there had been an agglomeration of lean-tos added to it with slanting walls and roofs of thin stratified rock. And there were cattle grazing on the green grass. The center of the grid was a pasture!

Save for the clutter about the grid-control building there were no structures, no dwellings, no homes anywhere in view. There was no longer even a highway leading to the grid. Calhoun threw on the outside microphones and there was no sound except a thin keening of wind in the steelwork overhead. But presently one of the cattle made a mournful bellowing sound.

Calhoun whistled as he went from one port to another.

"Murgatroyd," he said meditatively on his second round, "you observe—if you observe—one of the consequences of human error. I still don't know where I am, because I doubt that starplates have ever been made from this solar system, and I didn't take one for comparison anyhow. But I can tell you that this planet formerly had a habitability rating of something like oh point oh, meaning that if somebody wanted to live here it would be possible but it wouldn't be sensible. However, people did come here, and it was a mistake."

He stared at a human figure, far away. It was a woman, dressed in shapeless, badly draping garments. She moved toward a clump of dark-coated cattle and did something in their midst.

"The mistake looks pretty evident to me," added Calhoun, "and I see some possibilities I don't like at all. There is such a thing as an isolation syndrome, Murgatroyd. A syndrome is a complex of pathological symptoms which occur together as a result of some morbid condition. To us humans, isolation is morbid. You help me to endure it, Murgatroyd, but I couldn't get along with only your society—charming as it is —for but so long. A group of people can get along longer than a single man, but there is a limit for any small-sized group."

"Chee," said Murgatroyd.

"In fact," said Calhoun, frowning, "there's a specific health problem involved, which the Med Service recognizes. There can be partial immunity, but there can be some tricky variations. If we're up against a really typical case we have a job on hand. And how did these people get that dust-ring out in space? They surely didn't hang it out themselves!"

He sat down and scowled at his thoughts. Presently he rose again and once more surveyed the icy landscape. The curious green pasture about the landing grid was highly improbable. He saw glaciers overhanging this valley. They were giant ice rivers which should continue to flow and overwhelm this relatively sheltered spot. They didn't. Why not?

It was more than an hour before the spacephone clattered. When Calhoun threw the switch again a new voice came out of it. This was also a male voice, high-pitched as if from tension.

"We've been talking about you," said the voice. It quivered with agitation which was quite out of reason. "You say you're Med Service. All right. Suppose you prove it!"

The landed Med Ship should be proof enough for anybody. But Calhoun said politely:

"I have the regular identifications. If you'll go on vision, I'll show you my credentials."

"Our screen's broken," said the voice, "but we have a sick cow. It was dumped on us night before last. Cure her and we'll accept it as identification."

Calhoun could hardly believe his ears. This was an emergency situation—yet the curing of a sick cow was considered more convincing than a Med Ship man's regular credentials! Such a scale of values hinted at more than a mere isolation syndrome. There were thousands of inhabited worlds, now, with splendid cities and technologies which most men accepted with the same bland confidence with which they looked for sunrise. The human race was civilized. Suspicion of a Med Ship was unheard of. But here was a world—

"Why . . . certainly," said Calhoun blankly. "I suppose I may go outside to . . . ah . . . visit the patient?"

"We'll drive her up to your ship," said the high, tense voice. *"And you stay close to it!"* Then it said darkly. *"Men from Two City sneaked past our sentries to dump it on us. They want to wipe out our herd! What kind of weapons have you got?"*

"This is a Med Ship!" protested Calhoun. "I've nothing more than I might need in an emergency!"

"We'll want them anyhow," said the voice. *"You said you need to find out where you are. We'll tell you, if you've got enough weapons to make it worth while."*

Calhoun drew a deep breath.

"We can argue that later," he said. "I'm just a trifle puzzled. But first things first. Drive your cow."

He held his head in his hands. He remembered to throw off the spacephone and said:

"Murgatroyd, say something sensible! I never ran into anybody quite as close to coming apart at the seams as that! Not lately! Say something rational!"

Murgatroyd said, *"Chee?"* in an inquiring tone.

"Thanks," said Calhoun. "Thanks a lot."

He went back to the ports to watch. He saw men come out of the peculiar agglomeration of buildings that had been piled around the grid's sturdy control building. They were clothed in cloth that was heavy and very stiff, to judge by the way it shifted with its wearers' movements. Calhoun wasn't familiar with it. The men moved stolidly, on foot, across the incredible pasture which had been a landing area for ships of space at some time or other.

They walked toward a spot where a dark animal form rested on the ground. Calhoun hadn't noticed it particularly. Cattle, he knew, folded their legs and lay down and chewed cuds. They existed nearly everywhere that human colonies had been built. On some worlds there were other domestic animals descended from those of Earth. Of course there were edible plants and some wholesome animals which had no connection at all with humanity's remote ancestral home, but from the beginning human beings had been adjusted to symbiosis with the organic life of Earth. Foodstuffs of non-terrestrial origin could supplement Earth-food, of course. In some cases Earth-foods were the supplements and local, non-terrestrial food-stuffs the staples. But human beings did not thrive on a wholly un-Earthly diet.

The clump of slowly moving men reached the reclining cow. They pulled up stakes which surrounded her, and coiled up wire or cordage which had made the stakes into a fence. They prodded the animal. Presently it lurched to its feet and swung its head about foolishly. They drove it toward the Med Ship.

Fifty yards away they stopped, and the outside microphones brought the sound of their voices muttering. By then Calhoun had seen their faces. Four of the six were bearded. The other two were young men. On most worlds men prided themselves that they needed to shave, but few of them omitted the practice.

These six moved hastily away, though the two younger ones turned often to look back. The cow, deserted, stumbled to a reclining position. It lay down, staring stupidly about. It rested its head on the ground.

"I go out now, eh?" asked Calhoun mildly.

"*We're watching you!*" grated the spacephone speaker.

Calhoun glanced at the outside temperature indicator and added a garment. He put a blaster in his pocket, and went out the exit port.

The air was bitter cold, after two months in a heat-metered ship, but Calhoun did not feel cold. It took him seconds to understand why. It was that the ground was warm. Radiant heat kept him comfortable, though the air was icy. Heat ele-ments underground must draw power from the grid's tapping of the ionosphere and heat this pasture from underneath so forage plants could grow here. They did. The cattle fed on them. There would be hydroponic gardens somewhere else, probably underground. They would supply vegetable food in greater quantity. But in the nature of things human beings had to have animal food in a cold climate.

Calhoun went across the pasture with the frowning snowy mountains all about. He regarded the reclining beast with an almost humorous attention. He did not know anything about the special diseases of domestic animals. He had only the knowledge required of a Med Ship man. But that should be adequate. The tense voice had said that this beast had been "dumped," to "wipe out" the local herd. So there would be infection and there would be some infective agent.

He painstakingly took samples of blood and saliva. In a ruminant, certainly, any digestive-tract infection should show up in the saliva. He reflected that he did not know the normal bovine temperature, so he couldn't check it. Nor the respiration. But the Interstellar Medical Service was not often called on to treat ailing cows.

Back in the ship he diluted his samples and put droplets in the usual nutrient solutions. He sealed up droplets in those tiny slides which allow a culture to be examined as it grows. His microscope, of course, allowed inspection under light of any wave length desired, and so yielded information by the frequency of the light which gave clearest images of different features of microöganisms.

After five minutes of inspection he grunted and hauled out his antibiotic stores. He added infinitesimal traces of cillin to the culture-media. In the microscope, he watched the active microscopic creatures die. He checked with the other samples.

He went out to the listless, enfeebled animal, and made a wry guess at its body-weight, and used the injector. He went back to the Med Ship and called on the spacephone.

"I think," he said, "that your beast will be all right in thirty hours or so. Now, how about telling me the name of this sun?"

The voice said sharply:

"*There's a matter of weapons, too! Wait till we see how the cow does. Sunset will come in an hour. When day comes again, if the cow is better—we'll see!*"

There was a click. The spacephone cut off.

Calhoun pulled out the log-mike. There was already an audio record of all ship-operations and communications. Now he added comments—a description of the ribbon in the sky, the appearance of the planet, and such conclusions as he'd come to. He ended:

". . . The samples from the cow were full of a single coccus, which seemed to have no resistance to standard antibiotics. I pumped the beast full of cillin and called it a day. I'm concerned, though, because of the clear signs of an isolation syndrome here. They're idiotically suspicious of me and won't even promise a bargain, as if I could somehow overreach them because I'm a stranger. They've sentries out—they said somebody sneaked past them—against what I imagine must be Two City and Three City. I've an impression that the sentries are to enforce a quarantine rather than to put up a fight. It is probable that the other communities practice the same tactics—plus biological cold war if somebody did bring a sick cow here to infect and destroy the local herd. These people may have a landing grid, but they've an isolation syndrome and I'm afraid there's a classic Crusoe health problem in being. If that's so, it's going to be nasty!"

He cut off the log. The classic Crusoe problem would be extremely awkward if he'd run into it. There was a legend about an individual back on old Earth who'd been left isolated on an island by shipwreck for half a lifetime. His name was given to the public-health difficulties which occurred when accidental isolations occurred during the chaotic first centuries of galactic migration. There was one shipwreck to which the name was first applied. The ship was missing, and the descendants of the crew and passengers were not contacted until three generations had passed. Larger-scale and worse cases occurred later, when colonies were established by entrepreneurs who grew rich in the establishment of the new settlements, and had no interest in maintaining them. Such events could hardly happen now, of course, but even a Crusoe condition was still possible in theory. It might exist here. Calhoun hoped not.

It did not occur to him that the affair was not his business because he hadn't been assigned to it. He belonged to the Med Service, and the physical well-being of humans everywhere was the concern of that service. If people lived by choice in an inhospitable environment, that was not a Med man's problem, but anything which led to preventable deaths was. And in a Crusoe colony there were plenty of preventable deaths!

He cooked a meal to have something to occupy his mind. Murgatroyd sat on his haunches and sniffed blissfully. Presently Calhoun ate, and again presently darkness fell on this part of the world. There were new noises—small ones. He went to look. The pasture inside the landing grid was faintly lighted by the glowing ribbon in the sky. It looked like a many-times-brighter Milky Way and the girders of the landing grid looked very black against it.

He saw a dark figure plodding away until he vanished. Then he reappeared as a deeper black against the snow beyond the pasture. He went on and on until he disappeared again. A long time later another figure appeared where he'd gone out of sight. It plodded back toward the gird. It was a different individual. Calhoun had watched a changing of sentries. Suspicion. Hostility. The least attractive qualities of the human race, brought out by isolation.

There could not be a large population here, since such suspicions existed. And it was divided into—most likely—three again-isolated communities. This one had the landing grid, which meant power, and a spacephone but no vision screen attached to it. The fact that there were hostile separate communities made the situation much more difficult, from a medical point of view. It multiplied the possible ghastly features which could exist.

Murgatroyd ate until his furry belly was round as a ball, and settled to stuffed slumber with his tail curled around his nose. Calhoun tried to read. But he was restless. His own time-cycle on the ship did not in the least agree with the time of daylight on this planet. He was wakeful when there was utter quiet outside. Once one of the cattle made a dismal lowing noise. Twice or three times he heard cracking sounds, like sharp detonations, from the mountains. They would be stirrings in the glaciers.

He tried to study, but painstaking analysis of the methods by which human brains defeated their own ends and came up with wrong answers was not appealing. He grew restless.

It had been dark for hours when he heard rustling noises on the ground outside—through the microphones, of course. He turned up the amplification and made sure that a small party of men moved toward the Med Ship. From time to time they paused, as if in caution.

"Murgatroyd," he said dryly, "we're going to have visitors. They didn't give notice by spacephone, so they're unauthorized."

Murgatroyd blinked awake. He watched as Calhoun made sure of the blaster in his pocket and turned on the log-mike. He said:

"All set, Murgatroyd?"

Murgatroyd said *"Chee"* in his small shrill voice just as a soft and urgent knock sounded on the exit-lock door. It was made with bare knuckles. Calhoun grimaced and went into the lock. He undogged the door and began to open it, when it was whipped from his grasp and plunging figures pushed in. They swept him back into the Med Ship's cabin. He heard the lock-door close softly. Then he faced five roughly, heavily clothed men who wore cloaks and mittens and hoods, with cloth stretched tightly across their faces below the eyes. He saw knives, but no blasters.

A stocky figure with cold gray eyes appeared as spokesman.

"You're the man who got landed today," he said in a deep voice and with an effect of curtness. "My name's Hunt. Two City. You're a Med Ship man?"

"That's right," said Calhoun. The eyes upon him were more scared than threatening—all but the stocky man named Hunt. "I landed to find out where I was," he added. "The data-card for my astrogator had been punched wrong. What—"

"You know about sickness, eh?" demanded the stocky man evenly. "How to cure it and stop it?"

"I'm a Med Ship man," admitted Calhoun. "For whatever that may mean."

"You're needed in Two City," said the deep-voiced Hunt. His manner was purest resolution. "We came to get you. Get y'medicines. Dress warm. Load us down, if you like, with what you want to take. We got a sledge waiting."

Calhoun felt a momentary relief. This might make his job

vastly easier. When isolation and fear brings a freezing of the mind against any novelty—even hope—a medical man has his troubles. But if one community welcomed him—

"*Chee!*" said Murgatroyd indignantly from overhead. Calhoun glanced up and Murgatroyd glared from a paw-hold near the ceiling. He was a peaceable animal. When there was scuffling he got out of the way. But now he chattered angrily. The masked men looked at him with fear, but their deep-voiced leader growled at them.

"Just a animal." He swung back to Calhoun. "We got a need for you," he repeated. "We mean all right, and anything we got you can have if you want it. But you're coming with us!"

"Are your good intentions," asked Calhoun, "proved by your wearing masks?"

"They're to keep from catchin' your sickness," said the deep voice impatiently. "Point to what you want us to take!"

Calhoun's feeling of encouragement vanished. He winced a little as he saw that the isolation syndrome was fully developed. It was a matter of faith that strangers were dangerous. All men were assumed to carry contagion. Once, they'd have been believed to carry bad luck. But a regained primitiveness would still retain some trace of the culture from which it had fallen. If there were three settlements as the pasture-lands seen from space suggested, they would not believe in magic, but they would believe in contagion. They might have, or once have had, good reason. Anyhow, they would fanatically refrain from contact with any but their own fellow-citizens. Yet there would always be troubles to excite their terrors. In groups of more than a very few there would always be an impulse against the isolation which seemed the only possible safety in a hostile world. The effectiveness of the counter-instinct would depend in part on communications, but the urge to exogamy can produce ghastly results in a small culture gone fanatic.

"I think," said Calhoun, "that I'd better come with you. But the people here have to know I've gone. I wouldn't like them to heave my ship out to space in pure panic because I didn't answer from inside it!"

"Leave a writing," said Hunt's deep voice, as impatiently as before. "I'll write it. Make them boil, but they don't dare follow us!"

"No?"

"Think One City men," asked the stocky man scornfully, "will risk us toppling avalanches on them?"

Calhoun saw. Amid mountain-country in a polar zone, travel would be difficult at best. These intruders had risked much to come here for him. But they were proud of their daring. They did not believe that the folk of lesser cities—tribes —groups than theirs had courage like theirs. Calhoun recognized it as a part of that complex of symptoms which can begin with an epidemic and end with group-madness.

"I'll want this—and this—and that," said Calhoun. He wouldn't risk his microscope. Antibiotics might be useful. Antiseptics, definitely. His med-kit—"That's all."

"Your blankets," said Hunt. "Y'want them, too."

Calhoun shrugged. He clothed himself for the cold outside. He had a blaster in his pocket, but he casually and openly took down a blast-rifle. His captors offered no objection. He shrugged again and replaced it. Starting to take it was only a test. He made a guess that this stocky leader, Hunt, might have kept his community just a little more nearly sane than the group that had set him to the cure of a sick cow. He hoped so.

"Murgatroyd," he said to the *tormal* still clinging up near the control-room's top, "we have a professional call to make. You'd better come along. In fact, you must."

Murgatroyd came down then leaped to Calhoun's shoulder. He clung there, gazing distrustfully about. Calhoun realized that his captors—callers—whatever they were—stayed huddled away from every object in the cabin. They fingered nothing. But the scared eyes of most of them proved that it was not honesty which moved them to such meticulousness. It was fear. Of contagion.

"They're uncouth, eh?" said Calhoun sardonically. "But think, Murgatroyd, they may have hearts of gold! We physicians have to pretend to think so, in any case!"

"Chee!" said Murgatroyd as Calhoun moved toward the lock.

III

"Civilization is based upon rational thought applied to the purposes of men. Most mistakes occur in the process of thinking. But there can be a deep and fundamental error about purposes. It is simply a fact that the purposes of human beings are not merely those of rational animals. It is the profoundest of errors to believe otherwise—to consider, for example, that prosperity, or pleasure, or even survival, cannot be priced so high that their purchase is a mistake."

The Practice of Thinking
Fitzgerald

There was a sheet of paper fastened outside the combination lock of the Med Ship's exit port. It said that Calhoun had been taken away by men of Two City, to tend some sick person. It said that he would be returned. The latter part might not be believed, but the Med Ship might not be destroyed. The colony of the landing grid might try to break into it, but success was unlikely.

Meanwhile, it was an odd feeling to cross the grassy pastureland with hoarfrost crunching underfoot. The grid's steel girders made a harsh lace of blackness against the sky, with its shining ribbon slashing across it. Calhoun found himself reflecting that the underground heat applied to the thousand-acre pasture had been regulated with discretion. There was surely power enough available from the grid to turn the area into a place of tropic warmth, in which only lush and thick-leaved vegetation could thrive. But a storm from the frigid mountains would destroy such plants. Hardy, low-growing, semi-arctic grass was the only suitable ground-cover. The iciest of winds could not freeze it so long as the ground was warmed.

Tonight's wind was biting. Calhoun had donned a parka of synthetic fur on which frost would not congeal at any temperature, but he was forced to draw fur before his face and adjust heated goggles before his eyes would stop watering. Yet in the three-quarter-mile trudge to the edge of the snow, his feet became almost uncomfortably warm.

That, though, ended where a sledge waited at the edge of the snow. Five men had forced themselves inside the Med Ship. A sixth was on guard beside the sledge. Now the stocky man, Hunt, urged him to a seat upon the sledge.

"I'm reasonably able-bodied," said Calhoun mildly.

"You don't know where we're going—or how," growled Hunt.

Calhoun got on the sledge. The runners were extraordinarily long. He could not see small details, but it appeared that the sledge had been made of extreme length to bridge crevasses in a glacier. There were long thin metal tubes to help. At the same time, it looked as if it could be made flexible to twist and turn in a narrow or obstacle-strewn path.

The six clumsily-clad men pushed it a long way, while Calhoun frowned at riding. Then Murgatroyd shivered, and Calhoun thrust him inside the parka. There Murgatroyd wriggled until his nose went up past Calhoun's chin and he could sniff the outside air. From time to time he withdrew his nose—perhaps with frost-crystals on it. But always he poked his small black snout to sniff again.

Two miles from the pastureland, the sledge stopped. One man fumbled somewhere behind Calhoun's seat and a roaring noise began. All six piled upon the long, slender snow-vehicle. It began to move. Then, suddenly, it darted forward and went gliding up a steep incline, gathering speed. Twin arcs of disturbed snow rose up on either side, like bow-waves from a speeding water-skimmer. The sledge darted into a great ravine of purest white and the roaring sound was multiplied by echoes.

For better than half an hour, then, Calhoun experienced a ride which for thrills and beauty and hair-raising suspense made mere space-travel the stodgiest of transportation. Once the sledge shot out from beetling cliffs—all icy and glittering in the light from the sky—and hurtled down a slope of snow so swiftly that the wind literally whistled about the bodies of its occupants. Then the drive roared more loudly, and there was heavy deceleration, and abruptly the sledge barely crawled. The flexibility of the thing came into operation. Four of the crew, each controlling one segment of the vehicle, caused it to twist and writhe over the surface of a glacier, where pressure-ridges abounded and pinnacles of shattered, squeezed-up ice were not uncommon.

Once they stopped short and slender rods reached out and touched, and the sledge slid delicately over them and was itself a bridge across a crevasse in the ice that went down unguessably. Then it went on and the rods were retrieved. Minutes later the sledge-motor was roaring loudly, but it barely crawled up to what appeared to be a mountain crest— there were ranges of mountains extending beyond seeing in the weird blue-and-golden skylight—and then there was a breathtaking dash and a plunge into what was incredibly a natural tunnel beside the course of an ice-river—and abruptly there was a vast valley below.

This was their destination. Some thousands of feet down in the very valley-bottom there was a strange, two-mile-long patch of darkness. The blue-gold light showed no color there, but it was actually an artificially warmed pastureland like that within and about the landing grid. From this dark patch vapors ascended and gathered to form a misty roof—which was swept away and torn to tatters by an unseen wind.

The sledge slowed and stopped beside a precipitous upcrop of stone while still high above the valley bottom. A voice called sharply.

"It's us," growled Hunt's deep voice. "We got him. Everything all right?"

. . . "No!" rasped the invisible voice. "He broke out and got her loose, and they run off again. We shoulda killed 'em and had done with it!"

Everything stopped. The men on the sledge seemed to become still in the shock of pure disaster, pure frustration. Calhoun waited. Hunt was motionless. Then one of the men on the sledge spat elaborately. Then another stirred.

"Had your work for nothing," rasped the voice from the shadow. "The trouble that's started goes for nothing, too!"

Calhoun asked crisply:

"What's this? My special patients ran away?"

"That the Med man we heard about?" The invisible speaker was almost derisive with anger. "Sure! They've run off, all right! Man and girl together. After we made trouble with Three City by not killin' 'em and One City by sneakin' over to get you! Three City men'll come boiling over—" The voice raised in pitch, expressing scorn and fury. "Because they fell in love! We shoulda killed 'em right off or let 'em die in the snow like they wanted in the first place!"

Calhoun nodded almost imperceptibly to himself. When there is a syndrome forbidding association between societies, it is a part of the society's interior struggle against morbidity that there shall be forbidden romances. The practice of exogamy is necessary for racial health, hence there is an instinct for it. The more sternly a small population restricts its human contacts to its own members, the more repressed the exogamic impulse becomes. It is never consciously recognized for what it is. But especially when repressed, other-than-customary contacts trigger it explosively. The romantic appeal of a stranger is at once a wise provision of nature and a cause of incredible furies and disasters. It is notorious that spaceship crews are inordinately popular where colonies are small and strangers infrequent. It is no less notorious that a girl may be destitute of suitors on her own world, but has nearly her choice of husbands if she merely saves the ship fare to another.

Calhoun could have predicted defiances of tradition and law and quarantine alike, as soon as he began to learn the state of things here. The frenzied rage produced by this specific case was normal. Some young girl must have loved terribly, and some young man been no less impassioned, to accept expulsion from society on a world where there was no food except in hydroponic gardens and artificially warmed pastures. It was no less than suicide for those who loved. It was no less than a cause for battle among those who did not.

The deep-voiced Hunt said now, in leaden, heavy tones:

"Cap it. This is my doing. It was my daughter I did it for. I wanted to keep her from dying. I'll pay for trying. They'll be satisfied in Three City and in One alike if you tell 'em it's my fault and I've been drove out for trouble-making."

Calhoun said sharply:

"What's that? What's going on now?"

The man in the shadows answered—by his tone as much to express disgust as to give information.

"His daughter Nym was on sentry-duty against Three City sneaks. They had a sentry against us. The two of 'em talked across the valley between 'em. They had walkies to report with. They used 'em to talk. Presently she sneaked a vision screen out of store. He prob'ly did, too. So presently they figured it was worth dyin' to die together. They run off for the hotlands. No chance to make it, o'course!"

The hotlands could hardly be anything but the warm equatorial belt of the planet.

"We should've let them go on and die," said the stocky Hunt, drearily, "but I persuaded men to help me bring 'em back. We were careful against sickness! And we . . . I . . . locked them separate and I . . . I hoped my daughter mightn't die of the Three City sickness. I even hoped that young man wouldn't die of the sickness they say we have that we don't notice and they die of. Then we heard your call to One City. We couldn't answer it, but we heard all you said, even to the bargain about the cow. And . . . we'd heard of Med men who cured sickness. I . . . hoped you could save Nym from dying of the Three City sickness or passing it in our city. My friends risked much to bring you here. But . . . my daughter and the man have fled again."

"And nobody's goin' to risk any more!" rasped the voice from the shadow of the cliff. "We held a council; and it's decided. They're gone and we got to burn out the places they was in! You don't head the Council any more, either! We decided that, too. And no Med man! The Council ruled it!"

Calhoun nodded yet again. It is a part of fear, elaborately to ignore everything that can be denied about the thing feared. Which includes rational measures against it. This was a symptom of the state of things which constituted a Med Service emergency, because it caused needless deaths.

Hunt made a gesture which was at once commanding and filled with despair.

"I'll take the Med man back so One City can use him if they dare and not blame you for me taking him. I'll have to take the sledge—but he's used it so it'd have to be burned anyhow. You men be sure to burn your clothes. Three City'll be satisfied because I'm lost to balance for their man lost. The Med man will tell One City I'm drove out. You've lost me and my daughter too, and Three City's lost a man. One City'll growl and threaten, but they win by this. They won't risk a showdown."

Silence again. As if reluctantly, one man of the party that had abducted Calhoun moved away from the sledge and toward the deep shadow of the cliff. Hunt said harshly:

"Don't forget to burn your clothes! You others, get off the sledge. I'm taking the Med man back and there's no need for a war because I made the mistake and I'm paying for it."

The remaining men of the kidnaping-party stepped off the sledge into the trampled snow. One said clumsily:

"Sorry, Hunt. Luck!"

"What luck could I have?" asked the stocky man, wearily.

The roaring of the sledge's drive, which had been a mere muffled throbbing, rose to a booming bellow. The snow-vehicle surged forward, heading downward into the valley with the dark area beolw. Half a mile down, it began to sweep in a great circle to return upon its former track. Calhoun twisted in his seat and shouted above the roar. He made violent gestures. The deep-voiced Hunt, driving from a standing position behind the seat, slowed the sledge. It came nearly to a stop and hissing noises from snow passing beneath it could be heard.

"What's the matter?" His tone was lifeless. "What d'you want?"

"Two people have run away," said Calhoun vexedly. "Your daughter Nym and a man from Three City—whatever that is. You're driven out to prevent fighting between the cities."

"Yes," said Hunt, without expression.

"Then let's go get the runaways before they die in the

snow! After all, you got me to have me save them—and there's no need for anybody to die unless they have to."

Hunt said without any expression at all:

"They're heading for the hotlands—where they'd never get. It's my meaning to take you back to your ship, and then find them and give them the sledge so's they'll . . . so Nym will keep on living a while longer."

He moved to shift the controls and set the sledge again in motion. His state of mind was familiar enough to Calhoun— shock or despair so great that he could feel no other emotion. He would not react to argument. He could not weigh it. He'd made a despairing conclusion and he was lost to all thought beyond carrying it out. His intention was not simply a violent reaction to a single event, such as an elopement. He intended desperate means by which a complex situation could be kept from becoming a catastrophe to others. Three City had to be dealt with in this fashion, and One City in that, and it was requisite that he die, himself. Not only for his daughter but for his community. He had resolved to go to his death for good and sufficient reasons. To get his attention to anything else, he would have to be shocked into something other than despair.

Calhoun brought his hand out of its pocket holding his blaster. He pointed it to one side and pressed the stud. A half-acre of snow burst into steam. It bellowed upward and went writhing away in the peculiar blue-gold glow of this world at night.

"I don't want to be taken back to my ship," said Calhoun firmly. "I want to catch those runaways and do whatever's necessary so they won't die at all. The situation here has been thrown into my lap. It's a Med Service obligation to intervene in problems of public health, and there's surely a public-health problem here!"

Murgatroyd wriggled vigorously under Calhoun's parka. He'd heard the spitting of the blaster and the roaring of exploded steam. He was disturbed. The stocky man stared.

"What's that?" he demanded blankly. "You pick up—"

"We're going to pick up your daughter and the man she's with," Calhoun told him crossly. "There's an isolation syndrome and what looks like a Crusoe problem here, and it's got to be dealt with. As a matter of public health!"

The stocky Hunt started at him. Calhoun's intentions were unimaginable to him. He floundered among incredible ideas.

"We medics," said Calhoun, "made it necessary for men to invent interplanetary travel because we kept people from dying and the population on old Earth got too large. Then we made interstellar travel necessary because we continued to keep people from dying and one solar system wasn't big enough. We're responsible for nine-tenths of civilization as it exists today, because we produced the conditions that make civilization necessary. And since on this planet civilization is going downhill and people are dying without necessity, I have the plain obligation to stop it. So let's go pick up your daughter Nym and this sweetheart of hers, and keep them from dying and get civilization on the upgrade again!"

The former leader of the kidnapers said hoarsely:

"You mean—" Then he stammered. "Th-th-they're heading for the hotlands. No other way to go. Watch for their tracks!"

The drive-engine bellowed. The sledge raced ahead. And now it did not complete the circle that had been begun, to head back to the landing grid. Now it straightened and rushed in a splendid roaring fierceness down between the sides of the valley. It left behind the dark patch with its whirling mists. It flung aside bow-waves of fine snow, which made rainbows in the half-light which was darkness here. It rushed and rushed and rushed, leaving behind a depression which was proof of its passage.

Calhoun cringed against the wind. He could see nothing of what was ahead. The sprayed wings of upflung snow prevented it. Hunt, standing erect, could do better. Murgatroyd, inside the parka, again wriggled his nose out into the stinging wind and withdrew it precipitately.

Hunt drove as if confident of where to go. Calhoun began to fit things into the standard pattern of how such things went. There were self-evidently three cities or colonies on this planet. They'd been named and he'd seen three patches of pasture from the stratosphere. One was plainly warmed by power applied underground—electric power from the landing grid's output. The one now falling behind was less likely to be electrically heated. Steam seemed more probable because of the vapor-veil above it. This sledge was surely fuel-powered. At a guess, a ram-jet drove it. Such motors were simple enough to make, once the principle of air inflow at low speeds was known. Two City—somewhere to the rear—might operate on a fuel technology which could be based on fossil oil or gas. The power-source for Three City could not now be guessed.

Calhoun scowled as he tried to fill in the picture. His factual data was still limited. There was the misty golden ribbon in space. It was assuredly beyond the technical capacity of cities suffering from an isolation syndrome. He'd guessed at hydroponic gardens underground. There was surely no surface city near the landing grid, and the city entrance they'd just left was in the face of a cliff. Such items pointed to a limited technical capacity. Both, also, suggested mining as the original purpose of the human colony or colonies here.

Only mining would make a colony self-supporting in an arctic climate. This world could have been colonized to secure rare metals from it. There could be a pipeline from an oil field or from a gas well field near a landing grid. Local technological use of gas or oil to process ores might produce ingots of rare metal worth interstellar freight charges. One could even guess that metal reduced by heat-chemistry could be transported in oil suspension over terrain and under conditions where other forms of surface transportation were impractical.

If the colony began as a unit of that sort, it would require only very occasional visits of spacecraft to carry away its products. It could be a company-planet, colonized and maintained by a single interstellar corporation. It could have been established a hundred and fifty or two hundred years before, when the interstellar service organizations were in their infancy and only operated where they were asked to serve. Such a colony might not even be on record in the Medical Service files.

And that would account for everything. When for some reason the mines became unprofitable, this colony would not be maintained. The people who wished to leave would be taken off—of course. But some would elect to stay behind in the warmed, familiar cities they and their fathers had been born in. They couldn't imagine moving to a strange and unfamiliar world.

So much was normal reasoning. Now the strictly technical logic of the Med Service took over to explain the current state of things. In one century or less an isolated community could lose, absolutely, its defenses against diseases to which it was never exposed. Amerinds were without defense against smallpox, back on Earth. A brown race scattered among thousands of tiny islands was nearly wiped out by measles when it was introduced. Any contact between a long-isolated community and another—perhaps itself long-isolated—would bring out violently any kind of contagion that might exist in either.

There was the mechanism of carriers. The real frequency of disease-carriers in the human race had been established less than two generations ago. A very small, isolated population could easily contain a carrier or carriers of some infection. They could spread it so freely that every member of their group acquired immunity during infancy. But a different isolated group might contain a carrier of a different infection and be immune but distributive of it.

It was literally true that each of the three cities might have developed in their first century of isolation a separate immunity to one disease and a separate defenselessness against all others. A member of one community might be actually deadly to a member of either of the others whom he met face to face.

With icy wind blowing upon him as the sledge rushed on, Calhoun wryly realized that all this was wholly familiar. It was taught, nowadays, that something of the sort had caused the ancient, primitive human belief that women were perilous to men, and a man must exercise great precaution to avoid evil *mana* emanating from his prospective bride. When wives were acquired by capture and all human communities were small and fiercely self-isolated—why each unsanitary tribal group might easily acquire a condition like that assumed in cities One, Two, and Three. The primitive suspicion of women would have its basis in reality if the women of one tribe possessed immunity to some deadly microbe their skin or garments harbored—and if their successful abductors had no defense against it.

The speeding sledge swerved. It leaned inward against the turn. It swerved again, throwing monstrous sheets of snow aloft. Then the drive-jet lessened its roar. The shimmering bow-waves ceased. The sledge slowed to a mere headlong glide.

"Their trail!" Hunt cried in Calhoun's ear.

Calhoun saw depressions in the snow. There were two sets of pear-shaped dents in the otherwise virgin surface. Two man beings, wearing oblong frames on their feet, criss-crossed with cordage to support them atop the snow, had trudged ahead, here, through the gold-blue night.

Calhoun knew exactly what had happened. He could make the modifications the local situation imposed upon a standard pattern, and reconstitute a complete experience leading up to now.

A girl in heavy, clumsy garments had mounted guard in a Two City sentry-post above a snow-filled mountain valley. There were long and bitter-cold hours of watching, in which nothing whatever happened. Eternal snows seemed eternally the same, and there was little in life but monotony. But she'd known that across the valley there was another lonely watcher from an alien city, the touch of whose hand or even whose breath would mean sickness and death. She'd have mused upon the strangeness that protected her in this loneliness— because her touch or her breath would be contagion upon him, too. She'd have begun to feeling a vague dread of the other sentry. But presently, perhaps, there came a furtive call on the walkie-frequency used by sentries for communication with their own cities.

Very probably she did not answer at first. But she might listen. And she would hear a young man's voice, filled with curiosity about the sentry who watched as he did.

There'd come a day when she'd answer shyly. And there would be relief and a certain fascination in talking to some-one so much like herself—but so alien and so deadly! Of course there could be no harm in talking to someone who would flee from actual face-to-face contact as desperately as herself. The might come to joke about their mutual dangerousness. They might find it amusing that cities which dared not meet should hate. Then there'd come a vast curiosity to see each other. They'd discuss that frankly—because what possible evil could come, if two persons were deadly to each other should they actually approach?

Then there'd come a time when they looked at each other breathlessly in vision screens they'd secretly stolen from their separate cities' stores. There could be no harm. They were only curious! But she would see someone at once infinitely strange but utterly dear, and he would see someone lovely beyond the girls of his own city. Then they would regret the alienness which made them perilous to each other. Then they would resent it fiercely. They'd end by denying it.

So across the wide valley of eternal snow there would travel whispers of desperate rebellion, then firmly resolute murmurings, and then what seemed the most obvious of truth—that it would be much more satisfactory to die together than to live apart. Insane plannings would follow—arrangements by which two trembling young folk would meet secretly and flee. Toward the hotlands, to be sure, but without any belief than that the days before death, while they were together, were more precious than the lifetimes they would give up to secure them.

Calhoun could see all this very clearly, and he assured himself that he regarded it with ironic detachment. He asserted in his own mind that it was merely the manifestation of that blind impulse to exogamy which makes spacemen romantic in far spaceports and invests an outer-planet girl with glamour. But it was something more. It was also that strange and unreasonable and solely human trait which causes one to rejoice selflessly that someone else exists, so that his or her own life and happiness is put into its place of proper insignificance in the cosmos. It may begin in instinct, but it becomes an achievement only humans can encompass.

Hunt knew it—the stocky, deep-voiced despairing figure

who stared hungrily for the daughter who had defied him and for whom he was an exile from all food and warmth.

He flung out a mittened hand.

"There!" he cried joyously. "It's them!"

There was a dark speck in the blue-gold night-glow. As the sledge swept close, there were two small figures who stood close together. They defiantly faced the approaching sledge. As its drive-motor stopped and it merely glided on, its runners whispering on the snow, the girl snatched away the cold-mask which all the inhabitants of this planet wore out-of-doors. She raised her face to the man. They kissed.

And then the young man desperately raised a knife. It glittered in the light of the ribbon in the sky. And—

Calhoun's blaster made its inadequate rasping noise. The knife-blade turned incandescent for two-thirds of its length. The young man dropped the suddenly searing handle. The knife sank hissing into the snow.

"It's always thrilling to be dramatic," said Calhoun severely, "but I assure you it's much more satisfying to be sane. The young lady's name is Nym, I believe. I do not know the gentleman. But Nym's father and myself have come to put the technical resources of two civilizations at your disposal as a first step toward treatment of the pandemic isolation syndrome on this planet, which with the complications that have developed amounts to a Crusoe health problem."

Murgatroyd tried feverishly to get his head out of Calhoun's parka past his chin. He'd heard a blaster. He sensed excitment. His nose emerged, whiffing. Calhoun pushed it back.

"Hunt, tell them what we're here for and what you've done already!"

The girl's father told her unsteadily—almost humbly, for some reason—that the jet-sledge had come to take her and her sweetheart—to be her husband—to the hotlands where at least they would not die of cold. Calhoun added crossly that he believed there would even be food there—because of the ribbon in the sky.

Trembling and abashed, the fugitives got on the sledge. Its

motor roared. It surged toward the hotlands under the golden glow of that ribbon.

IV

"An action is normally the result of a thought. Since we cannot retract an action, we tend to feel that we cannot retract the thought which produced it. In effect, we cling desperately to our mistakes. In order to change our views we have commonly to be forced to act upon new thoughts, so urgent and so necessary that without disowning our former, mistaken ideas, we can abandon them tactfully without saying anything to anybody—even ourselves."

The Practice of Thinking
Fitzgerald

Murgatroyd came down a tree with his cheek-pouches bulged with nuts. Calhoun inserted a finger, and Murgatroyd readily permitted him to remove and examine the results of his scramble aloft. Calhoun grunted. Murgatroyd did have other and more useful abilities in the service of public health, but right here and now his delicate digestion was extremely convenient. His stomach worked so much like a human's, that anything Murgatroyd ate was safe for Calhoun to an incredible degree of probability. And Murgatroyd ate nothing that disagreed with him.

"Instead of 'physician, heal thyself,'" Calhoun observed, "it's amounted to 'physician, feed thyself' since we got past the frost-line, Murgatroyd. I am gratified."

"*Chee!*" said Murgatroyd complacently.

"I expected," said Calhoun, "only to benefit by the charm of your society in what I thought would be a routine check-trip to Merida Two. Instead, some unknown fumble-finger punched a wrong button and we wound up here. Not exactly here, but near enough. I brought you from the Med Ship because there was nobody to stay around and feed you, and now you feed us—at least by pointing out edible things we might otherwise miss."

"*Chee!*" said Murgatroyd. He strutted.

"Wish," protested Calhoun, "that you wouldn't imitate

that Pat character from Three City! As a brand-new husband he's entitled to strut a little, but I object to your imitating him! You haven't anybody acting like Nym!—gazing at you raptly as if you'd invented not only marriage but romance itself, impassioned falsehoods, and all other desirable things back to night and morning!"

Murgatroyd said, *"Chee?"* and turned to face away from Calhoun.

The two of them, just then, stood on a leaf-covered patch of ground which slanted down to the smooth and reflective water of a tiny bay. Behind and above them reared gigantic mountains. There was snow in blinding-white sheets overhead, but the snowline itself was safely three thousand feet above them. Beyond the bay was a wide estuary, with more mountains behind it, with more snowfields on their flanks. A series of leaping cascades jumped downward from somewhere aloft where a glacier-foot melted in the sun's heat. And everywhere that snow was not, green stuff shone in the sunlight.

Nym's father, Hunt, came toward the pair. He'd abandoned the thick felt cloak and heavy boots of Two City. Now he was dressed nearly like a civilized man, but he carried a sharpened stick in one hand and in the other a string of authentic fish. He wore an expression of astonishment. It was becoming habitual.

"Murgatroyd," said Calhoun casually, "has found another kind of edible nut. Terrestrial, too, like half the living things we've seen. Only the stuff crowding the glaciers seems to be native. The rest originated on Earth and was brought here, some time or another."

Hunt nodded. He seemed to find some difficulty in speaking.

"I've been talking to Pat," he said at last.

"The son-in-law," observed Calhoun, "who has to thank you not only for your daughter and his life, but for your public career in Two City which qualified you to perform a marriage ceremony. I hope he was respectful."

Hunt made an impatient gesture. "He says that you haven't done anything either to Nym or to him to keep them from dying!"

Calhoun nodded.

"That's true."

"But . . . they should die! Nym should die of the Three City sickness! And Three City people have always said that we had a sickness too . . . that did not harm us but they died of!"

"Which," agreed Calhoun, "is undoubtedly historical fact. Its current value is that of one factor in an isolation syndrome and consequently a complicating factor in the Crusoe health problem here. I've let Nym and Pat go untreated to prove it. I think there's only a sort of mass hypochondria based on strictly accurate tradition. Which would be normal."

Hunt shook his head.

"I don't understand!" he protested helplessly.

"Someday I'll draw a diagram," Calhoun told him. "It is complicated. Did you check with Pat on what Three City knows about the ribbon in the sky? I suspect it accounts for the terrestrial plants and animals here, indirectly. There wouldn't be an accidental planting of edible nuts and fish and squirrels and pigeons and rabbits and bumblebees! I suspect there was a mistake somewhere. What does Pat say?"

Hunt shrugged his shoulders.

"When I talk to him," added Calhoun, "he doesn't pay attention. He simply gazes at Nym and beams. The man's mad! But you're his father-in-law. He has to be polite to you!"

Hunt sat down. He rested his spear against a tree and looked over his string of fish. He wasn't used to the abundance of foodstuffs here, and the temperature—Calhoun estimated it at fifty degrees—seemed to him incredibly balmy. Now he separated one fish from the rest and with a new skill began to slice away two neatly boneless fillets. Calhoun had showed him the trick the day after a lesson in fish-spearing, which was two days after their arrival.

"Children in Three City," growled Hunt, "are taught the same as in Two City. Men came to this planet to work the mines. There was a company which sent them, and every so often it sent ships to take what the mines yielded, and to bring things the people wanted. Men lived well and happily. The company hung the ribbon in the sky so the hotlands could grow food for the men. But presently the mines could not deliver what they made to the ships when they came. The hotlands grow bigger, the glaciers flowed faster, and the pipes between the cities were broken and could not be kept repaired. So the company said that since the mine-products could no longer be had, it could not send the ships. Those who wanted to move to other worlds would be carried there. Some men went, with their wives and children. But the grandfathers of our fathers' grandfathers were contented here. They had homes and heat and food. They would not go."

Hunt regarded the pinkish brook trout fillet he'd just separated. He bit off a mouthful and chewed, thoughtfully.

"That really tastes better cooked," said Calhoun mildly.

"But it is good this way also," said Hunt. He waved the remainder of the fillet. "Then the ships ceased to come. Then sickness came. One City had a sickness it gave to people of Two and Three when they visited it. Two City had a sickness it gave to One and Three. Three City—" He grunted. "Our children in Two say only Two City people have no sickness. Three City children are taught that only Three City is clean of sickness."

Calhoun said nothing. Murgatroyd tried to gnaw open one of the nuts he'd brought down from the tree. Calhoun took it and another and struck them together. Both cracked. He gave them to Murgatroyd, who ate them with great satisfaction.

Hunt looked up suddenly.

"Pat did not give a Three City sickness to Nym," he observed, "so our thinking was wrong. And Nym has not given a Two City sickness to him. His thinking was wrong."

Calhoun said meditatively:

"It's tricky. But sickness can be kept by a carrier, just as you people have believed of other cities. A carrier has a sickness but does not know it. People around the carrier have the sickness on their bodies or their clothing from the carrier. They distribute it. Soon everybody in the city where there is a carrier—" Calhoun had a moment's qualm because he used the word "city." But to Hunt the idea conveyed was a bare few hundred people. "Soon everybody is used to the sickness. They are immune. They cannot know it. But somebody from another city can come, and they are not used to the sickness, and they become ill and die."

Hunt considered shrewdly.

"Because the sickness is on clothing? From the carrier?"

Calhoun nodded.

"Different carriers have different sicknesses. So one carrier in One City might have one disease, and all the people in One City became used to it while they were babies—became immune. There could be another carrier with another sickness in Two City. A third in Three City. In each city they were used to their own sickness—"

"That is it," said Hunt, nodding. "But why is Pat not dying? Or Nym? Why do you do nothing to keep them alive?"

"Suppose," said Calhoun, "the carrier of a sickness dies. What happens?"

Hunt bit again, and chewed. Suddenly he choked. He sputtered:

"There is no sickness to spread on the clothing! The people no longer have it to give to strangers who are not used to it! The babies do not get used to it while they are little! There is no longer a One City sickness or a Two City sickness or a Three!"

"There is," said Calhoun, "only a profound belief in them. You had it. Everybody else still has it. And the cities are isolated and put out sentries because they believe in what used to be true. And people like Nym and Pat run away in the snow and die of it. There is much death because of it. You would have died of it."

Hunt chewed and swallowed. Then he grinned.

"Now what?" His deep voice was respectful to Calhoun, so much younger than himself. "I like this! We were not fools to believe, because it was true. But we are fools if we still believe, because it is not true any more. How do we make people understand, Calhoun? You tell me. I can handle people when they are not afraid. I can make them do what I think wise—when they are not afraid. But when they fear—"

"When they fear," said Calhoun dryly, "they want a stranger to tell them what to do. You came for me, remember? You are a stranger to One City and Three City. Pat is a stranger to Two City. If the cities become really afraid—"

Hunt grunted, and watched Calhoun intently. Calhoun was reminded of the elected president of a highly cultured planet, who had exactly that intent way of looking at one.

"Go on!" said Hunt. "How frighten them into—this?"

He waved his hand about. Calhoun, his tone very dry indeed, told him. Words would not be enough. Threats would not be enough. Promises would not be enough. But rabbits and pigeons and squirrels and fish—fish that were frozen like other human food—and piles of edible nuts. . . . They would not be enough either, by themselves. But—

"An isolation syndrome is a neurotic condition, and a Crusoe problem amounts to neurotic hypochondria. You can do it—you and Pat."

Hunt grimaced.

"I hate the cold, now. But I will do it. After all, if I am to have grandchildren there should be other children for them to play with! And we will take you back to your ship?"

"You will," said Calhoun. "By the way, what is the name of this planet, anyhow?"

Hunt told him.

* * *

Calhoun slipped across the pasture inside the landing grid and examined the ship from the outside. There had been batterings, but the door had not been opened. In the light of the ribbon in the sky he could see, too, that the ground was trampled down but only at a respectful distance. One City was disturbed about the Med Ship. But it did not know what to do. So long as nothing happened from it . . .

He was working the combination lock-door when something hopped, low-down and near him. He jumped, and Murgatroyd said, *"Chee?"* Then Calhoun realized what had startled him. He finished the unlocking of the port, went in, and closed it behind him. The air inside seemed curiously dead, after so long a time outside. He flipped on the outside microphones and heard tiny patterings and mildly resentful cooings. He grinned.

When morning came, the people of One City would find their pastureland inhabited by small snowshoe rabbits and bush-tailed squirrels and fluttering pigeons. They would react as Two City and Three City had already done—with panic. And panic would inevitably call up the notion of the most-feared thing in their lives. Sickness. The most-feared thing is always a rare thing, of course. One cannot fear a frequent thing, because one either dies of it or comes to take it for granted. Fear is always of the rare or nonexistent. One City would be filled with fear of sickness.

And sickness would come. Hunt would call them, presently, on a walkie-talkie communicator. He would express deep concern because—so he'd say—new domestic animals intended for Two City had been dumped on One City pastureland. He'd add that they were highly infective, and Two City was already inescapably doomed to an epidemic which would begin with severe headaches, and would continue with cramps and extreme nervous agitation. And he would say that Calhoun had left medicines at Two City with which that sickness and all others could be cured, and if the sickness described should appear in One City—why—its victims could be cured if they traveled to Two City.

The sickness would appear. Inevitably. There was no longer sickness in the three communities. Arctic colonies, never visited by people from reservoirs of infection, become magnificently healthy by the operation of purely natural causes. But an isolation syndrome . . .

The people of One City would presently travel, groaning, to Two City. Their suffering would be real. They would dread the breaking of their isolation. But they'd dread sickness—even sickness they only imagined—still more. And when they reached Two City they would find themselves tended by Three City members, and they would be appalled and terrified. But mumbo-jumbo medication by Hunt and Pat—and Nym for the women—would reassure them. A Crusoe condition requires heroic treatment. This was it.

Calhoun cheerfully checked over the equipment of the Med Ship. He'd have to take off on emergency rockets. He'd have to be very, very careful in setting a course back to Headquarters to report before starting out again for Merida II. He didn't want to make any mistakes. Suddenly he began to chuckle.

"Murgatroyd," he said, "it's just occurred to me that the mistakes we make—that we struggle so hard to avoid—are part of the scheme of things."

"*Chee?*" said Murgatroyd inquiringly.

"The company that settled this planet," said Calhoun, grinning, "set up that ribbon out in space as a splendidly conservative investment to save money in freight charges. It was a mistake, because it ruined their mining business and they had to write the whole colony off. They made another mistake by not reporting to Med Service, because now they've abandoned the colony and would have to get a license to reoccupy—which they'd never be granted against the population already here. Somebody made a mistake that brought us here, and One City made a mistake by not accepting us as guests, and Two City made a mistake by sending Nym on sentry duty, and Three City made a mistake . . ."

Murgatroyd yawned.

"You," said Calhoun severely, "make a mistake in not paying attention." He strapped himself in, and stabbed an emergency-rocket control-button. The little ship shot heavenward on a pencil-thin stream of fire. Below him, people of One City would come pouring out of underground to learn what had happened, and they'd find the pasture swarming with friendly squirrels and inquisitive rabbits and cooing pigeons. They'd be scared to death. Calhoun laughed. "I'll spend part of the time in overdrive making a report on it. Since an isolation syndrome is mostly psychological, and a Crusoe condition is wholly so—I managed sound medical treatment by purely psychological means! I'll have fun with that!"

It was a mistake. He got back to Headquarters all right, but when his report was read they made him expand it into a book, with footnotes, an index, and a bibliography.

It was very much of a mistake!

MATE IN TWO MOVES

Winston K. Marks

There have been many kinds of epidemics throughout history, all of them bad. Bubonic plague, for one; and that curious, never-diagnosed dancing mania of the Middle Ages. Most plagues have defeated the physicians as well as the patients, at least up to the discoveries of Pasteur and his followers. Indeed, the one that Winston Marks describes here might well have defeated Pasteur: it took the development of much more modern medical science, including biochemistry and electron microscopy, to flatten this one. The plague he describes is, of course, a bit out of the ordinary—but not, epidemiologists assure us, necessarily impossible. And it must have been pretty dreadful to have, too. Perhaps even worse than the Real Thing!

Mate in Two Moves

I

LOVE CAME SOMEWHAT LATE to Dr. Sylvester Murt. In fact, it took the epidemic of 1981 to break down his resistance. A great many people fell in love that year—just about every other person you talked to—so no one thought much about Dr. Murt's particular distress, except a fellow victim who was directly involved in this case.

High Dawn Hospital, where 38-year-old Dr. Murt was resident pathologist, was not the first medical institution to take note of the "plague." The symptoms first came to the attention of the general practitioners, then to the little clinics where the G.P.'s sent their patients. But long before anything medical was done about it, the plague was sweeping North and South America and infiltrating every continent and island in the world.

Murt's assistant, Dr. Phyllis Sutton, spotted the first irregularity in the *Times* one morning and mentioned it to him. They were having coffee in Murt's private office-lab, after completing reports on two rush biopsies.

She looked up from the editorial page and remarked, "You know, someone should do a research on the pathology of pantie raids."

Murt spooned sugar into his mug of coffee and stared at her. In their six months' association, it was the first facetious remark she had made in his presence. To this moment, he had held an increasing regard for her quiet efficiency, sobriety, professional dignity and decorum. True, she wore her white coat more tightly belted than was necessary and, likewise, she refused to wear the very low hospital heels that thickened feminine ankles. But she wore a minimum of come-hither in both her cosmetic and personality makeup. This startling remark, then, was most unexpected.

"Pantie raids?" he inquired. "Whatever would justify an inquiry into such a patently behavioristic problem?"

"The epidemic nature and its increasing virulence," she replied soberly. "This spring, the thing has gotten out of hand, according to this editorial. A harmless tradition at a few of the more uninhibited campuses has turned into a national collegiate phenomenon. And now secondary effects are turning up. Instructors say that intramural romance is turning the halls of ivy into amatory rendezvous."

Murt sipped his coffee and said, "Be thankful you aren't a psychiatrist. Bacterial mutations are enough of a problem, without pondering unpredictable emotional disturbances."

His assistant pursued it further. "It says the classrooms are emptying into the marriage bureaus, and graduation exercises this year will be a mockery if something isn't done. What's more, statistics show a startling increase in marriages at the high school level."

Murt shrugged broad shoulders that were slightly bent from long hours over a microscope. "Then be thankful you aren't an over-worked obstetrician," he offered as an amendment.

She glanced up from the paper, with annoyance showing in her dark, well-spaced eyes. "Is it of no interest to you that several hundred thousand youngsters are leaving high school and college prematurely because they can't control their glands?"

"Be glad, then," Murt said coldly, "that you aren't an endocrinologist—now drink your coffee. I hear the microtome working. We'll have some business in a minute."

Dr. Phyllis Sutton rustled the pages of the *Times* together, folded it up and threw it at the wastebasket with more vigor than was necessary. The subject was momentarily closed.

His staff position at High Dawn paid less, but the life suited Dr. Murt better than the hectic, though lucrative, private practices of many of his colleagues. He arrived at the hospital early, seven o'clock each day, to be on hand for quick tissue examinations during the morning operations. By ten, the biopsies were usually out of the way, and he spent the rest of the morning and early afternoon checking material from the bacteriology section and studying post-operative dissections of tumorous tissues and organs removed in surgery.

It was engrossing, important work, and it could be accomplished in a normal work-day, leaving the pathologist considerable leisure to study, read and relax. Shortly after the pantie-raid conversation with Phyllis Sutton, he found the evening paper attracting more than his usual quick perusal.

This emotional fuss in the young human animal was beginning to preoccupy the newspaper world. Writers were raising their eyebrows and a new crop of metaphors at the statistics, which they described variously as alarming, encouraging, disheartening, provocative, distressing, romantic or revolting, depending upon the mood and point of view.

As June, the traditional mating month, wore into July, national statistics were assembled to reveal that marriages were occurring at almost double the highest previous rate, that the trend was accelerating rather than diminishing.

Jewelers and wholesale diamond merchants chalked up fabulous increases in the sale of engagement and wedding settings. Clergymen and qualified public officials were swamped with requests for religious and civil marriage ceremonies.

Parks, beaches and drive-in theaters were jammed with mooning and/or honeymooning couples, and amusement parks began expanding their overpatronized tunnel-of-love facilities.

The boom in houses, furniture, appliances and TV was on, and last year's glut of consumer goods for the home was rapidly turning into a shortage.

All was not good news, however. The divorce courts reported their calendars stacked months ahead of time, and an increasing number of lurid headlines were devoted to the love-triangular troubles of the rich, famous and notorious. Love-nest exposés and bigamous marriages rocketed in number.

The whole world, adolescent and adult, was falling in love, with the inevitable unrequited infatuations, the jealousies, infidelities and the bitter-sweetness of wholesale, illict, impossible love situations in which vulnerable people found themselves increasing astronomically.

Writers of popular newspaper psychology columns attributed the rampaging emotional fire to everything from mass-hysteria, caused by sunspots, to the paternalism of a government that gave increased income-tax deductions to married people.

Dr. Murt's growing interest was not entirely academic. His bachelorhood was no accident of fate, but rather a carefully contrived independence, for which he paid the price of eternal vigilance. As the world supply of eligible bachelors diminished sharply, his wariness increased, and he became more and more curt with nurses and female technicians at the hospital.

He revealed the depth of his leeriness one afternoon at the scrub-up sink, where he and his assistant were washing after a messy dissection. Phyllis Sutton remarked, "Holly, down in Personnel, showed me a tabulation she ran off for her own curiosity today, Doctor. Do you realize that in this whole hospital there are only *eight* unmarried female employees?"

Murt threw water droplets from his bare arms and muttered, "Yes, and every one of them's giving me the eye—to say nothing of half the married ones."

His aide dried her long arms and slender hands and looked at him with a crooked smile. "Not to underestimate your good looks, Doctor, but I am one of the unmarried females. I trust I'm not giving you too much trouble?"

He looked up, startled. "Yes—no, *no*—of course not. I'm referring to the nurses and the technicians. What's got into them? The whole lot seems to be on the make!"

Phyllis combed out her short dark hair and looked at him in the mirror. "I assure you the males are just as bad. These interns and four of the male nurses give me a physical with their eyes every time I happen to meet them."

"I suppose this ties in somehow with your pantie-raid theory."

"Well, what do *you* think?"

"I don't think. I just dodge. You'd do well to do the same," Murt told her, putting on his jacket and adjusting his tie.

She sat down in his oak swivel-chair and crossed her slender ankles. "Are you aware of the problem they have downstairs in the out-patient clinic?"

"Hadn't heard," Murt said.

She removed a file from her purse and touched up her short nails. "The outlying clinics are sending their overflow to us. They can't seem to diagnose the odd symptoms they're getting."

"I had noticed the large number of negative test results coming out of the lab," Murt acknowledged. "Haven't followed any of them through, though."

"I have," Phyllis said with a little frown. "Seems to be a psychosomatic nightmare down there."

"What are the symptoms?"

"Mostly neurotic," she said. "Listlessness, loss of appetite, palpitations, cold sweats and absent-mindedness."

"Why don't they go to the pychiatric clinics?"

"Overloaded. They're sending patients here."

"What age groups?"

"From puberty to senility. I'd like your permission to do a little special work on blood samples."

"Another theory?" he asked caustically.

"Yes. Will you give me your permission to test it?"

Murt adjusted his Panama straw in the mirror and noticed that the nostrils of his straight nose were flared for some reason. "Your time is your own after three P.M. every day. If you want to take time out from your thesis research, that's your business."

He crossed to the door and was opening it when he became aware that he had had no answer. He looked back at the profile of his assistant's body, which was now stretched out full length, suspended at three points—her higher-than-practical heels on the linoleum tile, her spine and curved hips using only an inch of the chair's edge, and her head tilted over the chair's back. She inhaled from a king-size filter-tip cigarette and blew a feather of smoke at the ceiling.

"*Yuh!*" she said finally. Her flat abdomen jumped at the exhaled syllable, and so did her generous breasts under the soft emerald-green street dress.

"Good *night!*" Murt closed the door behind him quickly and became aware of a sharp stab of what he defined as pure rut—the first he had suffered in fifteen years.

II

He taxied downtown to the athletic club, where he maintained his three-room apartment. The 20-story building was a citadel of masculinity—no females allowed—and recently it was an especial relief to enter the lobby and leave behind the world of turbulently mixed sexes.

The small but lush entry chamber had a deserted air about it this afternoon. At the room desk, Crumbley, the clerk, handed him his key with a pallid hand and returned to sigh over a colored picture in *Esquire*—it was the "fold-out" page, featuring a gorgeous blonde reclining at full length. Crumbley's expression, however, was far from the loose-lipped, lecherous leer that he normally exposed to such art. His eyes had a thin glaze over them, he breathed shallowly and, if Dr. Murt had not known the little man's cynically promiscuous nature so well, he'd have sworn Crumbley was in love.

Upstairs, Murt donned rubber-soled gym shoes and sweat clothes and rode the elevator back down to the gymnasium. Three times a week, he put his muscles through the whole routine—work on the bars, rings, the leather horse, the rope climb and a twenty-lap jog around the balcony racetrack. Afterward, he showered, took a dip in the swimming pool and retired to the health service department for a rubdown and some sunlamp.

Throughout the whole routine, he encountered not a single other member. While Charlie, the husky blond masseur, hammered and kneaded his muscles, Murt reflected on the abating interest in athletics at the club.

"Are we losing members, Charlie?" he asked.

"You'd think so from how dead it is up here," Charlie replied. "But Crumbley says we aren't. The guys just aren't exercising. Can't figure it, Doc. Even with the usual summer slump, it's never been this slow."

When he had absorbed all the punishment he could stand, Murt rolled off, went into the ultraviolet room, set an alarm clock and lay down by himself on one of the paper-covered tables. He adjusted the dark goggles and reflected thankfully that he didn't have to go to the beach for his sun and have sand kicked in his face by a procession of predatory females, ogling his long limbs and trying to attract his attention.

The clean smell of ozone was pleasant, the warmth of the lamps relaxed him, and he dozed off. He dreamed that he heard someone else come in and lie down on the next table and, when he raised his head to see who it was, was amazed to discover his assistant, Dr. Phyllis Sutton, stretched out like himself, wearing only shower-sandals and goggles.

The alarm clock wakened him from the disturbing dream. He was sweating profusely and took another shower, using the cold water at full needle force to dispel his shock at his subconscious.

Wrapping the robe around him, Murt returned to his apartment to dress for dinner. As he snapped the paper laundry band off a clean shirt, he caught himself wondering how old Phyllis Sutton was. Twenty-eight? Thirty? She appeared younger, but she was in her last year of residence to gain her specialty of pathology. That meant over eleven years of school and practice. She was a lovely creature, but she was no child.

He had half an impulse to phone her for dinner, then became lost in studying his own reaction to the thought. Pulse over a hundred, respiration quickening, irregular. There was a tensing of the abdomen, a faint burning in the pit of his stomach.

He remembered the urge at the office, the dream in the sunroom, the sudden sweat that had required five minutes under the cold needle shower.

After so many years of deliberate, scholarly celibacy, what was happening to him?

He stared at the phone. With six motions of one finger, he

could dial Phyllis Sutton's face into view, and suddenly he yearned to do that very ridiculous thing.

After staring at her, off and on, for the six months since she had transferred to High Dawn to complete her residency, now he wanted to see her face outside of working hours for some inexplicable reason.

Call her up, date her, take her dancing, proposition her—get this silly feeling off your chest!

Suppose she was busy or refused to go out with him? Suppose she already had a boy friend?

This last thought deepened the burn in the pit of his stomach, and he finished dressing listlessly. To hell with it! This was poker night. If he did succeed in dating his assistant, they'd inevitably talk shop. That was why he enjoyed a night of cards with his six non-medical brother clubmen, once a week. It was refreshing to break away from the professional point of view.

No, he wouldn't sacrifice that for any woman.

He ate alone, read the paper, joined the poker party at seven o'clock, played six hands of stud, cashed in his chips and returned to his room. In a mood of deep irritation, he found Phyllis Sutton's home phone number and rang it four times with no result.

He thought to try the hospital. She answered from the lab extension on audio only, but her voice and its frankly curious tone sent vertically polarized chills through him.

"I—I wanted to apologize for my rudeness this afternoon," he said with difficulty from a suddenly dry mouth.

There was a brief silence. "Have you been drinking, Dr. Murt?" He noticed that she did not call him Sylvester. Why was he so damned thirsty for some little sign of warmth and friendliness from her?

He cleared his throat. "No, I'm serious. It occurred to me that your interest in the out-clinic problem was commendable, and that I was rather short in my remarks to you."

"Oh! I take it I have your permission to work my project in during the day, then?"

"That's right, so long as it doesn't interfere with the routine." He sounded stuffy to himself, but he was entirely out of practice in speaking to please a female.

"Thanks," she said wryly, and the conversation ended.

Somehow, the brief talk with her restored his perspective. Once again she was his assistant, and the significance of her as a woman faded. She was a dedicated physician like himself. In another few years, she would find a residency of her own. She had no more inclination to knock off and become a woman than he had to squander his time and energy on attaining the status of family man.

It was with mounting admiration that he followed her new project in examining blood samples. As they came up from the clinic, she sorted the specimen tubes at once, putting a tiny snip of yellow Scotch tape under the label of each sample that belonged to a patient with the new undiagnosed disorder.

Then, after the requested hemoglobin, blood sugar and other standard tests had been run, she retrieved the samples from the technicians, grouped them in a special rack and devoted every spare minute to further examination.

She centrifuged, precipitated, filtered and stained over and over, using every qualitative procedure in the book. Murt signed her requisitions for exotic reagents and rare stains. He helped her balance out the large centrifuge to get the maximum r.p.m. from it. He let her use the most costly of the fine-porosity filters.

He had little hope of success, but it was good practice for her. She was required to identify every organism she found, bone up on its known effects, then determine that it could not cause the symptoms reported.

She did all this without impairing her usefulness to Murt. When he needed her, she was at his side, dissecting, taking down notes, preparing delicate sections and checking slides before they came to him.

In several weeks, she exhausted all known tests on the first samples. After lunch one day, she turned her palms up. "*Nichts da!*" she said, pulling a mashed cigarette from the huge pocket of her white smock.

He glanced at her and swiveled to stare out the window.

It was part of his tight campaign to prevent a disastrous recurrence of the emotional tempest he had suffered the day she had begun this research.

"It was a nice brush-up on your bacteriology," he said. "Have you saved the filtrates?"

"Yes, of course. Did I overlook anything?"

"Nothing that we could do here, but there's an electron microscope downtown at Ebert Industrial Labs. How about photomicrography? Could be a filtrable virus."

He knew that she was aware of the possibility, and also that she was reluctant to ask him for additional funds to go into a virus hunt with the expensive piece of equipment.

"Wonderful!" she told him. "I did hate to ask you, but it would be a shame to waste all that immaculate filtrate."

III

A week passed, during which a bulletin from the Government Health Service announced official suspicion that the human race was suffering a mysterious, pandemic affliction which was as yet undiagnosed. Although the symptoms, as reported by hundreds of clinics, were relatively mild, the effect on the nation's economy was growing serious.

Industry and business reported unprecedented absenteeism. Factory supervisors and insurance companies were frantic over the upsurge in accidents. It was estimated that almost fifty per cent of the population exhibited the symptoms of depression, absentmindedness, insomnia and loss of appetite.

Negligent driving was increasing the highway toll sharply. Educational institutions reported classroom discipline rapidly vanishing. Armed forces headquarters cautiously admitted a new high in desertions and AWOLs.

The consensus among psychiatrists and psychologists was that the condition stemmed from pathogenic causes.

Dr. Murt raised his eyebrows when he read this. Perhaps Phyllis Sutton was right, after all.

The bulletin continued, "All clinical pathologists are requested to be alert to the presence of any unusual organisms discovered in body fluids or tissues examined. Please report your findings to the U.S. Public Health Service."

Murt found Phyllis Sutton at the microtome, finishing a wax section, and showed her the bulletin.

"Score one for woman's intuition," he smiled. "Federal Health Service tends to agree with your theory."

"Now I *am* eager to see those pictures," she said.

Less than two hours later, a messenger brought the photomicrographs, and the two pathologists bent over them together. Phyllis had submitted eighteen samples, six of which were controls taken from healthy, unafflicted subjects. Per her instructions, smears of the specimens in various degrees of dilution had been photographed through the great electron microscope.

Murt muttered to himself as they compared the controls with the "infected specimens." The "healthy" samples were relatively clear, except for minute protein matter. Conversely, all twelve suspect specimens swarmed with shadowy six-sided dots.

Phyllis' eyes widened. "There *is* something there! Do you suppose it could be the Love Bug?"

"Love Bug?"

"Certainly. That bulletin didn't go into the psychologists' findings. The diagnosticians downstairs say that the symptoms appear to be no more than complaints of the lovesick."

"Are you back on the pantie-raid theme again?"

"I've never been off it," she replied. "From the first, I've had a notion that some organism was increasing glandular activity. Excess emotionalism often originates in overstimulated glands."

"Of course, but mental attitudes can trigger the glands, and they are interacting. How do you separate the effects? How could you guess that an organism was responsible?"

She shrugged. "It was a possibility within our specialty, so I set out to prove or disprove it. From the appearance of these photographs, I don't think we have *disproved* it."

It was a properly cautious statement that pleased Murt.

They were a long way from proving that their newly discovered virus was the culprit, but the research had definitely produced a question mark.

Murt ordered copies of the photomicrographs from Ebert Industrial Labs and arranged for a complete dossier to be forwarded to the U.S. Health Service.

That night, he was startled by a headline and lead story that quoted the government bulletin. The science editor had a field day, tying in speculation that "Doctors Suspect Love Bug Epidemic."

The next day, three reporters called upon him, each with the same query. "It's rumored that you are doing research on the Love Bug, Dr. Murt. Anything to report?"

He shooed them out angrily, after learning that someone at Ebert Labs had given them the tip. Phyllis smiled at him as he slammed the door after the last reporter.

"You still discount the Love-Bug idea, don't you?" she asked.

"I dislike sensationalism in a matter like this," he said. "Even if their assumptions were true, I wouldn't like it."

"You can't blame the papers. They're starved for some explanation. I pity your passion for anonymity if your virus proves to be the causative factor."

"*My* virus?"

"Certainly. The whole project is under your auspices and direction."

"See here, Phyl, *you* did the work."

"Don't you dare mention my name," she said. "You're my superior and senior pathologist and it's your duty to protect me against the press. I don't want columnists popping out of my bathroom any more than you do."

Murt gave up. "The argument is entirely anticipatory," he pointed out. "The virus might turn out to be a batch of dormant German measles. Would you consider having dinner with me tonight?"

"Why?" She shot the question back at him like a rebounding tennis ball. "Answer that first!"

Murt opened his mouth. He could not recall ever hearing

such a rude rejoinder to an invitation to dinner. Not that there had been a plethora of amenities between them, but this was unthinkable! The question was, why *should* she have dinner with him? Give her eight good reasons. What was his motive in asking her? In one word, *why?*

Murt searched her face, but only a quiet interest showed in her expression.

"Why does any man invite any woman to dinner?" he countered.

"You aren't *any* man, Dr. Murt. Nor am I *any* woman. I want your specific reason for inviting me to dinner. Is it to discuss professional matters or—what?"

"Good Lord, Dr. Sutton!" He followed her lead in using the formal address. "Man is a social animal! I would enjoy your company at dinner, that's all. At least, I thought I would."

She looked at him unrelentingly. "If the talk will be about baseball, books or billiards, I'm for it. If it's to be moonlight, roses and dimmed lights—no sale."

It was like asking one's grandfather for a date. His regard for her highly professional approach turned to resentment. After all, she was a woman, a woman who persisted in belting her smock too tightly and wearing sheer nylons. Why this absurd revulsion at his casual acknowledgment of her sex?

He almost withdrew the invitation, but changed his mind at the last moment. "You name the place and the subject for conversation."

She nodded. "Very well, I'll pick you up at seven."

He had his date—with an emancipated female, and she didn't let him forget it during the whole meal. The restaurant she picked was expensive, but about as romantic as a bus depot. She ordered beer instead of a cocktail, toyed wordlessly with a $5.00 steak, and argued over the check.

Only as they were preparing to leave did she betray a sign of femininity. A platinum blonde, two tables away, had been eying Murt. Suddenly, she lurched to her feet without a word to her escort, staggered over to the pathologist, slurred, "You're what I've b'n lookin' for all m'life," and planted a wet alcoholic kiss on his mouth before he could defend himself.

Her escort peeled her away with sad-eyed apologies. There was no jealousy or anger in his face, only a deep hurt. "She— she isn't well, I think," he said. "You know, this new— whatever it is that's going around."

Murt wiped off the lipstick and looked at Phyllis, expecting to find at best sardonic amusement, but she seemed pale and annoyed.

"I'm sorry I brought you here," she said.

"Think nothing of it," Murt told her. "You heard the man. This is what's going around. Do you think I'll catch it?"

Phyllis wasn't amused. She did let him ride the taxi to her apartment, but bade him a terse good-by at the door.

Except for the incident of the blonde and Phyl's reaction, the evening had been a bust. Murt wondered how he had ever visualized her as a warm-blooded, responsive female. He smiled at the evening of torment she had once given him.

She was entirely frigid or else so leery of men that she might as well have been one herself.

IV

The following morning, he presided at a specialists' conference at the hospital, during which he revealed the results of the blood research. They had all read the Health Service bulletin and were sharply interested in the photomicrographs.

When the meeting was over, Feldman, the bacteriologist, and Stitchell, an endocrinologist, volunteered to work with Murt. They gave Phyllis' "gland-irritation" theory more credence than Murt. He outlined a program. Both agreed to take the problem back to their own departments.

The conference set Murt behind in his work and he spoke scarcely five words to his assistant until he was ready to leave. As he finished scrubbing up, she handed him an early edition of the *Times.*

"Local Doctor Isolates Love Bug!" The story was sketchy and not half so positive as the headline, but it did name him and High Dawn Hospital, and described the new virus.

He stared at Phyllis Sutton. "Did you—"

"Of course not. The reporters were here, but I sent them away. I told them we were medicine men, not tobacco men."

"Your name isn't even mentioned," he said suspiciously.

"You signed the report to the Health Service," she pointed out. "The leak probably came at that end." She put her hand on his arm. "It wasn't your fault."

His fury cooled as he noted her gesture. Then she realized that he was looking down at her hand and withdrew it quickly.

The next few days were blindly busy. A note from the government acknowledged receipt of his report and pictures, and was followed by a message that the virus could not be identified. The implication was that there was a strong possibility that it was the causative factor in the new *malaise*.

Murt devoted more attention to the joint laboratory work on the virus. The newspapers continued to come up with confidential information they shouldn't have had, and they dubbed the Love Bug, *Murt's Virus*. The name stuck, and the pathologist found himself famous overnight.

Phyllis continued to force all the credit upon him, on threat of transferring out if he violated her confidence. Except for the nuisance of dodging reporters, the accolade was not entirely unpleasant.

His pictures—old ones, Lord knew where they had dug them up—began appearing in the papers. Instead of reproving him, the hospital board voted him a substantial salary increase and gave him a free hand in directing the research. A government grant was obtained to supplement his budget, and the work picked up speed.

Necessarily, the lead that Phyllis Sutton's early research had given them on the rest of the medical world was maintained largely because of the time lag in disseminating the information contained in Murt's report, and the additional time it took for other clinical laboratories to confirm it.

Cages of experimental animals began arriving along with several additional specialists. Ebert Industrial Labs, contrite over the original information leak, made available their electron microscope, and Murt assigned the new toxicologist to work over there with Feldman, the bacteriologist, studying ways to weaken or destroy the virus.

Stitchell, the endocrinologist, and a trio of psychologists from the State University began injecting monkeys with virus when Feldman found he could propagate it in sterile medium.

On September 12, 1981, Dr. Sylvester Murt became a victim of the virus which bore his name.

He had slept poorly and he awakened feeling empty. His first dismal thought was that Phyl wouldn't be at the hospital this morning. He had told her to spend a few hours down at Ebert Labs, getting notes on their progress.

As he shaved, dressed and breakfasted, this thought preyed on his mind. It wasn't until he had put in half the morning clock-watching and door-gazing that he stepped outside his wretchedness and took an objective look at his feelings.

It wasn't that he missed her help—he had plenty of personnel at his disposal now. He simply longed for the sight of her, for the sound of her voice and her heels clipping busily around his office-lab.

Here we go again, he thought, and then he came up short. The feeling was similar to the silly evening of infatuation he had allowed himself, but it was intensified tenfold. The burn in his stomach was almost painful. He caught himself sighing like a frustrated poet, and he grew to hate the sight of the hall door, through which she kept right on not appearing.

When she failed to show up by 11:30, and he gagged over his lunch, he knew he was sick.

He had Murt's Virus!

Now what? Did knowing you had it make it any easier? Easier to make a damned fool of himself, he supposed. He'd have to take hold of himself or he'd scare her off the grounds.

At the thought of her leaving him for good, something like a dull crosscut saw hacked across his diaphragm, and he dropped his forkful of potato salad.

Back at his office, he diluted 30 cc of pure grain alcohol with water and swallowed it. Some of the distress and anxiety symptoms were relieved, and he bent determinedly to his work.

When her distinctive steps finally came through the door, he refused to raise his head from the binocular microscope. "How are they making out over there?" he mumbled.

"It's slow," she said, dropping her notes on his desk. "They're halfway through the sulfas so far. No results yet."

Relief at having her near him again was so great, it was almost frightening. But he gained equal pleasure from finding his self-control adequate to keep from raising his head and devouring her with his eyes.

"Sylvester," her voice came from behind his stool, "if you don't mind, I'd rather not go over there again."

"Why not?"

Her voice was strangely soft. "Because I—I missed . . ."

At that instant, her hand rested on his shoulder and it sent a charge of high voltage through him. He stiffened.

"*Don't do that!*" he said sharply.

He could see her reflection dimly in the window glass. She took a step backward. "What's the matter, Sylvester?"

He fought back the confusion in his brain, considered explaining that he was making a fine adjustment on the scope. But he didn't. He turned and let her have it. "Because I've got the virus," he said in a flat voice. "And the object of my affection—or infected, overstimulated glands—is *you!*"

"Oh, dear! That blonde at the restaurant . . ." Phyl's face was pale, but she composed her features quickly. "Do you want me to leave?"

"Lord no! That magnifies the symptoms. Stay with me and —and just be yourself. I won't bother you. If I lay a finger on you, clobber me."

"Have you had your blood tested?"

"I don't have to. I've got all the symp—"

He broke off, realizing that he was taking for granted that the new virus *was* the cause of his feeling. Clinically, this was nowhere near proved yet. Slowly he rolled up his sleeve above the elbow. He dipped a swatch of gauze in alcohol and swabbed a vein.

"All right, Phyl, you're the doctor. Make with the syringe."

By nightfall, Murt came to understand the reasons for the

increase in industrial accidents, absenteeism and the rest of the social effects of the "mild" epidemic. Phyllis Sutton was in his mind constantly. He deliberately did not look at her. But he was aware of her every movement, the texture and shape of her hand when she handed him a slide, the scent of her powder, the sound of her heels.

When she left the room, he found himself awaiting her return and conjecturing on what she was doing every moment. Not that it was difficult to adjust his behavior—no, that was relatively easy. All he had to do was think about every remark he made to her, censoring word, inflection and tone of voice—and, by keeping his back to her, it was easy to prevent his eyes from darting glances at her profile and staring at the curve of her hip below the tight belt.

By staying busy, he fought off the depression until he left for the club, when it closed in on him like an autumn fog. He stopped at the club bar.

Curly, the bald-headed bartender, eyed him curiously when he ordered a double Scotch.

"Heavy going down at the hospital these days?" Curly asked.

Murt envied him his relaxed, carefree expression. He nodded. "Pretty busy. I suppose you're catching it, too. Lot of people drowning their sorrows these days?"

Curly looked up at the clock. "You said it! In about a half hour, the place'll be loaded. This epidemic is going to run the distilleries dry if it doesn't end pretty soon."

"Does liquor help any?"

"Seems to—a little. It's the damnedest thing! Everybody's in love with the wrong people—I mean ten times as bad as usual. Of course, not everybody. Take my wife—she's got it bad, but she's still in love with *me*. So it could be worse."

"What do you mean?" Murt asked, raising his head.

"I mean it's bad enough for the poor woman to have the guy she wants. It's the jealousy angle. Every minute I'm away, she sits at home wondering if I'm faithful. Calls me up six times a shift. I don't dare take her out anyplace. Every time another female comes in sight, she starts worrying. Kate's a damned good wife, always has been, or I wouldn't be putting up with it. That's what's happening to a lot of marriages. Some guys get fed up and start looking around. About that time, the bug bites *them* and look out, secretary!"

"But it's not her fault," Murt said emphatically.

"I know," Curly shrugged. "A lot of people don't make any allowances for it, though. You know Peter, the elevator boy? He and his wife both got it. For a while it was okay, but I guess they finally drove themselves nuts, keeping tabs on each other. Now they can't stand to be together and they can't stand to be apart. Poor joker ran the cage past the basement limit-switch three times today and had to be bailed out of the shaft. Mr. Johnson said he'd fire him if he could get another boy."

The implication was shocking to Murt. He had supposed that unhappiness would stem principally from cases of unrequited love, such as his own, but it was apparent that the disease magnified the painful aspects of mutual love as well. Over-possessiveness and jealousy were common reefs of marriage, so it was hardly illogical that the divorce courts were as busy as the marriage license bureaus, after all.

It helped a little to immerse himself in the troubles of others, but, after another double Scotch, he went to his apartment and immediately fell into despondency. The desire to phone Phyllis was almost overpowering, though he knew talking to her wouldn't help. Instead, he dressed and went to dinner. The club boasted a fine chef, but the food tasted like mucilage.

Later, he went to the bar and drank excessively. Yet he had to take a sedative to get to sleep.

He awoke in a stupor at ten o'clock. His phone was jangling persistently. It was Phyllis Sutton, and her face showed sharp concern.

"Are you all right, Sylvester?"

For a moment his hangover dominated, but then it all came back. "Good morning! I'm *great*!" he moaned.

"Stitchell and the new toxicologist think they have something to report," she said.

"So do I. Alcohol is positively not the answer."

"This is important. Your suggestion on the sulfa series seems to have paid off."

"I'll be right over," he said, "as soon as I amputate my head."

"Come down to the zoo. I'll be there."

The thought of a remedy that might relieve him was a fair hangover cure. He dressed quickly and even managed to swallow a little coffee and toast.

V

At the hospital, he went directly to the "zoo" in the basement. A knot of personnel, including Phyllis, Peterson, the toxicologist, and Feldman, opened to admit him to the cage under their inspection. A quick glance at the control cages showed no change in the undoctored monkeys. Males and females were paired off, huddling together miserably, chittering and sadly rubbing their heads together. Each couple eyed the other couples suspiciously. Even here, the overpossessiveness was evident, and Murt cringed from the pitiful, disconsolate expressions.

The cage before him, however, appeared normally animated. The monks were feeding and playing happily. Feldman was grinning. "Had to try a new derivative, Sylvester, but the sulfa series was the right approach."

Murt stared at the cage, red-eyed. "Hadn't realized you succeeded in producing the symptoms in monkeys."

Phyllis said, "Why, I gave you that report yester—" She broke off with an understanding glance.

Peterson was exclaiming, "I never saw such a rapid-acting remedy! And so far, there's no evidence of toxic effect."

"It must absorb directly into the gland tissue," Feldman added. "Hardly had time to materially reduce the virus content significantly."

Murt murmured words of congratulations to them, turned on his heel and stalked out. Phyllis followed him to his office.

"Get me some of the stuff and notes on the dosages they administered," he ordered.

"Certainly," she said. "But why didn't you ask—*Dr. Murt, you aren't going to try it on yourself?*"

"Why not?" he barked hoarsely.

"It'll be weeks before we can determine if it's safe," she protested, horrified.

"We haven't got weeks. People are falling apart. This thing's contagious."

Even while Murt said it, he felt it was the wrong approach. He knew his own perspective was shot, but Phyllis would probably try to protect him against himself.

She did not. Instead, her face softened with sympathy and something else he refused to identify. She said, "I'll be right back."

The pressure in his head throbbed down his neck into his body. He wanted her so much, it was difficult to resist following her out into the hall. She returned in a few minutes with a 500-cc glass-stoppered reagent bottle half full of a milky fluid.

"Oral administration?" he asked.

She nodded. "Fifteen cc for the monkeys."

She secured a small beaker and a tapered graduate from the glassware cabinet and set them before him. He poured 50 cc into the graduated measure and transferred it to the beaker.

"What do they call it?" he asked.

"Sulfa-tetradine," she replied. One of a series Peterson was testing. There is no physiological data on it yet. All he knows is that it inhibited the virus in culture. So they tried it on the monkeys."

Murt raised the beaker to his lips. It was against every sensible tenet of scientific procedure. He was amazed that Phyllis was silent as he swallowed the bland, chalky fluid. He heard a clink. Turning, he saw her raising the graduate to her lips. In it was a like quantity of sulfa-tetradine.

"What are you doing?" he half-shouted. "We don't need a test-control!"

"I'm not a control," she said softly, touching her lips with a scrap of gauze. "I've had the virus for months."

He stared at her unbelievingly. "How do you know?"

"One of the first test samples was my own blood," she said. "You saw it. It was one of the twelve positive."

"But the symptoms—you don't show a sign of—"

"Thanks," she said. "I started to break down yesterday, but you didn't notice. You see, you are my fixation and when you told me that you had it, too, I—"

"*Your* fixation!" The beaker slipped from his fingers and smashed to the tile. "*You're in love with me?*"

Her arms hung loosely at her sides and tears rimmed her eyes. "Pathologically or otherwise, I've been a case since before I started the blood tests."

They moved together and clung to each other. "Phyl, Phyl —why didn't you tell me?"

Fiercely, she closed his lips with her own, and her fingers dug deeply into his shoulders. His arms pulled her closer yet, trying to fill the void in him that was greater than the Universe. For a long minute, the knowledge of her love and physical contact with her straining body dispelled the bleak loneliness.

When their lips parted, they gasped for breath.

It was no good. It was like tearing at an itching insect bite with your fingernails. The relief was only momentary, and it left the wound bleeding and more irritated than ever. Even if they were married—look at Peter at the club—Peter and his wife, mutually in love and completely miserable. It wasn't normal love. It was the damned virus!

As well argue with gravity. He tried to tell her, but he couldn't make her understand. Her restraint had been magnificent, but when the dam broke, it was beyond stopping the flood of her emotion. And now he couldn't believe it himself. Nothing this wonderful could be destroyed by mere misunderstanding. He cursed the years of his celibacy. All that time wasted—lost!

It was six o'clock before they reached her apartment. The License Bureau had been a mob scene. Hours more, upstairs in the City Hall waiting for the judge, while they held hands like a pair of college sophomores, staring into each others' eyes, drinking, drinking the elixir of adoration with a thirst that wouldn't be sated.

Phyllis weakened first. In the cab, after the ceremony, she released his hand and wiped her damp forehead.

Then, in the elevator, Murt felt himself relaxing. The alchemy of sustained passion had exhausted them both, he decided.

As Phyllis slipped the key in the door, she looked up at him in surprise. "Do you know, I'm hungry. I'm starved—for the first time in months."

Murt discovered his own stomach was stirring with a prosaic pangful demand of its own. "We should have stopped to eat," he said, realizing they had forgotten lunch.

"*Steaks!* I have some beauties in my freezer!" Phyllis exclaimed. They peeled off their coats and she led him into the small kitchen. She pointed at the cupboard and silverware drawer. "Set the table. We'll eat in five minutes."

Slipping into an apron, she explored the freezer for meat and French fries, dropped them into the HF cooker and set the timer for 90 seconds. When it clicked off, she was emptying a transparent sack of prepared salad into a bowl.

"Coffee will be ready in 50 seconds, so let's eat," she announced.

For minutes, they ate silently, ravenously, face to face in the little breakfast nook. Murt had forgotten the pure animal pleasure of satisfying a neglected appetite, and so, apparently, had his wife.

Wife! The thought jolted him.

Their eyes met, and he knew that the same thing was in her mind.

The sulfa-tetradine!

With the edge barely off his hunger, he stopped eating. She did, too. They sipped the steaming coffee and looked at each other.

"I—feel better," Phyllis said at last.

"So do I."

"I mean—I feel differently."

He studied her face. It was new. The tenseness was gone

and it was a beautiful face, with soft lips and intelligent eyes. But now the eyes were merely friendly.

And it aroused no more than a casual pleasure in him, the pleasure of viewing a lovely painting or a perfect sunset. A peaceful intellectual rapport settled over them, inducing a physical lethargy. They spoke freely of their sensations, of the hypo-adrenal effects, and wondered that there was no unpleasant reaction. They decided that, initially at least, sulfa-tetradine was a miraculous success. Murt thought he should go back to the hospital and work out a report right away.

Phyllis agreed and offered to accompany him, but he said she had better get a night's sleep. The next day would be hectic.

After four hours at his desk, he called a taxi and, without hesitation, gave the address of his club. Not until he fell wearily into bed did he remember it was his wedding night.

By mutual agreement, the marriage was annulled the next day.

Feldman and Peterson were gratified at the efficacy of their drug, but both were horrified that Murt had chosen to experiment on himself. As usual, Phyl had insisted on being left out of the report.

After a week of close observation, one of the monkeys was chloroformed and tissue-by-tissue examination was made by an army of histologists. Blood samples showed completely clear of the virus, as did a recheck on Murt's own blood. No deleterious effects could be detected, so the results were published through the Government Health Service.

It was the day before Christmas before Dr. Sylvester Murt first noticed the approaching symptoms of a relapse, or reinfection—he couldn't guess which. The past weeks had been pleasantly busy and, as acclaimed authority on Murt's virus, he had had little time to think subjectively about his experience.

Sulfa-tetradine was now considered the specific for the affliction and was being produced and shipped by the carload all over the world. The press had over-generously insisted on giving him all the credit for the remedy as well as the isolation of the disease virus. He was an international hero.

The warning of another attack came to him at 3:30 in the afternoon, when Phyllis Sutton was leaving. She stuck her head back in the door and gave him an uncommonly warm smile and cried, "Merry Christmas, Doctor!"

He waved at her and, as the door closed, caught his breath. There was the burn in his stomach again. It passed away and he refused to give it further thought.

His own cab wound its way through the heavy Christmas Eve traffic an hour before store-closing time. Finally, the vehicle stalled in a jam. It was only six blocks to his club, so Murt paid off the driver and walked.

Part of his strategy of bachelorhood had been to ignore Christmas and the other sentimental seasons, when loneliness costs many a man his independence. But now it was impossible to ignore the snowflakes, the bustling, package-laden crowds and the street-corner Santa Clauses with their tinkling bells.

He found himself staring into department store windows at the gay decorations.

A pair of shimmering, nearly invisible nylons caught his eye. They were the most impalpable of substances, only their bare outline visible against the white background.

He thought of Phyllis and, on impulse, went into the store and bought a pair. The clerk had to pick a size at random for him. Outside, on the sidewalk, he stared at the prettily gift-wrapped package and finally acknowledged the tremor, the tension and the old ache in the region of his diaphragm.

Relapse!

He plodded three slushy blocks up a side-street before he found a cab. He gave Phyllis Sutton's address to the driver and sank back in the taxi as a wave of weakness overcame him. What if she weren't home? It was Christmas Eve. She would probably be visiting friends or relatives.

But she wasn't. She opened the door under his impatient knock, and her eyes widened cordially.

"Sylvester!" she exclaimed. "Merry Christmas! Is that for me?" She pointed to the package, clutched forgotten in his hands.

"Merry, hell!" he said dispiritedly. "I came to warn you to look out for a relapse. Mine's been coming on all day."

She drew him inside, made him take off his coat and sit down before she acknowledged his remark. The apartment was cozy, with a tiny Christmas tree decorated in the window. She returned from the hall closet and sat beside him.

"Look what I did—on impulse," he said and tossed the package on her lap. "That's what really turned it on."

She opened the nylons and looked up at him sideways.

He continued unhappily, "I saw them in a window. Made me think of you, and about that time the seizure began. I tried to kid myself that I was just getting you a little token of—of my esteem, but the symptoms are almost as bad as before already."

Apparently she refused to accept the seriousness of the situation. Her smile was fatuous, he thought, kissably fatuous.

"Don't you realize what this means?" he demanded. "Peterson and Feldman turned up a very distressing fact. Sulfatetradine deposits out in the endocrines, so a single dose is all a person can take. This relapse of mine means we have it all to do over again."

"Think, Dr. Murt! Just think a minute," she urged.

"About what?"

"If the sulfa deposits out in the very glands it's there to protect, how could you be suffering another attack?"

His arms ached to reach out and emphasize his argument. "I don't know. All I know is how I feel. In a way, this is even worse, because—"

"I know," Phyllis said and perversely moved close to him. "My relapse came last Tuesday when I bought you a tie for Christmas. I sent a blood sample over to Ebert Labs right away. And do you know what?"

"What?" Murt asked in a bewildered fog.

"It was negative. I don't have Murt's Virus." She slipped an arm around his waist and put her head on his shoulder. "All I've got is Murt himself."

BEDSIDE MANNER

William Morrison

Nothing new under the sun? Surgery with anesthesia is not much more than a century old; antibiotics less than a quarter-century. Within these short periods, we have learned more about mending the body and the mind than was known during the previous written history of man. So—why not imagine a truly advanced medical science, from a star culture eons older than ours? It would be as far ahead of the medicine imagined in Cyril Kornbluth's future of our own planet (see page 163) as his "little black bag" would be an improvement on the healing art as we know it today.

Bedside Manner

SHE AWOKE, and didn't even wonder where she was.

First there were feelings—a feeling of existence, a sense of still being alive when she should be dead, an awareness of pain that made her body its playground.

After that, there came a thought. It was a simple thought, and her mind blurted it out before she could stop it: *Oh, God, now I won't even be plain any more. I'll be ugly.*

The thought sent a wave of panic coursing through her, but she was too tired to experience any emotion for long, and she soon drowsed off.

Later, the second time she awoke, she wondered where she was.

There was no way of telling. Around her all was black and quiet. The blackness was solid, the quiet absolute. She was aware of pain again—not sharp pain this time, but dull, spread throughout her body. Her legs ached; so did her arms. She tried to lift them, and found to her surprise that they did not respond. She tried to flex her fingers, and failed.

She was paralyzed. She could not move a muscle of her body.

The silence was so complete that it was frightening. Not a whisper of sound reached her. She had been on a spaceship, but none of a ship's noises came to her now. Not the creak of an expanding joint, nor the occasional slap of metal on metal. Not the sound of Fred's voice, nor even the slow rhythm of her own breathing.

It took her a full minute to figure out why, and when she had done so she did not believe it. But the thought persisted, and soon she knew that it was true.

The silence was complete because she was deaf.

Another thought: The blackness was so deep because she was blind.

And still another, this time a questioning one: Why, if she could feel pain in her arms and legs, could she not move them? What strange form of paralysis was this?

271

She fought against the answer, but slowly, inescapably, it formed in her mind. She was not paralyzed at all. She could not move her arms and legs because she had none. The pains she felt were phantom pains, conveyed by the nerve endings without an external stimulus.

When this thought penetrated, she fainted. Her mind sought in unconsciousness to get as close to death as it could.

When she awoke, it was against her will. She sought desperately to close her mind against thought and feeling, just as her eyes and ears were already closed.

But thoughts crept in despite her. Why was she alive? Why hadn't she died in the crash?

Fred must certainly have been killed. The asteroid had come into view suddenly; there had been no chance of avoiding it. It had been a miracle that she herself had escaped, if escape it could be called—a mere sightless, armless and legless torso, with no means of communication with the outside world, she was more dead than alive. And she could not believe that the miracle had been repeated with Fred.

It was better that way. Fred wouldn't have to look at her and shudder—and he wouldn't have to worry about himself, either. He had always been a handsome man, and it would have killed him a second time to find himself maimed and horrible.

She must find a way to join him, to kill herself. It would be difficult, no doubt, without arms or legs, without any way of knowing her surroundings; but sooner or later she would think of a way. She had heard somewhere of people strangling themselves by swallowing their own tongues, and the thought cheered her. She could at least try that right now. She could—

No, she couldn't. She hadn't realized it before, but she had no tongue.

She didn't black out at this sudden awareness of a new horror, although she desperately wanted to. She thought: *I can make an effort of will, I can force myself to die. Die, you fool, you helpless lump of flesh. Die and end your torture, die, die, die . . .*

But she didn't. And after a while, a new thought came to

her: She and Fred had been the only ones on their ship; there had been no other ship near them. Who had kept her from dying? Who had taken her crushed body and stopped the flow of blood and tended her wounds and kept her alive? And for what purpose?

The silence gave no answer. Nor did her own mind.

After an age, she slept again.

When she awoke, a voice said, "Do you feel better?"

I can hear! She shouted to herself. *It's a strange voice, a most unusual accent. I couldn't possibly have imagined it. I'm not deaf! Maybe I'm not blind either! Maybe I just had a nightmare—*

"I know that you cannot answer. But do not fear. You will soon be able to speak again."

Who was it? Not a man's voice, nor a woman's. It was curiously hoarse, and yet clear enough. Uninflected, and yet pleasant. A doctor? Where could a doctor have come from?

"Your husband is also alive. Fortunately, we reached both of you at about the time death had just begun."

Fortunately? She felt a flash of rage. *You should have let us die. It would be bad enough to be alive by myself, a helpless cripple dependent upon others. But to know that Fred is alive too is worse. To know that he has a picture of me like this, ugly and horrifying, is more than I can stand. With any other man it would be bad enough, but with Fred it's unendurable. Give me back the ability to talk, and the first thing I'll ask of you is to kill me. I don't want to live.*

"It may reassure you to know that there will be no difficulty about recovering the use of the limbs proper to you, and the organs of sensation. It will take time, but there is no doubt about the final outcome."

What nonsense, she asked herself, was this? Doctors had done wonders in the creation and fitting of artificial arms and legs, but he seemed to be promising her the use of *real* limbs. And he had said, "organs of sensation." That didn't sound as if he meant that she'd see and hear electronically. It meant—

Nonsense. He was making a promise he couldn't keep. He was just saying that to make her feel better, the way doctors did. He was saying it to give her courage, keep her morale up, make her feel that it was worth fighting. But it *wasn't* worth fighting. She had no courage to keep up. She wanted only to die.

"Perhaps you have already realized that I am not what you would call human. However, I suggest that you do not worry too much about that. I shall have no difficulty in reconstructing you properly according to your own standards."

Then the voice ceased, and she was left alone. It was just as well, she thought. He had said too much. And she couldn't answer, nor ask questions of her own . . . and she had so many.

He wasn't human? Then what was he? And how did he come to speak a human language? And what did he mean to do with her after he had reconstructed her? And what would she look like after she was reconstructed?

There were races, she knew, that had no sense of beauty. Or if they had one, it wasn't like a human sense of beauty. Would he consider her properly reconstructed if he gave her the right number of arms and legs, and artificial organs of sight that acted like eyes—and made her look like some creature out of Hell? Would he be proud of his handiwork, as human doctors had been known to be, when their patients ended up alive and helpless, their bodies scarred, their organs functioning feebly and imperfectly? Would he turn her into something that Fred would look at with abhorrence and disgust?

Fred had always been a little too sensitive to beauty in women. He had been able to pick and choose at his will, and until he had met her he had always chosen on the basis of looks alone. She had never understood why he had married her. Perhaps the fact that she was the one woman he knew who *wasn't* beautiful had made her stand out. Perhaps, too, she told herself, there was a touch of cruelty in his choice. He might have wanted someone who wasn't too sure of herself, someone he could count on under all circumstances. She remembered how people had used to stare at them—the handsome man and the plain woman—and then whisper among themselves, wondering openly how he had ever come to marry her. Fred had liked that; she was sure he had liked that.

He had obviously *wanted* a plain wife. Now he would have an ugly one. Would he want *that?*

She slept on her questions, and waked and slept repeatedly. And then, one day, she heard the voice again. And to her surprise, she found that she could answer back—slowly, uncertainly, at times painfully. But she could speak once more.

"We have been working on you," said the voice. "You are coming along nicely."

"Am I—am I—" she found difficulty asking: "How do I look?"

"Incomplete."

"I must be horrible."

A slight pause. "No. Not horrible at all. Not to me. Merely incomplete."

"My husband wouldn't think so."

"I do not know what your husband would think. Perhaps he is not used to seeing incomplete persons. He might even be horrified at the sight of himself."

"I—I hadn't thought of that. But he—we'll both be all right?"

"As a medical problem, you offer no insuperable difficulty. None at all."

"Why—why don't you give me eyes, if you can? Are you afraid—afraid that I might see you and find you—terrifying?"

Again a pause. There was amusement in the reply. "I do not think so. No, that is not the reason."

"Then it's because—as you said about Fred—I might find myself horrifying?"

"That is part of the reason. Not the major part, however. You see, I am, in a way, experimenting. Do not be alarmed, please—I shall not turn you into a monster. I have too much knowledge of biology for that. But I am not too familiar with human beings. What I know I have learned mostly from your books, and I have found that in certain respects there are inaccuracies contained in them—I must go slowly until I can check what they say. I might mend certain organs, and then discover that they do not have the proper size or shape, or that they produce slightly altered hormones. I do not want to make such mistakes, and if I do make them, I wish to correct them before they can do harm."

"There's no danger—?"

"None, I assure you. Internally and externally, you will be as before."

"Internally and externally. Will I—will I be able to have children?"

"Yes. We ourselves do not have your distinctions of sex, but we are familiar with them in many other races. We know how important you consider them. I am taking care to see that the proper glandular balance is maintained in both yourself and your husband."

"Thank you—Doctor. But I still don't understand—why don't you give me eyes right away?"

"I do not wish to give you eyes that see imperfectly, and then be forced to take them away. Nor do I want you to watch imperfect arms and legs developing. It would be an unnecessary ordeal. When I am sure that everything is as it should be, then I shall start your eyes."

"And my husband—"

"He will be reconstructed in the same way. He will be brought in to talk to you soon."

"And you don't want either of us to see the other in—in imperfect condition?"

"It would be inadvisable. I can assure you now that when I have completed your treatment you will almost exactly be as you were in the beginning. When that time comes you will be able to use your eyes."

She was silent a moment.

He said, "Your husband had other questions. I am waiting to hear you ask them too."

"I'm sorry, Doctor . . . I wasn't listening. What did you say?"

He repeated his remarks, and she said, "I do have other questions. But—no, I won't ask them yet. What did my husband want to know?"

"About me and my race. How we happened to find you in time to save you. *Why* we saved you. What we intend to do with you after you are reconstructed."

"Yes, I've wondered about those things too."

"I can give you only a partial answer. I hope you do not find it too unsatisfactory. My race, as you may have gathered, is somewhat more advanced than yours. We have had a head start," he added politely.

"If you can grow new arms and legs and eyes," she said, "you must be thousands of years ahead of us."

"We can do many other things, of which there is no need to talk. All I need say now is that I am a physician attached to a scouting expedition. We have had previous contact with human beings, and have taken pains to avoid coming to their attention. We do not want to alarm or confuse them."

"But all the same, you rescued us."

"It was an emergency. We are not human, but we have, you might say, humanitarian feelings. We do not like to see creatures die, even inferior creatures—not that you are, of course," he added delicately. "Our ship happened to be only a few thousand miles away when it happened. We saw, and acted with great speed. Once you are whole again, we shall place you where you will be found by your own kind, and proceed on our way. By that time, our expedition will have been completed."

"When we are whole again—Doctor, will I be exactly the same as before?"

"In some ways, perhaps even better. I can assure you that all your organs will function perfectly."

"I don't mean that. I mean—will I look the same?"

She felt that there was astonishment in the pause. "Look the same? Does that matter?"

"Yes . . . oh, yes, it matters! It matters more than anything else."

He must have been regarding her as if she were crazy. Suddenly she was glad that she had no eyes to see his bewilderment. And his contempt, which, she was sure, must be there too.

He said slowly, "I didn't realize. But, of course, we don't know how you did look. How can we make you look the same?"

"I don't know. But you must! You must!" Her voice rose, and she felt the pain in her throat as the new muscles constricted.

"You are getting hysterical," he said. "Stop thinking about this."

"But I can't stop thinking about it. It's the only thing I *can* think of! I don't want to look any different from the way I did before!"

He said nothing, and suddenly she felt tired. A moment before she had been so excited, so upset; and now—merely tired and sleepy. She wanted to go to sleep and forget it all. *He must have given me a sedative,* she thought. *An injection? I didn't feel the prick of the needle, but maybe they don't use needles. Anyway, I'm glad he did. Because now I won't have to think, I won't be able to think—*

She slept. When she awoke again, she heard a new voice. A voice she couldn't place. It said, "Hello, Margaret. Where are you?"

"Who . . . Fred!"

"Margaret?"

"Y-yes."

"Your voice is different."

"So is yours. At first I couldn't think who was speaking to me!"

"It's strange it took us so long to realize that our voices would be different."

She said shakily, "We're more accustomed to thinking of how we look."

He was silent. His mind had been on the same thing.

"Your new voice isn't bad, Fred," she said after a moment. "I like it. It's a little deeper, a little more resonant. It will go well with your personality. The Doctor has done a good job."

"I'm trying to think whether I like yours. I don't know. I

suppose I'm the kind of guy who likes best what he's used to."

"I know. That's why I didn't want him to change my looks."

Again silence.

She said, "Fred?"

"I'm still here."

"Have you talked to him about it?"

"He's talked to me. He's told me about your being worried."

"Don't you think it matters?"

"Yes, I suppose it does. He told me he could do a good technical job—leave us with regular features and unblemished skins."

"That isn't what I want," she said fiercely. "I don't want the kind of regular features that come out of physiology books. I want my own features. I don't care so much about the voice, but I want my own face back!"

"That's a lot to ask for. Hasn't he done enough for us?"

"No. Nothing counts unless I have that. Do—do you think that I'm being silly?"

"Well—"

"I don't want to be beautiful, because I know you don't want me to be."

He sounded amazed. "Whoever told you that?"

"Do you think that after living with you for two years, I don't know? If you had wanted a beautiful wife, you'd have married one. Instead, you chose me. You wanted to be the good-looking one of the family. You're vain, Fred. Don't try to deny it, because it would be no use. You're vain. Not that I mind it, but you are."

"Are you feeling all right, Margaret? You sound—overwrought."

"I'm not. I'm being very logical. If I were either ugly or beautiful, you'd hate me. If I were ugly, people would pity you, and you wouldn't be able to stand that. And if I were beautiful, they might forget about you. I'm just plain enough for them to wonder why you ever married anyone so ordinary. I'm just the kind of person to supply background for you."

After a moment he said slowly, "I never knew you had ideas like that about me. They're silly ideas. I married you because I loved you."

"Maybe you did. But *why* did you love me?"

He said patiently, "Let's not go into that. The fact is, Margaret, that you're talking nonsense. I don't give a damn whether you're ugly or beautiful—well, no, that isn't strictly true. I do care—but looks aren't the most important thing. They have very little to do with the way I feel about you. I love you for the kind of person you are. Everything else is secondary."

"Please, Fred, don't lie to me. I want to be the same as before, because I know that's the way you want me. Isn't there some way to let the Doctor know what sort of appearance we made? You have—had—a good eye. Maybe you could describe us—"

"Be reasonable, Margaret. You ought to know that you can't tell anything from a description." His voice was almost pleading. "Let's leave well enough alone. I don't care if your features do come out of the pictures in a physiology textbook—"

"Fred!" she said excitedly. "That's it! Pictures! Remember that stereo shot we had taken just before we left Mars? It must be somewhere on the ship—"

"But the ship was crushed, darling. It's a total wreck."

"Not completely. If they could take *us* out alive, there must have been some unhurt portions left. Maybe the stereo is still there!"

"Margaret, you're asking the impossible. We don't know where the ship is. This group the Doctor is with is on a scouting expedition. The wreck of our ship may have been left far behind. They're not going to retrace their tracks just to find it."

"But it's the only way . . . the only way! There's nothing else—"

She broke down. If she had possessed eyes, she would have wept—but as it was, she could weep only internally.

They must have taken him away, for there was no answer to her tearless sobbing. And after a time, she felt suddenly that there was nothing to cry about. She felt, in fact, gay and cheerful—and the thought struck her: *The Doctor's given me another drug. He doesn't want me to cry. Very well, I won't. I'll think of things to make me happy, I'll bubble over with good spirits—*

Instead, she fell into a dreamless sleep.

When she awoke again, she thought of the conversation with Fred, and the feeling of desperation returned. *I'll have to tell the Doctor all about it,* she thought. *I'll have to see what he can do. I know it's asking an awful lot, but without it, all the rest he has done for me won't count. Better to be dead than be different from what I was.*

But it wasn't necessary to tell the Doctor. Fred had spoken to him first.

So Fred admits it's important too. He won't be able to deny any longer that I judged him correctly.

The Doctor said, "What you are asking is impossible."

"Impossible? You won't even try?"

"My dear patient, the wrecked ship is hundreds of millions of miles behind us. The expedition has its appointed task. It cannot retrace its steps. It cannot waste time searching the emptiness of space for a stereo which may not even exist any longer."

"Yes, you're right . . . I'm sorry I asked, Doctor."

He read either her mind or the hopelessness in her voice. He said, "Do not make any rash plans. You cannot carry them out, you know."

"I'll find a way. Sooner or later I'll find a way to do something to myself."

"You are being very foolish. I cannot cease to marvel at how foolish you are. Are many human beings like you, psychologically?"

"I don't know, Doctor. I don't care. I know only what's important to me!"

"But to make such a fuss about the merest trifle! The difference in appearance between one human being and another of the same sex, so far as we can see, is insignificant. You must learn to regard it in its true light."

"You think it's insignificant because you don't know anything about men and women. To Fred and me, it's the difference between life and death."

He said in exasperation, "You are a race of children. But sometimes even a child must be humored. I shall see what I can do."

But what could he do? she asked herself. The ship was a derelict in space, and in it, floating between the stars, was the stereo he wouldn't make an attempt to find. Would he try to get a description from Fred? Even the best human artist couldn't produce much of a likeness from a mere verbal description. What could someone like the Doctor do—someone to whom all men looked alike, and all women?

As she lay there, thinking and wondering, she had only the vaguest idea of the passage of time. But slowly, as what must have been day followed day, she became aware of strange tingling sensations all over her body. The pains she had felt at first had slowly diminished and then vanished altogether. What she felt now was not pain at all. It was even mildly pleasant, as if some one were gently massaging her body, stretching her muscles, tugging at her—

Suddenly she realized what it was: New limbs were growing. Her internal organs must have developed properly, and now the Doctor had gone ahead with the rest of his treatment.

With the realization, tears began to roll down her cheeks. *Tears,* she thought, *real tears—I can feel them. I'm getting arms and legs, and I can shed tears. But I still have no eyes.*

But maybe they're growing in . . . From time to time I seem to see flashes of light. Maybe he's making them develop slowly, and he put the tear ducts in order first. I'll have to tell him that my eyes must be blue. Maybe I never was beautiful, but I always had pretty eyes. I don't want any different color. They wouldn't go with my face.

The next time the Doctor spoke to her, she told him.

"You may have your way," he said good-naturedly, as if humoring a child.

"And, Doctor, about finding the ship again—"

"Out of the question, as I told you. However, it will not be necessary." He paused, as if savoring what he had to tell her. "I checked with our records department. As might have been expected, they searched your shattered ship thoroughly, in the hope of finding information that might contribute to our understanding of your race. They have the stereos, about a dozen of them."

"A *dozen* stereos? But I thought—"

"In your excitement, you may have forgotten that there were more than one. All of them seem to be of yourself and your husband. However, they were obviously taken under a wide variety of conditions, and with a wide variety of equipment, for there are certain minor differences between them which even I, with my non-human vision, can detect. Perhaps you can tell us which one you prefer us to use as a model."

She said slowly, "I had better talk about that with my husband. Can you have him brought in here, Doctor?"

"Of course."

She lay there, thinking. A dozen stereos. And there was still only one that she remembered. Only a single one. They had posed for others, during the honeymoon and shortly after, but those had been left at home on Mars before they started on their trip.

Fred's new voice said, "How are you feeling, dear?"

"Strange. I seem to have new limbs growing in."

"So do I. Guess we'll be our old selves pretty soon."

"Will we?"

She could imagine his forehead wrinkling at the intonation of her voice. "What do you mean, Margaret?"

"Hasn't the Doctor told you? They have the stereos they found on our ship. Now they can model our new faces after our old."

"That's what you wanted, isn't it?"

"But what do *you* want, Fred? I remember only a single

one, and the Doctor says they found a dozen. And he says that my face differs from shot to shot."

Fred was silent.

"Are they as beautiful as all that, Fred?"

"You don't understand, Margaret."

"I understand only too well. I just want to know—were they taken before we were married or after?"

"Before, of course. I haven't gone out with another girl since our wedding."

"Thank you, dear." Her own new voice had venom in it, and she caught herself. *I musn't talk like that,* she thought. *I know Fred, I know his weakness. I knew them before I married him. I have to accept them and help him, not rant at him for them.*

He said, "They were just girls I knew casually. Good-looking, but nothing much otherwise. Not in a class with you."

"Don't apologize." This time her voice was calm, even amused. "You couldn't help attracting them. Why didn't you tell me that you kept their pictures?"

"I thought you'd be jealous."

"Perhaps I would have been, but I'd have got over it. Anyway, Fred, is there any one of them you liked particularly?"

He became wary, she thought. His voice was expressionless as he said, "No. Why?"

"Oh, I thought that perhaps you'd want the Doctor to make me look like her."

"Don't be silly, Margaret! I don't want you to look like anybody but yourself. I don't want to see their empty faces ever again!"

"But I thought—"

"Tell the Doctor to keep the other stereos. Let him put them in one of his museums, with other dead things. They don't mean anything to me any more. They haven't meant anything for a long time. The only reason I didn't throw them away is because I forgot they were there and didn't think of it."

"All right, Fred. I'll tell him to use our picture as a model."

"The AC studio shot. The close-up. Make sure he uses the right one."

"I'll see that there's no mistake."

"When I think I might have to look at one of *their* mugs for the rest of my life, I get a cold sweat. Don't take any chances, Margaret. It's your face I want to see, and no one else's."

"Yes, dear."

I'll be plain, she thought, *but I'll wear well. A background always wears well. Time can't hurt it much, because there's nothing there to hurt.*

There's one thing I overlooked, though. How old will we look? The Doctor is rather insensitive about human faces, and he might age us a bit. He mustn't do that. It'll be all right if he wants to make us a little younger, but not older. I'll have to warn him.

She warned him, and again he seemed rather amused at her.

"All right," he said, "you will appear slightly younger. Not too much so, however, for from my reading I judge it best for a human face to show not too great a discrepancy from the physiological age."

She breathed a sigh of relief. It was settled now, all settled. Everything would be as before—perhaps just a little better. She and Fred could go back to their married life with the knowledge that they would be as happy as ever. Nothing exuberant, of course, but as happy as their own peculiar natures permitted. As happy as a plain and worried wife and a handsome husband could ever be.

Now that this had been decided, the days passed slowly. Her arms and legs grew, and her eyes too. She could feel the beginnings of fingers and toes, and on the sensitive optic nerve the flashes of light came with greater and greater frequency. There were slight pains from time to time, but they were pains she welcomed. They were the pains of growth, of return to normalcy.

And then came the day when the Doctor said, "You have

recovered. In another day, as you measure time, I shall remove your bandages."

Tears welled up in her new eyes. "Doctor, I don't know how to thank you."

"No thanks are needed. I have only done my work."

"What will you do with us now?"

"There is an old freighter of your people which we have found abandoned and adrift. We have repaired it and stocked it with food taken from your own ship. You will awaken inside the freighter and be able to reach your own people."

"But won't I—can't I even get the chance to see you?"

"That would be inadvisable. We have some perhaps peculiar ideas about keeping our nature secret. That is why we shall take care that you carry away nothing that we ourselves have made."

"If I could only—well, even shake hands—do something—"

"I have no hands."

"No hands? But how could you—how can you—do such complicated things?"

"I may not answer. I am sorry to leave you in a state of bewilderment, but I have no choice. Now, please, no more questions about me. Do you wish to talk to your husband for a time before you sleep again?"

"Must I sleep? I feel so excited . . . I want to get out of bed, tear off my bandages, and see what I look like!"

"I take it that you are not anxious to speak to your husband yet."

"I want to see myself first!"

"You will have to wait. During your last sleep, your new muscles will be exercised, their tones and strength built up. You well receive a final medical examination. It is most important."

She started to protest once more, but he stopped her. "Try to be calm. I can control your feelings with drugs, but it is better that you control yourself. You will be able to give vent to your excitement later. And now I must leave you. You will not hear from me after this."

"Never again?"

"Never again. Goodbye."

For a moment she felt something cool and dry and rough laid very lightly against her forehead. She tried to reach for him, but could only twitch her new hands on her new wrists. She said, with a sob, "Goodbye, Doctor."

When she spoke again, there was no answer.

She slept.

This time, the awakening was different. Before she opened her eyes, she heard the creaking of the freighter, and a slight hum that might have come from the firing of the jets.

As she tried to sit up, her eyes flashed open, and she saw that she was lying in a bunk, strapped down to keep from being thrown out. Unsteadily, she began to loosen the straps. When they were half off, she stopped to stare at her hands. They were strong hands, well-shaped and supple, with a healthily tanned skin. She flexed them and unflexed them several times. Beautiful hands. The Doctor had done well by her.

She finished undoing the straps, and got to her feet. There was none of the dizziness she had expected, none of the weakness that would have been normal after so long a stay in bed. She felt fine.

She examined herself, staring at her legs, body—staring as she might have done at a stranger's legs and body. She took a few steps forward and then back. Yes, he had done well by her. It was a graceful body, and it felt fine. Better than new.

But her face!

She whirled around to locate a mirror, and heard a voice: "Margaret!"

Fred was getting out of another bunk. Their eyes sought each other's faces, and for a long moment they stared in silence.

Fred said in a choked voice, "There must be a mirror in the captain's cabin. I've got to see myself."

At the mirror, their eyes shifted from one face to the other and back again. And the silence this time was longer, more painful.

√

A wonderful artist, the Doctor. For a creature—a person—who was insensitive to the differences in human faces, he could follow a pattern perfectly. Feature by feature, they were as before. Size and shape of forehead, dip of hairline, width of cheeks and height of cheekbones, shape and color of eyes, contour of nose and lips and chin—nothing in the two faces had been changed. Nothing at all.

Nothing, that is, but the overall effect. Nothing but the fact that where before she had been plain, now she was beautiful.

I should have realized the possibility, she thought. *Sometimes you see two sisters, or mother and daughter, with the same features, the faces as alike as if they had been cast from the same mold—and yet one is ugly and the other beautiful. Many artists can copy features, but few can copy with perfect exactness either beauty or ugliness. The Doctor slipped up a little. Despite my warning, he's done too well by me.*

And not well enough by Fred. Fred isn't handsome any more. Not ugly really—his face is stronger and more interesting than it was. But now I'm the good-looking one of the family. And he won't be able to take it. This is the end for us.

Fred was grinning at her. He said, "Wow, what a wife I've got! Just look at you! Do you mind if I drool a bit?"

She said uncertainly, "Fred, dear, I'm sorry."

"For what? For his giving you more than you bargained for—and me less? It's all in the family!"

"You don't have to pretend, Fred. I know how you feel."

"You don't know a thing. I *asked* him to make you beautiful. I wasn't sure he could, but I asked him anyway. And he said he'd try."

"You *asked* him—oh, no!"

"Oh, yes," he said. "Are you sorry? I hoped he'd do better for me, but—well, did you marry me for my looks?"

"You know better, Fred!"

"I didn't marry you for yours either. I told you that before, but you wouldn't believe me. Maybe now you will."

Her voice choked. "Perhaps—perhaps looks aren't so important after all. Perhaps I've been all wrong about everything. I used to think was essential."

"You have," agreed Fred. "But you've always had a sense of inferiority about your appearance. From now on, you'll have no reason for that. And maybe now we'll both be able to grow up a little."

She nodded. It gave her a strange feeling to have him put around her a pair of arms she had never before known, to have him kiss her with lips she had never before touched. *But that doesn't matter*, she thought. *The important thing is that whatever shape we take, we're us. The important thing is that now we don't have to worry about ourselves—and for that we have to thank* him.

"Fred," she said suddenly, her face against his chest. "Do you think a girl can be in love with two—two people—at the same time? And one of them—one of them not a man? Not even human?"

He nodded, but didn't say anything. And after a moment, she thought she knew why. *A man can love that way too*, she thought—*and one of them not a woman, either*.

I wonder if he . . . she . . . it knew. I wonder if it knew.

THE SHOPDROPPER

Alan Nelson

In this, our second basically supernatural item (vide **Dr. Dance's** The Brothers) *we see our author taking an unfair swipe at psychoanalysts—fair game, indeed. We like it because it is such a tasty example of pot calling kettle black and getting potted as a reward. As background, you might like to know that* **Dr. Manly J. Departure** *first appeared in a lovely little item called* "Narapoia," *which told of the young man who was convinced that* he was following someone, *and that people were always plotting to* do him good. *As a result of his handling of the narapoiac, Dr. Departure himself had an enforced stay in a mental institution, but he came out of it well enough, as the following story indicates.*

The Shopdropper

"I'M A KLEPTO-KLEPTOMANIAC, Doctor." Dr. Manly J. Departure, bursting with vitamins and energy after his year's leave of absence, gazed with professional cordiality at the angular young man across the desk who was kneading preposterously long fingers and scowling.

"Well, that's not too serious, Mr. Flint," Dr. Departure replied, permitting himself an affable chuckle. "There seems to be a lot of kleptomania going around this season. As for the stuttering . . ."

Mr. Flint did not smile.

"Not kleptomania, Doctor. *Klepto*-kleptomania." The young man continued to massage his fingers as though smoothing out invisible wrinkles. "I steal only from other kleptomaniacs," he said earnestly.

Dr. Departure's chuckle dribbled away.

"If I understand you," Dr. Departure began very slowly, "you have a pathological impulse to steal. But instead of stealing from department stores as does the normal kleptom . . . rather, the *usual* kleptomaniac, you feel impelled to steal the things other kleptomaniacs have already stolen?"

"That's right," the man answered. "I sneak into their rooms when they're out. They're getting harder and harder to find, too. Of course it's all stuff I have no particular use for. Look!"

He reached down, hauled up a bulky paper sack and handed it across the desk. Dr. Departure opened it and extracted, among other things, an egg beater, a plastic thimble, a pencil sharpener, a bottle of permanent wave lotion and an ocarina.

"I just . . . just can't help myself, Doctor." Flint flexed his long lean fingers, frowned at them, then looked up once more at the doctor. "This urge I get—it's irresistible. And getting worse all the time. You've got to help me."

Dr. Departure laid the bag down and began running his finger over the small brass clock his wife had given him for

Christmas; it always steadied him to focus his attention a moment or so on the little instrument ticking off the dollars like a taxi meter. Presently he lifted his eyes and studied the man: thin pallid face, a shaving cut over the Adam's apple, conservative dresser. Nothing remarkable execpt his preoccupation with those very long fingers.

"Just a few routine questions, first," Dr. Departure said, picking up a pencil.

Flint, it turned out, was 37, graduated from high school, employed as an insurance clerk, unmarried. All very usual.

At the end of the hour the doctor arose and smiled reassuringly.

"Shall we say Tuesday at 10?" he said, seeing Flint to the door.

Shortly before 10 the following Tuesday, as Dr. Departure stepped out of the elevator to keep his appointment with Flint, he bumped into his brother-in-law, Dr. Bert Schnappenhocker, a tall, assertive psychiatrist with aggressive front teeth and iron gray hair, who specialized in rich divorcees, and whose very presence in the office adjoining his own caused Departure a kind of permanent, bristling hostility. If it weren't for the fact he was Emily's brother . . .

"Glad to see you back, Manly," Schnappenhocker boomed in that loathsome, hearty voice. "How'd they treat you at the asylum?"

"It was a rest home," Dr. Departure replied coldly, moving down the hall toward his own office.

"Well, if you begin to feel shaky again, feel free to drop in. Professional discount, of course." He laughed raucously and pounded Departure on the shoulder. "By the way, did I tell you I'm speaking before the Institute of Psychiatry banquet next month? Hope you can make it."

Quack! Dr. Departure muttered angrily, closing the door against Schnappenhocker's imbecilic and tuneless whistle outside. Then, shaking off his irritation, he called Flint in from the waiting room.

"Now!" he began brightly, after Flint seated himself and placed another bulky paper sack down beside the desk. "Now, about this . . . this kleptomania." He refused to utter that ridiculous word *klepto-kleptomania*. Since Flint's first visit, he'd been unable to find anything in the literature to cover the problem, but at length he reassured himself the thing wasn't as weird as it first appeared; after all, kleptomania was kleptomania, no matter who it was you stole from—possibly this man's case might be a little more complicated, that was all.

"I'd like you to start at the beginning, if you will, Mr. Flint, and tell me how this problem got started."

Flint looked troubled and poked the trinket-filled bag with his foot.

"It's the gloves," he said. "Never had any trouble until I started wearing the gloves. Then I began having this urge to snatch things off department store counters. Didn't take two weeks, though, until I couldn't get any kicks out of that any more. Then I started on the kleptos. . . ."

Dr. Departure smiled and felt the problem begin to unravel right then and there. So typical, this childish process of blaming inanimate objects for our own defects. Just last night his little niece had accused her rag doll of shattering the vase.

"Where are these gloves?" he inquired kindly.

Flint lifted his hands above the desk.

"I have them on," he said.

Dr. Departure blinked, leaned forward and gazed at the long, pink hands with the wrinkled knuckles, tapering fingers and well care-for finger nails. They were as naked as billiard balls.

"I don't see any gloves," the doctor said in a moment.

"I know," Flint replied evenly. "They're invisible."

Ah, the pieces are beginning to fall into place, Dr. Departure thought. A case of guilt projection complicated by delusionary ideas. Ten to one there will be some flights of fantasy involving sorcery showing up soon.

"Where did you get these . . . these gloves?" he asked in a soft persuasive voice.

"I bought them from a gypsy who bought them from a three-fingered Brazilian witch doctor named Bessie."

"And where did the witch doctor get them?"

"She brewed them out of a stunted guayule bush that had

been struck twice by lightning and injected three times with the blood of an insane virgin."

"And what was the . . . the purpose of these gloves?"

"To make it easier for the witch doctor's son to steal pigeon eggs." Flint looked away with troubled eyes. "The gloves are defective though. They're too strong."

This could go on forever, Dr. Departure thought sadly. If I ask him why he simply doesn't take the gloves off, he'll say he can't get them off.

"The worst of it is, Doctor—I can't get them off. See?" Flint raised one hand, plucked futilely at the pink skin with the thumb and forefinger of the other. Suddenly, he leaned across the desk confidentially. "There's only one way they'll come off, Doctor."

"And what's that?"

"First I have to find a witch doctor who ranks as high in *his* community as Bessie does in hers. That's you."

"Now, just a moment!" Dr. Departure protested huffily.

From his pocket Flint whipped a piece of paper and a small box of white powder which he laid before the doctor.

"Then I have to get you to sprinkle this powder over the gloves while saying these words and making a gesture like this. After that I can peel them right off."

"Please!" Dr. Departure said firmly, holding up his hand. He'd had quite enough of invisible gloves—except, of course, in a symbolic sense.

"Let me tell *you* how to get those . . . those invisible gloves off." He paused, polished his glasses, cleared his throat and glanced oratorically at the ceiling. "First, what do the gloves represent? Nothing more than . . ."

For a solid hour, Dr. Departure probed, prodded and pronounced. He spoke eloquently on phobias; on fantasies; on fixations; and the little brass clock jumped when he pounded the table for emphasis. Flint watched and listened intently, then at last when Dr. Departure paused to wipe his forehead and glance significantly at his watch, he leaned forward.

"That's all very well, Doctor," he said. "But are you, or are you not, going to cast this spell?"

These things take time, Dr. Departure told himself wearily. Time and patience . . .

"Because if you're not," Flint continued, half rising from the chair. "I'm going some place else. There's another man down the hall here. A Dr. Schnapp . . . Schnappen . . ."

Hastily, Dr. Departure motioned the man back into the chair. Every time he'd lost a patient to Dr. Schnappenhocker, his brother-in-law through some fantastic freak of luck had been able to clear up the problem in practically no time. The crowing that went on afterwards was unbearable. The man had even written up one case for the *American Journal*.

Dr. Departure looked distastefully at the box of powder and studied the words on the slip of paper. Well, if he had to demonstrate the impotence of spell casting, he had to—that was all.

"If I cast this . . . this spell," he finally said, trying to get a deeper meaning into the words, "will you promise to really *try* to remove these imaginary gloves—shed them like you would so much dead skin—skin you no longer need?"

"Yes! Yes!" Flint agreed eagerly.

"EEDO! QUEEDO! SKIZZO LIBIDO!" Dr. Departure intoned, sprinkling powder over Flint's outstretched hands and making a certain gesture with his own. Then he sat back and smiled indulgently.

"Thanks!" Flint breathed gratefully. Then with a *zip-snick-snap!* he deftly peeled a transparent rubbery glove from each hand quite as if he were shedding so much dead skin, and tossed them both on the desk. In amazement, Dr. Departure gazed at this tiny mound of sheer limp rubber that had collapsed his psychological house of cards with such a nasty little plop.

"This should cover the fee," Flint was saying happily, placing three twenties on the blotter. "And thanks again." He went out, slammming the door.

Dr. Departure closed his eyes a moment and listened to the tick of the brass clock. Of course the man could be perpetrating an elaborate practical joke. It was even possible that that loud-mouth charlatan, that hand holder of rich nymphomaniacs, that psychoanalytical peeping tom, Dr. Schnappenhocker had put him up to it. No, on second thought it couldn't have been a practical joke. No one—not even Bert Schnappenhocker himself—would be willing to pay $25 an hour for that meager pleasure.

He picked up one glove and examined it. It was inside out now—peeling it off had done that—but both sides seemed practically the same. Never had he touched anything so wonderfully soft and delicate, so light and completely transparent! He turned it over and over. It had no more body than a cobweb, yet it was as resilient as a rubber girdle. He put his fingers into it tentatively. Remarkable how snug and comfortable it was! He pulled it completely on. Why you scarcely knew it was there! He picked up the other glove, pulled it on to. . . .

The reason I can't get these gloves off, Dr. Departure told himself the next day staring at his fingers, is that the rubber sticks so close to the skin I can't get a good grip on it. If only I had longer finger nails.

The door opened suddenly and through it popped the beaming face of Dr. Schnappenhocker.

"Morning, Manly!" he boomed. "Just out drumming up a little business and right off I thought of you." He laughed heartily.

"Don't you ever knock?" Dr. Departure growled.

"No offense, Doctor. Thought I'd leave you a program for next month's Institute banquet. Did I tell you I was guest speaker?" He dropped a folder on the chair and disappeared.

Dr. Departure turned his attention back to the gloves. It *was* odd he couldn't get them off. Very odd. Not that this bothered him particularly—they were so snug and light you scarcely knew you had them on. Tonight he'd get Emily to peel them off. It *was* a bit disconcerting, though, not to be able to do it yourself.

Of course he'd had no impulse toward kleptomania—absolutely none at all. He smiled to himself. As a matter of fact—of you permitted yourself such a wild thought—it was just the other way around. Last night he'd left a book on the bus and this morning he'd misplaced his favorite pipe in the coffee shop. Odd. Very odd.

His eyes drifted to the two sacks of stolen articles Flint had left. Have to return *those,* he told himself—not good to have them lying around. He scooped up the bags and pawing through them discovered from price tags that most of them came from Snow Brothers' Department Store. It was lunch time; he'd drop them off right now.

A pre-inventory sale was raging in Snow Brothers'; its aisles throbbed with a squirming horde of women shoppers, and Dr. Departure, hugging two paper sacks, burrowed his way determinedly toward the accommodation desk.

It was in Women's Purses that the whim suddenly seized him. He fought it off. It returned—more powerfully, more insistently—and in a moment it swelled into a wild, unreasoning, clamoring urge that made his fingers tingle and his whole body quiver.

He found himself edging over to a counter, reaching into the sack he carried. His breathing came faster as he removed the first article his fingers touched—a windshield wiper. Furtively, he looked about. No one was watching. With a quick darting motion he sneaked the wiper between two leather bags on the counter. Then glancing nervously about once more, he hurried away with a pounding heart, feeling an odd tingling triumph.

"Opposite of kleptomania—that's what you have!" Mrs. Departure was accusing her husband in a loud hysterical voice two weeks later at dinner time. She was a large resolute woman with steely eyes and sensible shoes. At the moment, however, she was considerably unstrung. "You're an *un*-kleptomaniac, and you've *got* to do something about it!"

"And I tell you it's these damn gloves!" the doctor shouted pacing back and forth. His dinner lay cold and untouched. His hair was rumpled. His eyes glittered with strange lights. His hands had a strange plucking motion one against the other.

"You shoplifter . . . I mean . . . you shopdropper!" Her

long, usually solid jaw quivered with anguish. "Sneaking into department stores, leaving trinkets all over the place. My blue vase! The pruning shears! Almost the entire silverware set! Even your little brass clock! All gone!"

"It's the gloves, I tell you!" Vainly he tugged, plucked and snatched at his finger tips. "I put them on backwards. Inside out! . . . Damn! If I could only get a grip on them!"

"And today the public library called again," she cried shrilly. "Not a day passes but what you sneak three or four of your own books onto their shelves!"

"Well, if you'd helped me get these things off that first night like I asked you to, maybe I wouldn't be in this fix!"

"But this evening!" Mrs. Departure's lips twitched, her voice shrilled ever higher. "On the bus—that was the last straw! I saw you with my own eyes. The way you sneaked that man's wallet out of his pocket, stuffed it with four of your own dollar bills, then put it back! I tell you, Manly, you've got to see some one!"

"And I tell you there's nothing wrong with me! It's the gloves! When Flint skinned them off, it turned them inside out. They're on backwards! Can't you get that through your head!" He jammed a cigarette in his mouth.

"Gloves! Gloves! Gloves! I tell you for the hundredth time you haven't any gloves on!"

"Where *is* that cigarette lighter," Dr. Departure growled, slapping his pockets. "I had it right in my vest this morning."

"The question is," she said, laughing a bit hysterically and throwing back the flaps of his coat, "where is your vest? . . . Manly, I might as well tell you—I've already made an appointment for you. Tomorrow."

She dug in her purse and handed him a card.

"Schnappenhocker!" he screamed.

"Bert was really very nice about it."

"I will *not* go to that revolting brother of yours," Dr. Departure shrieked, turning a shiny purple. "Not even if he was the last doctor on earth! That pompous witch doctor! That . . ." Suddenly in mid-sentence he let out his breath and stared into space a moment, a pleased and reflective expression beginning to relax his face. Witch doctor? There was still a little powder left. . . . Why hadn't he thought of palming the gloves off on Bert before? That loud mouth wit-snapper was always trying on other people's garments for a laugh—ladies' hats, little boys' bow ties, Dr. Departure's own rather conservative rain shoes. The man simply couldn't *resist* a pair of rubber gloves!

"You will go," his wife was saying in a low vibrant voice.

"Most certainly I will go!" Dr. Departure replied in an equally vibrant voice, the sweet smile of anticipation growing on his face.

Never were doctor and patient ever happier to see one another than the following day when Dr. Departure entered the softly shaded inner sanctum of Dr. Bert Schnappenhocker. Dr. Schnappenhocker beamed at his rival with the undisguised eagerness of an anatomy student about to dissect an especially interesting species of tailless amphibia, while Dr. Departure gazed back with the smirky innocence of one all set to administer an emotional hot-foot. For two full minutes they wrung each other's hands.

"Well!" Dr. Schnappenhocker finally said heartily, impatient to make the initial incision. "Emily tells me you have a little problem."

"I hate to bother you with it, really," Dr. Departure replied, trying to keep from grinning.

For almost an hour Dr. Departure allowed his brother-in-law to worm the whole unlikely story out of him, then finally when he gave the instructions and pushed the little box of white powder across the desk, he watched Schappenhocker shake his head with a coy gesture of hopelessness and settle back in his chair.

"Manly, old man," Schnappenhocker said. "Another six months of absolute rest and quiet ought to do it for you. Maybe eight. You owe it to Emily, you know. *And* to yourself." He reached for the telephone.

Dr. Departure was prepared for this. Wild lights shining from his eyes—or what he *hoped* were wild lights—he leapt from the chair, seized the copper letter opener and leaned across the desk breathing hard.

"Are you going to cast that spell or aren't you!" he shouted, digging the opener into the mahogany desk top.

Dr. Schnappenhocker blinked apprehensively.

"Sure, Manly. Sure!" he placated. "I'll cast the spell, *then* I'll make your reservation." He picked up the box of powder and glanced nervously at the slip of paper.

"EEDO! SQUEEDO! SKIZZO LIBIDO!"

With a *zip-snick-snap!* Dr. Departure peeled off the glove from the left hand. Then, as he fumbled with the right hand, an agonizing decision suddenly leapt out at him: should he make a shoplifter out of his brother-in-law, or a shopdropper? Should he leave the gloves right side out or wrong side out? Each alternative offered such dazzling possibilities that for a moment Dr. Departure felt himself almost torn in two by the exquisite but mutually exclusive choices. Then the answer came to him. What if he left one glove right side out, the other wrong side out . . .?

"Why Bert!" Mrs. Departure said, opening the door to her brother Dr. Schnappenhocker a week later. "Come on in!"

"I can't, Dr. Schnappenhocker replied, handing her a cardboard carton filled with assorted articles. "Just thought I'd drop these off. They're a few more things Manly deposited in my office when he was . . . well, before I cured him."

Mrs. Departure took the carton.

"I must say you're a miracle man, Bert. Just one treatment and now he's as fit as a fiddle."

"It was nothing," Schappenhocker said, backing down the steps nervously. There was a tenseness about his eyes and he kept jerking at the ends of his fingers.

Mrs. Departure closed the door and returned to the dining room where her husband was wolfing down a tremendous dinner.

"That was Bert," she explained. "With another carton of junk. You know, I'm worried about the man. He keeps bringing all this stuff over here insisting it's yours, but it all belongs to him! Here's his fountain pen, his copper letter opener, even his appointment book! And what makes it even stranger," she went on, shaking her head, "every time he deposits a load, he manages to sneak off with an armful of *our* stuff!"

She went to the window and peeked through the Venetian blinds. "Look at him out there! Unscrewing the nozzle of the hose! Why, the man's turning into a human pack rat!"

"Probably been working too hard on that speech," Dr. Departure said, beaming and helping himself to another pork chop. "Always knew Schnappenhocker would crack up someday."

FAMILY RESEMBLANCE

Alan E. Nourse, M.D.

There is some question in our minds whether this tale should be called science fiction or not, so true is it to the ways of medical students and the thought patterns of pompous professors. On the other hand, it is not exactly likely to happen, we hope, and furthermore, it did appear in a science fiction magazine, and, to complete our case, it is a lot of fun. So we have included it here, regardless of whether it is strictly a science fictional kosher pig or not. (Read on, and you'll catch that reference.) It would be an interne who would think up a tale like this! Dr. Nourse is by now, of course, a full-fledged physician.

Family Resemblance

IT REALLY started off as a prank, as so many things do, and it would have remained a prank if Dr. Herman Tally hadn't happened into the hospital nursery at precisely the moment he did—or if he hadn't had a fight with Dr. Hogan just before, which worked his mind into fertile ground for the seed to fall. And there wouldn't have *been* even a prank if it hadn't been Tuesday, and if Miss Henderson had been somewhat less inclined to squeal when excited.

But it *was* Tuesday, in the early summer, when life for a hospital interne was reaching its nadir, and many a fledgling doctor, like Dr. Barret, for instance, was practically driven to schemes to relieve the humdrum routine of patients and case histories. A most unimaginative cook was really to blame, for the three doctors were sitting about the internes' table at St. Christopher's Hospital that day, eating the inevitable Tuesday fare of pig-in-blanket and sauerkraut, and wondering dully what to discuss next.

"What," said Dr. Barret, in a moment of inspiration, viewing his dinner plate, "makes more noise than a pig under a gate?"

"Two pigs," muttered Dr. Hines, munching thoughtfully. "Or three pigs under a blanket. You're out of date."

"Oh, no," smiled Dr. Barret, the faintest gleam in his young hazel eyes. "For your information the answer is: Miss Henderson, when she's suffered an emotional shock!"

Miss Henderson, the newest proby nurse at St. Christopher's, was at present assigned to uneasy duty with Dr. Barret on the maternity ward, and had suffered numerous emotional shocks, it seemed, under that gentleman's tender care. Miss Henderson was, as they put it, a lush dish; she was also not too bright.

Dr. Barrett chuckled in unashamed malice: "You should have heard her," he grinned, "when she spotted that wiggly green lizard jiggling down my jacket front the other day. She squealed like five pigs under a gate!" The doctors laughed, and leaned closer to Dr. Barret, sensing a scheme under construction. "Now, Miss Henderson is in the nursery this afternoon," he speculated softly. "What do you suppose she would do if she found—"

It was very simple to arrange. Dr. Barret took a quick trip across the campus to the Agricultural Experiment Station after lunch, and returned to the hospital as unobtrusively as possible through a rear entrance, hoping that none of the staff would notice the odd bulge under his interne's jacket. Five minutes later he exhibited his prize to his fellow conspirators in their rooms, where they scrubbed it with soap and water and sprinkled it liberally with baby powder, amid much outraged squealing, until the barest whiff of chloroform sedated it into a snuffing and uneasy sleep. Then the other two internes waylaid Miss Henderson, giggling and self-conscious, in the chart room while Dr. Barret placed the prize in a baby basket in the nursery, neatly wrapping it in a blue baby blanket, and arranging it between the basket tagged "Child Harrison" and the one labeled "Child Wojikowsky." He left it there with a small but distinctly legible tag at the bottom of the basket: "Child Porker."

The three were watching from the nursery door, maintaining a studied and valiant calm, when Miss Henderson, still giggling and meditating future dates with handsome doctors, marched into the nursery with the two-o'clock bottles for Child Harrison and Child Wojikowsky. Her reaction was gratifying indeed. She stopped in her tracks, let out the prize squeal of her eighteen years, and fainted dead away.

It would have remained a prank if at precisely that moment Dr. Herman Tally, Professor of Anthropology, student of infant development, and chief whipping-boy of Dr. Hogan's anthropological research staff, had not made his weekly rounds of St. Christopher's nursery. Dr. Tally was essentially a mild man, calmly gratified if his daily routine was allowed to run its course without too many ragged edges, from rising in the morning to retiring at night. He was decidedly *not* mentally prepared for three startled internes, a bewildered nurse, and the apparition in the baby basket as he climbed the nursery stairs that afternoon.

He was muttering to himself at the most recent indignities suffered at the hands of his chief. The lazy pig! It wasn't enough that Dr. Hogan required him to type, rewrite, proofread, index, and play public relations supervisor for the Book—he had to collect the man's research data for him, too, when Dr. Hogan didn't feel like hoisting his porcine bulk down to St. Christopher's nursery on a hot Tuesday afternoon. Dr. Tally sighed tiredly. For three years now the Book had occupied the entire working hours of the whole anthropology staff.

" 'Back to the Apes,' " Dr. Hogan would beam, expounding enthusiastically, "will be the last word on the Origin of Man conflict—the *last word,* I say, the crowning blow to all opposing theories!" He would puff and wheeze, then, smiling his fat smile beneficently upon anyone who was still listening. "The final work will be published in 'Back to the Apes,' proving, I say *proving* that Man and Ape alike can smile back on a common ancestor!" And then he would beam some more.

Dr. Tally grimaced. He was so tired of going back to the apes. The title wasn't even Dr. Hogan's idea, and some of the harebrained ideas that *were* his, like these recent tests on infant reactions—Dr. Tally reached the top of the stairs unenthusiastically, and walked into the nursery.

Miss Henderson was already enjoying the solicitous attention of the three young internes, so Dr. Tally looked immediately for the cause of her sudden collapse, and the squeal he had heard clear down the stairs. The sight of the basket took him quite aback. For a moment he stared at it in disbelief, until in a flash of insight he recognized all the earmarks of an interne's sense of humor. Nevertheless, he still stared at the basket. And stared, and stared.

The idea trickled into his mind, almost frightening him. Something there struck a chord, a beautiful harmony, far back in his memory. Some resemblance to something he had seen, or read—he ran a trembling hand through his sparse hair as he thought, probing the vast store of incidental and disorganized material in his mind. There had been so much to learn in anatomy, or physiology—or was it embryology? The more he studied Child Porker, snuffing in its basket, the stronger the idea became, forcing itself into his mind, carrying him closer and closer to the familiar link—

Embryology! That was it! His heart was suddenly beating in his throat, and he jammed his hat on his head, beating a hasty retreat down the stairs. Embryology! Out of the depths of his mind, he knew excitedly, there was something about embryology. If he could only find the book—

Dr. Tally was late for supper, and when he came up the walk from his battered Chevvy, arms loaded with books, he viewed dinner with a certain degree of abstraction. It had been embryology, indeed, and much, much more. The afternoon had been spent in the library stacks, checking first one embryology text, then another. It was after an hour there that he grew certain that he had a trail to follow, but a complex trail, with many devious twistings. It took him into anatomy, into physiology, into biochemistry—He kissed his wife, hardly seeing her, and settled down to his belated supper, opening Benson's "Parasitology" on one side of his plate, and Best and Taylor's "Physiological Basis for Medical Practice" on the other side. In a matter of moments he was immersed, his thin shoulders trembling with agitation.

"Dear," said Mrs. Tally, hopefully, "are you enjoying your chops? They're very expensive, nowadays."

"Chops?"

"Pork chops. What you're eating. Aren't they delicious?"

He looked up from his books, first at his wife, then at the chops, his face slightly green. "My dear," he said, pushing his plate away gently but with finality. "I'm afraid I just can't enjoy the . . . dinner . . . this evening. I've a great deal of work to do, and I'd like to be undisturbed tonight." He rose unsteadily from the table, books under his arm, and beat a hasty retreat into his study.

The trail was unmistakable, clear and distinct. For years people had nodded sagely and accepted authority unchallenged, even when they had walked past the trail in a dozen places. It was here, winding its way through a dozen books, never examined, never correlated—but here! Anyone with half an eye could find it. They had just missed it because they hadn't dared to look. And all the palaver about scientific method! He pored over the "Parasitology," then checked several chapters of human physiology. Darwin's *Origin of Species* came next, then the embryology again and a huge text on dental surgery. Three large tomes on psychological conditioning and reflex reactions occupied him for almost an hour before he tossed them aside with a sigh and sought out a chapter on human nasal surgery. All here, all so clear— and nobody had thought to make the necessary correlation! His heart was in his throat, his whole mind afire with the expanse of his vision when his wife brought in a sandwich and milk, well past midnight. And she saw a gleam in her husband's eye that she hadn't seen in ten years under Dr. Hogan's tyranny.

"Darling," said Dr. Tally, after munching for a while on the sandwich, "how would you like to go away for a while— take an extended vacation, for instance?"

"Go away?" She looked up in surprise. "Why, Herman! We haven't been on a vacation in ten years! Where to?"

A faraway look came into the doctor's eyes. "Some beautiful island, maybe in the South Pacific. Maybe we could go to New Zealand, or Central Africa. I hear they need anthropologists in Central Africa—"

Here eyes were wide, and she brushed back her graying hair with studied care. "Herman, you aren't yourself tonight. What's wrong? Are you in trouble?"

He stood up, swelling his thin chest with air. "The biggest trouble in ten years, my dear, and the most wonderful! I've found something that may lose me my job so fast I won't know what hit me!"

"Something that will oppose Dr. Hogan?"

"Oppose him! It'll knock him and his theories right out the door. And it'll get me fired on the spot. The Board of Trustees may throw me out on my ear, if I can't convince them, but I'm going to do it if they put me on a spit and roast me! The great Dr. Hogan has been rooting in my corn-field for years—and now I've got a stick big enough to drive him out!"

Dr. Horace Hogan's office was the largest, brightest, best equipped office-lab in the Zoology Building. His first book, "The Essence of the Ape," had given him the laboratory, and the prestige, and the power over his subordinates, as well as altogether too much to eat in the past five years or so. He hoisted his blubbery bulk around in the swivel chair to face Dr. Tally, his fat red face heavy with annoyance.

"Yes, yes, Dr. Tally—what is it? You know I'm not to be disturbed when I'm writing."

"Dr. Hogan, I have a question to ask you." Dr. Tally's face was drawn tight, a cold light of determination in his eyes. He wondered, abstractedly, how Dr. Hogan would look roasted, with an apple in his mouth.

"Well, you'll have to see me later. 'Back to the Apes' comes first in this office, you know. I've a deadline to make."

"Bother the deadline," said Dr. Tally succinctly. "You won't need to make it. And I want my question answered here"—he drew himself up straight and proud—"and now!"

The fat man spluttered and swung back to face him. "All right," he said testily. "Out with it, man. What's the trouble?"

"What is the complete biological classification of Man?"

Dr. Hogan's face went blank with surprise. "Chordata, Craniata, Mammalia, Primata, Hominidae, Homo sapiens," he snapped mechanically. "Our freshman pre-medics were asked that question on their first-hour quiz, Dr. Tally."

"Yes," said Dr. Tally softly. "I suppose they were also asked to trace the human evolutionary chain back to a common ancestor with the apes, weren't they?"

"Of course they were! That is undoubtedly the most precious and fundamental single item of knowledge they will ever have occasion to encounter!" The fat man quivered, his face red.

Dr. Tally sniggered audibly. "But if they give *your* answer, they might be all wrong!"

"*Dr. Tally!*" Dr. Hogan started to get to his feet, thought better of it, and assumed a pose of militant indignation from a sitting position. "Such a remark is heresy, Dr. Tally. Rank hersey!"

Dr. Tally pulled a sheaf of papers from his briefcase. "Listen to me for a moment, Dr. Hogan, and correct me if I'm wrong. In tracing the evolutionary line of any creature, we look to generalized rather than specialized forms, isn't that right? And for that reason we consider Man from the point of view of the biological family, Hominidae, rather than the specialized genus and species Homo sapiens."

"That's right."

"And we look to the ancestral form with similar generalized characteristics when we want to find the progenitor of Man?"

"Of course. You know that."

"And are you wholeheartedly satisfied that Man's evolutionary root was unquestionably of the Tarsius family, now represented by certain monkeys and apes?"

Dr. Hogan wheezed in agitation. "For the dignity of Man, I am inalterably convinced, Dr. Tally. 'Back to the Apes,' I always say. All the evidence points—"

"Not *all* the evidence, Dr. Hogan! The evidence found in anthropology, perhaps, and paleontology—but there are other lines of evidence, modern evidence, unmistakable evidence. You can't twist scientific methods around a pole to suit your whims. There is evidence that does not point to Tarsius or the apes at all. It points directly and unmistakably to the *Suidae!*"

Dr. Hogan gasped, his hoglike jowls bobbing up and down. "Preposterous!" he gasped. "Of course there may be certain faint resemblances, but to relate human beings—*human beings*, mind you, to PIGS—"

Dr. Tally grinned a wicked grin. "There certainly are resemblances. Your evidence for the apes is anthropological, paleontological—but I have anatomical, physiological, and embryological evidence." He settled down in a chair. "Look at the evidence, Dr. Hogan. I remembered, from back in my college days, that somebody had once remarked, during an embryology course, that we studied the embryos of pigs rather than human beings, because they were more easily available, and *essentially the same!* I checked it. They are indubitably the same, Dr. Hogan, in almost every way. Only in the last few weeks of gestation does a pig embryo become distinguishable from a human embryo. And after birth, what anatomical relation is there? The organs, the viscera, the internal arrangement of the pig is *practically identical* with that of Man! The same size, placement, shape, function, for all the organs. The apes present a very different anatomical picture. Both men and pigs have similar vermiform appendixes—apes do not. Human teeth have either one root or two in the premolars and molars, while in monkeys and apes these same teeth have three roots. In pigs these teeth are rooted the same as in man. And other things—men and pigs have little or no vestigial tails, while apes and monkeys have either short or long tails. Men and pigs are essentially hairless; monkeys and apes, even up to the gorillas, all have hair in abundance—"

Dr. Hogan's face was turning a dangerous vermilion hue, his eyes bulging from their sockets. "Superficialities!" he hissed, wiping his forehead with a pudgy hand. "Of all the impertinent, disgraceful ideas—"

"But there are other 'superficialities,'" Dr. Tally cut in. "Pigs and men have cartilage all round their noses, while monkeys and apes have slit noses. Pigs and men have that odd bit of useless tissue, the uvula, tacked on to the back of their palates, while there is little or no uvula among monkeys and apes. These are superficialities, of course, but doesn't science demand attention to little things? Now—"

"Preposterous!" sputtered Dr. Hogan.

". . . Now, let's go a little deeper. How about parasites? Ever hear of Trichina? Or Macracanthorynchus, and other hook-headed worms? What mammalian forms do these parasites attack? Man and pig, but never apes and monkeys. How about serological comparisons—blood serum and cells, and the like? Man stands no farther serologically from pigs than from apes—I could go on for hours, Dr. Hogan, but there's one comparison that puts the clincher on the whole thing. We've talked about paleontology and anatomy and physiology —how about *psychology?*"

"Well, *what* about psychology?" roared Dr. Hogan, his whole body trembling.

A sly smile appeared on Dr. Tally's face. "Why are pigs used for conditioning experiments now, in preference to rats and dogs and cats? *Because they react more like Man*. The pig stands far above cats and dogs and rats and many monkeys on the intelligence scale. And what other animal, Dr. Hogan, besides man, is so consistently lazy, gluttonous, dirty, selfish, treacherous or pugnacious?"

Dr. Hogan was not merely sitting in his chair, he was fairly quivering, his round fat face damp with small beads of perspiration. "You . . . you'd never dare to publish such a thing!" he said in a hoarse whisper. "What would it do to our culture? What would people think, what would they say? They'd never believe it or accept it. We'd have to rearrange our entire thinking processes, our philosophical values. It would throw the world into chaos, Dr. Tally—why, you'd have almost every religious group in the country down on our necks."

Dr. Tally was smiling. "And I might, just possibly, make people wonder if Horace Hogan isn't just a bit of a goat with his 'Back to the Apes' theory, mightn't I?"

Dr. Hogan purpled, his voice laboring under the strain of civility. "Now, Herman, we've been friends for years—associates in our work—almost brothers, you might say," he wheezed, his little pig eyes watching Tally shrewdly. "I know you wouldn't want to discredit me, who has done so much for you, and I *know* you wouldn't want to start any such storm as this. Now, I could make you an Associate Professor, and see that you get a substantial raise in salary—"

Dr. Tally shook his head, grinning widely. "There's something I'd much rather do," he said. "I'd rather see Horace Hogan grow thin—with worry, perhaps. You can't talk me out of it, Horace. I'm going to put the skids under that book of yours."

This time the fat man did hoist himself out of his seat, his face deep purple. "Traitor!" he screamed. "Ingrate! Get out! You're fired. Get out! Do your worst! But you won't get anywhere. The Board of Trustees will throw you out on your ear, and you'll be the laughingstock of the scholarly world. Pigs, indeed!" Frantically he fumbled for a telephone, his face apoplectic. "I'll call the Board right now, and you'll be through—"

Dr. Tally coughed gently. "Dr. Hogan. You won't have to call the Board. As a matter of fact, they're waiting out in the office right now. I've already told them, you see, and they're —interested. Yes, you might say they're interested, and I've taken the liberty to arrange a little tour for them. Over at St. Christopher's Hospital—"

They were five elderly gentlemen. All five were tall, and all were lean, with narrow hawk noses and stooped shoulders, and sharp blue eyes peering disapprovingly at Dr. Horace Hogan as they made their way up the stairs to the hospital nursery. Dr. Hogan waddled ahead of them, panting and spluttering, for all the world like an overfed sow routed from her wallow. His pudgy face was damp, and his hands trembled as he worked his way up the steps, stopping periodically to pant a few spluttered words of protest. "Pigs! Can you imagine, gentlemen, the temerity of this man—"

"Yes, yes, Dr. Hogan, but if, as he says, there is some reason to believe—"

"Preposterous! My work has been most scientific, there have been no loopholes. All the important evidence points—"

One of the elderly gentlemen looked down his lean nose at Dr. Hogan. "But surely a man with your acquaintance with scientific methods should be willing at least to listen!"

Dr. Tally sprinted up the stairs ahead of them, his face pale, lines of worry on his forehead. At the top of the stairs he showed the men to seats in the anteroom. "If you'll just be seated, gentlemen. I'll check to make sure we aren't disturbing feeding—" He disappeared through a white-painted door, and almost collided with Dr. Barret.

The interne looked up, and grabbed at Dr. Tally's sleeve nervously. "Look, Doc—that's the Board of Trustees out there! They hire and fire around here! You didn't tell me it would be *them* when you called this morning—you just said some old fogies—"

Dr. Tally nodded his head vigorously. "You've got everything arranged?"

The interne looked worriedly over his shoulder. "Sure, everything's just like you said, but you'll never get away with it—"

"I've *got* to get away with it! I've planted the seed in fertile minds, and they'll see what they want to see. And particularly, they'll see Horace Hogan—" He patted the interne nervously on the arm and hurried back to the waiting room. "Now, gentlemen, if you'll just come with me."

Slowly they walked through the door and down the darkened corridor, past the viewing windows, to the very last room. The five members of the Board and Dr. Hogan filed up to the window and looked in, and silence fell abruptly over the party.

Inside, a subdued Miss Henderson moved efficiently from basket to basket, gently turning back the pink and blue blankets—

"What—"

"Impossible! Why, if I didn't see it with my own eyes—"

"There *is* a resemblance! Unmistakable! Why, how could this have been missed all these years? Dr. Tally, this is the most remarkable—"

Suddenly in the corridor there was a choked roar of anguish and despair, ending in a little gurgle and a heavy thud. This time Dr. Hogan fainted dead away. The elderly men looked around in alarm as several overnervous internes appeared to ease Hogan's bulk onto a stretcher and start work resuscitating him, and Dr. Tally herded his charges gently out into the bright light of the anteroom once again.

"Basically unstable," he whispered, jerking a thumb over his shoulder. "Couldn't bear to have his ideas refuted. But I'm sure you can see, gentlemen, that here is something worthy of careful investigation."

The five elderly gentlemen looked at each other, and back at Dr. Tally, and suddenly there appeared five broad and understanding smiles. "Yes, Dr. Tally. We're quite sure."

"What I can't see," said Dr. Barret later, as Dr. Tally helped him lug the heavy, squealing crates back toward the Agricultural Experiment Station, "is how you can reconcile this sort of thing with the 'scientific method' you're always yapping about. So maybe men came from pigs—it seems quite possible—but this is a funny way to prove it."

"Oh, it's *quite* possible. But this wasn't supposed to prove anything at all, really. Merely to give me a chance to try. We won't be bothered by Dr. Hogan and his wretched book any more." Dr. Tally turned twinkling eyes toward the young interne. "Though I'm afraid my methods of convincing would have insulted one of the greatest minds Man has ever turned out—the very father of the scientific method."

Dr. Barret looked up sharply. "You mean—"

Dr. Tally nodded apologetically. "Roger Bacon," he said.

FACTS IN THE CASE OF M. VALDEMAR

Edgar Allan Poe

Do we have to introduce Edgar Allan Poe? Or his classic tale of the results of an experiment in mesmerism? We think not!

Facts in the Case of M. Valdemar

OF COURSE I shall not pretend to consider it any matter for wonder, that the extraordinary case of M. Valdemar has excited discussion. It would have been a miracle had it not—especially under the circumstances. Through the desire of all parties concerned, to keep the affair from the public, at least for the present, or until we had further opportunities for investigation—through our endeavors to effect this—a garbled or exaggerated account made its ways into society, and became the source of many unpleasant misrepresentations; and, very naturally, of a great deal of disbelief.

It is now rendered necessary that I give the *facts*—as far as I comprehend them myself. They are, succinctly, these:

My attention, for the last three years, had been repeatedly drawn to the subject of Mesmerism; and, about nine months ago, it occurred to me, quite suddenly, that in the series of experiments made hitherto, there had been a very remarkable and most unaccountable omission:—no person had as yet been mesmerized *in articulo mortis*. It remained to be seen, first, whether, in such condition, there existed in the patient any susceptibility to the magnetic influence; secondly, whether, if any existed, it was impaired or increased by the condition; thirdly, to what extent, or for how long a period, the encroachments of Death might be arrested by the process. There were other points to be ascertained, but these most excited my curiosity—the last in especial, from the immensely important character of its consequences.

In looking around me for some subject by whose means I might test these particulars, I was brought to think of my friend, M. Ernest Valdemar, the well-known compiler of the "Bibliotheca Forensica," and author (under the *nom de plume* of Issachar Marx) of the Polish versions of "Wallenstein" and "Gargantua." M. Valdemar, who has resided principally at Harlem, N.Y., since the year of 1839, is (or was) particularly noticeable for the extreme spareness of his per-

321

son—his lower limbs much resembling those of John Randolph; and, also, for the whiteness of his whiskers, in violent contrast to the blackness of his hair—the latter, in consequence, being very generally mistaken for a wig. His temperament was markedly nervous, and rendered him a good subject of mesmeric experiment. On two or three occasions I had put him to sleep with little difficulty, but was disappointed in other results which his peculiar constitution had naturally led me to anticipate. His will was at no period positively, or thoroughly, under my control, and in regard to *clairvoyance*, I could accomplish with him nothing to be relied upon. I always attributed my failure at these points to the disordered state of his health. For some months previous to my becoming acquainted with him, his physicians had declared him in a confirmed phthisis. It was his custom, indeed, to speak of his approaching dissolution, as of a matter neither to be avoided nor regretted.

When the ideas to which I have alluded first occurred to me, it was of course very natural that I should think of M. Valdemar. I knew the steady philosophy of the man too well to apprehend any scruples from *him*; and he had no relatives in America who would be likely to interfere. I spoke to him frankly upon the subject; and, to my surprise, his interest seemed vividly excited. I say to my surprise; for, although he had always yielded his person freely to my experiments, he had never before given me any tokens of sympathy with what I did. His disease was of that character which would admit of exact calculation in respect to the epoch of its termination in death; and it was finally arranged between us that he would send for me about twenty-four hours before the period announced by his physicians as that of his decease.

It is now rather more than seven months since I received, from M. Valdemar himself, the subjoined note:

"MY DEAR P——

"You may as well come *now*. D—— and F—— are agreed that I cannot hold out beyond to-morrow midnight; and I think they have hit the time very nearly.

VALDEMAR"

I received this note within half an hour after it was written, and in fifteen minutes more I was in the dying man's chamber. I had not seen him for ten days, and was appalled by the fearful alteration which the brief interval had wrought in him. His face wore a leaden hue; the eyes were utterly lustreless; and the emaciation was so extreme, that the skin had been broken through by the cheek-bones. His expectoration was excessive. The pulse was barely perceptible. He retained, nevertheless, in a very remarkable manner, both his mental power and a certain degree of physical strength. He spoke with distinctness—took some palliative medicines without aid —and, when I entered the room, was occupied in penciling memoranda in a pocket-book. He was propped up in the bed by pillows. Doctors D—— and F—— were in attendance.

After pressing Valdemar's hand, I took these gentlemen aside, and obtained from them a minute account of the patient's condition. The left lung had been for eighteen months in a semi-osseous or cartilaginous state, and was, of course, entirely useless for all purposes of vitality. The right, in its upper portion, was also partially, if not thoroughly, ossified, while the lower region was merely a mass of purulent tubercles, running one into another. Several extensive perforations existed; and, at one point, permanent adhesion to the ribs had taken place. These appearances in the right lobe were of comparatively recent date. The ossification had proceeded with very unusual rapidity; no sign of it had been discovered a month before, and the adhesion had only been observed during the three previous days. Independently of the phthisis, the patient was suspected of aneurism of the aorta; but on this point the osseous symptoms rendered an exact diagnosis impossible. It was the opinion of both physicians that M. Valdemar would die about midnight on the morrow (Sunday.) It was then seven o'clock on Saturday evening.

On quitting the invalid's bedside to hold conversation with myself, Doctors D—— and F—— had bidden him a final farewell. It had not been their intention to return; but, at my request, they agreed to look in upon the patient about ten the next night.

When they had gone, I spoke freely with M. Valdemar on

the subject of his approaching dissolution, as well as, more particularly, of the experiment proposed. He still professed himself quite willing and even anxious to have it made, and urged me to commence it at once. A male and a female nurse were in attendance; but I did not feel myself altogether at liberty to engage in a task of this character with no more reliable witnesses than these people, in case of sudden accident, might prove. I therefore postponed operations until about eight the next night, when the arrival of a medical student, with whom I had some acquaintance (Mr. Theodore L——l), relieved me from further embarrassment. It had been my design, originally, to wait for the physicians; but I was induced to proceed, first, by the urgent entreaties of M. Valdemar, and secondly, by my conviction that I had not a moment to lose, as he was evidently sinking fast.

Mr. L——l was so kind as to accede to my desire that he would take notes of all that occurred; and it is from his memoranda that what I now have to relate is, for the most part, either condensed or copied *verbatim*.

It wanted about five minutes of eight when, taking the patient's hand, I begged him to state, as distinctly as he could, to Mr. L——l, whether he (M. Valdemar) was entirely willing that I should make the experiment of mesmerizing him in his then condition.

He replied feebly, yet quite audibly: "Yes, I wish to be mesmerized"—adding immediately afterward: "I fear you have deferred it too long."

While he spoke thus, I commenced the passes which I had already found most effectual in subduing him. He was evidently influenced with the first lateral stroke of my hand across his forehead; but, although I exerted all my powers, no further perceptible effect was induced until some minutes after ten o'clock, when Doctors D—— and F—— called, according to appointment. I explained to them, in a few words, what I designed and as they opposed no objection, saying that the patient was already in the death agony, I proceeded without hesitation—exchanging, however, the lateral passes for downward ones, and directing my gaze entirely into the right eye of the sufferer.

By this time his pulse was imperceptible and his breathing was stertorous, and at intervals of half a minute.

This condition was nearly unaltered for a quarter of an hour. At the expiration of this period, however, a natural although a very deep sigh escaped from the bosom of the dying man, and the stertorous breathing ceased—that is to say, its stertorousness was no longer apparent; the intervals were undiminished. The patient's extremities were of an icy coldness.

At five minutes before eleven, I perceived unequivocal signs of the mesmeric influence. The glassy roll of the eye was changed for that expression of uneasy *inward* examination which is never seen except in cases of sleep-waking, and which it is quite impossible to mistake. With a few rapid lateral passes I made the lids quiver, as in incipient sleep, and with a few more I closed them altogether. I was not satisfied, however, with this, but continued the manipulations vigorously, and with the fullest exertion of the will, until I had completely stiffened the limbs of the slumberer, after placing them in a seemingly easy position. The legs were at full length; the arms were nearly so, and reposed on the bed at a moderate distance from the loins. The head was very slightly elevated.

When I had accomplished this, it was fully midnight, and I requested the gentlemen present to examine M. Valdemar's condition. After a few experiments, they admitted him to be in an unusually perfect state of mesmeric trance. The curiosity of both the physicians was greatly excited. Dr. D—— resolved at once to remain with the patient all night, while Dr. F—— took leave with a promise to return at daybreak. Mr. L——l and the nurses remained.

We left M. Valdemar entirely undisturbed until about three o'clock in the morning, when I approached him and found him in precisely the same condition as when Dr. F—— went away—that is to say, he lay in the same position; the pulse was imperceptible; the breathing was gentle (scarcely noticeable, unless through the application of a mirror to the lips); the eyes were closed naturally; and the limbs were as rigid and as cold as marble. Still, the general appearance was certainly not that of death.

As I approached M. Valdemar I made a kind of half effort to influence his right arm into pursuit of my own, as I passed the latter gently to and fro above his person. In such experiments with this patient, I had never perfectly succeeded before, and assuredly I had little thought of succeeding now; but to my astonishment, his arm very readily, although feebly, followed every direction I assigned it with mine. I determined to hazard a few words of conversation.

"M. Valdemar," I said, "are you asleep?" He made no answer, but I perceived a tremor about the lips, and was thus induced to repeat the question, again and again. At its third repetition, his whole frame was agitated by a very slight shivering; the eyelids unclosed themselves so far as to display a white line of a ball; the lips moved sluggishly, and from between them, in a barely audible whisper, issued the words:

"Yes;—asleep now. Do not wake me!—let me die so!"

I here felt the limbs, and found them as rigid as ever. The right arm, as before, obeyed the direction of my hand. I questioned the sleep-waker again:

"Do you still feel pain in the breast, M. Valdemar?"

The answer now was immediate, but even less audible than before:

"No pain—I am dying!"

I did not think it advisable to disturb him further just then, and nothing more was said or done until the arrival of Dr. F——, who came a little before sunrise, and expressed unbounded astonishment at finding the patient still alive. After feeling the pulse and applying a mirror to the lips, he requested me to speak to the sleep-waker again. I did so, saying:

"M. Valdemar, do you still sleep?"

As before, some minutes elapsed ere a reply was made; and during the interval the dying man seemed to be collecting his energies to speak. At my fourth repetition of the question, he said very faintly, almost inaudibly:

"Yes; still asleep—dying."

It was now the opinion, or rather the wish, of the physicians, that M. Valdemar should be suffered to remain undisturbed in his present apparently tranquil condition, until death should supervene—and this, it was generally agreed, must now take place within a few minutes. I concluded, however, to speak to him once more, and merely repeated my previous question.

While I spoke, there came a marked change over the countenance of the sleep-waker. The eyes rolled themselves slowly open, the pupils disappearing upwardly; the skin generally assumed a cadaverous hue, resembling not so much parchment as white paper; and the circular hectic spots which, hitherto, had been strongly defined in the centre of each cheek, *went out* at once. I use this expression, because the suddenness of their departure put me in mind of nothing so much as the extinguishment of a candle by a puff of the breath. The upper lip, at the same time, writhed itself away from the teeth, which it had previously covered completely; while the lower jaw fell with an audible jerk, leaving the mouth widely extended, and disclosing in full view the swollen and blackened tongue. I presume that no member of the party then present had been unaccustomed to death-bed horrors; but so hideous beyond conception was the appearance of M. Valdemar at this moment, that there was a general shrinking back from the region of the bed.

I now feel that I have reached a point of this narrative at which every reader will be startled into positive disbelief. It is my business, however, simply to proceed.

There was no longer the faintest sign of vitality in M. Valdemar; and concluding him to be dead, we were consigning him to the charge of the nurses, when a strong vibratory motion was observable in the tongue. This continued for perhaps a minute. At the expiration of this period, there issued from the distended and motionless jaws a voice—such as it would be madness in me to attempt describing. There are, indeed, two or three epithets which might be considered as applicable to it in part; I might say, for example, that the sound was harsh and broken and hollow; but the hideous whole is indescribable, for the simple reason that no similar sounds have ever jarred upon the ear of humanity. There were two particulars, nevertheless, which I thought then, and still think, might fairly be stated as characteristic of the intonation —as well adapted to convey some idea of its unearthly peculiarity. In the first place, the voice seemed to reach our ears— at least mine—from a vast distance, or from some deep cavern within the earth. In the second place, it impressed me (I fear, indeed, that it will be impossible to make myself comprehend) as gelatinous or glutinous matters impress the sense of touch.

I have spoken both of "sound" and of "voice." I mean to say that the sound was one of distinct—of even wonderfully, thrillingly distinct—syllabification. M. Valdemar *spoke*— obviously in reply to the question I had propounded to him a few minutes before. I had asked him, it will be remembered, if he still slept. He now said:

"Yes;—no;—I *have been* sleeping—and now—now—*I am dead*."

No person present even affected to deny, or attempted to repress, the unutterable, shuddering horror which these few words, thus uttered, were so well calculated to convey. Mr. L——l (the student) swooned. The nurses immediately left the chamber, and could not be induced to return. My own impressions I would not pretend to render intelligible to the reader. For nearly an hour, we busied ourselves, silently— without the utterance of a word—in endeavors to revive Mr. L——l. When he came to himself, we addressed ourselves again to an investigation of M. Valdemar's condition.

It remained in all respects as I have last described it, with the exception that the mirror no longer afforded evidence of respiration. An attempt to draw blood from the arm failed. I should mention, too, that this limb was no further subject to my will. I endeavored in vain to make it follow the direction of my hand. The only real indication, indeed, of the mesmeric influence, was now found in the vibratory movement of the tongue, whenever I addressed M. Valdemar a question. He seemed to be making an effort to reply, but had no longer sufficient volition. To queries put to him by any other person than myself he seemed utterly insensible—although I endeavored to place each member of the company in mesmeric *rapport* with him. I believe that I have now related all that is necessary to an understanding of the sleep-waker's state at this epoch. Other nurses were procured; and at ten o'clock I left the house in company with the two physicians and Mr. L——l.

In the afternoon we all called again to see the patient. His condition remained precisely the same. We had now some discussion as to the propriety and feasibility of awakening him; but we had little difficulty in agreeing that no good purpose would be served by so doing. It was evident that, so far, death (or what is usually termed death) had been arrested by the mesmeric process. It seemed clear to us all that to awaken M. Valdemar would be merely to insure his instant, or at least his speedy, dissolution.

From this period until the close of last week—*an interval of nearly seven months*—we continued to make daily calls at M. Valdemar's house, accompanied, now and then, by medical and other friends. All this time the sleep-waker remained *exactly* as I have last described him. The nurses' attentions were continual.

It was on Friday last that we finally resolved to make the experiment of awakening, or attempting to awaken him; and it is the (perhaps) unfortunate result of this latter experiment which has given rise to so much discussion in private circles —to so much of what I cannot help thinking unwarranted popular feeling.

For the purpose of relieving M. Valdemar from the mesmeric trance, I made use of the customary passes. These for a time were unsuccessful. The first indication of revival was afforded by a partial descent of the iris. It was observed, as especially remarkable, that this lowering of the pupil was accompanied by the profuse out-flowing of a yellowish ichor (from beneath the lids) of a pungent and highly offensive odor.

It was now suggested that I should attempt to influence the patient's arm as heretofore. I made the attempt and failed. Dr. F—— then intimated a desire to have me put a question. I did so, as follows:

"M. Valdemar, can you explain to us what are your feelings or wishes now?"

There was an instant return of the hectic circles on the cheeks: the tongue quivered, or rather rolled violently in the mouth (although the jaws and lips remained rigid as before), and at length the same hideous voice which I have already described, broke forth:

"For God's sake!—quick!—quick!—put me to sleep—or, quick!—waken me!—quick!—*I say to you that I am dead!*"

I was thoroughly unnerved, and for an instant remained undecided what to do. At first I made an endeavor to recompose the patient; but, failing in this through total abeyance of the will, I retraced my steps and as earnestly struggled to awaken him. In this attempt I soon saw that I should be successful—or at least I soon fancied that my success would be complete—and I am sure that all in the room were prepared to see that patient awaken.

For what really occurred, however, it is quite impossible that any human being could have been prepared.

As I rapidly made the mesmeric passes, amid ejaculations of "dead! dead!" absolutely *bursting* from the tongue and not from the lips of the sufferer, his whole frame at once—within the space of a single minute, or less, shrunk—crumbled—absolutely *rotted* away beneath my hands. Upon the bed, before that whole company, there lay a nearly liquid mass of loathsome—of detestable putrescence.

EMERGENCY OPERATION

Arthur Porges

This report of a micro-micro-surgical exploit by a micro-micro-surgeon is straight, serious stuff. How can any of us know what is possible and what is impossible in the universe around us? Certainly there is no reason why the human-sized brain should be the only intelligent one there is: and here we give you a vivid story of medical heroism and intelligence on an infinitesimal scale.

Emergency Operation

THE CHIEF SURGEON made a crisp, authoritative gesture, and the medical students straightened in their seats. On the TV screen of the auditorium, which covered an entire wall, he was an impressive figure: tall, bony, white-haired, and intensely alive, with time-grooved lines of character on his mobile face. The laughter and conversation died away to an expectant hush. Word had gone around of an unusual case, one that was apparently luring even the senior staff members from their swank offices. As if to emphasize that point, Hoffman and Ball, two major officials of the American College of Surgeons, were walking sedately into the amphitheater to seat themselves among the fourth year students.

The chief surgeon began to speak with the slow, precisely enunciated words of a practiced lecturer. "As you know," he said, "we are confronted today with a rare, but not unique medical problem. The patient, on his way to the operating room right now, suffered a slight abrasion of the left thumb this morning at work."

He paused for a moment, presumably to organize his thoughts, but his hesitation produced an unexpected anti-climax, and many of the younger listeners snickered, taking his remark for humor. Recognizing this reaction, the surgeon frowned.

"No, gentlemen," he said wryly, "I wasn't trying to be funny, however the statement sounded. The point is that this man, dealing with atomics—and rather carelessly, it would appear—rubbed the lesion and managed to contaminate the wound with a tiny particle—less then a ten-thousandth of a milligram, we understand—of plutonium."

There was a sudden nodding of heads among the upper-classmen.

"Normally," the surgeon went on, "a quick, high amputation is indicated, since such a fragment, being highly radioactive, cannot be permitted to enter the main circulatory system. That sounds radical, I know, but it's been our only recourse in the past. The deadliness of this type of isotope, with a long half-life, is almost past belief; the size of the particle is irrelevant. Literally any mass of plutonium, however small, is invariably a killer inside the body.

"In this case, however, the patient was not sufficiently alerted to the dangers of his job, and on going off shift in the afternoon, he was found to be in a dangerous condition. The plutonium had already left his extremity and lodged elsewhere, behaving," he added a little ponderously, "with the typical perverseness of such foreign bodies."

He broke off, stepping aside, so that they could see the large, complex operating table glide in, under automatic control, on its rubberized tracks. It carried the anesthetized body of a burly, middle-aged man. Over the audio system they could hear his faintly whistling breath, typical of the new drug, prontocaine. More intriguing was the rhythmic purr of a pump. A fifty gallon plastic container of whole blood lay in its metal rack above the patient, and they could see the level fall slowly as the efficient little motor helped his heart drive fresh blood through the man's circulatory system. A plastic tube led from a vein in his right arm to a sump in the tiled floor.

"Yes," the lecturer continued, as if sensing their reaction through the operating room's own smaller screen which kept him in touch with his audience, "the best we can do at the moment is to keep renewing his entire blood supply. In that way, impossible with the ordinary closed circulation, we prevent the corpuscles from being repeatedly irradiated by the plutonium. The excess, which you see being drained off, will be banked and re-processed.

"If you wonder why nothing more positive is being attempted at this time, the explanation is that the particle has lodged in a tiny blood vessel, a capillary, in intimate contact with the posterior part of the optic nerve, where it branches out in the brain.

"Now, if we had two hours, modern techniques of brain surgery would enable us, with every hope of success, to reach that area and remove the foreign body; but the operation is quite difficult, as you professors of anatomy will testify, and in that time, gentlemen, the damage to the optic nerve—it's the right one—and the contiguous brain tissue would be so extensive that blindness of one eye would surely result immediately, to be followed later, as so often happens, by sympathetic atrophy of the left optic nerve, and total loss of sight. The brain lesions would produce less predictable symptoms, but undoubtedly serious ones. A very delicate situation, indeed. Our only hope, therefore, is more rapid action of a sort especially called for in this case. A geiger counter check has located the plutonium at the point I mentioned; and there being no other alternative, we have sent for a distinguished colleague who is uniquely competent to handle this emergency. It is while awaiting his arrival that I am able to give you this detailed summary of the problem."

There was an outburst of sibilant conversation. Many now guessed what was coming. It was a fortunate medical student who witnessed a case like this one. The last in this school had occurred almost six years earlier, and involved a normally inoperable glioma, one of the deadliest of brain tumors.

As one man the audience stiffened. A glittering speck, like a sunlit mote, was sailing majestically across the dustless, sterile air of the operating room. They could hear a shrill, pulsing beat as of tiny engines. The gleaming dot hovered momentarily, and then swooped down to alight on the stage of a TV microscope. On the auxiliary screen, which came to life immediately, the students saw the magnified image of a metal spheroid. A minute port flickered open, a ramp thrust out, and down this gangway came a microscopic organism. The size and approximate shape of a red blood corpuscle, it moved on dozens of whiplike cilia. Two eye-spots, immense in proportion to the creature's size, glowed symmetrically on each quadrant of the little disc. Lidless and bright, they were aglow with intelligence. A transparent sort of harness made a geometric pattern enclosing the saucer of protoplasm; its webbing held numerous complex instruments.

"Gentlemen," the chief surgeon boomed, "this is one of our newly trained colleagues from Ilkor—Dr. M'lo. He is about to enter the patient's blood stream and remove the particle of plutonium."

A technician came forward with a sparkling hypodermic syringe. They saw the hollow needle, a giant, glittering tube under the microscope, come to rest just before the Ilkerian doctor. A lipless slit at the upper center of the disc seemed to twist in a grimace of comical distaste. One could sense a feeling like that before an unwilling plunge into chilly water. The alien organism wrestled for a moment with the tough surface film at the point of the needle, and noting this difficulty, the technician drew back the plunger a trifle. M'lo was sucked through the opening, and a moment later could be seen swimming nonchalantly about in the clear tonic salt solution of the transparent syringe.

The magnified image vanished from the screen, and the audience saw the technician step alongside the patient. He gave the chief surgeon a questioning glance. "Go ahead, Joel," his superior ordered, and the technician expertly, in a single deft motion, found the great outer vein in the neck which drains the brain itself, and drove the plunger home.

"All we can do now is wait," the surgeon said. "There is no way Dr. M'lo can communicate with us at present. Even under ideal circumstances a very complicated electronic set-up is necessary. But while we're waiting, let me refresh your memories about our Ilkorian allies. As you may recall, it was only thirty years ago, in 1990, that the first organisms from Ilkor, a planet of Procyon, landed on earth. Luckily our worst period of nationalism was just over, and we made no serious blunders in our treatment of these altogether civilized beings. They are true seekers after knowledge, and before long they made enormously valuable contributions to many phases of our culture. A number of Ilkorians have devoted their best efforts to learning human anatomy and physiology, despite obstacles both in communication and size-differential.

This has been accomplished not only through study and consultation, but actual research within the bodies of human volunteers. Being the size of red blood corpuscles and free from bacterial infestation, they make ideal on-the-spot experts in microbiology.

"A few of them—all too few, unfortunately; but they are more interested in theory than practice—have made themselves available as actual medical specialists, aiding in difficult operations. They are in great demand. Dr. M'lo, for example, is kept very busy, so that we were lucky to obtain his services today. He's the one, oddly enough, who in this very room, six years ago, entered the brain of that famous patient and destroyed, in situ, with devices of his own invention, an "inoperable" tumor. He is an expert on radiation as well as a highly competent student of human physiology, which makes his assistance invaluable in this present emergency. By now, I hope, he is nearing the fragment of plutonium."

This was, in fact, the case. Swimming rapidly through the venous blood stream, battling its current, which while not of arterial strength was considerable, buffeted by corpuscles as bulky as himself, but less solid, Dr. M'lo knew he was getting close. The radiation detector on his webbing had its narrow bubble quivering against the stop. He paused in the rushing flood, annoyed by brittle platelets dashing against him in great numbers. He flailed his cilia vigorously, and huddled against the wall of the vessel where the blood moved more slowly. There was no light from the outside, of course, but to his ultra-sensitive eyespots every bit of living tissue gave off a faint glow. It was luminescence characteristic of life itself, although far below man's visual threshold and known to him only through the long-neglected researches of Gurwitch.

Just ahead, the vein branched, and it was necessary to take a reading. There was no time to retrace false steps. Every second the plutonium was bombarding the patient's tissues with missiles of tremendous energy and destructiveness. The left branch; no doubt of that. He studied the configuration carefully, drawing on his profound knowledge of human anatomy. Somewhere just a few inches away, there should be a smaller vein, and beyond it the very capillary, nestling against the optic nerve, in which the deadly fragment was wedged, stopped on its journey to the heart. M'lo, however, did not jump to conclusions. No one knew better than he how great were individual differences in the microscopic structure of humans. The major organs seldom varied in their relative locations, but capillary networks were not so obliging. Ah! Here was that last vein, all right. M'lo winced as a shower of nuclei battered his body. He could hear the crackling beat of atomic projectiles impinging on tissue; there was an aura of light ahead, painful to his eyes. He moved forward more slowly, almost with reluctance. What they didn't know, the doctors out there, was the personal agony of an operation like this one. To be sure, he was relatively immune to the worst effects of radioactivity, but the pain was hellish. The lancing electromagnetic rays were like summer sunlight on an inflamed conjunctiva; and a sharp-edged hail of nuclear rubbish, already disintegrated by its passage through tissue and water, pounded his tender body mercilessly.

Suddenly he stopped. A nuisance—a time waster, especially in this narrow capillary, where red corpuscles went single file. Just ahead loomed a white mass, a leucocyte, hurrying no doubt to the aid of the tortured cells, and suspecting somewhere in its vague intelligence a bacterial invasion. Just in advance of M'lo it had slipped through the vessel's wall, and now blocked his path. In its dim consciousness it seemed to recognize him as an alien, with no business in the blood stream. Although he was too big to engulf, it closed in, pseudopodia reaching for him. M'lo had no desire to grapple with the thing, moist, sticky and fetid. His eye-spots were cavities of pain; his whole body cringed under that terrible, relentless rain of atomic bullets. He wanted no more complications. The leucocyte was tenacious and strong, and even though it couldn't easily hurt him, it might immobilize many of his cilia, causing a delay fatal to the patient.

M'lo tried half-heartedly to escape through the cell wall, but he was less plastic than a red corpuscle, and couldn't quite make it at this point in the capillary. Well, there was no more time to waste. With a pair of cilia he whipped a projectile gun from his harness, pressed a stud, and under the thrust of highly compressed argon, a crystalline needle flashed through the plasma to imbed itself in the leucocyte's foamy mass. Instantly the tiny arrow dissolved; it was extremely, but locally, toxic. The white corpuscle knotted itself into an agonized blob. Then its almost invisible membrane burst, spilling loose protoplasm into the rushing fluid. A vacuole collapsed with a faint pop. But by that time, M'lo was on his way again.

The faint aura became a miniature sun; his eye-spots smarted even through the shields he fitted over them. Not too close. Even he couldn't take plutonium at short range. Nasty stuff. He made a quick, expert estimate of the damage; they'd want to know. The optic nerve was badly injured, but not hopelessly. He could see its pale surface right through the translucent capillary wall, itself a mass of lesions. There were drugs that would help those tissues mend. The brain was beyond his observation, but judging from the quantity and hardness of the radiation, there was some chance that the patient would suffer lifelong ataxia. M'lo hoped not.

He took a special grappler from his webbing, unreeling a length of metallic, flexible cord, and swimming as near the fiery, sputtering mass as he dared, sent the device gliding through the luminous fluid, almost at rest here in this far outpost of the circulatory system. It needed several tries, but finally the ingenious claws made a sort of cage about the plutonium, and M'lo pulled the cord tight. His plans were made. There was no time to drag the particle back by the circuitous route he had used in locating it. No, better to haul it away from the optic nerve immediately, and then take the direct, shortest way out.

He swam strongly, tugging at the cord, but the fragment, almost as big as he and incredibly dense, was tightly jammed. Inflammation of the capillary had closed the swollen tissue about it. With a little hiss of annoyance, M'lo snatched a wheeled instrument from his webbing, made a hasty inspection of the vein wall nearest him, and went to work. A few expert slashes with a sturdy knife, and a trio of holes gaped in the tough tissue. In a matter of moments he lashed the device —a simple block-and-tackle unit giving a mechanical advantage of four—in place, and threading the free end of the cord through, gave a savage tug.

There was the sound of ripping cells; the lacerated capillary loosed its grip, and the radioactive lump, sizzling and sparking viciously, was tumbling downstream at him. There was nothing else to do, unless he wanted that red-hot mass to bowl him over. M'lo dropped the cord and fled.

Coldly angry, reproachful of his own blunder, he ducked down a side branch to let the plutonium grate past. He was worried. Suppose the damned thing stuck in a worse place? Ruefully he began to trace it. Luckily the abandoned pulley was no problem; made of titanium alloy, it would be covered by venous tissue without causing inflammation.

Good! A break at last. He found the particle firmly jammed in another capillary, a minute vessel close by. Only the plutonium's weight and irregularity had diverted it from the main stream; otherwise he might be chasing it through the lungs by now.

Better get out of here. Taking another grappler from his web, he captured the fragment again, made a quick estimate of the situation, and with scalpels in four adjacent cilia, began to slice his way to the skin. The openings he made were too small to bleed; often he managed to slip, corpuscle-like, through a slacker wall of tissue. Only his great strength and dexterity, plus the array of manipulative instruments he carried, made it possible for him to bring the plutonium along. To a man, his task would have compared with that of hauling a loaded boxcar through several miles of tropical jungle. A final slash of the keen blades, and he was out, dragging the radioactive mass after, and standing on the patient's gently heaving chest with a white fold of sterile sheet like a ghastly sky above him.

The watchers saw the technician bend over with a powerful hand microscope, catch the plutonium in a bit of lead wool, and carry it triumphantly away. Beside the almost invisible specialist, waiting wearily on the patient's body, a single tiny spot of crimson welled. It was the only blood shed in the operation.

A MATTER OF ETHICS

J. R. Shango

This story appeared in the November, 1954, issue of the Magazine of Fantasy and Science Fiction, with an introductory note by Editor Anthony Boucher which read in part: "Despite an occasional classic . . . even Groff Conklin would find it impossible to assemble a specialized collection of medical s. f." Whereupon both of your editors at once wrote Mr. Boucher, protesting that each one could, indeed, produce just such an anthology. Mr. Boucher thereupon put Dr. F. and Mr. C. in touch with each other: and the result is the book you are now reading.

As for this story, which brought your collaborators together: there has rarely, if ever, been a more incisive commentary upon the dangers of unlimited power inherent in special knowledge than this bitter narrative of the discovery and criminal misuse of the Martian scalpels.

A Matter of Ethics

IT HAPPENED in the transition from planet-gravity to free-space drive. Mendez's last words had been a not too polite jest about a Martian dancer they'd seen the night before. And now he was sprawled there, clutching his chest, his face the color of sour milk.

Colby fixed the time on his watch. The transition period hadn't been more than a minute at most.

"What is it, Doctor Mendez?" Colby felt for his pulse. Fast, thready, shocky. Mendez's lips were compressed so tightly together there was a ring of white around them where the blood had been forced away.

"Pain in your chest?" Colby thought he saw a slight attempt to nod his head. With the icy ringing pain crushing his heart, it took a strong man to even nod.

Swiftly Colby got the Cardisev from the emergency locker in the cabin bulkhead, broke off the plastic guard and injected two cc's intramuscularly. Then he pulled gently on Mendez's arm, holding up the syrette so Mendez could see what he wanted. Slowly Mendez let his arm come out straight. Colby grabbed across the biceps muscle of the upper arm and squeezed, engorging the veins. Deftly he inserted the needle into the bulging cephalic vein and injected a small amount directly into the bloodstream. Almost instantly Mendez relaxed, then went deeper and deeper into unconsciousness. Colby watched him carefully, took a small ophthalomscope out of his pocket and examined the vessels on the retina to see how constricted they were. Finally he took the syrette out of the vein and threw it away. He sat down beside Mendez and found himself wet with perspiration, his hand trembling, his knees and elbows stiff from the strain. He didn't work on a patient of Mendez's eminence every day.

He checked the time on his watch again. Ten minutes. It was certainly a coronary. Mendez wasn't too old, but he was in a position of wealth and authority. He no longer needed to worry about pleasing other people so he'd let his body go. A common enough situation with specialists; no inherent sense of artistry except in connection with one thing. They could be perfectionists in fire sculpture, hypothalamic surgery, or Venusian phonetics, but they didn't carry over their perfectionism to the care of their bodies and this was what happened. The coronary vessels of the heart wall had lost their resiliency—perhaps foolish or capricious eating habits had thickened the vessel walls—and now, a sudden stress, the cushioned acceleration of the space drive, and a slight alarm reaction, the coronary vessels constrict, stopping the flow of blood to the heart wall, pain in the heart, more alarm, more constriction, more pain. A vicious circle, and if it lasts over a minute, clots start forming in the vessels, and cells in the heart wall begin to die from lack of oxygen. If the lack is long enough a large area of the heart wall will die. If it is large enough, nothing can save the victim except immediate intervention by a skilled mural cardiosurgeon, like Mendez.

Colby sighed. Yes, like Mendez. Not like Colby. He'd only had five years residency in surgery, then five years in cardiology, then three years in mural cardiosurgery. Thirteen years in labs, autopsy rooms, surgical amphitheaters. Thirteen years of emergency call, interrupted sleep, hasty meals, and class four subsistence level pay. Thirteen years and then he'd taken his examination for the Intergalactic Board of Mural Cardiosurgery.

And what had Mendez said? Mendez, the president of that august body! "It would be criminal for you to operate on humans at this stage in your development." Criminal! And what had the Board recommended? Five more years of special supervised training under a Board man!

Five more years of crap from Harkaway!

Colby checked the time and the pulse and the respirations. Quieting down a bit. Nothing to do for the moment but wait and let the vessels relax, adjust the Cardisev dosage to fit the changing physiology.

Colby picked up the phone and told the operator to summon the rocket's doctor. Then he waited and while he waited he thought. He'd put in three of those five extra years already. Three onerous, wasted years with that nut Harkaway. Three years doing over the things he'd learned and relearned and rerelearned. It would be different if he'd taken up valvular cardiosurgery. There you had four valves to mess with and quite a variety of techniques and operations. But no, he'd specialized in mural cardiosurgery. The walls of the heart. Only one technique, really only one successful operation: the Chauncey operation. It seemed simple enough. Excise the bloodless, dying area of the heart wall under deep hibernative anesthesia and sew in a plastic patch with the edges in healthy tissue. The patch was contractile and conductive to electrical impulses. It simulated the action of the branching cardiac muscle fibrils perfectly, and it preserved the continuity of the electrochemical network that initiated and synchronized the heart action. *When* it worked. And it always worked, said the Board, when the operation was correctly performed.

And how many times had he performed the operation? Thousands. On all sorts of living animals. On numerous post mortem human hearts. On three condemned psycho-resistant criminals. On seven Adromedan humanoid P.W.'s. The films were in the records to show his deftness, his meticulousness, his skill. He'd always been good with his hands, but after that much training even an adiadokokinetic cretin would have been good. And how many times had the patch worked for him? Not once.

Because, said the Board: 1) the patch is designed and balanced to fit the physiology of the damaged heart, not the healthy; 2) only diplomates of the Board have the finesse to fit it properly in place.

The light flashed over the door and the clicking started. He pressed the button on the chair arm and the rocket's doctor came in.

He looked at Mendez. Felt his pulse. Picked up the Cardisev syrette and turned to Colby, his eyebrows raised, his lids slightly wider than they'd been at dinner listening to Mendez the surgical god.

"Caught him during the drive transition," said Colby.

Jorgenson pursed his lips and held the syrette up to the lighter ceiling area, estimating the amount used.

"I gave him a heavy dose, but I'm inclined to think the area is extending. Held him too long for it to be just temporary vessel spasm."

Jorgenson shook his head. "I'm glad you're along this trip."

"I can't do any more than you can. I'm not a diplomate of the Board. Just eligible. They'd slap me with a manslaughter charge just as fast as they would you."

Jorgenson started. "Suppose he goes out?"

"What would you do? It's not only a violation of law, it's a violation of ethics. I'd lose my license. I'd lose sixteen years of specialty training. And I'd get psychiatric alteration as well."

Jorgenson sucked in the inside of his cheek and chewed on it a little. "The operation may be performed only by a Board man or under direct supervision of a Board man," he quoted more or less accurately from the law.

"And you can't supervise under hibernative anesthesia," said Colby.

Jorgenson shook his head. "Nope. Guess he's got himself. We could take him down to surgery and operate and if he died say we did it post mortem. I have the authority to post anyone in flight, for reasons of planetary medical security. But if he lived until we jetted in and then died, you'd be socked for manslaughter."

"And breach of ethics," added Colby. "How about getting the cardioscope up and we'll see if we can see anything yet?"

It was a somewhat risky job for the crew, getting the cardioscope out of the unshielded storage space, but they got it. It was a small machine which fed the multiple electrocardiograph leads to an integrating device that projected a composite oscillogram for direct reading. They watched the light lines form, fluctuate, waver, strengthen, finally the pattern hardened. There was the depressed S-T segment, the cove plane inversion of the T wave. At first it wasn't too clear, but after about an hour the pattern was diagnostic, even without any knowledge of his normal gram. Occlusion of the coronary vessel supplying the anterior wall of the heart. They had to administer Cardisev a number of times in small doses before it looked as though it had stopped spreading.

"If you want me for anything, Doctor, just call," said Jorgenson.

Colby busied himself with a chart of the dosages, and the pulse and cardiogram changes. Finally he thought he could risk bringing Mendez up. The flaccid face muscles pulled the sagging face together as they gained tone. It was like watching putty assume form under the artist's hands. The dominant, incisive nose even seemed to gain in size as Mendez came up. The rock-like chin grew sturdier, the deep lines deeper. Finally his eyes opened, swept across the ceiling, wavered, closed again, opened again and came over to Colby. For a while he just looked at him. Checked each feature. Fastened lastly on his eyes.

"How bad?" Mendez said softly.

"Anterior. Not too large and not extending."

Mendez closed his eyes. His chin seemed to grow larger, set more firmly. The jaw muscles in his cheeks bunched as though he was testing them. He turned when Colby gave him another shot of Cardisev.

"How much?" asked Mendez.

Colby told him. It was just enough to keep his vessels relaxed now, it wouldn't be enough to disturb his conscious faculties.

Mendez took some deep breaths experimentally, smiled at Colby.

"Never realized how good that Cardisev was." Suddenly the shadows in the corners of his eyes seemed to deepen and his chin slid to one side as though he was thinking.

"Colby! What were you going to do if it had extended?"

Colby looked down at his hands. Licked his lips with a tentative tongue. What did the old bastard want him to say? Might make a big difference on his Boards.

He looked at him. "Ethically, there isn't much I could do, but . . ." He hesitated over the words, gingerly testing each one as he spoke.

"But what?" said Mendez. He said it very softly. To Colby there seemed a hopeful, encouraging note in it. The same sort of note he'd heard before when he was exploring a theory that Mendez didn't like during the examination.

"But I wished there was some way I could have helped you."

"Humph!" snorted Mendez and lifted his eyes back to the ceiling.

"Let's see the cardioscope," he said.

Colby turned it so he could see it and switched it on.

Mendez didn't like it. It was more definite now, and perhaps a bit larger. It was getting near the critical level. Anything could tip him now.

Suddenly Mendez swung his beaky face back to him.

"How about the deceleration transition?"

It stunned Colby. He hadn't thought of that. Mendez might not be able to stand the shock. The margin of safety was not large enough to experiment with. If he lost any more tissue during the deceleration there would be no time to operate. The heart would either fibrillate, or so much muscle be involved that it could not contract and express an adequate amount of blood. He would be dead before they could get through the pericardium.

The realization of death flowed between them. He takes it well, thought Colby with that little bit of mind that seems to stand apart from conscious processes to comment on them.

Mendez's narrow lips seemed to grow narrower.

"That's it, eh, Colby! That's what you're thinking, isn't it, Colby?"

Colby looked away. "Not necessarily. You stand a fair chance." The words sounded artificial as a funeral wreath.

"You know what you'd get if you told me that on an exam, Colby!"

Colby didn't answer. But he knew. It was a chance no one would take who knew anything about the matter. It was graver than that. There was the imminent possibility of something happening in flight. Right now. Anything might exhaust his reserve. A sudden shift in course, a fright, a fall, any of a hundred thousand little things, a nightmare, a difficult b.m., a sneeze, anything from excessive worry to laughter. No, the best thing to do was to operate immediately. Rocket landings weren't intended for bum hearts. If he survived without a patch it would be a fluke.

"How long was I out?"

"About two and a half hours," said Colby.

"From transition?"

"From transition."

"We have plently of time then." He was silent. Calculating something, Colby thought. His will, probably. It would be pretty meaty if he was a typical Board man. They're all very wealthy. Should be, judging by the number of operations they do and the astronomical fees they charge. And they don't overwork, in spite of the high incidence of coronaries among humanoids. Plenty of trusted and trained dogs like me, mused Colby, to carry the burden of the diagnostic work and the emergency preparation. A few minutes at the crucial part of the operation was enough work for them, sometimes they observed the rest, sometimes not. You'd think with a future like that everyone strong enough to stand at an operating table would be trying to get into mural cardiosurgery. Yet they weren't. Probably the lengthy training and the arduous reviewing for the exams had something to do with it. But the singular fact that year in and year out, regardless of the number of examinees, the number of living members of the Board never seemed to increase probably had a good deal more to do with it.

Perhaps they're right in their exclusiveness, shrugged Colby with his forebrain. Certainly whenever the procedure was attempted by a surgeon who was not a Board diplomate the patient died. The Board invariably said he had not evaluated the criteria correctly or his technique was faulty. It was a good twenty years now since it had been made part of interplanetary law that an automatic charge of manslaughter be preferred against anyone performing the operation other than Board men or under their direct supervision. The medical profession generally felt the law was superfluous since ethics covered the situation fairly well, but the interplanetary legal administrators apparently didn't agree.

"You'll have to try it, Colby." Mendez's voice was quietly determined.

Try it, Colby. Go ahead, try it. You've got nothing to lose. Except your frontal lobes. When the psychs get through with you you won't even remember trying it. They'll give you a nice easy machine to operate for the rest of your life.

This wouldn't be like Chauncey; they'd had no automatic manslaughter law in those days. Colby looked at Mendez's hands. The hands that had operated on Chauncey. Chauncey, the discoverer of the technique, known as widely for his philosophical writings as for his famous operation. The man who, after the disappointing failure of the highly touted embryological transplants, had revived interest in the possibilities of a surgical treatment for coronaries. Chauncey had died the week after he published the operation. Of a coronary. Mendez, his assistant, had operated, but he'd been unable to save him. It had extended too far. Shortly thereafter Mendez had founded the Board, and he'd been either president or secretary of the Board for alternate terms ever since.

"I . . . I don't know."

Mendez curled his lip. "What don't you know? This is what you've been wanting, isn't it? You've wanted to be a mural cardiosurgeon! You've trained long enough, God knows. Well, here's your chance!"

Colby felt himself begin to tingle. His palms were wet again. By Solar, there may be a way yet. If Mendez wanted him to do it enough he could make him a Board member here and now. A bargain! Before, all he'd had to offer Mendez was competition. Make me a Board member and I'll compete with you for cases. I'll set up a clinic of my own. I'll share your fame and fortune. No wonder he hadn't been anxious to welcome him in, any more than master jetmen welcome apprentice jetmen, or master plumbers apprentice plumbers. But now! He could offer him his life in return. A bargain. A simple bargain. And like all bargains it would be wise to get all the details out of the way. Colby raised his eyes to Mendez's.

"You yourself said I wasn't ready yet." Colby watched Mendez's lids flick up. "In fact, you said it would be criminal for me to operate. That it would be better for me to let the man die normally than to kill him with surgery I was incapable of. Kill him, you said."

Mendez's cold eyes winked shrewdly. "Yes," he said slowly, "yes, I recall saying that. But that was three years ago." He paused. "Since then many things have changed. Techniques have changed. You have changed. Harkaway tells me you are much improved."

"He told me a couple more years."

"Perhaps he is too conservative. I will go over the procedure with you step by step. You will use my instruments. I have watched you work with me on this lecture trip and I have confidence in you."

He paused, cocked his head analytically, looking toward the golden future. "You know what this will mean, when you are successful. It practically insures your admission to the Board. Possibly a year or so more training under Harkaway since he is your superior and we can't go over his head. But I can practically guarantee your admission the next time your name comes up."

Practically! Sure, practically. Harkaway may not recommend me. The police may say I'm a criminal guilty of attempted murder. Colby could imagine Mendez shrugging his shoulders, smiling with mock rue. "You know I'm sorry, Colby, but after all I'm not the law."

Colby shook his head. "I don't see how I can do it, I really don't."

Mendez suddenly tightened up and lay back, his head twisted on his neck, his lips a thin faint line.

Colby quickly found a vein and shot the Cardisev in. He took his wrist and checked the pulse rate . . . dropping gradually, gradually. Mendez slowly relaxed, slowly the stiffness left his neck, slowly he turned back to Colby, his face a bloodless, pain-etched mask of tallow. In those few minutes he had aged horribly.

He opened his mouth and breathed through it a few times before he spoke. "We'll have to chance it, Colby." His voice was a hoarse whisper. "It's the only chance I have. It may be too late in five minutes. It may extend while we're talking."

"Like Chauncey," Colby said, almost unconsciously.

"Why did you say that?" spat Mendez so vehemently that

Colby sprang back away from the bed. "Why? Damn you! Why?"

"Why . . . why . . . it just struck me that you were then the student operating on the master, and now I'm to be the student operating on the master."

Mendez looked at him a moment, then his lips drew back from his teeth and his eyes squinted up. "Sometimes, Colby, I wonder what you young fellows think about!" His face became all deep wrinkles, seeming to center out from his mouth. It was a way he had of speaking through his teeth whenever he was excited. It almost seemed he was afraid to move his jaw for fear he'd bite the person he was speaking to. "What fantastic, sadistic, libelous dreams must wander around in your skulls!"

Colby listened outwardly. But he was used to tirades of all kinds. Sixteen years of residency work had inured him to the most biting sarcasm and the most personal obscenities. His objective was Board qualification and these things were all part of the initiation. They annoyed him and aroused bitterness in him, but once he'd made up his mind to take whatever came they only made him cling more resolutely to his course. It was the only way a resident could survive.

Mendez's face had a thin shine of perspiration all over it. He switched on the cardioscope and the lines flickered a moment then solidified. Rate a little faster, slight deepening of the T wave, but essentially the gram was the same.

"Don't believe it's wise for you to keep looking at that thing," said Colby.

"What did you decide?"

"You know the law: an automatic charge of manslaughter lodged against anyone attempting the operation who is not a Board member." Let the bastard sweat a while. Colby remembered the nausea before the exams. The constant attacks of diarrhea. The almost suicidal depressions after they announced his failure. Let him sweat.

"Listen, Colby. Have the rocket's captain and the doctor come down. I'll make a statement before them requesting that you perform it. That will protect you. As president of the Board I'll endorse your operating on me."

That could do it. He was getting close. Armed with that statement and a successful operation on a human, not an ordinary human, but a Board president, he couldn't be flunked again. Maybe he'd be able to avoid those last two years of Harkaway's castrating insolence and demeaning orders. The ridiculous way he raced around—"all the time you want up to twenty seconds." The man was insane.

But that could do it. That could get him Board qualification. *Could?* Colby wanted something that would, not could! Something he could count on. The Board was all powerful; what it giveth, it could also taketh away. He could hear Mendez weaseling out of it some way.

Colby looked at the deck. Have to phrase this right, no sense in twisting it off in him. He did look paler and tenser than was good. If it extended now and he died . . . Two years, a golden opportunity rusted away.

"Don't you think it would be better to have it down in writing, just in case . . ."

"Certainly, certainly. Have the captain and the doctor come down and I'll dictate it. But you won't need it, Colby. Nothing will happen to me. You'll do it, won't you!" It was a statement, not a question. His color was better now. His eyes glinted with the hard shine of polished steel. He thought Colby would do it.

Colby looked up at the security indicator set in the bulkhead. "It still doesn't fulfill the letter of the law. It says a Board member or under direct supervision of a Board member. They could still prosecute me under the criminal code."

"Well, I certainly can't supervise you while you're working on my heart." There was more than a little despair mixed with the sarcasm.

"No," said Colby softly. "No, that's true. But you can make me a member of the Board."

The words seemed to hang there, in the air between them. Though there were no echoes in that place of gleaming plast-alloy and smooth curves, still they seemed to resonate and play in the recesses.

Mendez looked steadily down at his own feet, biting speculatively on the inside of his lip. Thinking, thinking. Colby could almost hear him thinking.

"I'd like to, Colby. Believe me, I would. And if I could, I would. But you know it takes four members to make an examining panel. Besides, there . . . besides . . ." The sentence trailed off somewhere in space.

Besides! Sure, besides! *Besides the Board is full!* Colby's mind completed the sentence. *There are no vacancies! There have been no vacating deaths among the membership.* That was the way it was. Besides! After he was well and down on earth and in the saddle again he'd dream up a lot more *besides*. He and that cockroach, Harkaway.

"I don't know," said Colby. "I'll have the captain and the doctor come down, and then I think I'll go into the chapel and pray for guidance."

"Guidance!" Mendez's eyebrows shot up into the air. "Listen, Colby, you don't need any guidance. You were good enough when you took your exam three years ago." A thin note of desperation pierced his voice. "Three years ago! Do you understand?"

"Take it easy, Doctor. I'll give you a bit more Cardisev."

"No, wait! I want to convince you, get your answer now. You don't need guidance." Mendez had long ago decided he himself was as much of a god as there was in the universe. "The Board is a sort of union. We keep the membership down to a limited number. For economic reasons. The operation itself is simple."

"Simple! Sixteen years now . . ."

"I know, I know. But there has been a . . . a . . . a new development." He seized on the words and raced ahead. "A new development that simplifies it considerably."

"I know of nothing new lately, other than the Peterman creatinine chain exposure. And that didn't help the technique any."

"No, no, not that. Only the Board men know about it. It's the scalpel blade."

Maybe he'd had too much Cardisev. Maybe he was going off his rocker. Have to operate fast, before he got hallucinatory and violent and blew the thing out. Colby started over to the emergency locker.

"No, wait, Colby! This is the truth. The blade is made of an isotopal alloy and acts as a catalytic agent. It catalyzes the reaction which seals the edges of the plastic patch to the heart wall. The sutures are just window dressing."

Could it be . . . Could the bastard be telling the truth?

"What is this alloy?"

"It's quite complex." The words fairly burst out of Mendez now, as out of a neurotic who has decided to confess all. "Contains a small amount of a radioactive isotope of the Martian elemental metal, Maranium. It acts on the trace metals in the muscle tissue, linking them ionically through their salts with the metals in the patch. Makes a continuous conductive pathway for the electrical component of the stimulating impulses. That, plus the tight seal, makes it work."

He pointed at his bag. "In there, in the little lead box on top, are twelve blades. Practically indestructible. One would last a lifetime. This lecture trip to Mars was just a cover. They're made up there to my specifications. I'm picking them up and taking them to earth. They're cheap, but I have to keep them limited. They're the secret of the whole thing. Without them the patch won't fuse and blows out every time."

"Every time?"

"Every time."

"Then even back when I took my exam . . . Even before that . . . "

"Yes, I lied." Mendez didn't hesitate, nor blush, nor falter, nor seem embarrassed. He was used to lying. "It's not new. Chauncey found it by accident. Didn't even know what he had. But you see how simple it is. You'll do it now, won't you?"

"Yes, I'll do it." There was strange new resolution in Colby's voice.

"Good. Then when we get back to earth, I'll see that you pass your exam."

"I'll want to take my exam right away."

Mendez looked away. "Well, Harkaway may have something to say about that. Have you ever done anything to antagonize Harkaway?"

Colby thought about it.

"No matter," Mendez hastened on. "We couldn't very well hurry it up. Would look very strange now that it's in the records that you have the five year period to serve."

"But what's the point? Now that I know the . . ."

Mendez cut in. "I'll have to ask you on your honor as a physician not to reveal any of this material." His eyes had that metallic luster again and his color was almost florid. He had Colby now. He was going to operate. He had dangled the Boards in front of him and he was his goat again. "It's an ethical problem of course. Medical ethics. Should you disregard my wishes in this matter you would probably shortly lose your license for breach of ethics." Suddenly his face relaxed into a smile.

"But why am I talking this way to you, John! No need to brief you on ethics. Not a man with your training."

"I'll get the captain," Colby said.

The captain came and the doctor, and the statement was taken and signed by everyone present. Colby tucked it way in his pocket, got the box of blades out of Mendez's bag and took them to his cabin where he put the box and the statement in his personal bulkhead safe.

The operating room was ready. Mendez was on the table, the field was prepared, and Colby was in the anteroom mixing the anesthetic. This first dose would be given intravenously, then the hypothermia apparatus on the table itself would rapidly bring the patient's body temperature down to hibernative levels where the blood flowed slowly, heart action was markedly decreased, and the oxygen demand was less. Colby swirled the anesthetic solution in the decanter, then slowly, meticulously he added 30 drops of epinephrine. Then he thought about it and added double that amount again. Epinephrine, the chemical of shock. The adrenals shot it into the bloodstream when the organism was threatened. It keyed it up, tensed it, stimulated it for the final supreme struggle. A few drops made the surface vessels constrict, the heart beat faster, the fingers quiver. A few drops. Thirty drops would jolt him the way breaking his legs with a baseball bat would jolt him. Sixty drops would make his myocardium quiver like the *recti abdominis* of an Egyptian belly dancer. What would ninety drops do? Colby thought it would do enough. He filled the syringe and went into the O.R.

Colby wrote out a consultant's report and clipped it to the death certificate. "Patient expired during anesthetic induction. Undoubtedly due to an extension of the coronary occlusion." They would perform an autopsy on earth and what would they find? Evidence of an enormous coronary probably. Epinephrine is a normal constituent of blood and no one would run quantitative determinations. If they did no one would consider the matter other than a final massive shock reaction.

Communications relayed the sad news as soon as the rocket reached the ionosphere. When the rocket jetted down on the salt flats, Mendez's widow was waiting. And with her were two Board men, Harkaway and Gehman. Harkaway took Mendez's bag and nodded curtly to Colby. Colby returned the nod even more curtly.

The same day he requested an immediate examination in a visiogram to the secretary of the Board in Boston. He followed it with a visiostat of the Mendez statement. He got his reply at his apartment the next day.

"In view of the circumstances, the Board will make up a special panel and examine you as you request. But you must understand that in the event of failure, you will automatically be ineligible for reexamination for ten years, and in ad—" Colby didn't bother to read any further. He went over to Harkaway's office and got his scrub shoes and some things he kept in his locker. Harkaway sat there and watched him. Not saying a word. As Colby left he made a short prayer that he might never see the dyspeptic bastard again.

But when Colby arrived in Boston a week later, there was Harkaway in the examination room, his eyes glittering, his lips barely visible, his chin set stiff as concrete in his corroded face. He had got on the panel of examiners for this special session by personal request. He crouched at his place at the table, clasping and unclasping his hands, hunching his shoulders forward and rocking on the edge of his seat like an edgy boxer in his corner waiting to get at his opponent. The panel, by some common consent, let him ask Colby the first question.

He began with evident satisfaction. Almost smiling. "Describe in detail,"—he lingered lovingly over *detail*—"giving accurately the amounts of all agents used according to the apothecaries' system, the method of standardizing crude digitalis leaf which employed the terminology 'cat units.'" He sat back glowing.

Digitalis, thought Colby, one of the ancient "natural" drugs used by witch doctors. And the apothecaries' system of measurement, a system known now only to antiquarians and esoteric Ph.D.'s. It would be nice to be able to give him the goddamn answer.

"Do you know the answer, Colby?" Harkaway jarred him out of his reverie.

"I think so, Harkaway."

Harkaway jumped like a galvanized muscle wehen Colby left off the *Doctor*. His nostrils flared sharply, and Colby could hear the breath whistling in and out.

"Well, what is it?" He bit the words off.

Colby took his time, looked up at the ceiling, let his gaze slide slowly back down to Harkaway . . . and smiled.

Harkaway was dead white, almost off his chair, his hands clenched before him, his pupils so dilated with rage that his eyes looked space black against the pallor of his skin. He opened his mouth to say something, but only a hoarse, cracked sound came out.

"Don't have a coronary, Harkaway," Colby chuckled. "There's one vacancy on the Board already."

"Would you kindly answer the question, Colby!" It was Feldman, the secretary.

Colby smiled at him too.

"It's all in the scalpel blade. A matter of a catalyzed reaction involving trace metals."

Feldman reached out and clicked off the recorder which kept the permanent records of the examinations.

They spent some time haggling over the details, but in the end everything was settled with nice attention to the ethical principles involved. Harkaway had to be given restoratives before he was able to leave the examination room. Colby passed, of course.

The press paid very little attention to his appointment. In fact, even in medical circles there was no noticeable reaction when Colby was admitted to the Board. Perhaps it was this very lack of any previous publicity that so focused every news purveyor's hungry eye upon him when his monograph was published; in any event, they blazoned his name across space like a comet's tail. Suddenly every academic honor, and a good many unacademic ones, avalanched down on him for his discovery of a fact that, by their own admission, had previously escaped the notice of all the members of the Board, namely that the largest part of their success was due to their use of a rather unique scalpel blade. This revelation plus the simplified technique described by Colby in his monograph, made it possible for any general surgeon to perform the Chauncey operation successfully. Immediately there was a revision in interplanetary law, a marked drop in the mortality figure due to coronaries, and an even greater drop in the incomes of the members of the Board of Mural Cardiosurgery.

In the years that have passed since then, neither of these developments seems to have discomfited Colby. The blade, now professionally known as the Colby blade, is made exclusively by the Colby factory on Mars; and the tremendous galaxy-wide sale has made him a tidy fortune.

A good deal of this money he has generously devoted to aiding indigent surgical residents, alleviating a good deal of suffering in this almost universally oppressed group. In the light of this and his many other philanthropies, it is difficult for some to understand his persistent refusal to contribute to the Intergalactic Fund for the Rehabilitation of Board Mural Cardiosurgeons, a fund called into being by the affliction of increasing numbers of Board cardiosurgeons with acute forms of paranoia. Indeed, so many Board men have shown symptoms of this malady that it has come to be regarded in clinical circles as an occupational hazard.

On this basis the clinicians find it logical that the highest incidence is among the older members, but applying the same logic, they find it difficult to explain why one of the most frequent manifestations of the disease seems to be a fixed delusion that Colby is persecuting them. This delusion is particularly persistent and refractory to treatment, and the number of Board cardiosurgeons ultimately requiring psychiatric alteration has surprised even the psychiatrists, those arcanic practitioners who have so long and so frequently maintained that nothing could surprise them.

An equally astonishing number of Board men succumb each year to coronary disease. These deaths have also been attributed statistically to their paranoia, for the Board men display an amazing and obstinate reluctance to allow Colby or any of their former residents to operate on them, preferring to take their chances on physiologic survival. This can only be explained on the basis of lunatic doubts of the skill of their former residents, for they certainly could have no other reason to fear them.

BOLDEN'S PETS

F. L. Wallace

Negative symbiosis? Never heard of it? Most symbiotes keep each other alive. Contrariwise, if one is bad for the other, the relationship is called antipathetic symbiosis, or parasitism. But did you ever hear of a positive parasite?—a parasite that enjoyed dying for you, rather than living off you? That was the novelty Bolden found to be so blessedly real out on Van Daamas' planet—a novelty which the doctors could hardly believe, but which nevertheless was forced upon them by the fact that Bolden got well, which he never should have. For the physicians involved, it was a kind of embarrassing mistake of nature. For the patient, it was a natural miracle.

Bolden's Pets

HIS HANDS were shaking as he exhibited the gifts. If he were
on Earth, he would be certain it was the flu; in the Centaurus
system, kranken. But this was Van Daamas, so Lee Bolden
couldn't say what he had. Man hadn't been here long enough
to investigate the diseases with any degree of thoroughness.
There were always different hazards to overcome as new
planets were settled.

But whatever infection he had, Bolden was not greatly concerned as he counted out the gifts. He had felt the onset of
illness perhaps an hour before. When he got back to the
settlement he'd be taken care of. That was half a day's flight
from here. The base was equipped with the best medical
facilities that had been devised.

He stacked up the gifts to make an impressive show: five
pairs of radar goggles, seven high-velocity carbines, seven
boxes of ammunition. This was the natives' own rule and
was never to be disregarded—it had to be an odd number of
gifts.

The Van Daamas native gazed impassively at the heap. He
carried a rather strange bow and a quiver was strapped to his
thigh. With one exception, the arrows were brightly colored,
mostly red and yellow. Bolden supposed this was for easy recovery in case the shot missed. But there was always one
arrow that was stained dark blue. Bolden had observed this
before—no native was ever without that one somber-looking
arrow.

The man of Van Daamas stood there and the thin robe that
was no protection against the elements rippled slightly in the
chill current of air that flowed down the mountainside. "I
will go talk with the others," he said in English.

"Go talk," said Bolden, trying not to shiver. He replied in
native speech, but a few words exhausted his knowledge and
he had to revert to his own language. "Take the gifts with
you. They are yours, no matter what you decide."

The native nodded and reached for a pair of goggles. He

tried them on, looking out over fog and mist-shrouded slopes. These people of Van Daamas needed radar less than any race Bolden knew of. Living by preference in mountains, they had developed a keenness of vision that enabled them to see through the perpetual fog and mist far better than any Earthman. Paradoxically it was the goggles they appreciated most. Extending their sight seemed more precious to them than powerful carbines.

The native shoved the goggles up on his forehead, smiling with pleasure. Noticing that Bolden was shivering, he took his hands and examined them. "Hands sick?" he queried.

"A little," said Bolden. "I'll be all right in the morning."

The native gathered up the gifts. "Go talk," he repeated as he went away.

Lee Bolden sat in the copter and waited. He didn't know how much influence this native had with his people. He had come to negotiate, but this might have been because he understood English somewhat better than the others.

A council of the natives would make the decision about working for the Earthmen's settlement. If they approved of the gifts, they probably would. There was nothing to do now but wait—and shiver. His hands were getting numb and his feet weren't much better.

Presently the native came out of the fog carrying a rectangular wicker basket. Bolden was depressed when he saw it. One gift in return for goggles, carbines, ammunition. The rate of exchange was not favorable. Neither would the reply be.

The man set the basket down and waited for Bolden to speak. "The people have talked?" asked Bolden.

"We have talked to come," said the native, holding out his fingers. "In five or seven days, we come."

It was a surprise, a pleasant one. Did one wicker basket equal so many fine products of superlative technology? Apparently it did. The natives had different values. To them, one pair of goggles was worth more than three carbines, a package of needles easily the equivalent of a box of ammunition.

"It's good you will come. I will leave at once to tell them

at the settlement," said Bolden. There was something moving in the basket, but the weave was close and he couldn't see through it.

"Stay," the man advised. "A storm blows through the mountains."

"I will fly around the storm," said Bolden.

If he hadn't been sick he might have accepted the offer. But he had to get back to the settlement for treatment. On a strange planet you never could tell what might develop from a seemingly minor ailment. Besides he'd already been gone two days searching for this tribe in the interminable fog that hung over the mountains. Those waiting at the base would want him back as soon as he could get there.

"Fly far around," said the man. "It is a big storm." He took up the basket and held it level with the cabin, opening the top. An animal squirmed out and disappeared inside.

Bolden looked askance at the eyes that glowed in the dim interior. He hadn't seen clearly what the creature was and he didn't like the idea of having it loose in the cabin, particularly if he had to fly through a storm. The man should have left it in the basket. But the basket plus the animal would have been two gifts—and the natives never considered anything in even numbers.

"It will not hurt," said the man. "A gentle pet."

As far as he knew, there were no pets and very few domesticated animals. Bolden snapped on the cabin light. It was one of those mysterious creatures every tribe kept in cages near the outskirts of their camps. What they did with them no one knew and the natives either found it impossible to explain or did not care to do so.

It seemed unlikely that the creatures were used for food and certainly they were not work animals. And in spite of what this man said, they were not pets either. No Earthman had ever seen a native touch them nor had the creatures ever been seen wandering at large in the camp. And until now, none had been permitted to pass into Earth's possession. The scientists at the settlement would regard this acquisition with delight.

"Touch it," said the native.

Bolden held out his trembling hand and the animal came to him with alert and friendly yellow eyes. It was about the size of a rather small dog, but it didn't look much like one. It resembled more closely a tiny slender bear with a glossy and shaggy cinnamon coat. Bolden ran his hands through the clean-smelling fur and the touch warmed his fingers. The animal squirmed and licked his fingers.

"It has got your taste," said the native. "Be all right now. It is yours." He turned and walked into the mist.

Bolden got in and started the motors while the animal climbed into the seat beside him. It was a friendly thing and he couldn't understand why the natives always kept it caged.

He headed straight up, looking for a way over the mountains to avoid the impending storm. Fog made it difficult to tell where the peaks were and he had to drop lower, following meandering valleys. He flew as swiftly as limited visibility would allow, but he hadn't gone far when the storm broke. He tried to go over the top of it, but this storm seemed to have no top. The region was incompletely mapped and even radar wasn't much help in the tremendous electrical display that raged around the ship.

His arms ached as he clung to the controls. His hands weren't actually cold, they were numb. His legs were leaden. The creature crept closer to him and he had to nudge it away. Momentarily the distraction cleared his head. He couldn't put it off any longer. He had to land and wait out the storm—if he could find a place to land.

Flexing his hands until he worked some feeling into them, he inched the ship lower. A canyon wall loomed at one side and he had to veer away and keep on looking.

Eventually he found his refuge—a narrow valley where the force of the winds was not extreme—and he set the land anchor. Unless something drastic happened, it would hold.

He made the seat into a bed, decided he was too tired to eat, and went directly to sleep. When he awakened, the storm was still raging and the little animal was snoozing by his side.

He felt well enough to eat. The native hadn't explained what the animal should be fed, but it accepted everything

Bolden offered. Apparently it was as omnivorous as Man. Before lying down again, he made the other seat into a bed, although it didn't seem to matter. The creature preferred being as close to him as it could get and he didn't object. The warmth was comforting.

Alternately dozing and waking he waited out the storm. It lasted a day and a half. Finally the sun was shining. This was two days since he had first fallen ill, four days after leaving the settlement.

Bolden felt much improved. His hands were nearly normal and his vision wasn't blurred. He looked at the little animal curled in his lap, gazing up at him with solemn yellow eyes. If he gave it encouragement it would probably be crawling all over him. However, he couldn't have it frisking around while he was flying. "Come, Pet," he said—there wasn't anything else to call it—"you're going places."

Picking it up, half-carrying and half-dragging it, he took it to the rear of the compartment, improvising a narrow cage back there. He was satisfied it would hold. He should have done this in the beginning. Of course he hadn't felt like it then and he hadn't had the time—and anyway the native would have resented such treatment of a gift. Probably it was best he had waited.

His pet didn't like confinement. It whined softly for a while. The noise stopped when the motors roared. Bolden headed straight up, until he was high enough to establish communication over the peaks. He made a brief report about the natives' agreement and his own illness, then he started home.

He flew at top speed for ten hours. He satisfied his hunger by nibbling concentrated rations from time to time. The animal whined occasionally, but Bolden had learned to identify the sounds it made. It was neither hungry nor thirsty. It merely wanted to be near him. And all he wanted was to reach the base.

The raw sprawling settlement looked good as he set the copter down. Mechanics came running from the hangars. They opened the door and he stepped out.

And fell on his face. There was no feeling in his hands and none in his legs. He hadn't recovered.

Doctor Kessler peered at him through the microscreen. It gave his face a narrow insubstantial appearance. The microscreen was a hemispherical force field enclosing his head. It originated in a tubular circlet that snapped around his throat at the top of the decontagion suit. The field killed all microlife that passed through it or came in contact with it. The decontagion suit was non-porous and impermeable, covering completely the rest of his body. The material was thinner over his hands and thicker at the soles.

Bolden took in the details at a glance. "Is it serious?" he asked, his voice cracking with the effort.

"Merely a precaution," said the doctor hollowly. The microscreen distorted sound as well as sight. "Merely a precaution. We know what it is, but we're not sure of the best way to treat it."

Bolden grunted to himself. The microscreen and decontagion suit were strong precautions.

The doctor wheeled a small machine from the wall and placed Bolden's hand in a narrow trough that held it steady. The eyepiece slid into the microscreen and, starting at the finger tips, Kessler examined the arm, traveling slowly upward. At last he stopped. "Is this where feeling ends?"

"I think so. Touch it. Yeah. It's dead below there."

"Good. Then we've got it pegged. It's the Bubble Death."

Bolden showed concern and the doctor laughed. "Don't worry. It's called that because of the way it looks through the X-ray microscope. It's true that it killed the scouting expedition that discovered the planet, but it won't get you."

"They had antibiotics. Neobiotics, too."

"Sure. But they had only a few standard kinds. Their knowledge was more limited and they lacked the equipment we now have."

The doctor made it sound comforting. But Bolden wasn't comforted. Not just yet.

"Sit up and take a look," said Kessler, bending the eyepiece around so Bolden could use it. "The dark filamented lines are nerves. See what surrounds them?"

Bolden watched as the doctor adjusted the focus for him. Each filament was covered with countless tiny spheres that isolated and insulated the nerve from contact. That's why he couldn't feel anything. The spherical microbes did look like bubbles. As yet they didn't seem to have attacked the nerves directly.

While he watched, the doctor swiveled out another eyepiece for his own use and turned a knob on the side of the machine. From the lens next to his arm an almost invisible needle slid out and entered his flesh. Bolden could see it come into the field of view. It didn't hurt. Slowly it approached the dark branching filament, never quite touching it.

The needle was hollow and as Kessler squeezed the knob it sucked in the spheres. The needle extended a snout which crept along the nerve, vacuuming in microbes as it moved. When a section had been cleansed, the snout was retracted. Bolden could feel the needle then.

When the doctor finished, he laid Bolden's hand back at his side and wheeled the machine to the wall, extracting a small capsule which he dropped into a slot that led to the outside. He came back and sat down.

"Is that what you're going to do?" asked Bolden. "Scrape them off?"

"Hardly. There are too many nerves. If we had ten machines and enough people to operate them, we might check the advance in one arm. That's all." The doctor leaned back in the chair. "No. I was collecting a few more samples. We're trying to find out what the microbes react to."

"*More* samples? Then you must have taken others."

"Certainly. We put you out for a while to let you rest." The chair came down on four legs. "You've got a mild case. Either that or you have a strong natural immunity. It's now been three days since you reported the first symptoms and it isn't very advanced. It killed the entire scouting expedition in less time than that."

Bolden looked at the ceiling. Eventually they'd find a cure. But would he be alive that long?

"I suspect what you're thinking," said the doctor. "Don't overlook our special equipment. We already have specimens in the sonic accelerator. We've been able to speed up the life processes of the microbes about ten times. Before the day is over we'll know which of our anti and neobiotics they like the least. Tough little things so far—unbelievably tough—but you can be sure we'll smack them."

His mind was active, but outwardly Bolden was quiescent as the doctor continued his explanation.

The disease attacked the superficial nervous system, beginning with the extremities. The bodies of the crew of the scouting expedition had been in an advanced state of decomposition when the medical rescue team reached them and the microbes were no longer active. Nevertheless it was a reasonable supposition that death had come shortly after the invading bacteria had reached the brain. Until then, though nerves were the route along which the microbes traveled, no irreparable damage had been done.

This much was good news. Either he would recover completely or he would die. He would not be crippled permanently. Another factor in his favor was the sonic accelerator. By finding the natural resonance of the one-celled creature and gradually increasing the tempo of the sound field, the doctor could grow and test ten generations in the laboratory while one generation was breeding in the body. Bolden was the first patient actually being observed with the disease, but the time element wasn't as bad as he had thought.

"That's where you are," concluded Kessler. "Now, among other things, we've got to find where you've been."

"The ship has an automatic log," said Bolden. "It indicates every place I landed."

"True, but our grid coordinates are not exact. It will be a few years before we're able to look at a log and locate within ten feet of where a ship has been." The doctor spread out a large photomap. There were several marks on it. He fastened a stereoscope viewer over Bolden's eyes and handed him a pencil. "Can you use this?"

"I think so." His fingers were stiff and he couldn't feel, but he could mark with the pencil. Kessler moved the map nearer and the terrain sprang up in detail. In some cases, he could see it more clearly than when he had been there, because on the map there was no fog. Bolden made a few corrections and the doctor took the map away and removed the viewer.

"We'll have to stay away from these places until we get a cure. Did you notice anything peculiar in any of the places you went?"

"It was all mountainous country."

"Which probably means that we're safe on the plain. Were there any animals?"

"Nothing that came close. Birds maybe."

"More likely it was an insect. Well, we'll worry about the host and how it is transmitted. Try not to be upset. You're as safe as you would be on Earth."

"Yeah," said Bolden. "Where's the pet?"

The doctor laughed. "You did very well on that one. The biologists have been curious about the animal since the day they saw one in a native camp."

"They can *look* at it as much as they want," said Bolden. "Nothing more on this one, though. It's a personal gift."

"You're sure it's personal?"

"The native said it was."

The doctor sighed. "I'll tell them. They won't like it, but we can't argue with the natives if we want their cooperation."

Bolden smiled. The animal was safe for at least six months. He could understand the biologists' curiosity, but there was enough to keep them curious for a long time on a new planet. And it was his. In a remarkably short time, he had become attached to it. It was one of those rare things that Man happened across occasionally—about once in every five planets. Useless, completely useless, the creature had one virtue. It liked Man and Man liked it. It was a pet. "Okay," he said. "But you didn't tell me where it is."

The doctor shrugged, but the gesture was lost in the shapeless decontagion suit. "Do you think we're letting it run in the streets? It's in the next room, under observation."

The doctor was more concerned than he was letting on. The hospital was small and animals were never kept in it. "It's not the carrier. I was sick before it was given to me."

"You had something, we know that much, but was it this? Even granting that you're right, it was in contact with you and may now be infected."

"I think life on this planet isn't bothered by the disease. The natives have been every place I went and none of them seemed to have it."

"Didn't they?" said the doctor, going to the door. "Maybe. It's too early to say." He reeled a cord out of the wall and plugged it into the decontagion suit. He spread his legs and held his arms away from his sides. In an instant, the suit glowed white hot. Only for an instant, and it was insulated inside. Even so it must be uncomfortable—and the process would be repeated outside. The doctor wasn't taking any chances. "Try to sleep," he said. "Ring if there's a change in your condition—even if you think it's insignificant."

"I'll ring," said Bolden. In a short time he fell asleep. It was easy to sleep.

The nurse entered as quietly as she could in the decontagion outfit. It awakened Bolden. It was evening. He had slept most of the day, "Which one are you?" he asked. "The pretty one?"

"All nurses are pretty if you get well. Here. Swallow this."

It was Peggy. He looked doubtfully at what she held out. "All of it?"

"Certainly. You get it down and I'll see that it comes back up. The string won't hurt you."

She passed a small instrument over his body, reading the dial she held in the other hand. The information, he knew, was being recorded elsewhere on a master chart. Apparently the instrument measured neural currents and hence indirectly the progress of the disease. Already they had evolved new diagnostic techniques. He wished they'd made the same advance in treatment.

After expertly reeling out the instrument he had swallowed, the nurse read it and deposited it in a receptacle in the wall. She brought a tray and told him to eat. He wanted to question her, but she was insistent about it so he ate. Allowance had been made for his partial paralysis. The food was liquid. It was probably nutritious, but he didn't care for the taste.

She took the tray away and came back and sat beside him. "Now we can talk," she said.

"What's going on?" he said bluntly. "When do I start getting shots? Nothing's been done for me so far."

"I don't know what the doctor's working out for you. I'm just the nurse."

"Don't try to tell me that," he said. "You're a doctor yourself. In a pinch you could take Kessler's place."

"And I get my share of pinches," she said brightly. "Okay, so I'm a doctor, but only on Earth. Until I complete my off-planet internship here, I'm not allowed to practice."

"You know as much about Van Daamas as anyone does."

"That may be," she said. "Now don't be alarmed, but the truth ought to be obvious. None of our anti or neobiotics or combinations of them have a positive effcct. We're looking for something new."

It should have been obvious; he had been hoping against that, though. He looked at the shapeless figure sitting beside him and remembered Peggy as she usually looked. He wondered if they were any longer concerned with him as an individual. They must be working mainly to keep the disease from spreading. "What are my chances?"

"Better than you think. We're looking for an additive that will make the biotics effective."

He hadn't thought of that, though it was often used, particularly on newly settled planets. He had heard of a virus infection common to Centaurus that could be completely controlled by a shot of neobiotics plus aspirin, though separately neither was of any value. But the discovery of what substance should be added to what antibiotic was largely one of trial and error. That took time and there wasn't much time. "What else?" he said.

"That's about it. We're not trying to make you believe this isn't serious. But don't forget we're working ten times as fast as the disease can multiply. We expect a break any moment." She got up. "Want a sedative for the night?"

"I've got a sedative inside me. Looks like it will be permanent."

"That's what I like about you, you're so cheerful," she said, leaning over and clipping something around his throat. "In case you're wondering, we're going to be busy tonight checking the microbe. We can put someone in with you, but we thought you'd rather have all of us working on it."

"Sure," he said.

"This is a body monitor. If you want anything just call and we'll be here within minutes."

"Thanks," he said. "I won't panic tonight."

She plugged in the decontagion uniform, flashed it on and then left the room. After she was gone, the body monitor no longer seemed reassuring. It was going to take something positive to pull him through.

They were going to work through the night, but did they actually hope for success. What had Peggy said? None of the anti or neobiotics had a positive reaction. Unknowingly she had let it slip. The reaction was negative; the bubble microbes actually grew faster in the medium that was supposed to stop them. It happened occasionally on strange planets. It was his bad luck that it was happening to him.

He pushed the thoughts out of his mind and tried to sleep. He did for a time. When he awakened he thought, at first, it was his arms that had aroused him. They seemed to be on fire, deep inside. To a limited extent, he still had control. He could move them though there was no surface sensation. Interior nerves had not been greatly affected until now. But outside the infection had crept up. It was no longer just above the wrists. It had reached his elbows and passed beyond. A few inches below his shoulder he could feel nothing. The illness was accelerating. If they had ever thought of amputation, it was too late, now.

He resisted an impulse to cry out. A nurse would come and sit beside him, but he would be taking her from work that might save his life. The infection would reach his shoulders and move across his chest and back. It would travel up his throat and he wouldn't be able to move his lips. It would paralyze his eyelids so that he couldn't blink. Maybe it would blind him, too. And then it would find ingress to his brain.

The result would be a metabolic explosion. Swiftly each bodily function would stop altogether or race wildly as the central nervous system was invaded, one regulatory center after the other blanking out. His body would be aflame or it would smolder and flicker out. Death might be spectacular or it could come very quietly.

That was one reason he didn't call the nurse.

The other was the noise.

It was a low sound, half purr, half a coaxing growl. It was the animal the native had given him, confined in the next room. Bolden was not sure why he did what he did next. Instinct or reason may have governed his actions. But instinct and reason are devisive concepts that cannot apply to the human mind, which is actually indivisible.

He got out of bed. Unable to stand, he rolled to the floor. He couldn't crawl very well because his hands wouldn't support his weight so he crept along on his knees and elbows. It didn't hurt. Nothing hurt except the fire in his bones. He reached the door and straightened up on his knees. He raised his hand to the handle, but couldn't grasp it. After several trials, he abandoned the attempt and hooked his chin on the handles, pulling it down. The door opened and he was in the next room. The animal was whining louder now that he was near. Yellow eyes glowed at him from the corner. He crept to the cage.

It was latched. The animal shivered eagerly, pressing against the side, striving to reach him. His hands were numb and he couldn't work the latch. The animal licked his fingers.

It was easier after that. He couldn't feel what he was doing, but somehow he managed to unlatch it. The door swung open and the animal bounded out, knocking him to the floor.

He didn't mind at all because now he was sure he was right. The natives had given him the animal for a purpose. Their own existence was meager, near the edge of extinction. They could not afford to keep something that wasn't useful. And this creature was useful. Tiny blue sparks crackled from the fur as it rubbed against him in the darkness. It was not whining. It rumbled and purred as it licked his hands and arms and rolled against his legs.

After a while he was strong enough to crawl back to bed, leaning against the animal for support. He lifted himself up and fell across the bed in exhaustion. Blood didn't circulate well in his crippled body. The animal bounded up and tried to melt itself into his body. He couldn't push it away if he wanted. He didn't want to. He stirred and got himself into a more comfortable position. He wasn't going to die.

In the morning, Bolden was awake long before the doctor came in. Kessler's face was haggard and the smile was something he assumed solely for the patient's benefit. If he could have seen what the expression looked like after filtering through the microscreen, he would have abandoned it. "I see you're holding your own," he said with hollow cheerfulness. "We're doing quite well ourselves."

"I'll bet," said Bolden. "Maybe you've got to the point where one of the antibiotics doesn't actually stimulate the growth of the microbes?"

"I was afraid you'd find it out," sighed the doctor. "We can't keep everything from you."

"You could have given me a shot of plasma and said it was a powerful new drug."

"That idea went out of medical treatment a couple of hundred years ago," said the doctor. "You'd feel worse when you failed to show improvement. Settling a planet isn't easy and the dangers aren't imaginary. You've got to be able to face facts as they come."

He peered uncertainly at Bolden. The microscreen distorted his vision, too. "We're making progress though it may not seem so to you. When a mixture of a calcium salt plus two antihistamines is added to a certain neobiotic, the result is that the microbe grows no faster than it should. Switching the ingredients here and there—maybe it ought to be a potassium salt—and the first thing you know we'll have it stopped cold."

"I doubt the effectiveness of those results," said Bolden. "In fact, I think you're on the wrong track. Try investigating the effects of neural induction."

"What are you talking about?" said the doctor, coming closer and glancing suspiciously at the lump beside Bolden.

"Do you feel dizzy? Is there anything else unusual that you notice?"

"Don't shout at the patient." Bolden waggled his finger reprovingly. He was proud of the finger. He couldn't feel what he was doing, but he had control over it. "You, Kessler, should face the fact that a doctor can learn from a patient what the patient learned from the natives."

But Kessler didn't hear what he said. He was looking at the upraised hand. "You're moving almost normally," he said. "Your own immunity factor is controlling the disease."

"Sure. I've got an immunity factor," said Bolden. "The same one the natives have. Only it's not inside my body." He rested his hand on the animal beneath the covers. It never wanted to leave him. It wouldn't have to.

"I can set your mind at rest on one thing, Doctor. Natives are susceptible to the disease, too. That's why they were able to recognize I had it. They gave me the cure and told me what it was, but I was unable to see it until it was nearly too late. Here it is." He turned back the covers and exposed the animal sleeping peacefully on his legs; it raised its head and licked his fingers. He felt that.

After an explanation the doctor tempered his disapproval. It was an unsanitary practice, but he had to admit that the patient was much improved. Kessler verified the state of Bolden's health by extensive use of the X-ray microscope. Reluctantly he wheeled the machine to the wall and covered it up.

"The infection is definitely receding," he said. "There are previously infected areas in which I find it difficult to locate a single microbe. What I can't understand is how it's done. According to you, the animal doesn't break the skin with its tongue and therefore nothing is released into the bloodstream. All that seems necessary is that the animal be near you." He shook his head behind the microscreen. "I don't think much of the electrical analogy you used."

"I said the first thing I thought of. I don't know if that's the way it works, but it seems to me like a pretty fair guess."

"The microbes *do* cluster around nerves," said the doctor.

"We know that neural activity is partly electrical. If the level of that activity can be increased, the bacteria might be killed by ionic dissociation." He glanced speculatively at Bolden and the animal. "Perhaps you do borrow nervous energy from the animal. We might also find it possible to control the disease with an electrical current."

"Don't try to find out on me," said Bolden. "I've been an experimental specimen long enough. Take somebody who's healthy. I'll stick with the natives' method."

"I wasn't thinking of experiments in your condition. You're still not out of danger." Nevertheless he showed his real opinion when he left the room. He failed to plug in and flash the decontagion suit.

Bolden smiled at the doctor's omission and ran his hand through the fur. He was going to get well.

But his progress was somewhat slower than he'd anticipated though it seemed to satisfy the doctor who went on with his experiments. The offending bacteria could be killed electrically. But the current was dangerously large and there was no practical way to apply the treatment to humans. The animal was the only effective method.

Kessler discovered the microbe required an intermediate host. A tick or a mosquito seemed indicated. It would take a protracted search of the mountains to determine just what insect was the carrier. In any event the elaborate sanitary precautions were unnecessary. Microscreens came down and decontagion suits were no longer worn. Bolden could not pass the disease on to anyone else.

Neither could the animal. It seemed wholly without parasites. It was clean and affectionate, warm to the touch. Bolden was fortunate that there was such a simple cure for the most dreaded disease on Van Daamas.

It was several days before he was ready to leave the small hospital at the edge of the settlement. At first he sat up in bed and then he was allowed to walk across the room. As his activity increased, the animal became more and more content to lie on the bed and follow him with its eyes. It no longer frisked about as it had in the beginning. As Bolden told the nurse, it was becoming housebroken.

The time came when the doctor failed to find a single microbe. Bolden's newly returned strength and the sensitivity of his skin where before there had been numbness confirmed the diagnosis. He was well. Peggy came to walk him home. It was pleasant to have her near.

"I see you're ready," she said, laughing at his eagerness.

"Except for one thing," he said. "Come, Pet." The animal raised its head from the bed where it slept.

"Pet?" she said quizzically. "You ought to give it a name. You've had it long enough to decide on something."

"Pet's a name," he said. "What can I call it? Doc? Hero?"

She made a face. "I can't say I care for either choice, although it did save your life."

"Yes, but that's an attribute it can't help. The important thing is that if you listed what you expect of a pet you'd find it in this creature. Docile, gentle, lively at times; all it wants is to be near you, to have you touch it. And it's very clean."

"All right, call it Pet if you want," said Peggy. "Come on, Pet."

It paid no attention to her. It came when Bolden called, getting slowly off the bed. It stayed as close as it could get to Bolden. He was still weak so they didn't walk fast and, at first, the animal was able to keep up.

It was almost noon when they went out. The sun was brilliant and Van Daamas seemed a wonderful place to be alive in. Yes, with death behind him, it was a very wonderful place. Bolden chatted gaily with Peggy. She was fine company.

And then Bolden saw the native who had given him the animal. Five to seven days, and he had arrived on time. The rest of the tribe must be elsewhere in the settlement. Bolden smiled in recognition while the man was still at some distance. For an answer the native shifted the bow in his hand and glanced behind the couple, in the direction of the hospital.

The movement with the bow might have been menacing, but Bolden ignored that gesture. It was the sense that something was missing that caused him to look down. The animal was not at his side. He turned around.

The creature was struggling in the dust. It got to its feet and wobbled toward him, staggering crazily as it tried to reach him. It spun around, saw him, and came on again. The tongue lolled out and it whined once. Then the native shot it through the heart, pinning it to the ground. The short tail thumped and then it died.

Bolden couldn't move. Peggy clutched his arm. The native walked over to the animal and looked down. He was silent for a moment. "Die anyway soon," he said to Bolden. "Burned out inside."

He bent over. The bright yellow eyes had faded to nothingness in the sunlight. "Gave you its health," said the man of Van Daamas respectfully as he broke off the protruding arrow.

It was a dark blue arrow.

Now every settlement on the planet has Bolden's pets. They have been given a more scientific name, but nobody remembers what it is. The animals are kept in pens, exactly as is done by the natives, on one side of town, not too near any habitation.

For a while, there was talk that it was unscientific to use the animal. It was thought that an electrical treatment could be developed to replace it. Perhaps this was true. But settling a planet is a big task. As long as one method works there isn't time for research. And it works—the percentage of recovery is as high as in other common ailments.

But in any case the animal can never become a pet, though it may be in the small but bright spark of consciousness that is all the little yellow-eyed creature wants. The quality that makes it so valuable is the final disqualification. Strength can be a weakness. Its nervous system is too powerful for a man in good health, upsetting the delicate balance of the human body in a variety of unusual ways. How the energy-transfer takes place has never been determined exactly, but it does occur.

It is only when he is stricken with the Bubble Death and needs additional energy to drive the invading microbes from the tissue around his nerves that the patient is allowed to have one of Bolden's pets.

In the end, it is the animal that dies. As the natives knew, it is kindness to kill it quickly.

It is highly regarded and respectfully spoken of. Children play as close as they can get, but are kept well away from the pens by a high, sturdy fence. Adults walk by and nod kindly to it.

Bolden never goes there nor will he speak of it. His friends say he's unhappy about being the first Earthman to discover the usefulness of the little animal. They are right. It is a distinction he doesn't care for. He still has the blue arrow. There are local craftsmen who can mend it, but he has refused their services. He wants to keep it as it is.

EXPEDITION MERCY

J. A. Winter, M.D.

And here is what may happen on planets where there are no "negative symbiotes," as there were in the previous story. This was one of the two tales the late Dr. Winter ever wrote, and the first one published. All the more remarkable, then, its skillful plotting and its sharp characterizations. As for the medicine, naturally it's accurate as far as earthbound pathology goes, and even when it becomes science fiction, as it is bound to on an alien planet, it retains all the circumstantial reality that a skilled physician could bring to it. And for the ending of the story: it will be as true tomorrow and at the farthest ends of the universe as it is today and here, that one should never *draw positive conclusions from insufficient evidence.*

Expedition Mercy

THE BRAZEN CLANGOR of the alarm bell reverberated through the Cupromagneloy bulkheads. "O.K., you dopes. Prepare for landing. Next stop Minotaur. End of the line. All out."

A hard flung boot narrowly missed the head of the grinning space pilot. "Save your opprobrious epithets for your brother space lice. When you speak to us doctors call us gentlemen."

"Yes, gentlemen," Tom Kelly bowed low in a mock salaam. He straightened up to the position of attention, removed his rakish Navy cap and announced in stentorian tones, "The Navy detachment in charge of the spaceship *Mercy* wishes to announce that in approximately one hour we will be the second ship to land on the planet Minotaur. And, if you pill-rollers don't get into your deceleration gear pretty quick, you'll be taking care of each other for the next month."

"Yes, admiral. We hear your words of wisdom."

In spite of this good-natured banter it was obvious that the five doctors were wasting no time in preparing themselves for the stresses of landing. This wasn't going to be an easy landing like the ones at the spaceport at Luna City or Mars Port. There would be no space tugs whose added mass would help deceleration and which could help ease them onto the landing strip. There were no spaceports on Minotaur. It was very probable that there were no men on Minotaur, in spite of the fact that Expedition I had landed there only six months ago.

Dr. Bob Edwards finished strapping himself to his bunk and sighed. "For this I went to medical school." A veteran of countless planetary landings, he knew how rigorous a landing such as they would be making could be.

"The rest of you fellows all set? Irv, better get that pad straightened out under your feet. We'll be turning in a few minutes and then you won't be able to."

The discordant jangle of the alarm bell rang out sharply again, to be followed by the high-pitched whine of the gyroscopes as the ship was rotated for her stern-first landing. Then the rockets blasted out and further speech was impossible.

The next hour was one of tense activity for the crew members, easing the ship down to her landing on the broad, vegetation-free plateau which had been chosen. For the five doctors strapped into their bunks it was a period of alternate haziness, stomach-wrenching free fall and an occasional respite of unconsciousness.

Dr. Bob, who was more accustomed to the strains of deceleration, took advantage of this period of enforced immobility by going over once again his plans for the expedition.

"Let's see, now. It was about two months before the first expedition stopped communicating. That would probably rule out any bacterial infection—too long a period of incubation. Vegetable spores? Possibly. Probably not food—those guys were certainly given strict instructions not to eat any of the plant life here."

The ability to think in straight lines, to evaluate and correlate, was an integral part of Edwards' mental equipment. If he hadn't had this ability, he would never have reached the rank of Senior Synthesist in the Solarian Public Health Service. He was a Synthesist because he had the true synthetic mind—the innate ability to absorb the findings of the various specialists, arrange them in the order of importance of influence and finally come up with a diagnosis which was accurate and not prejudiced by enthusiasm for any one specialty.

He represented the epitome of the general practitioner—a medical jack-of-all-trades and a master of them all. And even if he hadn't been appointed the leader of the medical contingent in this rescue expedition, he would have automatically been conceded first place. He was obviously, inherently and involuntarily a born leader.

"But to be on the safe side we have to keep as free from contamination as possible. We certainly have to use our own food and water; we'll have to keep on breathing this canned air until we can be sure that there are no spores. I hope our decontamination air lock is going to work all right."

A particularly violent surge from the rockets brought him to semiconsciousness, blotting out his thoughts.

The next thing Bob felt was the jar as the ship settled to the ground. He began to extricate himself from his deceleration harness, noticing that the others were doing the same.

Tom Kelly entered the room and saluted with a flourish. "Dr. Edwards, in accordance with the orders received from the Spacenavy Department I hereby end my tour of duty as commander of this expedition and pass my command to you." He grinned; it's hard to be formal with another man when you've been cooped up together in a spaceship for three months. "And be sure that you take good care of all the little boys."

"Thanks, Tom," replied Edwards. "You've done a good job so far, except for that lousy landing. Doesn't the Navy teach you how to land a ship without dismembering the passengers?"

"Now, grandfather—if I just hadn't forgotten about your brittle bones," Tom gave an exaggerated sigh. "And to think that a fragile old man like you is now CO!"

"O.K., fellas," said Bob, "let's get down to business." He could always take kidding but now there was a serious problem confronting him. "Come on and sit down and let's run through our plan of camping. I know we've all hashed this over before, but we'll do it again. We can't afford to make any mistakes."

The members of the expedition grouped themselves around the table. Bob looked them over with a strong sense of pride in the vast medical talent represented there. In addition to himself and the Navy captain, there was Jack Livingston, one of the cleverest young surgeons of Terra, the innovator of the practice of transplanting limbs from cadavers to the living. Sharp and incisive as his own scalpels, he was, next to Edwards, the obvious understudy for command. Then there was Irving Mandel: listed on the roll as a psychiatrist, he was actually an expert on psychosomatic medicine, an expert linguist and a very fine musician. Sensitive to the moods of others, sweet tempered and soft spoken, he was at home and well liked in any sort of group. The specialist in internal medicine was Wilhelm Schultz—and with a name like that, he was the obvious target for nicknames; at present he answered most frequently to the labels "Bilious" and "Dutchie." He was, in addition to his abilities in the field of exotic diseases, an expert endocrinologist. He was a phenomenal diagnostician; he knew more about a patient after taking his pulse than most doctors would after a complete physical examination. He and Kelly were a lot alike in their clowning and ham acting—a good balance for the more serious members. The last one of the medical group was the pathologist, Dr. David Charles Thomas. He was especially well equipped for membership in this expedition; it was part of his professional training to be able to perform an autopsy, do chemical analyses of the blood and recognize pathogenic spore forms. His hobby of the chemistry of radioactive substances made him an even bigger asset. He was a fastidious dresser, and his words were as clipped and neat as the trim mustache on his upper lip.

Yes, thought Bob, they were good guys and formed a group that was practically unbeatable. If anyone could solve the mystery of what happened to Expedition I, they should.

"Now," said Bob, "to recapitulate. Expedition I landed here about six months ago. Their reports were, medically speaking, essentially negative until about six weeks thereafter. Then they all began having attacks of nausea, vomiting and weakness. By this time the reports were a little sketchy and lacking in the sort of detail we'd like, but we do know that at least two of the men had sustained fractures. Why they didn't have a doctor with them I don't know. Yes, Tom, I know they had a pharmacist's mate with them; the Navy does a good job of training those boys for emergencies, but they haven't the knowledge to cope with something like this."

Having thus forestalled Tom's automatic objection to any possible criticism of his beloved Navy, Edwards was able to continue.

"It is doubtful that this could be anything but some form

of disease. We can discount the possibility of influence by indigenous life forms. Captain Henderson was very explicit in one of his early reports to say that they were unable to find any form of anthropoid, humanoid or intelligent life here. Apparently Minotaur is still a baby, as planets go, and intelligent life still hasn't evolved."

"Tom, may I ask a question?" It was Irv Mandel, the psychiatrist, speaking. "I noticed you've been studying the transcript of the radio messages. Did you get any more clues since we talked it over the last time?"

"No, I didn't, Irv. The only conclusion is the one I've been stressing right along—we *must* be careful, so careful it'll seem silly, not to expose ourselves to anything on this planet until we're completely certain it's safe."

"You're right, Tom," Livingston spoke up, "but I don't have to *like* wearing a spacesuit, and breathing this canned air. I've been breathing this same air so long I can recognize every molecule as it hits my alveoli."

"I'm afraid you'll just have to keep on greeting your little molecular friends for a while. Until we find out what happened to the others and what caused it we can't take any chances. You men realize as well as I do the sort of dangers that might exist here. There's no point in enlarging on the obvious. So my first order must be—no one is to leave this ship or to have any contact with anything on this planet unless he is specifically commanded to do so. Tom, please pass this along to the members of your crew. Now—any questions?"

There was silence in the room. Even the irrepressible Schultz hadn't any remarks to make.

Edwards stood up. "Well, we'd better get started. The first big job will go to Death-House Davey. Dr. Thomas, will you get your crew started on air analysis? And don't hesitate to do animal inoculations with any suspicious spores or bacteria. We have plenty of guinea pigs and hamsters. Schultz will help you. Tom and Irv and I will put on our rompers and go out and see what we can see. Jack, you'll be in command while we're gone. Try to restrain yourself from carving up the crew."

Jack grinned back at Edwards. He was always the recipient of good-natured chaffing for his interest in the surgical approach. "O.K., synthetic; I'll try. Be a good boy when you go out and come home immediately when Momma calls."

"Yeah," added Schultz, as the three doctors left for the laboratory, "don't forget to take a hankie with you."

In the meantime Tom had spread a pile of charts out on the table. "Here are those charts they sent us by facsimile. Apparently there's no magnetic poles here; they've specified an arbitrary North Pole at the axis of counter-clockwise rotation. They did a pretty fair job of mapping this area, too."

Bob was studying the maps with his usual intensity. "Seems very complete to me. Where are we now?"

Tom put the tip of his pencil on a point on the chart. "We're on this little plateau. The location of their base camp is about two kilometers at seventy degrees."

"Hm-m-m—we could walk it in twenty minutes or a half hour. Guess we'd better do that. No point in taking the flitter out yet."

"That's right," said Tom. "I'd like the chance to get out and stretch my legs a little. And by the way—I'm having the boys rig direction finders on the bow and stern. The ship is lying pretty close to due north and south, so we can get our bearing by triangulation."

"Good idea, Tom. I'd hate like the devil to get lost. Well, let's get to going."

Within a few minutes the outer door of the air lock had clanged shut and the three men set their booted feet on the soil of Minotaur.

Tom's voice crackled over the intercom headsets. "Testing —one, two, three, four—are your radios O.K., gents?"

"All right."

"No trouble, I hope." This last was from Mandel, the cautious.

"O.K., Carson?" Tom was speaking to the radioman within the ship.

"Yes, sir. I have the directional beam on at azimuth 75. If you don't hear it by the time you get fifty meters from the ship, please let me know."

"All right, Carson. Turn on the recorder, and we'll put this on the tape as we go along."

They walked a short distance from the ship, then turned until the faint, regular *beep beep* of the directional beam told them they were headed correctly and started off. It seemed so silly to be wearing spacesuits. From the appearance of the landscape they might have thought that they were still on Earth, perhaps in the Washito mountain region of Oklahoma. There were some slight differences, of course. There were twin suns, quite close to each other in the sky, and the light given off gave everything a noticeably yellow tinge. And you couldn't be sure if the vegetation was made up of large plants or small trees—but a quick glance would still make one think of Earth. It seemed a shame to be cooped up in a spacesuit on a lovely, cloudless, sunny day—but they knew that death for humans was hiding on this planet. And until they could determine its hiding place—well, eternal vigilance is the price of freedom, especially freedom from death.

Gravity of Minotaur was slightly less than that of Earth, so walking, even with the encumbrance of spacesuits, was quite pleasurable. They wasted no breath on useless conversation as they strode along. The silence was broken only by occasional laconic comments on the terrain, dictated by Tom to the recording apparatus back at the ship. Once Bob saw a large flying insect, but was unable to obtain a good description of it. They saw no other living animals.

The way they took wound downward from a low plateau towards what seemed to be a watercourse lined by vegetation. They soon reached this river valley with its rich greenish soil and began walking through a field of brush. The ground was firm and springy beneath their feet. The silence was broken only by the hiss of their respirators and the faint beeping of the beam changing its rhythm as an occasional obstacle would force them from their course.

After about a quarter of an hour they glimpsed a shining metallic cylinder ahead of them.

Bob pointed. "There she is, fellows. Now to find out why we came on this little buggy ride."

They strode along a little faster until Tom suddenly said: "Hey, look here!"

In a little clearing stood ten markers, each set up at one end of a rectangular mound of earth. Irv bent over the nearest and read, "Herman Jesperson; died April 12, 2245." He moved over to the next. "David Carter; died April 16, 2245."

"Do you notice how each grave is progressively cruder? The first man that died had a lot of attention given to his burial; the last man was apparently just covered over. Guess that as the expedition grew weaker they just couldn't make the effort any more."

"But listen," said Tom. "There were twelve men in the expedition and there are only ten graves here. We'll have to do a little more looking."

"Yes," agreed Bob, "we'll have to come back here later."

Another few minutes brought them to the spaceship. The outer door hung open; the inner door of the space lock opened without difficulty. A few lights were still burning. That meant nothing, as the power supply on these ships was practically inexhaustible. Other than that, the first glance at the interior of the ship showed nothing remarkable. The old Navy tradition of keeping things shipshape had still operated, in spite of the illness of the crew.

"Let's look it over," said Bob. "Tom, you take the forward end, Irv the engine room and I'll plow around amidships."

A few minutes of silence, punctuated by the opening and closing of doors, then two voices spoke up simultaneously. "Here's the ship's log," reported Tom.

"Hey, there's a body here!" Irv called.

"Come on aft, Tom, and bring the log with you and we'll see what Irv has found," commanded Bob.

It wasn't a pleasant sight; the processes of putrefaction and desiccation don't make the human body a thing of beauty. It bothered Tom to look at what remained of this mass of dissolving protoplasm, and he mentally noted his thanks that he was breathing the air of his spacesuit. It would have been just too much for him to have been exposed to the odor of this corpse.

The two doctors weren't bothered, of course; they had seen human bodies in all degrees of dissolution and disrepair countless times before. But they were shocked at the appearance. The arms and legs looked as though they had been broken in at least twenty places. The toes of one foot pointed toward the bunk, although the body was lying on its back. The body looked as if it had been twisted in the hands of a vindicative giant. And the skull was studded with numerous protuberances like warts on a schoolboy's hands.

"Are you thinking what I'm thinking?" asked Mandel.

"It sure looks like it, doesn't it?" said Bob. "Well, we can come back to this later. This is a job for Thomas—and won't he love it? Let's get out of here before our naval friend gets *mal de corpse*."

They left the room, to Tom's complete satisfaction. "Say," said he, "while you ghouls were looking over that poor devil in there, I just glanced at the log. Look what I found."

Inside the front cover, in large, shaky, painful-looking letters were the words, "Look in refrigerator."

"I don't suppose that someone was trying to tell us that the cook left some ice cream for us," said Bob. "Maybe we'd better follow this up before going any further. Tom, where do they keep the galley on this type can?"

"It should be right in here," replied Tom, opening a door.

It was the galley. It was, as everything else on this ship, spotlessly clean and reflected efficiency in every inch of its design. Along one wall was the huge refrigerator chest used for the storage of frozen dehydrated foods. Bob strode over and gave the heavy lid a heave up and looked inside.

"Irv—Tom."

"What is it? What is it?" asked the other two as they crowded up.

Inside was another corpse. Dressed carefully in a crisp white uniform, preserved by the minus fifteen degree centigrade cold, it was as though Death had been arrested at the moment of occurrence. It would have been prettier if it hadn't, too. The limbs gave evidence of numerous fractures, had that same twisted look that the other body had; the face still showed the dusky bluish discoloration that means asphyxiation. And a stick with a piece of string tied to it, lying beside the body, gave mute witness to the fact that he had died by slowly smothering in the dark frigid depths of the refrigerator.

"Do you have this figured the same way I do?" asked Bob. "This man, seeing that he was going the same way as the others, preferred to commit suicide in the refrigerator so that his body would be preserved for our examination. And it must have been a perfect hell for him to have gone up to the control room, written that note and then come back here and climbed in. Look at those legs—I don't see how he could have *crawled*, let alone hoist himself into this box. And once inside, he pulled the string, the stick holding up the lid came out. Boy, what guts this boy must have had!"

"He sure did," said Tom. "I know him. That's Mattson, one of the best pharmacist's mates the Navy ever had. He was just the sort of guy who would realize that doing something like this would be a help to those who came to investigate."

"What sublime courage. Imagine—the last man on a planet, dying here alone in the cold and blackness, without air and without hope. 'Greater love hath no man—' " and Irv shook his head slowly in profound admiration.

Bob let the lid fall again with an air of finality. "We'd better just leave him there until Thomas is ready to have his post-mortem. And I guess we'll get on with our search. I'll pick up any likely looking specimens of food or liquid, and you guys pick up all the documents you can find—letters, diaries and so on. There's not much doubt about the diagnosis, but how it could happen to all these men in such a short time is beyond me."

Within a few minutes the three men were gathered outside the ship. "Did you find anything else?" Bob asked.

"Nothing very important, I guess," replied Tom. "I took a quick look at the navigation and operation charts and there's nothing out of line there, so I left them."

"I got a couple of diaries and some letters," Irv added. "The rest of the stuff was, if I may use the phrase, apparently noncontributory."

"I checked over the galley pretty closely," Bob said. "They had been eating nothing but standard food. I couldn't find any evidence of experimentation with any of the native food-stuffs. They had been using local water, however, but they had run it through a Berkefeld porcelain filter according to standard operating procedure. I brought along a specimen anyhow. Just a minute—I want to get a bottle full of river water, too."

That took just a few seconds and soon the three men were on their way back to the *Mercy*. It was noticeable that they were no longer under the strain that had weighed them down on their first walk. Now they had the terms of the problem laid out before them, had some data to work on. Like good investigators should, they shifted their minds into neutral until the data could be studied, without wasting time in circular cerebration.

"Tom," spoke up Irv, "I've often wondered, how does it happen that such anachronistic terms as 'pharmacist's mate' and 'galley' are still a part of naval vocabulary?"

"To tell you the truth," answered Tom, "I can't tell you. I suppose it's just another example of the persistence of tradition. Those names probably meant something at one time, but I've never thought to inquire."

"I'll bet that you don't know the significance of the salute, either," Bob remarked.

"That one you can't fool me on. It's a hold over from the time when a knight would raise his vizor to identify himself as a friend—a mark of respect to someone he met."

Bob spoke up. "It's funny how your conversation ties in with what I've been thinking about. I've been mulling over the fact that disease patterns persist for even longer than traditions. If the situation here is what I suspect it is, it's a disease which was first described about 1890—more than three hundred fifty years ago."

"Are you one of those characters who says that there's nothing new under the sun?" Tom asked.

"No," replied Bob, "I wouldn't be as arbitrary as that; but it's quite obvious that men haven't changed their modes of response to pathogenic stimuli for a long, long time."

He broke off this train of thought to look ahead of him. "There's the ship again. I'd better warn them that we're in sight. Carson!"

"Yessir," came back a voice over the radio.

"We're bringing back some written material that I don't want to bring aboard ship. Have the boys rig the microfilm camera at the analysis port; they'd better toss out a pager, too. We can decontaminate that easier than we can the books. And tell them that I'm bringing in some water specimens, so they can have some suction tubes hanging out. Are you all set for decontaminating us?"

"Clean up crew is standing by, sir. We'll be ready for you."

When they reached the ship they could see a small port opened near the underside. Two short lengths of plastic tubing hung out; the blank eye-on-a-stalk of a camera gazed at the ground and nearby was a compact piece of apparatus whose function was not immediately obvious.

Bob uncapped one specimen bottle and held it up so that the tubing could reach the bottom. "Specimen number one: water used for drinking; taken from collection chamber of filter of Ship I. Take her away." The water level in the bottle immediately descended.

"Specimen number two: water from the river near Ship I. It's yours!" And this specimen disappeared into the ship.

"Finished with suckers." A gush of antiseptic solution spewed forth from the tubing; an ingenious device clipped off the lengths of tube which protruded and the discarded ends fell to the ground. Anything which came in contact with the planet was either discarded or decontaminated.

In the meantime Irv had arranged all the loose sheets of paper under the eye of the camera, which was busily transferring what it saw on to microfilm. That task having been completed, he arranged the books on the pager. This was a device which automatically turned the pages, hesitating just long enough between turns to allow the entire page to be photographed. After making sure that the machine was working satisfactorily, he joined the others in entering the air lock.

The technicians who had perfected this arrangement for insuring that nothing foreign could be brought aboard had surpassed themselves. First, from numerous tiny openings in the ceiling, walls and floor there issued a fine mist of a detergent solution. Of low surface tension, it penetrated every nook and cranny of the spacesuits of the occupants of the lock, then fell to the floor, from whence it was ejected from the ship. Then the chamber was completely filled with a strong fluoro-mercuric-phenol solution, completely submerging the three men. They knew that their spacesuits protected them against it, and would permit them to live under water or even under nitrohydrochloric acid for days, yet they all felt that slight sense of panic and claustrophobia. Agitators began to swirl the liquid around them, cleansing every crevice, then with a *woosh* it was forced out to the ground beneath the ship. Finally the interior of this room was bathed in strong ultraviolet light at a temperature of 100° C; even with the efficient temperature regulators of the suits the men felt the sweat droplets gathering on their foreheads and trickling down their backs.

"Well, by now we should be nice and sweet and clean," said Bob. "We don't want to bring any nasty old bugs aboard our nice clean ship."

"No, never let the fair ship *Mercy* be sullied by any indigenous stuff and things," Tom agreed.

In spite of their light-hearted attitudes, they still realized that even with all their precautions, they might be bringing Death aboard ship. And the type of Death that had caught up with the previous expedition was not one to be desired.

Having rid themselves of their spacesuits, they opened the inner door of the air lock and entered the ship, where they were greeted by the other three doctors.

"How did you make out?" asked Livingston. "Did you see anything worth operating on?"

"There speaks Jack Livingston, the tomomaniac—nuts about cuts."

In a few succinct phrases Bob filled in the gaps of his report which had been heard over the ship's speakers. He concluded by saying: "Dave, get your autopsy kit ready and get organized to go out and examine those bodies. Jack can assist you—he'll enjoy doing some slicing even though there won't be any gore. And Bilious—"

"*Zu befehl, mein Herr*," replied Schultz, stiffening to a travesty of the position of attention.

"You'd better go along to observe and report. I have a sneaking suspicion that this situation is going to fall right into your favorite field of endocrinology."

"Just a suspicion, Bob? Why, any second-year medical student could make that diagnosis with his eyes closed. Tell me, does that M.S. degree of yours mean Master of Stupidity?"

"Stop your prattle, little boy," laughed Bob. "Say—if I might make a suggestion it might not be a bad idea to get some chow before you take off. By the way, Tom, how much more daylight can we expect?"

Tom consulted the clock. "It's about two hours and a half before sunset. Then there'll be about nine hours of darkness. The period of rotation is about eighteen hours Earth time."

The pathologist grunted an amorphous sound of vague disapproval. It offended his meticulous sense of the fitness of things to realize that all planets did not have a twenty-four-hour day. The entire trip was, in fact, a major dislocation of his life. The only consolation was that he had the finest laboratory equipment in the solar system. And now—he was going to get a chance to use it.

"Schultz—Livingston," he rapped out, "let's eat and get

started while we still have daylight. The technicians will be up all night cutting and staining sections as it is." And he turned and left for the galley.

The others, at a more leisurely pace, followed him. It was a silent meal, with each man immersed deeply in his own thoughts, and soon finished. Like most doctors they didn't dawdle over their food; they just seemed to surround the calories like amoebas.

After the other three doctors had finished their meal and had left for the other ship, Bob and Irv returned to the cabin and spent a couple of hours in concentrated study of the documents brought back from the ill-fated craft. Mandel made copious notes; Bob was content to read and absorb, automatically sifting out the kernels of relevant fact.

They had almost finished when Tom wandered in. "Aren't you guys ever going to get any sleep?" he asked.

"Pretty soon," answered Bob. "What do you hear from the others?"

"They've finished with Mattson and are ready to start on the other. That guy Thomas—'we are encountering some technical difficulties due to the frozen condition of the body.' What a bunch of grave robbers I have with me this trip!"

Bob shrugged; he had long since given up expecting anything but an emotional bias against autopsies from the laity. "How else can we find out anything?"

"Guess you're right," Tom conceded. "By the way, I wouldn't be surprised if there was a storm brewing. The barometric pressure has dropped about 10 mm. in the last hour. If we were on Earth, I'd say we were due for a hurricane."

Bob pondered a moment. "I don't suppose that you have any idea of what we might expect in the line of storms."

"I'm afraid I haven't," answered Tom. "The first expedition didn't report any storms at all, but that doesn't mean that they're nonexistent here."

"Well, we can't afford to take any chances," Bob decided. "Let's go up to the radio room and talk to the boys."

They entered the radio room where a loud-speaker was crackling out the report dictated by Thomas from the other ship. The recording apparatus was spinning, making a permanent record of his findings.

"Edwards calling Livingston—Edwards calling Livingston."

"Livingston here. What's on your mind, Bob?"

"Tom tells me that there's a possibility of a storm coming up. You'd better plan on spending the night there. It might not be so smart trying to come back here in the darkness."

"O.K., if you think so," assented the surgeon. "But we'll have to get out of our spacesuits, you know."

"Huh? Why? Oh, yeah." For a moment Bob had forgotten that the problem of elimination while in a spacesuit had not been solved.

"Just a second, Jack." Bob mused for a short interval, his mind racing over the problem, weighing one possibility against another. Then, "Under the circumstances I'd still say that you should stay there. I've got a very good idea of what caused the death of those boys and I'm quite certain you'll be safer in that ship that you would outside. Just one thing, though—don't eat or drink anything that's aboard that ship."

"O.K., Bob; if you say it'll be all right, that's good enough for me."

"Hail, Edwards! We who are about to become guinea pigs salute you!" That was Schultz, of course. And his gay remark didn't make Bob feel any better. He *thought* he was right; he was *almost* certain that his advice wouldn't prove harmful, but there was still that little lingering doubt. The mantle of responsibility is seldom a comfortable garment.

"We'll keep a man on duty at the radio at all times, fellows," concluded Bob. "Let us know if you need anything. I'm going to turn in now and I'll call you in the morning."

When Bob rolled into his bunk he fell asleep immediately. The rigors of landing, the unaccustomed exercise of the walk to the other ship and the nervous tension engendered by the problem in hand had all conspired to exhaust him. In spite of his heavy slumber, however, he was awakened during the night by the sound of rain pounding on the hull of the ship.

"There's that storm that Tom promised us," he thought sleepily. Then he realized that this must be the granddaddy of all rainstorms if he could hear it through the hull. The thick tough plating, the numerous layers of insulation and dead air spaces which were necessary to shield the crew members against the cold of interstellar space and the inferno of the suns—you couldn't hear the sound of an ordinary rain through that. But that wouldn't bother the ship—she'd be safe at the bottom of the ocean. So he rolled over and went back to sleep.

The next thing he knew, he was being shaken, not too gently, by Tom. "Whuzza matter—is it morning?" he asked drowsily.

"The clock says it is, but this is the poorest imitation of daylight I've ever seen. Come on, get up, and let's get a look outside."

With a prodigious yawn Bob clambered out of his bunk, slipped into his uniform, gave the zipper a twitch and was fully dressed.

"O.K., early bird—let's go."

Tom led the way to the observation chamber on the top of the ship. He carefully dogged down the airtight door and pressed the button which caused the outer plates of the hull to slide back, revealing the transparent ceiling. The drumming of the rain became thunderous. Tom started the pump which raised the air pressure within the room, blowing the tough, transparent and highly elastic polymer into a dome which protruded from the ship's back like a soap bubble on top of a watermelon. They took their seats in the observation chairs, which shot up until their heads were almost touching the dome.

It was difficult to remember that it wasn't necessary to flinch as the huge drops of rain, driven with machine-gun force, pelted against the dome. Visibility was no greater than fifty meters, and then only when the force of the wind abated temporarily. During the furious gusts it seemed as though they were at the bottom of some deep, murky and turbulent body of water.

"It's letting up some, now," said Tom, judiciously. "Those

puffs aren't any harder than seventy kilometers an hour. During the night I'll bet the wind was better than one hundred and fifty."

"No wonder there's no humanoid life on this planet. I don't see how anything could survive this sort of weather. I'm certainly glad that I told the others to stay at the ship. How are they making out?" Bob asked.

"Pretty good, I guess," answered Tom. "Their ship is completely under water, though, and reception is rather faint. Last thing I heard clearly was that Schultz was hungry."

While they were talking the rain had gradually decreased, although the wind continued with unabated fury. For a moment the two men could see around them in a thousand meter radius. And what a sight! The plateau on which the *Mercy* was rested was now an island. Vast torrents of water swirled around the base of the outcrop. There might have been waves—but every time a crest of water tried to rear itself, its top was amputated by the screaming knife of the wind and hurled into the dimness which lay beyond their field of vision. The vegetation which had carpeted the floor of the valley was totally submerged.

They had just a glimpse of their surroundings, then the rain began again. It pounded with mighty fists against the dome while the wind screamed a challenge to the puny humans who dared to challenge its might by their presence.

"Dr. Edwards," said Tom, "it looks as if we might have a heavy dew one of these days."

"I agree," answered Bob gravely. "The weather appears to be a mite threatening—inclement, you might say."

He took a deep breath, then exhaled slowly; annoyance, frustration and concern for the welfare of his men were all inherent in that sigh. "Guess that there's nothing to do but relax and wait for this storm to subside. There's one consolation—we'll all be safe inside."

The next three days of enforced idleness were much worse, by far, than the months consumed in traversing deep space. Bob and Irv played chess; they studied and re-studied the records from the other ship; they wandered in and out of the laboratory, suggesting further tests to be run on the specimens of water of Minotaur; and at least three or four times a day they inflated the dome and looked out at the climatic convulsions of Minotaur. To make matters less endurable they were no longer in communication with the men in the other ship; the suit radios were not powerful enough to penetrate the water in which the ship was submerged. They might have used the ship's communications system, but no one of the doctors was enough of a radio expert to operate it.

But finally the rain stopped, the wind ceased to howl like a demented banshee and the sunlight made a hesitant and apologetic appearance. The flood waters subsided rapidly and soon the radio carried the welcome words, "We're on our way back!"

"And be sure to have some food ready for us," added Schultz.

Bob, with a noble effort, refrained from asking any questions until his colleagues had been fed to the bursting point. Then Livingston began his report.

"That was quite an experience—being under water in a spaceship. It wasn't too bad, though. The only time when it looked as if it might be a little tough was when we ran out of water."

"You didn't drink any of the native water, I hope," said Bob anxiously.

"Well, not exactly. We talked it over for some time before deciding what would be best to do. We didn't believe that filtration would be safe, and we weren't even quite sure about how safe distillation would be. So we finally rigged up a gadget for electrolysis and then recombined the hydrogen and oxygen. There was plenty of power on the ship, so it wasn't difficult."

"Good boy," said Bob. "I'm sure that that's a safe method. Well, we'd better get to work. I don't suppose that you're tired—you've had nothing to do but sleep for the last three days. Davey, how long will it take you to get your sections stained and studied?"

"About two hours, Bob," replied the pathologist. "We can eliminate the study of the noncontributory tissues."

"Then let's plan on having a conference in about two hours. Maybe we can lick this problem today."

At the end of the appointed interval the group gathered around the table in the main cabin again.

Bob began, "I think that we all have a pretty good idea of what caused the deaths of the first expedition but for the sake of the record we'll start reviewing the evidence. Irv, tell the boys about the documents we studied. What did you get out of them?"

"The evidence from all sources is pretty consistent, with allowances made for differing degrees of accuracy of observation. The first complaints were noted about a month after landing and consisted in muscular weakness and extreme fatigability. Most of the men complained of pain and tenderness in the muscles and bones. They became apathetic, and as a consequence the task of exploring the planet was given up. It must have taken all their energy just to do routine work around the ship. Most of the men suffered a loss of appetite and several of them had numerous seizures of severe abdominal pain and vomiting. The captain realized, after it was too late, that he should have asked for help or tried to leave the planet, but he was apparently just too weak to attempt the effort. And that's all there was of interest, medically speaking. From the standpoint of heroic courage, however—well, these records beat anything I've ever heard of. This Expedition I—and I say this without any attempt to be flowery—should be an inspiration to all spacemen."

"Thanks, Mandel," said Bob. "I agree with you. And I'll make that as strong as possible in my report. Now, Livingston, I'll ask you what you boys found on autopsy."

"Well," began Jack, "you all saw the gross appearance of the two bodies—numerous fractures of the extremities. The salient points of diagnosis were the softening and fragility of the bones, areas of decalcification, and cystic degeneration of the bones of the skull. There were numerous areas of calcification in muscles and organs and large calculi in the kidneys. We couldn't determine the immediate cause of death in the unidentified body; it was too far gone. In the case of Mattson, of course, it was anoxemia."

"That certainly substantiates my suspicions," Bob said. "O.K., Davey, now maybe you'd give us the laboratory findings."

"There were only a few tests I thought were necessary to confirm the diagnosis. The blood calcium was 18 mgm. per 100 cc. and the blood phosphorus was 2.5 mgm. I cut a few frozen sections but didn't see anything of interest." Dr. Thomas leaned back in his chair again; his reports were always noteworthy for their briefness.

"Now, Schultzie," said Bob. "This disease looks like your baby. Suppose you tell us all about it."

"We've all been beating around the bush," said Schultz, "acting as though we were afraid to give this disease a name. You all know what it is—it's hyperparathyroidism. There, I've said it and I'm glad. Glad, do you hear me? Glad!"

A round of applause greeted this ham acting. Schultz was always good for a laugh.

"But seriously, fellows. These are typical cases of osteitis fibrosa cystica which we know is due to hyperparathyroidism. The funny thing about it, though, is that there were no changes in the parathyroids. How do you explain that, O Senior Synthesist?"

Bob pondered awhile before answering. "The only possible answer I can see to that is that the oversupply of parathyroid hormone came from the outside. Since it is an unusual disease on Earth, aboard spaceships and on the other inhabited planets I think we are safe in assuming that something here on this planet caused it. Thomas, how about giving us your report on the analysis of the atmosphere?"

"It certainly is nothing spectacular," answered Thomas. "All the gases here are within two percent of the values found on Earth. The carbon dioxide content is a little lower; that's probably due to the fact that no men are cluttering up the planet. There is no evidence of radioactivity in excess of what we can tolerate. The cosmic ray concentration is likewise low. As far as I'm concerned this air is completely nontoxic."

"You're probably right, Davey," Bob said. "Oh, by the way, you didn't mention bacteria content. What about that?"

"I didn't mention air-borne bacteria because there weren't any. If it weren't for the fact that there are twelve dead men out there to disprove it, I'd say that this was an unusually healthful place to live."

Again Bob pondered for awhile. "What about those water specimens I brought in—anything unusual in them?"

"Well, now, there might be. Mineral content is low. Bacteria count is practically negligible. The coloration is due to the presence of what might be called diatoms which, of course, are not seen in the specimen that had been filtered. The only unusual thing is the presence of a substance similar to albumen; very probably protein in nature. It's there in sufficient concentration to give a positive nitric acid ring test with both specimens."

"That," said Bob, "is the crux of the entire problem. We have to find out what that substance is before we do anything else. And incidentally, that's why I was so insistent that you didn't drink any of the local water."

"Did you do any more work on this while we were gone?" asked Thomas.

"No, Davey," Bob replied, "I wanted to give you a chance to use your favorite gilhickey. I thought we could inject a few animals with the water and put them in the metabolic accelerator and see what happens."

"Just a minute, Bob," Tom interrupted, "I've managed to keep my head above water so far, in spite of all the technical terms you've been throwing around. But would you mind telling a poor brokendown spacedog what is a metabolic accelerator?"

Bob laughed, "I don't wonder you've never heard about that. There are only two models in existence and we have one of them. It's a fancy sort of incubator in which you can, by controlling temperature, humidity, glandular function and numerous other factors, speed up the rate of living. You can literally make an animal live its entire life span in less than a week. Some bright boys who were doing mutation research figured that they could get the answers a lot faster if the animals would live faster. I've seen it a few times and it's really startling to see a cat put in there and die of old age in less than a week."

"Hm-m-m, quite a gadget," said Tom.

"It sure is," replied Bob, "and if it works it'll speed things up for us. Remember, it took the men of Expedition I about six weeks to develop their illness. If we're on the right track, we ought to be able to reproduce that effect in guinea pigs in about half an hour."

By the time Tom and Bob had reached the laboratory the other men were already there. A technician was just entering the room with a box in which there were eight of the world's most stupid animal, the guinea pig.

"How many are you going to use, Dave?" asked Bob.

"I thought that eight would be good to start with. We'll inject two with straight river water and two with the filtered water you brought. I had one of the boys distill some of the river water and we'll see what that does. And, of course, we'll use two more for controls."

"Here's an idea. Why don't you give the water intraperitoneally by drip? If we just give 'em one shot of water, that wouldn't imitate the continuous exposure that the men had."

"You're right, Bob," answered the pathologist. "How about you fellows helping to expose the femorals on these pigs?"

And so for the next little while the five doctors were busy immobilizing the guinea pigs, each on his own board. An incision was made in the groin and the femoral vein isolated and a cannula inserted. Through this tiny tube would flow the concentrated nutrient solution; at the rate at which metabolism would proceed the animals would starve to death in a few minutes unless their diet was augmented. They wouldn't be able to eat fast enough to keep up with tissue catabolism. The solution also contained thyroxin, testosterone, estradiol, a mixture of the adrenal corticosteroids plus a delicately adjusted amount of the pituitary trophins.

At last the guinea pigs were completely prepared and were placed in the capacious maw of the machine. Connections were made for the intravenous and the intraperitoneal solutions. Then the doors were closed and the switches thrown.

It seemed as though that next half-hour would never end. The dials were scrutinized every five seconds, innumerable cigarettes were smoked—three puffs and the butts ground out—and they all but pushed the second hand of the clock. But at last the time was up and the machine was opened. The eight trays were puts out on a table.

Thomas studied the labels. "Pigs one and two—river water—both dead. Pig three—filtered water—dead. Pig four—likewise filtered water—alive . . . no, dead. Pigs five and six—distilled water—old but healthy. Pigs seven and eight—controls—old but healthy. O.K., men, let's do a bunch of autopsies."

Tom and Irv looked on while the other four men opened up the little furry bodies and examined them.

Bob finally got up, washed and dried his hands, lit a cigarette and leaned back against the table. The smoke drifted up before his face as he squinted his eyes and spoke slowly.

"Well, fellows, I guess that's that. We'll have to do a little more work in confirmation of our findings here, but I think you'll all agree that the source of this parathyroid-hormone-like substance is the river water. It'll be one very sweet problem to determine the exact structure of this stuff. Just as a guess, I'll bet that its structural formula isn't anything like that of parathormone. It'll probably be like diethyl stilbestrol and estradiol—same physiologic effect, but entirely different structure. And then'll come the job of determining the source of the stuff. It looks like we're going to be ecologists and biochemists for a while, instead of M.D.s."

He sighed and shifted his position. "So I suppose that if we want to go running around outside without spacesuits, we can do it. Tom, be sure to warn the men in the crew that under no circumstances are they to drink any water on this planet unless we've checked it first."

He sighed again. "This is so anticlimatic. Well, that's the way it goes. Nice work, boys. Now we can take it easy for a while until we get orders from Earth. Tommy, my boy, let's get at that radio."

The message was soon coded and sent. While they were waiting for the necessary twenty minutes to elapse between sending the message and getting a confirmation of reception, Tom started quizzing Bob.

"Doc, that was a very swell piece of work. It beats me how you guys can do it—but I suppose that you wonder how I can calculate a transorbital course, too. But how can it be so easy?"

"Tommy, you will now receive Dr. Edwards' famous indoctrination course on how not to be surprised at exotic diseases. There can't be any new diseases. You see, the human organism is capable of acting in only certain ways. For example, the blood pressure can go up, it can come down or it can remain the same. The temperature can be elevated, it can be subnormal, or it can be normal. And so it goes for every function of the body—it can change only within the limits of its own capacity to function.

"When we study exotic diseases the difficulty, therefore, is to find the causative agent. The disease itself is probably greatly similar to one with which we have been familiar on Earth for hundreds of years."

"Oh, I see," said Tom. "The roads it may travel on might be new, but it's the same disease that's doing the traveling."

"Exactly," replied Bob. "To give you another example: the body is capable of only certain color changes. The skin might turn brown, due to the presence of melanin, one of the normally found pigments. Or it might turn any one of the colors seen in the degradation of hemoglobin. You know, those fascinating color changes of dark blue to green to yellow and all shades in between that you see in a bruise—or in that shiner that I saw you wearing last year.

"No," he continued, without giving Tom a chance to explain that he got the black eye from bumping into a door in the dark, "we could never expect to see a man turn an aquamarine blue. There just isn't a precursor for that color in the body. So we'll never see an exotic disease where the skin is aquamarine or we'll never see a disease where a man reacts outside of the normal limitations of response."

"So that's it," mused Tom. "Yes, what is it?" He turned around as a knock came at the door.

It was one of the crew members. "Sorry to interrupt, sir, but I'd like to have Dr. Edwards take a look at me. My skin is kind of a funny color."

Edwards turned around. Like the Bay of Naples on a sunny day, or Lake Superior in July, the man's skin was a beautiful, vivid aquamarine blue.